A WOMAN'S EYE

A WOMAN'S EYE

edited by
Sara Paretsky

**Delacorte
Press**

Published by
Delacorte Press
The Bantam Doubleday Dell Publishing Group, Inc.
666 Fifth Avenue
New York, New York 10103

Published by
Delacorte Press
Bantam Doubleday Dell Publishing Group, Inc.
666 Fifth Avenue
New York, New York 10103

0-385-30000-X

CONTENTS

EYE OF A WOMAN: AN INTRODUCTION   vii

LUCKY DIP *by Liza Cody*   1

"FULL CIRCLE" *by Sue Grafton*   20

BENNY'S SPACE *by Marcia Muller*   32

THE PUPPET *by Dorothy Salisbury Davis*   48

THE SCAR *by Nancy Pickard*   65

MURDER WITHOUT A TEXT *by Amanda Cross*   81

DISCARDS *by Faye Kellerman*   97

GETTING TO KNOW YOU *by Antonia Fraser*   114

A MATCH MADE IN HELL *by Julie Smith*   124

THEFT OF THE POET *by Barbara Wilson*   139

DEATH AND DIAMONDS *by Susan Dunlap*   152

KILL THE MAN FOR ME *by Mary Wings*   167

THE CUTTING EDGE *by Marilyn Wallace*   178

LOOKING FOR THELMA *by Gillian Slovo*   194

DEBORAH'S JUDGMENT *by Margaret Maron*   212

A MAN'S HOME *by Shelley Singer*   229

HER GOOD NAME *by Carolyn G. Hart*   237

GHOST STATION *by Carolyn Wheat*   251

WHERE ARE YOU, MONICA? *by Maria Antonia Oliver*   263

SETTLED SCORE *by Sara Paretsky*   284

THAT SUMMER AT QUICHIQUOIS *by Dorothy B. Hughes*   300

EYE OF A WOMAN

an introduction by Sara Paretsky

"My dear, you are a young woman. You are writing about a book that has been written by a man. Be sympathetic; be tender; flatter; deceive; use all the arts and wiles of our sex. Never let anybody guess that you have a mind of your own."

The Angel in the House spoke these words to Virginia Woolf when Woolf first tried to write for publication. The Angel was a phantasm, but its speech crystallized all the voices Woolf had heard from childhood on, telling her that women should never have a mind or wish of their own. Woolf says she struggled with this Angel for years, trying to kill it so that she could find her own voice. "She died hard," the artist reports. "Her fictitious nature was of great assistance to her. It is far harder to kill a phantom than a reality."

Women have been wrestling with that Angel for many centuries. It is a difficult phantom to overpower because it speaks in so many voices and with so much authority behind it. In some cases the authority is quite specific. John Winthrop, the first governor of Massachusetts Bay, wrote in 1645 that the poet Anne Hopkins "has fallen into a sad infirmity, the loss of her understanding and reason, . . . by occasion of giving herself wholly to read-ing and writing, and had written many books." He added that "if she had attended her household affairs, and such things as belong to women . . . she had kept her wits."

This kind of authority, this active pressure to keep women doing "such things as belong to women," made it difficult for women to join the ranks of storytellers. Of course, we all look admiringly at the poet Sappho—all except the Athenian men who destroyed much of her work because she was praised more highly than their favorite Pindar. And we see the Lady Murasaki, the eleventh-century creator of the first novel, whose father—recognizing her talent—lamented she had not been born a boy. She only had the minor hurdle of learning to write by secretly looking over her brothers' shoulders— her lamenting father had forbidden her direct education.

By 1700 we find more than one woman writer per century, but to see a continuous chain of female storytellers we can look back only two hundred years. During those two centuries women struggled hard for the right to be published and read. In the nineteenth century they often wrote under men's names to gain an audience—Acton, Currer, and Ellis Bell for the Brontë sisters; George Eliot for Mary Ann Evans; and George Sand for Lucie Dupin Dudevant. George Sand wrote most of her enormous oeuvre at night, starting work at two or three in the morning after finishing with the management of her large household or her numerous lovers. And it is only in this century that we find enough women writing that we no longer see ourselves as odd, or worry, like the seventeenth-century poet Anne Finch, that the masculine art of poetry is making us crabbed and unwomanly.

In some cases, women struggling to express themselves faced a bombardment of wholesale anger—furious reviews, social ostracism, public excoriation —so intense that they stopped writing. Kate Chopin experienced this reaction after publishing *The Awakening* in 1899. The anger against her was so intense that she wrote nothing else for publication. She died five years later at the age of fifty-three, broken by the forcible silencing of her voice.

Edna Pontellier, the heroine of *The Awakening,* married, with two children, leaves her husband in order to paint—and in so doing falls in love with a younger man. She commits suicide in the end, but this fate did not exonerate her or her creator, either in 1900 or today. Over and over reviewers have castigated Chopin for Edna's "selfishness." In 1970 George Spangler condemned Chopin for Edna's "ruthless determination to go her own way" that is "disturbing, even alienating."

Contrast Chopin's fate, and that of her heroine, with Goethe and Faust. At the end of a long life of debauchery Faust *"ist gerichtet, ist gerettet"*—he is judged and saved—a fate his creator, who glorified his own numerous seductions in poems and journals, no doubt expected for himself. Do any biographers of Goethe take him to task for "selfishness" or find Faust "disturbing, even alienating"? The strong expression of sexual desire is not just condoned in the male hero—it makes him more heroic.

In a woman that desire is a sign at best of selfishness, at worst of psychosis. The character Glenn Close plays in *Fatal Attraction*, Alex Forrest, shows that we still find female sexuality—outside of marriage, and specifically married maternity—so shocking and debasing that the character must be deranged. And as with Chopin's Edna Pontellier, the only fitting end for Alex Forrest is death.

It is the struggle to find a voice, to kill the Angel, to figure out what women really want, what our stories really are, that absorbs the energy of many women writers. The voices that tell us we can't do it, or we shouldn't do it, continue to blare at us. They may be loud and raucous, like Norman Mailer, addressing International PEN a few years ago while head of PEN USA, and saying that it isn't possible for women to write as well as men. It's not hard to imagine what threat women present to Mailer's vision of his masculinity that drives him to insist that you "have to have balls" to write well; it is hard to understand why an organization dedicated to freeing imprisoned writers should elect him president.

Mailer's statements are so extreme that many people laugh at him, but he's far from alone in pushing down women's voices. Other people merely express themselves more softly. Women who write strong, even angry stories are no longer told that they are "unwomanly" or "selfish." Today, as Carolyn Heilbrun points out, we hear that we are "shrill," "strident," or, worst of all, feminists. We also find most women excluded from the sacred mystical canon that Allan Bloom, Mortimer Adler, and others keep firing. And a Chicago area critic recently explained that feminists by definition cannot write great books.

In addition to needing considerable courage even to tell stories, we women have also had to figure out what our stories are. The image of ourselves as inconstant, duplicitous, stupid, illogical, using our bodies to seduce and subvert men is such an ancient, ingrained part of our tradition, reinforced in fairy tales, epics, history, that to counteract these images by telling women's stories makes for very heavy work. Writers as different as George Eliot and Virginia Woolf suffered from migraines brought on by the stress of this work and the self-doubts that come from countering so widely accepted an authority.

It was Virginia Woolf who first clearly spelled out the central problem of the female artist: the conflict between her interior vision and the expectation that she subordinate that vision to her perceived primary role as a self-sacrificing angel.

Just being able to articulate this problem was an important step toward resolving it. But many women artists—including the crime writer—continue to experience stress in taking their own visions seriously. Agatha Christie, who wrested total artistic control for production from her publishers in the twenties, and whose residuals brought in over a million pounds a year at her death, often told reporters that she regarded herself as a wife first, a writer second. One should take this statement seriously: as a sign not of poormouthing, but of internal conflict between her success and what she thought her womanly role should be.

In writing mysteries, women for many years created primarily male heroes: Sayers with Wimsey, Tey with Grant, Marsh with Alleyn. When the detectives were women, they were women who did not upset male stereotypes. Jane Marple is everybody's elderly spinster aunt, essentially asexual. While sharp and perceptive, she uses her insights to shore up the patriarchal society in which she lives and operates on its fringes rather than as a professional crime investigator. Lady Molly of Scotland Yard was a bit more daring, but Baroness Orczy assures us repeatedly that Lady Molly never lost her feminine daintiness. Dorothy Sayers created a complex character in Harriet Vane, but could not allow her—or the female dons of Shrewsbury—to solve their own problems. They fester in an environment of fear and mutual suspicion for almost a year before Peter Wimsey arrives. He is able to see through the situation at a glance and in a matter of days resolves the problem for them.

Since Sayers created Harriet Vane sixty years ago women have developed active careers in many spheres. In 1878 the U.S. Supreme Court barred women lawyers because of their "natural timidity and delicacy." Now we have a woman Justice. When I started my first book twelve years ago, Chicago women were fighting for the right to be homicide detectives and patrol officers instead of matrons at the women's jails. Today ten percent of the force is female. We don't think twice about seeing women on the beat, in the courtroom, the operating room, or other exciting arenas.

It's because we see women doing so much that the horizons of our fiction have expanded. We can create heroines who act independently without guilt —not Jane Marples, or even Harriet Vanes—but Kate Fansler, Sharon McCone, or Kinsey Millhone, who are all present in this anthology. And our unmarried women can have affairs without needing to kill themselves afterward, or turning out to be villains like Brigid O'Shaughnessy or Chandler's Dolores Gonzalez.

Does that make this group of writers better than Sayers? By no means. Nor in terms of craft and talent does she have many equals today. But what we do have is the freedom to present an independent woman hero without fear of excoriation.

Kate Chopin, the Brontës, and other pioneers made it possible for us to believe in the female artist. They turned publishing into a routine, accessible, acceptable business—they obviated the need to publish under the cloak of an anonymous lady, as Austen had to, or under a man's name, as Sand and Eliot felt compelled to. Sayers, Woolf, and others, taking advantage of this ease of publication, made us start thinking about what a genuine woman's voice might be.

Twenty-five years ago Amanda Cross delighted readers with Kate Fansler in *In the Final Analysis*. Kate, professional, witty, feminine, took over where Dorothy Sayers left Harriet Vane: she could solve her own problems. She could investigate and resolve a murder. She could have a warm and wonderful lover but stand apart from him. Cross presented the hero we'd been waiting for all our lives.

What began as a trickle of strong women a quarter of a century ago—with Christy Oper working a New York Transit Authority beat, followed by Cordelia Gray doing an *Unsuitable Job for a Woman*—has grown into a great outpouring of women's stories. Marcia Muller gave us Sharon McCone in *Edwin of the Iron Shoes* in 1977. Five years later Sue Grafton and I flung Kinsey Millhone and V. I. Warshawski on an unsuspecting world; English PI Anna Lee joined us at the same time. Since then the number of interesting women heroes has grown past counting. They range from the private eyes to Julie Hayes in Dorothy Salisbury Davis's books, whose efforts to find her own strength mirror the struggles many American women have gone through in the last twenty years.

This book gathers together a sample of what women have to say about women in the final decade of our century. The collection begins with Liza Cody's story "Lucky Dip." Being homeless and on the street are issues that we all worry about. Cody goes beyond worry to show us through Crystal's eyes what that life is really like. A street girl, Crystal is presented without gloss or sentimentality. The horrors she witnesses, and how she copes with them, may chill you, but will also give you food for serious thought.

The collection ends with another young girl in a different situation. Emma, in Dorothy B. Hughes's "That Summer at Quichiquois," is trying to sort out the passions of the adults around her. This haunting story shows us many different ways to view people, passion, and even forensic evidence.

Between Cody and Hughes we see women struggling with a range of problems. Nancy Pickard takes a new look at jealousy and possessiveness in "The Scar." The New Zealand setting is unusual and arresting, but the feelings, brought to life with delicate realism, have been with us for thousands of years. Private eyes Kinsey Millhone, Sharon McCone, Kiernan O'Shaughnessy, and Lònia Guiu solve cases that are far from conventional. Famous amateurs like Jemima Shore, Julie Hayes, and Kate Fansler are here. Along with these professional crime solvers are mothers, grandmothers, battered wives, social workers, and Barbara Wilson's startling story about one of the world's most revered dead poets. We have the debut of Carolyn Wheat's new hero, New York Transit cop Maureen Gallagher, whose struggles with sobriety and authority are as important as the torched subway bums she fights for.

Mary Wings's "Kill the Man for Me" is guaranteed to provoke late-night discussions: how far is it permissible to go in seeking justice or revenge? And if her solution shocks you, ask yourself if you were also offended by Charles Bronson in *Death Wish*.

The one thing these stories have in common is the message that there is no one way to view women. Nor is there one way women see themselves. What we have all learned in the last three hundred and fifty years is that the reading and writing of books are "such things as belong to women."

A WOMAN'S EYE

LUCKY DIP

Liza Cody

 He was sitting against a bit of broken wall, looking almost normal. I could see him because of the full moon. It was a lovely moon with wispy clouds like old lady's hair across its face.

I watched the man for a couple of minutes, but he didn't move. Well, he wouldn't, would he? I could see he didn't belong—he was far too well dressed—and I wondered how he got there. This is not a part of the city men dressed like him go.

He had not been dead long. You could tell that at a glance because he still had his shoes on. If you die here you won't keep your shoes for ten minutes. You won't keep your wallet for ten seconds, dead or alive.

With this in mind I had a quick look, right and left, for anyone lurking in the shadows. If I'd seen anyone bigger than me, I'd have stayed where I was. Moon shadows are blacker than hearses, and I knew I wasn't the only one out that night. But in the Trenches only the big are bold, and someone big would have been rummaging in the remains already. So I hopped out from behind my pile of rubble and made a run for it.

I reached him in no time at all and grabbed his left lapel. Seven out of ten men are right-handed, and the chances are seven to three anything valuable will be in a left-hand inside pocket. I took a swift dip and came up with the winnings.

By now I could hear stirrings—a snap of rotten wood, a slide of brick dust. I flicked his watch off his wrist and almost in the same motion made a dive into his jacket pocket. Then I got on my toes and legged it.

I legged it out of the Trenches completely, because, although there are plenty of places to hide, the people I wanted to hide from know them as well as I do. The Trenches are useful as long as it's only the law you want to avoid. Robbing a corpse isn't nice, and I didn't want to take all that trouble only to be robbed myself.

It was just a quick jog to the High Street. On the way I stopped under a street lamp to look at what I had in my hand. The wallet was fat snakeskin, the watch was heavy gold, and the loose change was all pound coins and fifty-pence pieces. For once in my short life I'd struck oil.

All the same you don't break old habits for the sake of one lucky dip, and when I saw all those plump taxpayers doing their late Christmas shopping on the High Street, I stuck out my hand as usual.

"Got any spare change, please?" I said, as always. "For a cup of tea. For a bed for the night. For a hot meal."

And as always they coughed up like princes or told me to get myself a job. It was nice that night. I perform best when there's no pressure, and by the time I'd worked my way down to the station, I'd made a nice little pile. But it doesn't do to loll around and count your takings in public, so I jumped a tube to Paddington.

My sister has this room in Paddington. She lives in Camberwell with her boyfriend, so this room's just for business. I don't trust my sister's boyfriend, but I do trust my sister, up to a point, which was why I went to her business address. You may meet all sorts of funny blokes there, but you won't meet her boyfriend, and that suits me. It suits him, too, if you want to know the truth: he doesn't like me any more than I like him.

When we first came down to the city, Dawn and me, we relied on each other; we didn't have anyone else to turn to. But after she took up with him and he set her up in business, she didn't need me like she used to, and we drifted apart.

The trouble with Dawn is she always needs a man. She says she doesn't feel real without one. Feeling real is important to Dawn so I suppose I shouldn't criticize. But her men have been nothing but a disappointment. You could say I'm lucky to have an older sister like Dawn: she's an example to me. I'd rather die than turn out like her.

Still, she is my sister, and we've been through a lot together. Especially in this last year when we came down to the city together. And before that, when our mum kicked us out, or rather, kicked Dawn out because of the baby. And after that when Dawn's boyfriend kicked Dawn out because of the baby.

I have never been hungrier than I was last year trying to look after Dawn. She lost the baby in the end, which was a bit of a relief to me. I don't know how we would have managed if she'd had it. I don't think she would have coped very well either. It's much harder to get a man when you've got a little baby to look after.

Anyway, that's all in the past, and now Dawn has business premises in Paddington.

I waited outside until I was sure she was alone, and then I went up and knocked on the door.

"Crystal!" she said when she opened the door. "What you doing here? You got to be more careful—I might've had company."

"Well, you haven't," I said. And she let me in, wrinkling her nose and pulling her kimono tight. I don't like that kimono—it's all hot and slippery. Since she got her hair streaked, Dawn has taken to wearing colors that would look all right on a tree in autumn but turn her hard and brassy.

"Gawd," she said, "you don't half look clatty. Can't you get your hair cut? That coat looks like it's got rats living in it."

I took the coat off, but she didn't like the one underneath either.

"What a pong," she said.

"I had a wash last week," I told her. "But I would like to use your bathroom." I wanted somewhere private to look at what I'd got off the dead man.

"You can't stop around here," she said, worried. "I got someone coming in half an hour." She looked at her watch.

I sat in her bathroom and looked at the dead man's watch. It had *Cartier* written on the face, and it really was proper gold. Quality, I thought, and felt a bit sad. By rights a man with a watch like that shouldn't end up in the Trenches without a stitch on. Because that's how he'd be by now, pale and naked in the moonlight. Nobody would recognize him without his coat and suit and shoes. He'd just look like anyone. We're into recycling in the Trenches.

To cheer myself up I looked at his wallet, and when I counted up I found I had 743 pounds and 89 pence. And I couldn't use half of it.

Imagine me trying to change a fifty-pound note! There's a chance in a million a cat with cream on his whiskers milked a cow, but that's good odds compared to the chance I'd come by a fifty-quid note honestly. I couldn't even pop the watch. One look at a watch like that and any honest pawnbroker would turn me in. A dishonest one would rip me off quick as a wink. Either way the watch was no good for me.

I borrowed my sister's toothbrush and had a fast swipe with her deodorant before I joined her again. You never know when you're going to find clean water next so it pays to make use of what there is.

"Do me a favor, Crystal," she said, when she saw me. "Bugger off before you frighten the horses."

"Brought you a Christmas present," I said and handed her the watch.

"You're barmy, Crystal." She stared at the watch like it was a spider in her bed. "Who'd you nick this off?"

"I never," I told her. "I found it." And it was true because the feller was dead. It wasn't as if it was his property because there wasn't a him anymore for it to belong to. When you're dead you're gone. And that's final. Dead men don't own watches.

Even with a Christmas present, Dawn wouldn't let me stop for the night. It's a funny thing, if I hadn't had 743 pounds, 89 pence in my pocket, I wouldn't have wanted to. If it had just been the 89 pence, I'd've been quite happy sleeping out.

But having things is dangerous. Having things makes you a mark. It's like being pretty. If you don't believe me, look at Dawn. She's pretty and she's been a mark from the time she was eleven. Being pretty brought her nothing but trouble. She's always had to have someone to protect her. I'm glad I'm not pretty.

There's a hospital down the Harrow Road so I went there. I couldn't decide what to do, so I sat in Casualty till they chucked me out. It's a pity there aren't more places you can go and sit in at night to have a quiet think. It's hard to think on the hoof, and if you are cold or hungry, thinking is not on your mind at all.

It seemed to me, after a while, that the best place to go was where I slept last night. Some might say it was a daft idea to go back to a place that was rousted, but I thought if the police had been there last night, it would be deserted tonight.

Twenty-seven Alma-Tadema Road is a condemned house. They say it's unsafe. There are holes in the roof and holes in the floors, but it is perfectly safe if you are sober, tread carefully, and don't light fires. That was what went wrong last night: we had a couple of winos in, and one of them got cold just before daybreak.

When I got there, I saw that they had nailed more boards across the front door and downstairs windows. I could get in, but it would take time. There were still people up and about so, to be on the safe side, I would have to come back later if I wanted more than a few minutes' kip.

I walked on past and went down to the Embankment. It is quite a long walk, and by the time I got there I was hungry. Actually, I'm hungry all the time. Dawn says she thinks I must have worms and I probably do, but mostly I think it's just my age. Someone like Bloody Mary does almost as much walking as I do, but she doesn't seem to need half the fuel. She stopped growing years ago.

There are a lot of women like Bloody Mary, but I mention her because she was the one I picked up on the Embankment that night, huffing and puffing along with her basket on wheels.

"Oh, me poor veins," she said, and we walked on together. I slowed down a bit so she could keep up.

"There's a stall open by the Arches," she said. "Couldn't half murder a cuppa."

She used to sing in the streets—walk up and down Oxford Street bellowing "Paper Moon" with her hand held out—but after a bad dose of bronchitis last year her voice went.

At the Arches I got us both a cup of tea and a sausage sandwich.

"Come into money, Crys?" Johnny Pavlova asked. It is his stall and he has a right to ask, because now and then when there's no one around to see, he gives me a cup free. As he always says, he's not a charitable institution, but catch him in the right mood and he'll slip you one like the best of them.

All the same it reminded me to be careful.

"Christmas," I said. "They were feeling generous down the High Street."

"Down the High Street?" he said. "You ain't been on that demolition site, have you? I heard they found this stiff bollock-naked there this evening."

"Did they?" I said as if I couldn't care less. "I didn't hear nothing. I was just working the High Street."

I went over and sat with Bloody Mary under the Arches. Johnny Pavlova doesn't like us hanging too close round his stall. He says we put the respectable people off their hot dogs.

"Will you look at that moon," Bloody Mary said, and she pulled her coats tight.

It was higher in the sky now and smaller, but there was still a good light to see by.

"Where you kipping tonight, Crystal?" she asked. I knew what she meant. A moon like that is a freezing moon this time of year.

Just then, Brainy Brian came slithering in beside us so I didn't have to answer. He was coughing his lungs out as usual, and he didn't say anything for a while. I think he's dying. You can't cough like that and live long. He used to go to college in Edinburgh, but then he started taking drugs and he failed all his exams. He did all right down here in the city because to begin with he was very pretty. But druggies don't keep their looks any longer than they keep their promises. Now he's got a face like a violin and ulcers all over his arms and legs.

When he recovered his breath he said, "Share your tea, Crystal?"

We'd already finished ours so we didn't say anything for a while. But Brian was so sorry-looking, in the end I went to get another two, one for him and one for Bloody Mary. While they were sucking it up I slipped away.

"Watch yourself, Crys," Johnny Pavlova said as I went by. He gave me a funny look.

The first thing you do when you break into a house is find another way out. A good house has to have more than one way out because you don't want to go running like the clappers to get out the same door the Law is coming in.

The house on Alma-Tadema Road has a kitchen door through to the garden. I loosened the boards on that before lying down to sleep. I also made sure I had the snakeskin wallet safe.

I had made the right decision: there was no one but me there. A heap of damp ashes marked the spot where the winos had lit their fire, and they blew in little eddies from the draught. Otherwise nothing stirred.

I went over the house collecting all the paper and rags I could find to build myself a nest, then I curled up in it and shut my eyes.

Nighttime is not the best time for me. It's when I can't keep busy and in control of my thoughts that bad memories and dreams burst out of my brain. It's hard to keep cheerful alone in the dark, so I need to be very, very tired before I'll lie down and close my eyes. Sometimes I say things over and over in my head until I get to sleep—things like the words of a song or a poem I learned at school—over and over so there's no spare room in my brain for the bad stuff.

That night I must have been very tired because I only got part of the way through "What's Love Got to Do with It," when I dropped off. Dawn used to play that song all the time when we were still living at home. She played it so often it used to drive me up the wall. But it is songs like that, songs I didn't even know I'd learned the words to, that help me through the night nowadays.

The next thing I knew someone was coughing. I opened my eyes but it was still dark, and there was this cough, cough, cough coming my way. Brainy Brian, I thought, and relaxed a bit. It's something you have to watch out for —people coming up on you when you're alone in the dark.

"It's cold," he said when he found me. "It's hard, hard cold out there." He crawled into my nest. I was quite warm and I didn't want to leave but I knew his coughing would keep me awake.

"Give us a cuddle, Crystal," he said. "I got to get warm."

"Shove off," I said. His hands remind me of a fork. Some people do it to keep warm. Not me. I've seen too much and I want to die innocent.

He started coughing again. Then he said, "You got any dosh, Crystal?"

"Enough for a tea in the morning," I said. I really did not want to go. It was one of my better nests and it didn't seem fair to give it up to Brian.

"They're looking for you," he said. "Someone saw you in the Trenches."

"Not me," I said. "Who saw me?"

"You know that little kid?" he said. "Marvin, I think he's called. Well, they hurt him bad. He said he saw you."

"Who wants to know?" I sat up.

"Lay down," he said, "I got to get warm." He grabbed me and pulled me down, but he didn't start anything so I kept still.

After a while he said, "Johnny Pavlova says you got dosh. They asked him too."

I waited till he finished coughing. Then I said, "Who's asking? The Law?"

"Not them," he said. He knew something, I thought. And then I thought, he talked to Johnny Pavlova, he's talked to Marvin, and Marvin saw me in the Trenches. Maybe Brian talked to whoever is looking for me.

I said, "Did they send you, Brian? Did they send you to find me?"

He doubled over, coughing. Later he said, "You don't understand, Crystal. I got to get some money. I lost my fixings, and I haven't scored for days."

So that was that. I left him and went out the kitchen way. Brian was right —it was hard cold outside. And I was right, too—having things makes you a mark. I dumped the snakeskin wallet in the garden before I climbed over the fence. And then I climbed right back and picked it up again. Dumping the wallet wouldn't stop anyone looking for me. Not having it would be no protection. Marvin didn't have it and he got hurt. I wondered why they picked on Marvin to clobber. Perhaps he got the dead man's shoes, or his coat. Perhaps they saw a little kid in a big thick coat and they recognized the coat.

No one ever looked for me before. There was no one interested. I thought maybe I should run away—somewhere up north, or maybe to the West Country. But when I ran away the first time, it was me and Dawn together. And it was difficult because we didn't know the city. It took us ages to get sorted.

I thought about it walking down the road. The moon had gone and the sky had that dirty look it gets just before day. My nose was runny from the cold and I was hungry, so I went to the Kashmir takeaway. The Kashmir is a good one because it has a bin not twenty paces away. What happens is that when the pubs close a lot of folks want an Indian takeaway, but because they've been drinking they order too much and chuck what's left over in this bin. I've had breakfast there many times. The great thing about a Kashmir breakfast is that although the food is cold by the time you get it, the spices are still hot, and it warms you up no end. From this point of view Indian food is the best in the city.

I felt much more cheerful after breakfast, and I found a lighted shopwindow with a doorway to sit in. It was there I had a proper look at the wallet. Before, at Dawn's business premises, I only counted the money and redistributed it in the pockets of my coats. Now I studied the credit cards, library cards, and business stuff.

These are not things I am normally interested in. I can't use them. But this time, it seemed to me, the only way out of trouble was to give them back. The dead man in the Trenches might be dead but he was still dangerous.

His name was Philip Walker-Jones. He belonged to a diners club, a bridge club, and a chess club. He had two business cards—Data Services Ltd. and Safe Systems Plc. He was managing director twice over, which seemed quite clever because both companies had the same address in Southwark Road. Southwark Road is not far from where I found him. Maybe he walked out of his office and died on the way to the station. But that didn't explain what he was doing in the Trenches. Nobody like him goes in the Trenches.

I thought about Philip Walker-Jones sitting in the moonlight against the broken brickwork. He had looked as if he'd just sat down for a bit of a breather. But he wasn't resting. He was dead. There wasn't a mark on him that I could see. It didn't look as if anyone had bumped him—he was just sitting there in all his finery. Quite dignified, really.

Little Marvin would have been there watching like I was, and probably a few others too—waiting to see if it was safe to take a dip. We were wrong, weren't we?

I didn't want to go back too close to the Trenches, but if I was going to give the wallet back I had to. It was too early yet for public transport so I started walking. A good breakfast does wonders for the brain, so while I was walking I went on thinking.

I didn't know anything about data and systems except that they sounded like something to do with computers, but I do know that dining, bridge, and chess are all things you do sitting down. Philip Walker-Jones didn't have any cards saying he belonged to a squash club or a swimming club, and if he spent all that time sitting down, maybe he wasn't very fit. If he wasn't very fit, and he started to run suddenly, he could have had a heart attack.

It was a satisfying bit of thinking that took me down to the river without really noticing. Crossing over, it occurred to me that computers, bridge, and chess were things that really brainy people did, and in my experience brainy people all wear glasses and don't run around much. A really brainy man would not go running into the Trenches after dark, unless he was being chased. A scared, unfit man running in the Trenches would have no bother getting a heart attack. Easy.

The wind off the river was sharp and cold, but it wasn't the only thing making me shiver. Because if Philip Walker-Jones had a reason to be scared to death, so did I.

Give the rotten wallet back, I thought, *and do it double quick. Say, "Here's your money, now leave me be." And then do a runner.* I'm good at that.

I stopped for a pint of milk to fuel up. And I went through my pockets to find some of the fifty-pound notes, which I stuffed back in the wallet to make it look better.

I felt quite good. I had made my plan and it was almost as if I didn't have the wallet anymore. It was as good as gone, and by the time I reached Southwark Road I wasn't bothering much about keeping out of sight. It was daylight now and there were other people in the streets, and cars on the roads, and as usual no one seemed to notice me.

All the same, I gave the Trenches a miss. I walked down Southwark Road bold as brass looking at numbers and signs. And when I found one that read *Safe Systems Plc*, I walked right up to the door.

It was a new door in an old building, and it was locked. Perhaps it was too early. Not having a watch myself, I don't keep track of office hours. I stood there wondering if I should hike on to the station where there's a clock and a cup of tea, and just then the door opened from the inside. It gave me such a fright I nearly legged it. But the person opening the door was a young woman, and usually women don't give me much trouble. This one had red rims to her eyes and a really mournful expression on her face. She also had a nasty bruise on her cheekbone that made me think of Little Marvin.

She said, "Where do you think you're going?" She wasn't friendly but she looked as if she had other things on her mind.

"Safe Systems Plc," I said.

"What do you want?" she said. "The office is closed. And haven't you ever heard of a thing called soap and water?"

"I've got something for Safe Systems," I said, and held out the wallet.

"Jesus Christ!" she said and burst into tears.

We stood there like that—me holding the wallet and her staring at it, crying her eyes out.

At last, she said, "I don't want it. Take it away." And she tried to slam the door.

But I stuck my foot in there. "What do I do with it?" I said.

"Lose it," she said, and because I wouldn't let her close the door, she went on, "Look, you silly little cow, don't you come near me with that thing. Drop it in the river—you can give it to Steve for all I care. I'm finished with all that."

She started banging the door on my foot so I hopped back. The door crashed shut and she was gone.

I was so surprised I stood there gawping at the door and I didn't see the big feller coming up behind until he dropped a hand on my shoulder.

"You the one they call Crystal?" he said from a great height.

"Not me," I said. "Never heard of her." I got the wallet back under my top coat without him noticing.

"What you doing at that office then?" he said, not letting go.

"The lady sometimes gives me her spare change," I said, and watched his feet. It's no good watching their eyes. If you want to know what a bloke's going to do, watch his feet. The big man's feet were planted. I did not like him knowing my name.

"What is your name then?" he said.

I nearly said, "Dawn," but I bit it off just in time.

"What?" he said.

"Doreen," I said. "Who's asking?" If he was Steve, I would give him the wallet and run.

"Detective Sergeant Michael Sussex," he said. It was even worse than I thought. Now even the Law knew my name. It made me sweat in spite of the cold.

"I've got a few questions for you," he said, and he tightened his hand on my shoulder.

"I don't know anything," I said. "What about?"

"About where you was last night," he said. "And who you saw."

"I never saw nothing," I said, really nervous.

"Course you didn't," he said. "Come on. I'll buy you breakfast and then we can talk." And he smiled.

Never, never trust the Law when it smiles.

None of this had ever happened to me before. If you must know, I've hardly ever talked to a policeman in my life. I'm much too fast on my feet.

"Where do you live, Crystal?" he said, starting to walk.

"The name's Doreen," I said, and tried to get out from under the big hand.

"Where do you live . . . Doreen?" he said.

The thing you have to know about the Law is that they ask questions and you answer them. You've got to tell them something or they get really upset. It's the same with social workers. If they want an answer, give them an answer, but keep the truth to yourself. I told Detective Sergeant Michael Sussex the address of a hostel in Walworth.

He was walking us in the direction of the Trenches, and I didn't want to go there. So I said, "I've had my breakfast and I ought to go because I've got an appointment with my social worker."

It was a mistake because then he wanted to know who my social worker was and what time I had to be there. Lies breed. It's much better if you don't talk to the Law because then you can keep to the truth.

After a while he said, "Aren't you a bit young to be living on your own . . . Doreen?"

"I'm eighteen," I said. I felt depressed. I hadn't spoken one honest word to the man since he dropped his big hand on my shoulder. Well, you can't, can you? I talked to a social worker once and she tried to put Dawn and me in care. Never again. They would have split us up and then Dawn would never have found herself a man. Say what you like about Dawn's boyfriend, but he did set her up in business, and she does make good money. She feels real. No one can feel real in care.

We were right next to the Trenches by now. For a change it looked completely deserted—no winos, no bonfires, none of us picking through the rubbish dumped there in the night. It's just a big demolition site, really, but since no one is in any hurry to build there, it's become home to all sorts of people.

Detective Sergeant Michael Sussex stopped. He said, "We found a body in there last night."

I said nothing. I couldn't see the bit of wall the dead man had been sitting by, but I knew where it was.

"Yes," he said, as if he was thinking about something else. "Stripped clean, he was. When it comes my turn I'd like to be somewhere no one can get their thieving hands on me."

I was still watching his feet, and now even his boots looked as if they were thinking about something else. So I took off.

I broke clear of his hand. I dodged between two people passing by and hopped over the wire. Then I dropped down into the Trenches.

It was the last place I wanted to be, but it was the only place I could go.

I heard him come down behind me, and as I ran through the rubble I could feel his feet thudding on the ground. He was awfully fast for a big man.

"Stop!" he yelled, and I kept running. This way, that way, over the brickwork, round the rubbish tips, into cellars, up steps. And all the time I could hear his feet and his breath. I couldn't get free of him.

I was getting tired when I saw the drain. I put on one more sprint and dived head first into it. It was the only thing I could think of to do. It was the only place he couldn't come after me.

It was the only place I couldn't get out of.

I know about the drain. I've been in there before to get out of the wind, but it doesn't go anywhere. There is a bend about ten yards from the opening, and after that it's very wet and all stopped up with earth.

Anyway, like it or not, I dived straight in and crawled down. There wasn't much room even for me. I had to get all the way to the bend before I could turn round.

It was totally dark in the drain. There should have been a circle of light at the opening, but Detective Sergeant Michael Sussex had his head and shoulders wedged in it.

He said, "Don't be a fool, Crystal. Come out of there!" His voice boomed.

"Look, I only want a chat," he said. "I'm not going to hurt you."

He wasn't going to hurt me as long as I stayed in the drain and he stayed out of it.

"Come and get me," I said. I would have felt quite cheerful if it hadn't been so dark and wet.

"I don't know what you think you're up to, Crystal," he said. "But you're in a lot of trouble. I can help you."

I nearly laughed. "I don't know any Crystals," I said. "How can you help me?"

"You've got enemies," he said. "The bloke who died had the same enemies. You took something off him and now they're looking for you. They're rough people, Crystal, and you need my help."

"I don't know any dead blokes," I said. "I didn't take anything. What am I supposed to have nicked?"

"You're wasting my time," he said.

"All right," I said. "Then I'll go." There wasn't anywhere to go, but I didn't think he'd know that.

"Wait," he said. "Don't go anywhere till you've heard what I have to say." He fell silent. It was what I always thought. You tell them things. They'd rather eat worms before they tell you something back.

After a bit he said, "You still there?"

"I'm still here," I said. "But not for long. I'm getting wet."

"All right," he said. "You won't understand this but I'll tell you anyway. The dead bloke was a systems analyst."

"What's one of them?" I asked.

"He was a computer expert." Detective Sergeant Michael Sussex sighed. I could hear it from my end of the drain. Sound travels in a drain.

"He wrote programs for computers. He debugged programs. But most of all he wrote safe programs." He sighed again.

"This doesn't mean anything to you," he said. "Why don't you just come out of there like a good girl and give me the number."

"What number?" I said. He was right. I didn't understand. I was very confused. I thought I was in trouble because I'd taken the wallet. I tried to give it back but the woman wouldn't take it. That was confusing. Whoever heard of anyone not taking money when it was offered.

"It doesn't matter what number," he said, sounding angry. "This bloke, this Philip Walker-Jones, he worked for some very funny types. These types don't keep their dealings in books or ledgers anymore. Oh no. They stick them on computer tape, or discs where your average copper won't know how to find them. It's all bleeding high tech now."

He sounded very fed up, and I couldn't tell if it was because I was in a drain out of reach, or because he didn't understand high tech any more than I did.

Just then I heard footsteps, and someone said, "What you doing down there, boss?"

"Taking a bleeding mudbath," Detective Sergeant Michael Sussex said. "What does it look like I'm doing?"

"Did you lose her, then?" the other voice said.

"Course not. This is a new interview technique. Orders from on high: 'Do it in a bleeding land-drain.'" He sounded so down I almost laughed.

"Are you still there?" he said.

"No," I said. "Good-bye." And I scrambled into the bend of the pipe and pulled my knees up to my chest so that I couldn't be seen.

"Shit!" Detective Sergeant Michael Sussex said. "You've scared her off, you bleeding berk."

I could hear him heaving and cursing, and then he said, "You'd better give me a pull out of here, Hibbard."

There was some more heaving and cursing, and then I heard his voice from further off saying, "Where does this bleeding drain come out?"

"Buggered if I know, boss," Hibbard said. "Could be the river for all I know."

"Well, bleeding go and look," Detective Sergeant Michael Sussex said. "And if you find her don't lose her or I'll have you back in uniform quicker than you can say 'crystal balls.'"

"You sure you had the right one?" Hibbard said. He sounded reluctant to go tramping around the Trenches looking for the other end of a drain.

"You saw the description—there can't be two like her."

I didn't like the way he said that, and I didn't like the way he made fun of my name. I was freezing cold and soaked through, but I wasn't going to come out for anyone with that sort of attitude.

So that's where we stayed, him outside in the Trenches and me scrunched up at the end of the drain waiting for him to give up and go away. Sometimes he shone a torch in—to keep himself busy, I suppose. But I stayed stone-still and never made a sound.

Sometimes he paced up and down and muttered foul language to himself. He reminded me of our mum's boyfriend when he thought I'd pinched something off him. We were all at it in those days. He'd pinch things out of our mum's handbag and Dawn and me pinched things off him. We used to hide under the stairs, Dawn and me, while he raged around swearing he'd leather the lights out of us. Sometimes I'd hide from the truant officer too.

I'm used to hiding. All it takes is a bit of patience and a good breakfast in your belly. Don't try it somewhere wet and cold, though—that calls for real talent and I wouldn't recommend it to beginners.

At one stage Hibbard came back. He didn't sound half so cocky now.

"She'll be long gone," he said. "I can't find where this thing comes out."

"It's got to come out somewhere," Detective Sergeant Michael Sussex said. "Use your radio. Get more bodies. Make a bleeding effort."

He stayed where he was, and I stayed where I was.

Another time, Hibbard said, "Why don't we get in the Borough Engineers to dig this whole fucking site up and be done with it?"

And another time Detective Sergeant Michael Sussex said, "Comb the bleeding area. She could've dropped it or stashed it." He was sounding cold and tired too.

"All this for a bleeding number," he said. "And if we don't get it our whole case goes down the bleeding bog. Why couldn't the silly sod pick somewhere else to pop his clogs?"

Hibbard said, "Why are we so sure he had it on him? And why are we so sure she's got it now?"

"We know he had it because he was bringing it to me," Detective Sergeant Michael Sussex said. "And we know she got it because she swiped his wallet. We've got everything else back except that, and unless he had the number tattooed to his bleeding skull under his bleeding hair that's where it is."

"Couldn't he have just had it in his head?" Hibbard said. "Remembered it."

"Twenty-five bleeding digits? Do me a favor. He said it was written down and he said I could have it. You just want to go indoors for your dinner. Well, no one gets any dinner till I get that kid."

So we all sat there without our dinners. Detective Sergeant Michael Sussex made everyone go hungry for nothing. Because I didn't have any number twenty-five digits long.

But it's no use worrying about what you don't have, especially when what really worries you is what you might get. I was worried I might get pneumonia. If you get sick you can't feed yourself. If you can't feed yourself you get weak, and then either the officials grab you and put you in a hospital, or you die. I've seen it happen.

And I'll tell you something else—a very funny thing happened when I got out of the drain. Well, it wasn't a thing, and it didn't really happen. But I thought it did, and it really frightened me.

I became an old woman.

It was when I looked round the bend and couldn't see the circle of light at the end of the drain. I strained my ears and I couldn't hear anything moving out there. And suddenly I thought I'd gone deaf and blind.

I tried to move, but I was so stiff with cold it took me ages to inch my way along to the opening. I didn't care if Detective Sergeant Michael Sussex caught me. In fact I called out to him, and my voice had gone all weak and husky. I wanted him to be there, if you can believe that. I actually wanted him to help me, see, because I thought I'd gone blind, and I was scared.

But he wasn't there, and it was dark and teeming down with rain. And I couldn't straighten up. My back was bent, my knees were bent. There was no strength in my legs. I couldn't have run if they'd set the dogs on me.

I was an old woman out there in the dark—looking at the puddles in the mud, shuffling along, bent over. And I thought about Bloody Mary and the way she is first thing of a morning. There are some of them even older than she is who never have to bend over to look in dustbins because that's the shape they always are.

Of course I come to my senses soon enough. I got my circulation back and I rubbed the stiffness out of my legs. And I knew it was truly dark. I hadn't gone blind. But I did not stop being scared.

Even standing upright I felt helpless. Even with 743 pounds, 89 pence on me. The Law was after me. The bastards who beat up Little Marvin were after me. And I had nowhere to go. I was sick and old, and I needed help. What I needed, I thought, was a mark of my own.

Once having thought that, I became a little more cheerful. Not a lot, mind, because I hadn't had anything to eat since that curry before daybreak, and being hungry brings on the blues like nothing else can. But I pulled myself together and went looking for my mark.

I didn't know her name, but I knew where to find her. It was up the other end of the northern line. I couldn't have walked it that night, not for love nor money. So I caught the tube to Chalk Farm, and I hung around outside one of those bookshops.

I thought I had her once, but she tightened her grip on her shopping and hurried away. It was a mistake I put down to hunger. Usually I don't go wrong on middle-aged women.

But I saw her at last. She was wearing a fawn-colored raincoat and a tartan scarf. She had a green umbrella and she was struggling with her Christmas shopping.

I said, "Carry your bags for you, missus?"

She hesitated. I knew her. She's the one who has her handbag open before you even ask. She doesn't give you any mouth about finding a job or spending money on drink. She just looks sort of sorry and she watches you when you walk away.

She hesitated, but then she gave me a bag to carry. Not the heaviest one either. She's nice. She wants to trust me. At least she doesn't want to distrust me. I knew her. She was my mark.

She said, "Thank you very much. The car is just round the corner."

I followed her, and stood in the rain while she fumbled with her umbrella and car keys. I put her bag in the boot and helped her with the other one.

She looked at me and hesitated again. Not that she'd dream of going off without giving me something. This one just wants to find a polite way of doing it.

She said, "Well, thanks very much," and she started to fumble in her handbag again. I let her get her money out, and then I said, "I don't want your money, missus, thanks all the same for the thought."

She said, "Oh, but you must let me give you something."

I just stood there shaking my head, looking pitiful.

"What is it?" she asked, with that sorry expression on her face.

It was the crucial time. I said. "I've got some money, missus, but I can't spend it." And I held out one of the fifty-pound notes.

She looked at the money and she looked at me.

I said, "I know what you're thinking. That's why I can't spend it. I want to get some decent clothes because I can't get a job looking like this. But every time I try they look at me like I stole the money and they go to call the Law. No one trusts people like me."

She went on looking first at me and then at the money, and said, "I don't mean to sound suspicious, but where *did* you get a fifty-pound note?"

"A nice lady give it to me," I said. "She must've thought it was a fiver. She was a really nice lady because no one's ever given me a fiver before. But when I went in to buy a cup of tea and some chips, the man went to call the Law and I saw she must have made a mistake."

"I see," she said.

"You don't," I said. "Having this money is worse than not having anything."

"I can see that," she said. "How can I help?"

I had her. "Please, missus," I said. "Please help me spend it. All I want's a good coat and some shoes. There's a charity shop just round the corner and I been hanging around for ages but I can't bring myself to go in on my own."

She was good as gold, my lady mark. She bought me a big wool coat for only a couple of quid and she talked to the women in the shop while I looked for jeans and jerseys.

It was all quality stuff and probably it was all donated to the charity by women like her. They don't give any old rubbish to charity. And I'll tell you something else—my lady mark was having the time of her life. It was like a dream come true to her. Someone really and truly wanted her help with something she approved of. She didn't have to worry I was spending her money on drink or drugs because it wasn't her money and I was there under her nose spending it on warm clothes.

Even the women behind the counter had a sort of glow on them when I came out from behind the racks with my arms full. She'd probably told them my story in whispers when my back was turned. And that was why I really had needed her help. Because those nice ladies behind the counter would have chased me out if I'd gone in on my own. They'd have been afraid I'd pinch their charity.

It was still coming down in buckets when we left the shop. This time it was me carrying all the bags.

I was about to go when she said, "Look, don't be insulted, but what you need is a hot bath and somewhere to change." She said it in a rush as if she really was afraid of hurting my feelings.

"I live up the hill," she said. "It won't take any time at all."

"Nah," I said. "I'll get your car seats all dirty."

"It doesn't matter," she said. "Please."

And I thought, why not? She deserved the satisfaction.

She ran me a hot bath and squirted loads of scented oil in. She gave me her shampoo and a whole heap of clean towels. And then my lovely lady mark left me alone in her bathroom.

I swear she had tears in her eyes when I came out in my new clothes.

"Crystal," she said, "you look like a new person." This was just what I wanted to hear.

"You look quite like my own daughter when she was younger," she said. Which was a good thing because the Law and the bastards who beat Marvin up weren't looking for someone who looked like my lady mark's daughter. And no one would bat an eyelash if she had a fifty-pound note. My lady mark's daughter would not turn into an old woman who had to bend over to root around in dustbins.

And nor, I thought, would I, if I could help it.

She cooked me eggs and potatoes for my tea, and when I left she gave me a fiver and her green umbrella.

It was a shame really to have pinched her soap. But you can't break old habits all at once.

She even wanted to give me another ride in her car. But I wouldn't let her. She was a lovely lady, but I didn't think she'd understand about Dawn. Lovely ladies don't.

I could give lessons about what to do when you find your mark, and the last one would be—don't push your luck. Because if you push your luck and let them take over, they start giving you what they think you need instead of what you want. If my lady mark knew too much about Dawn and what was really going on, she'd have got in touch with the Social Services all over again. And far from being a lovely lady she'd have turned into an interfering old cow.

I was doing her a favor, really. I'm sure she'd rather be a lovely lady than an interfering old cow.

No one who saw me knocking at Dawn's door in Paddington would have known I'd spent all day down a drain. Dawn didn't.

" 'Struth, Crystal," she said when she opened up. "You look like one of those girls from that snob school up the hill from ours."

I knew what she meant and I didn't like it much. But I was lucky really. I'd caught her at a slack time when she was just lying around reading her comic and playing records. And now I was all clean and respectable, she didn't mind if I sat on her bed.

"You still need your hair cut," Dawn said.

She got out her scissors and manicure set, and we sat on her bed while she cut my hair and did my nails. Dawn could be a beautician if she wanted. The trouble is she'd never stand for the training and the money wouldn't be enough. She's used to her creature comforts now, is Dawn.

It was a bit like the old days—Dawn and me together listening to records, and her fiddling with my hair. I didn't want to spoil it but I had to ask about the watch.

Because when I was in the lovely lady's bathroom I'd had another search through Philip Walker-Jones's wallet.

Dawn said, "What about the watch?" And she rubbed round my thumb with her little nail file.

"It was real gold," I said, to remind her. "Your Christmas present."

"I can't wear a man's watch," she said. Dawn likes to be very dainty sometimes.

"Where is it?" I said.

"You want it back?" she asked. "Fine Christmas present if you want it back."

I looked at her and she looked at me. Then she said, "Well, Crystal, if you must know, I was going to give it to my boyfriend for Christmas."

"It wasn't for him," I said. "It was for you."

"A man's watch?" she said, and laughed. "I was going to get his name engraved on the back. 'Eternal love, from Dawn.' But there wasn't room. There were all these numbers on the back, and the man at the jewelers said I'd lose too much gold having them rubbed down."

"Hah!" I said. I felt clever. Because all it takes is some good hot food to help you think. And it had come to me in a flash just after I'd put down my last mouthful of egg and potato.

I said, "Bet there were twenty-five of them."

"Loads of numbers," she said. She put the nail file back in her manicure set.

"If you must know, Crystal," she said, "I popped it. And I bought him a real gold cigarette lighter instead."

And she gave me the pawn ticket.

She hadn't got much for a solid gold watch. Dawn isn't practical like I am, so the pawnbroker cheated her. Not that it mattered. It wasn't her watch in the first place, and besides, it would cost me less to get back. If I wanted it back.

Poor Dawn. She needs me to take care of her. She doesn't think she does because she thinks her boyfriend's doing it. She's not like me. She doesn't want to look after herself. That's not her job. And if I told her what I'd been through today to solve my own problems she'd say I was a fool.

But look at it this way—I'd given Detective Sergeant Michael Sussex the slip. I'd dressed up so he wouldn't know me again if I ran slap-bang into him. Nor would Brainy Brian. So he couldn't finger me to the bastards who beat up little Marvin. I'd had a bath and I'd had eggs and potatoes for my tea. I had enough money to sleep in a bed for as many nights as I wanted. And now I had the watch.

Or I could have it any time I wanted. But it was safer where it was. I still didn't know why the number was so important but I was sure it would be worth something to me sooner or later.

I saw Dawn looking at me.

"Don't get too cocky, Crystal," she said. "You might *look* like a girl from the snob school, but you're still just like me."

That's how much she knew.

SUE GRAFTON's private eye Kinsey Millhone is, along with Sara Paretsky's V. I. Warshawski and Marcia Muller's Sharon McCone, one of three female investigators who revolutionized crime fiction in the 1980s. Her alphabetized book titles, beginning with *"A" is for Alibi* and now extending through *"G" is for Gumshoe,* have proved enormously popular. Ms. Grafton lives in Santa Barbara, California, a community much like Kinsey's "Santa Teresa."

"FULL CIRCLE"

A Kinsey Millhone Short Story

Sue Grafton

 The accident seemed to happen in slow motion . . . one of those stop-action sequences that seem to go on forever though in truth no more than a few seconds have elapsed. It was Friday afternoon, rush hour, Santa Teresa traffic moving at a lively pace, my little VW holding its own despite the fact that it's fifteen years out of date. I was feeling good. I'd just wrapped up a case and I had a check in my handbag for four thousand bucks, not bad considering that I'm a female private eye, self-employed, and subject to the feast-or-famine vagaries of any other free-lance work.

I glanced to my left as a young woman, driving a white compact, appeared in my side view mirror. A bright red Porsche was bearing down on her in the fast lane. I adjusted my speed, making room for her, sensing that she meant to cut in front of me. A navy-blue pickup truck was coming up on my right, each of us jockeying for position as the late afternoon sun washed down out of a cloudless California spring sky. I had glanced in my rearview mirror, checking traffic behind me, when I heard a loud popping noise. I snapped my attention back to the road in front of me. The white compact veered abruptly back into the fast lane, clipped the rear of the red Porsche, then hit the center divider and careened directly into my path. I slammed on my brakes, adrenaline shooting through me as I fought to control the VW's fishtailing rear end.

Suddenly a dark green Mercedes appeared from out of nowhere and caught the girl's car broadside, flipping the vehicle with all the expertise of a movie stunt. Brakes squealed all around me like a chorus of squawking birds and I could hear the successive thumps of colliding cars piling up behind me in a drumroll of destruction. It was over in an instant, a cloud of dust roiling up from the shoulder where the girl's car had finally come to rest, right side up, half-buried in the shrubbery. She had sheared off one of the support posts for the exit sign that now leaned crazily across her car roof. The ensuing silence was profound.

I pulled over and was out of my car like a shot, the fellow from the navy-blue pickup truck right behind me. There must have been five of us running toward the wreckage, spurred by the possibility of exploding gasoline, which mercifully did not ignite. The white car was accordion-folded, the door on the driver's side jammed shut. Steam billowed out from under the hood with an alarming hiss. The impact had rammed the girl head first into the windshield, which had cracked in a star-burst effect. She was unconscious, her face bathed in blood. I willed myself to move toward her though my instinct was to turn away in horror.

The guy from the pickup truck nearly wrenched the car door off its hinges in one of those emergency-generated bursts of strength that can't be duplicated under ordinary circumstances. As he reached for her, I caught his arm. "Don't move her," I said. "Let the paramedics handle this."

He gave me a startled look but drew back as he was told. I shed my windbreaker and we used it to form a compress, stanching the flow of blood from the worst of her cuts. The guy was in his twenties, with dark curly hair and dark eyes filled with anxiety.

Over my shoulder, someone was asking me if I knew first aid, and I realized that others had been hurt in the accident as well. The driver from the green Mercedes was already using the roadside emergency phone, presumably calling police and ambulance. I looked back at the guy from the pickup truck, who was pressing the girl's neck, looking for a pulse.

"Is she alive?" I asked.

"Looks like it."

I jerked my head at the people on the berm behind me. "Let me see what I can do down there until the ambulance comes," I said. "Holler if you need me."

He nodded in reply.

I left him with the girl and moved along the shoulder toward a writhing man whose leg was visibly broken. A woman was sobbing hysterically somewhere close by and her cries added an eerie counterpoint to the moans of those in pain. The fellow from the red Porsche simply stood there numb, immobilized by shock.

Meanwhile, traffic had slowed to a crawl and commuters were rubbernecking as if freeway accidents were some sort of spectator sport and this was the main event. Sirens approached. The next hour was a blur of police and emergency vehicles. I spotted my friend John Birkett, a photographer from the local paper, who'd reached the scene moments behind the paramedics. I remember marveling at the speed with which news of the pileup had spread. I watched as the girl was loaded into the ambulance. While flashbulbs went off, several of us gave our accounts of the accident to the highway patrol officer, conferring with one another compulsively as if repetition might relieve us of tension and distress. I didn't get home until nearly seven and my hands were still shaking. The jumble of images made sleep a torment of sudden awakenings, my foot jerking in a dream sequence as I slammed on my brakes again and again.

When I read in the morning paper that the girl had died, I felt sick with regret. The article was brief. Caroline Spurrier was twenty-two, a senior psychology major at the University of California, Santa Teresa. She was a native of Denver, Colorado, just two months short of graduation at the time of her death. The photograph showed shoulder-length blond hair, bright eyes, and an impish grin. According to the paper, six other people had suffered injuries, none fatal. The weight of the young woman's death settled in my chest like a cold I couldn't shake.

My office in town was being repainted, so I worked at home that next week, catching up on reports. On Thursday, when the knock came, I'd just broken for lunch. I opened the door. At first glance, I thought the dead girl was miraculously alive, restored to health, and standing on my doorstep with all the solemnity of a ghost. The illusion was dispelled. A close look showed a blond woman in her midforties, her face etched with weariness.

"I'm Michelle Spurrier," she said. "I understand you were a witness to my daughter's accident."

I stepped back. "Please come in. I'm sorry for your loss, Mrs. Spurrier. That was terrible."

She moved past me like a sleepwalker as I closed the door.

"Please sit down. Can I get you anything?"

She shook her head, looking around with bewilderment as if she couldn't quite remember what had brought her here. She set her purse aside and sank down on my couch, placing her cupped hands across her nose and mouth like an oxygen mask.

I sat down beside her, watching as she breathed deeply, struggling to speak. "Take your time," I said.

When the words came, her voice was so low I had to lean closely to hear her. "The police examined Caroline's car at the impound lot and found a bullet hole in the window on the passenger side. My daughter was shot." She burst into tears.

I sat beside her while she poured out a grief tinged with rage and frustration. I brought her a glass of water and a fistful of tissues, small comfort, but all I could think to do. "What are the police telling you?" I asked when she'd composed herself.

She blew her nose and then took another deep breath. "The case has been transferred from traffic detail to homicide. The officer I talked to this morning says it looks like a random freeway shooting, but I don't believe it."

"God knows they've had enough of those down in Los Angeles," I remarked.

"Well, I can't accept that. For one thing, what was she doing speeding down the highway at that hour of the day? She was supposed to be at work, but they tell me she left abruptly without a word to anyone."

"Where was she employed?"

"A restaurant out in Colgate. She'd been waiting tables there for a year. The shift manager told me a man had been harassing her. He thinks she might have left to try to get away from him."

"Did he know who the guy was?"

She shook her head. "He wasn't sure. Some fellow she'd been dating. Apparently, he kept stopping by the restaurant, calling her at all hours, making a terrible pest of himself. Lieutenant Dolan tells me you're a private detective, which is why I'm here. I want you to find out who's responsible for this."

"Mrs. Spurrier, the police here are very competent. I'm sure they're doing everything possible."

"Skip the public relations message," she said with bitterness. "I have to fly back to Denver. Caroline's stepfather is very ill and I need to get home, but I can't go unless I know someone here is looking into this. Please."

I thought about it briefly, but it didn't take much to persuade me. As a witness to the accident, I felt more than a professional interest in the case. "I'll need the names of her friends," I said.

I made a note of Mrs. Spurrier's address and phone number, along with the name of Caroline's roommate and the restaurant where she'd worked. I drew up a standard contract, waiving the advance. I'd bill her later for whatever time I put in. Ordinarily I bypass police business in an attempt to stay out of Lieutenant Dolan's way. As the officer in charge of homicide, he's not crazy about private eyes. Though he's fairly tolerant of me, I couldn't imagine what she'd had to threaten to warrant the referral.

As soon as she left, I grabbed a jacket and my handbag and drove over to the police station, where I paid six dollars for a copy of the police report. Lieutenant Dolan wasn't in, but I spent a few minutes chatting with Emerald, the clerk in Identification and Records. She's a heavy black woman in her fifties, usually wary of my questions but a sucker for gossip.

"I hear Jasper's wife caught him with Rowena Hairston," I said, throwing out some bait. Jasper Sax is one of Emerald's interdepartmental foes.

"Why tell me?" she said. She was pretending disinterest, but I could tell the rumor cheered her. Jasper, from the crime lab, is forever lifting files from Emerald's desk, which only gets her in trouble when Lieutenant Dolan comes around.

"I was hoping you'd fill me in on the Spurrier accident. I know you've memorized all the paperwork."

She grumbled something about flattery that implied she felt flattered, so I pressed for specifics. "Anybody see where the shot was fired from?" I asked.

"No ma'am."

I thought about the fellow in the red Porsche. He'd been in the lane to my left, just a few yards ahead of me when the accident occurred. The man in the pickup might be a help as well. "What about the other witnesses? There must have been half a dozen of us at the scene. Who's been interviewed?"

Emerald gave me an indignant look. "What's the matter with you? You know I'm not allowed to give out information like that!"

"Worth a try," I said equably. "What about the girl's professors from the university? Has Dolan talked to them?"

"Check it out yourself if you're so interested," she snapped.

"Come on, Emerald. Dolan knows I'm doing this. He was the one who told Mrs. Spurrier about me in the first place. I'll make it easy for you. Just one name."

She squinted at me suspiciously. "Which one's that?"

I took a flier, describing the guy in the pickup, figuring she could identify him from the list by age. Grudgingly, she checked the list and her expression changed.

"Uh-oh," she said. "I might know you'd zero in on this one. Fellow in the pickup gave a phony name and address. Benny Seco was the name, but he must have made that up. Telephone was a fake, too. Looks like he took off and nobody's seen him since. Might have been a warrant out against him he was trying to duck."

"How about the guy in the Porsche?"

I heard a voice behind me. "Well, well, well. Kinsey Millhone. Hard at work, I see."

Emerald faded into the background with all the practice of a spy. I turned to find Lieutenant Dolan standing in the hallway in his habitual pose: hands

shoved down in his pants pockets, rocking on his heels. He'd recently celebrated a birthday, his baggy face reflecting every one of his sixty years.

I folded the police report and tucked it in my bag. "Mrs. Spurrier got in
touch with me and asked me to follow up on this business of her daughter's
death. I feel bad about the girl."

His manner shifted. "I do, too," he said.

"What's the story on the missing witness?"

Dolan shrugged. "He must have had some reason to give out a phony
name. Did you talk to him at the scene?"

"Just briefly, but I'd know him if I saw him again. Do you think he could
be of help?"

Dolan ran a hand across his balding pate. "I'd sure like to hear what the
fellow has to say. Nobody else was aware that the girl was shot. I gather he
was close enough to have done it himself."

"There's gotta be a way to track him down, don't you think?"

"Maybe," he said. "No one remembers much about the man except the
truck he drove. Toyota, dark blue, maybe four or five years old from what
they say."

"Would you object if I checked back with the other witnesses? I might get
more out of them since I was there."

He studied me for a moment, then reached over to the file and removed
the list of witnesses, which he handed to me without a word.

"Don't you need this?" I said, surprised.

"I have a copy."

"Thanks. This is great. I'll let you know what I find out."

Dolan pointed a finger. "Keep in touch with the department. I don't want
you going off half-cocked."

I drove out to the campus area to the restaurant where Caroline Spurrier
had worked. The place had changed hands recently, the decor downgraded
from real plants to fake as the nationality of the food changed from Mexican
to Thai. The shift manager, David Cole, was just a kid himself, barely
twenty-two, tall, skinny, with a nose that belonged on a much larger face.

I introduced myself and told him I was looking into Caroline's death.

"Oh, yeah, that was awful. I talked to her mom."

"She says you mentioned some guy who'd been bugging her. What else
can you tell me?"

"That's about all I know. I mean, I never saw the guy myself. She was
working nights for the last couple months and just switched back to days to
see if she could get away from him."

"She ever mention his name?"

"Terry something, I think. She said he used to follow her around in this green van he drove. She really thought the dude was bent."

"Bent?"

"You know . . . twisted." He twiddled an index finger beside his head to indicate his craziness.

"Why'd she go out with him?"

"She said he seemed like a real nice guy at first, but then he got real possessive, all jealous and like that. In the end, I guess he was totally nuts. He must have showed up on Friday, which is why she took off."

I quizzed him, but couldn't glean much more from his account. I thanked him and drove over to the block of university housing where Caroline had lived. The apartment was typical of student digs; faintly shabby, furnished with mismatched items that had probably been languishing in someone's garage. Her roommate was a young woman named Judy Layton, who chatted despondently as she emptied kitchen cabinets and packed assorted cardboard boxes. I kept the questions light at first, asking her about herself as she wrapped some dinner plates in newspaper, shoving each in a box. She was twenty-two, a senior English major with family living in town.

"How long did you know Caroline?"

"About a year," she said. "I had another roommate, but Alice graduated last year. Caroline and I connected up through one of those roommate referral services."

"How come you're moving out?"

She shrugged. "Going back to my folks'. It's too late in the school year to find someone else and I can't afford this place on my own. My brother's on his way over to help me move."

According to her, Caroline was a "party-hearty" who somehow managed to keep her grades up and still have a good time.

"Did she have a boyfriend?"

"She dated lots of guys."

"But no one in particular?"

She shook her head, intent on her work.

I tried again. "She told her mom about some guy harassing her at work. Apparently she'd dated him and they'd just broken up. Do you have any idea who she might have been talking about?"

"Not really. I didn't keep track of the guys in her life."

"She must have mentioned this guy if he was causing such a fuss."

"Look. She and I were not close. We were roommates and that was it. She went her way and I went mine. If some guy was bugging her, she didn't say a word to me."

"She wasn't in any trouble that you knew about?"

"No."

Her manner seemed sullen and it was getting on my nerves. I stared at her. "Judy, I could use a little help. People get murdered for a reason. It might seem stupid or insignificant to the rest of us, but there was *something* going on. What gives?"

"You don't know it was murder. The policeman I talked to said it might have been some bozo in a passing car."

"Her mother disagrees."

"Well, I can't help you. I already told you everything I know."

I nailed her with a look and let a silence fall, hoping her discomfort would generate further comment. No such luck. If she knew more, she was determined to keep it to herself. I left a business card, asking her to phone me if she remembered anything.

I spent the next two days talking to Caroline Spurrier's professors and friends. From the portrait that emerged, she seemed like a likable kid, funny, good-natured, popular, and sweet. She'd complained of the harassment to a couple of classmates without giving any indication who the fellow was. I went back to the list of witnesses at the scene of the accident, talking to each in turn. I was still tantalized by the guy in the pickup. What reason could he have to falsify his identity?

I'd clipped out the news account of Caroline Spurrier's death, pinning her picture on the bulletin board above my desk. She looked down at me with a smile that seemed more enigmatic with the passing days. I couldn't bear the idea of having to tell her mother my investigation was at an impasse, but I knew I owed her a report.

I was sitting at my typewriter when an idea came to me, quite literally, in a flash. I was staring at the newspaper picture of the wreckage when I spotted the photo credit. I suddenly remembered John Birkett at the scene, his flash going off as he shot pictures of the wreck. If he'd inadvertently snapped one of the guy in the pickup, at least I'd have something to show the cops. Maybe we could get a lead on the fellow that way. I gave Birkett a call. Twenty minutes later, I was in his cubbyhole at the Santa Teresa *Dispatch*, our heads bent together while we scanned the contact sheets.

"No good," John said. "This one's not bad, but the focus is off. Damn. I never really got a clear shot of him."

"What about the truck?"

John pulled out another contact sheet that showed various views of the wrecked compact, the pickup visible on the berm behind. "Well, you can see it in the background, if that's any help."

"Can we get an enlargement?"

"You looking for anything in particular?"

"The license plate," I said.

The California plate bore a seven-place combination of numbers and letters that we finally discerned in the grainy haze of the two blowups. I should have called Lieutenant Dolan and had him run the license number, but I confess to an egotistical streak that sometimes overrides common sense. I didn't want to give the lead back to him just yet. I called a pal of mine at the Department of Motor Vehicles and asked him to check it out instead.

The license plate was registered to a 1984 Toyota pickup, navy blue, the owner listed as Ron Cagle with an address on McClatchy Way.

The house was stucco, dark gray, with the trim done in white. My heart was pounding as I rang the bell. The fellow's face was printed so indelibly in my memory that when the door was finally opened, I just stood there and stared. Wrong man. This guy was probably six foot seven, over two hundred pounds, with a strong chin, ruddy complexion, blue eyes, auburn hair, red moustache. "Yes?"

"I'm looking for Ron Cagle."

"I'm Ron Cagle."

"You are?" My voice broke in astonishment like a kid reaching puberty. "You're the owner of a navy-blue Toyota pickup?" I read off the number of the license plate.

He looked at me quizzically. "Yes. Is something wrong?"

"Well, ! don't know. Has someone else been driving it?"

"Not for the last six months."

"Are you sure?"

He half laughed. "See for yourself. It's sitting on the parking pad just behind the house."

He pulled the door shut behind him, leading the way as the two of us moved off the porch and down the driveway to the rear. There sat the navy-blue Toyota pickup, without wheels, up on blocks. The hood was open and there was empty space where the engine should have been. "What's going on?" he asked.

"That's what I'm about to ask you. This truck was at the scene of a recent accident where a girl was killed."

"Not this one," he said. "This has been right here."

Without another word, I pulled out the photographs. "Isn't that your license plate?"

He studied the photos with a frown. "Well, yes, but the truck isn't mine. It couldn't be." He glanced back at his pickup, spotting the discrepancy. "There's the problem . . ." He pointed to the license. The plate on the truck was an altogether different set of numbers.

It took me about thirty seconds before the light finally dawned. "Somebody must have lifted your plates and substituted these."

"What would be the point?"

I shrugged. "Maybe someone stole a navy-blue Toyota truck and wanted plates that would clear a license check if he was stopped by the cops. Can I use your telephone?"

I called Lieutenant Dolan and told him what I'd found. He ran a check on the plates for the pickup sitting in the drive that turned out to match the numbers on a vehicle reported stolen two weeks before. An APB was issued for the truck with Cagle's plates. Dolan's guess was that the guy had left the state, or abandoned the pickup shortly after the accident. It was also possible that even if we found the guy, he might not have any real connection with the shooting death. Somehow I doubted it.

A week passed with no results. The silence was discouraging. I was right back where I started from with no appreciable progress. If a case is going to break, it usually happens fast, and the chances of cracking this one were diminishing with every passing day. Caroline Spurrier's photograph was still pinned to the bulletin board above my desk, her smile nearly mocking as the days went by. In situations like this, all I know to do is go back to the beginning and start again.

Doggedly I went through the list of witnesses, calling everybody on the list. Most tried to be helpful, but there was really nothing new to add. I drove back to the campus to look for Caroline's roommate. Judy Layton had to know something more than she'd told me at first. Maybe I could find a way to worm some information out of her.

The apartment was locked, and a quick peek in the front window showed that all the furniture was gone. I picked up her forwarding address from the manager on the premises and headed over to her parents' house in Colgate, the little suburb to the north.

The house was pleasant, a story and a half of stucco and frame, an attached three-car garage visible at the right. I rang the bell and waited, idly scanning the neighborhood from my vantage point on the porch. It was a nice street, wide and treelined, with a grassy divider down the center planted with pink and white flowering shrubs. I rang the bell again. Apparently no one was home.

I went down the porch steps and paused in the driveway, intending to return to my car, which was parked at the curb. I hesitated where I stood. There are times in this business when a hunch is a hunch . . . when a little voice in your gut tells you something's amiss. I turned with curiosity toward the three-car garage at the rear. I cupped my hands, shading my eyes so I could peer through the side window. In the shadowy interior, I saw a pickup, stripped of paint.

I tried the garage's side entrance. The door was unlocked and I pushed my way in. The space smelled of dust, motor oil, and primer. The pickup's license plates were gone. This had to be the same truck, though I couldn't think why it hadn't been dumped. Maybe it was too perilous to attempt at this point. Heart thumping, I did a quick search of the cab's interior. Under the front seat, on the driver's side, I saw a handgun, a .45. I left it where it was, eased the cab door shut, and backed away from the truck. Clearly, someone in the Layton household had been at the murder scene.

I left the garage at a quick clip, trotting toward the street. I had to find a telephone and call the cops. I had just started my car, shoving it into gear, when I saw a dark green VW van pass on the far side of the divider and circle back in my direction, headed toward the Laytons' drive. The fellow driving was the man I'd seen at the accident. Judy's brother? The similarities were obvious, now that I thought of it. No wonder she'd been unwilling to tell me what was going on! He slowed for the turn, and that's when he spotted me.

If I'd had any doubts about his guilt, they vanished the minute he and I locked eyes. His surprise was replaced by panic, and he gunned his engine, taking off. I peeled after him, flooring it. At the corner he skidded sideways and recovered, speeding out of sight. I went after him, zigzagging crazily through a residential area that was laid out like a maze. I could almost chart his course ahead of me by the whine of his transmission. He was heading toward the freeway.

At the overpass, I caught a glimpse of him in the southbound lane. He wasn't hard to track, the boxy shape of the van clearly visible as we tore toward town. The traffic began to slow, massing in one of those inexplicable logjams on the road. I couldn't tell if the problem was a fender-bender in the northbound lane, or a bottleneck in ours, but it gave me the advantage I needed. I was catching him.

As I eased up on his left, I saw him lean on the accelerator, cutting to his right. He hit the shoulder of the road, his tires spewing out gravel as he widened the gap between us. He was bypassing stalled cars, hugging the shrubbery as he flew down the berm. I was right behind him, keeping as close to him as I dared. My car wasn't very swift, but then neither was his van. I jammed my accelerator to the floor and pinned myself to his tail. He was watching me steadily in his rear-view mirror, our eyes meeting in a deadlock of determination and grit.

I spotted the maintenance crew just seconds before he did; guys in bright orange vests working with a crane that was parked squarely in his path. There was no way for him to slow in time and no place else to go. His van plowed into the rear of the crane with a crash that made my blood freeze as I slammed on my brakes. I was luckier than he. My VW came to a stop just a kiss away from death.

Like a nightmare, we repeated all the horror of the first wreck. Police and paramedics, the wailing of the ambulance. When I finally stopped shaking, I realized where I was. The road crew was replacing the big green highway sign sheared in half when Caroline Spurrier's car had smashed into it. Terry Layton died at the very spot where he killed her.

Caroline's smile has shifted back to impishness in the photograph above my desk. I keep it there as a reminder, but of what I couldn't say. The brevity of life, perhaps, the finality of death . . . the irony of events that sometimes connect the two. We live in a world in which justice is skewed.

Regarded as the person most responsible for introducing the new, realistic, and modern woman detective, **MARCIA MULLER** has three exciting series characters—Sharon McCone, in *Eye of the Storm* and others; Joanna Stark, in *There Hangs the Knife* and others; and Elena Oliverez in powerful novels like *The Tree of Death*. These three characters all exhibit a keen ability to understand themselves as well as their suspects. Ms. Muller lives in Sonoma, California.

BENNY'S SPACE

Marcia Muller

 Amorfina Angeles was terrified, and I could fully empathize with her. Merely living in the neighborhood would have terrified me—all the more so had I been harassed by members of one of its many street gangs.

Hers was a rundown side street in the extreme southeast of San Francisco, only blocks from the drug- and crime-infested Sunnydale public housing projects. There were bars over the windows and grilles on the doors of the small stucco houses; dead and vandalized cars stood at the broken curbs; in the weed-choked yard next door, a mangy guard dog of indeterminate breed paced and snarled. Fear was written on this street as plainly as the graffiti on the walls and fences. Fear and hopelessness and a dull resignation to a life that none of its residents would willingly have opted to lead.

I watched Mrs. Angeles as she crossed her tiny living room to the front window, pulled the edge of the curtain aside a fraction, and peered out at the street. She was no more than five feet tall, with rounded shoulders, sallow skin, and graying black hair that curled in short, unruly ringlets. Her shapeless flower-printed dress did little to conceal a body made soft and fleshy by bad food and too much childbearing. Although she was only forty, she moved like a much older woman.

Her attorney and my colleague, Jack Stuart of All Souls Legal Cooperative, had given me a brief history of his client when he'd asked me to undertake an investigation on her behalf. She was a Filipina who had emigrated to the states with her husband in search of their own piece of the good life that was reputed to be had here. But as with many of their countrymen and -women, things hadn't worked out as the Angeleses had envisioned: first Amorfina's husband had gone into the import-export business with a friend from Manila; the friend absconded two years later with Joe Angeles's life savings. Then, a year after that, Joe was killed in a freak accident at a construction site where he was working. Amorfina and their six children were left with no means of support, and in the years since Joe's death their circumstances had gradually been reduced to this two-bedroom rental cottage in one of the worst areas of the city.

Mrs. Angeles, Jack told me, had done the best she could for her family, keeping them off the welfare rolls with a daytime job at a Mission district sewing factory and nighttime work doing alterations. As they grew older, the children helped with part-time jobs. Now there were only two left at home: sixteen-year-old Alex and fourteen-year-old Isabel. It was typical of their mother, Jack said, that in the current crisis she was more concerned for them than for herself.

She turned from the window now, her face taut with fear, deep lines bracketing her full lips. I asked, "Is someone out there?"

She shook her head and walked wearily to the worn recliner opposite me. I occupied the place of honor on a red brocade sofa encased in the same plastic that doubtless had protected it long ago upon delivery from the store. "I never see anybody," she said. "Not till it's too late."

"Mrs. Angeles, Jack Stuart told me about your problem, but I'd like to hear it in your own words—from the beginning, if you would."

She nodded, smoothing her bright dress over her plump thighs. "It goes back a long time, to when Benny Crespo was . . . they called him the Prince of Omega Street, you know."

Hearing the name of her street spoken made me aware of its ironic appropriateness: the last letter of the Greek alphabet is symbolic of endings, and for most of the people living here, Omega Street was the end of a steady decline into poverty.

Mrs. Angeles went on, "Benny Crespo was Filipino. His gang controlled the drugs here. A lot of people looked up to him; he had power, and that don't happen much with our people. Once I caught Alex and one of my older boys calling him a hero. I let them have it pretty good, you bet, and there wasn't any more of *that* kind of talk around this house. I got no use for the gangs—Filipino or otherwise."

"What was the name of Benny Crespo's gang?"

"The *Kabalyeros*. That's Tagalog for Knights."

"Okay—what happened to Benny?"

"The house next door, the one with the dog—that was where Benny lived. He always parked his fancy Corvette out front, and people knew better than to mess with it. Late one night he was getting out of the car and somebody shot him. A drug burn, they say. After that the *Kabalyeros* decided to make the parking space a shrine to Benny. They roped it off, put flowers there every week. On All Saints Day and the other fiestas, it was something to see."

"And that brings us to last March thirteenth," I said.

Mrs. Angeles bit her lower lip and smoothed her dress again.

When she didn't speak, I prompted her. "You'd just come home from work."

"Yeah. It was late, dark. Isabel wasn't here, and I got worried. I kept looking out the window, like a mother does."

"And you saw . . . ?"

"The guy who moved into the house next door after Benny got shot, Reg Dawson. He was black, one of a gang called the Victors. They say he moved into that house to show the *Kabalyeros* that the Victors were taking over their turf. Anyway, he drives up and stops a little way down the block. Waits there, revving his engine. People start showing up; the word's been put out that something's gonna go down. And when there's a big crowd, Reg Dawson guns his car and drives right into Benny's space, over the rope and the flowers.

"Well, that started one hell of a fight—Victors and *Kabalyeros* and folks from the neighborhood. And while it's going on, Reg Dawson just stands there in Benny's space acting macho. That's when it happened, what I saw."

"And what was that?"

She hesitated, wet her lips. "The leader of the *Kabalyeros*, Tommy Dragón —the Dragon, they call him—was over by the fence in front of Reg Dawson's house, where you couldn't see him unless you were really looking. I was, 'cause I was trying to see if Isabel was anyplace out there. And I saw Tommy Dragón point this gun at Reg Dawson and shoot him dead."

"What did you do then?"

"Ran and hid in the bathroom. That's where I was when the cops came to the door. Somebody'd told them I was in the window when it all went down and then ran away when Reg got shot. Well, what was I supposed to do? I got no use for the *Kabalyeros* or the Victors, so I told the truth. And now here I am in this mess."

Mrs. Angeles had been slated to be the chief prosecution witness at

Tommy Dragón's trial this week. But a month ago the threats had started: anonymous letters and phone calls warning her against testifying. As the trial date approached, this had escalated into blatant intimidation: a fire was set in her trash can; someone shot out her kitchen window; a dead dog turned up on her doorstep. The previous Friday, Isabel had been accosted on her way home from the bus stop by two masked men with guns. And that had finally made Mrs. Angeles capitulate; in court yesterday, she'd refused to take the stand against Dragón.

The state needed her testimony; there were no other witnesses, Dragón insisted on his innocence, and the murder gun had not been found. The judge had tried to reason with Mrs. Angeles, then cited her for contempt— reluctantly, he said. "The court is aware that there have been threats made against you and your family," he told her, "but it is unable to guarantee your protection." Then he gave her forty-eight hours to reconsider her decision.

As it turned out, Mrs. Angeles had a champion in her employer. The owner of the sewing factory was unwilling to allow one of his long-term workers to go to jail or to risk her own and her family's safety. He brought her to All Souls, where he held a membership in our legal-services plan, and this morning Jack Stuart had asked me to do something for her.

What? I'd asked. What could I do that the SFPD couldn't to stop vicious harassment by a street gang?

Well, he said, get proof against whoever was threatening her so they could be arrested and she'd feel free to testify.

Sure, Jack, I said. And exactly why *hadn't* the police been able to do anything about the situation?

His answer was not surprising: lack of funds. Intimidation of prosecution witnesses in cases relating to gang violence was becoming more and more prevalent and open in San Francisco, but the city did not have the resources to protect them. An old story nowadays—not enough money to go around.

Mrs. Angeles was watching my face, her eyes tentative. As I looked back at her, her gaze began to waver. She'd experienced too much disappointment in her life to expect much in the way of help from me.

I said, "Yes, you certainly are in a mess. Let's see if we can get you out of it."

We talked for a while longer, and I soon realized that Amor—as she asked me to call her—held the misconception that there was some way I could get the contempt citation dropped. I asked her if she'd known beforehand that a balky witness could be sent to jail. She shook her head. A person had a right to change her mind, didn't she? When I set her straight on that, she seemed to lose interest in the conversation; it was difficult to get her to focus long enough to compile a list of people I should talk with. I settled for enough names to keep me occupied for the rest of the afternoon.

I was ready to leave when angry voices came from the front steps. A young man and woman entered. They stopped speaking when they saw the room was occupied, but their faces remained set in lines of contention. Amor hastened to introduce them as her son and daughter, Alex and Isabel. To them she explained that I was a detective "helping with the trouble with the judge."

Alex, a stocky youth with a tracery of moustache on his upper lip, seemed disinterested. He shrugged out of his high school letter jacket and vanished through a door to the rear of the house. Isabel studied me with frank curiosity. She was a slender beauty, with black hair that fell in soft curls to her shoulders; her features had a delicacy lacking in those of her mother and brother. Unfortunately, bright blue eyeshadow and garish orange lipstick detracted from her natural good looks, and she wore an imitation leather outfit in a particularly gaudy shade of purple. However, she was polite and well-spoken as she questioned me about what I could do to help her mother. Then, after a comment to Amor about an assignment that was due the next day, she left through the door her brother had used.

I turned to Amor, who was fingering the leaves of a philodendron plant that stood on a stand near the front window. Her posture was stiff, and when I spoke to her she didn't meet my eyes. Now I was aware of a tension in her that hadn't been there before her children returned home. Anxiety, because of the danger her witnessing the shooting had placed them in? Or something else? It might have had to do with the quarrel they'd been having, but weren't arguments between siblings fairly common? They certainly had been in my childhood home in San Diego.

I told Amor I'd be back to check on her in a couple of hours. Then, after a few precautionary and probably unnecessary reminders about locking doors and staying clear of windows, I went out into the chill November afternoon.

The first name on my list was Madeline Dawson, the slain gang leader's widow. I glanced at the house next door and saw with some relief that the guard dog no longer paced in its yard. When I pushed through the gate in the chain link fence, the creature's whereabouts quickly became apparent: a bellowing emanated from the small, shabby cottage. I went up a broken walk bordered by weeds, climbed the sagging front steps, and pressed the bell. A woman's voice yelled for the dog to shut up, then a door slammed somewhere within, muffling the barking. Footsteps approached, and the woman called, "Yes, who is it?"

"My name's Sharon McCone, from All Souls Legal Cooperative. I'm investigating the threats your neighbor, Mrs. Angeles, has been receiving."

A couple of locks turned and the door opened on its chain. The face that peered out at me was very thin and pale, with wisps of red hair straggling over the high forehead; the Dawson marriage had been an interracial one, then. The woman stared at me for a moment before she asked, "What threats?"

"You don't know that Mrs. Angeles and her children have been threatened because she's to testify against the man who shot your husband?"

She shook her head and stepped back, shivering slightly—whether from the cold outside or the memory of the murder, I couldn't tell. "I . . . don't get out much these days."

"May I come in, talk with you about the shooting?"

She shrugged, unhooked the chain, and opened the door. "I don't know what good it will do. Amor's a damned fool for saying she'd testify in the first place."

"Aren't you glad she did? The man killed your husband."

She shrugged again and motioned me into a living room the same size as that in the Angeles house. All resemblance stopped there, however. Dirty glasses and dishes, full ashtrays, piles of newspapers and magazines covered every surface; dust balls the size of rats lurked under the shabby Danish modern furniture. Madeline Dawson picked up a heap of tabloids from the couch and dumped it on the floor, then indicated I should sit there and took a hassock for herself.

I said, "You *are* glad that Mrs. Angeles was willing to testify, aren't you?"

"Not particularly."

"You don't care if your husband's killer is convicted or not?"

"Reg was asking to be killed. Not that I wouldn't mind seeing the Dragon get the gas chamber—he may not have killed Reg, but he killed plenty of other people—"

"What did you say?" I spoke sharply, and Madeline Dawson blinked in surprise. It made me pay closer attention to her eyes; they were glassy, their pupils dilated. The woman, I realized, was high.

"I said the Dragon killed plenty of other people."

"No, about him not killing Reg."

"Did I say that?"

"Yes."

"I can't imagine why. I mean, Amor must know. She was up there in the window watching for sweet Isabel like always."

"You don't sound as if you like Isabel Angeles."

"I'm not fond of flips in general. Look at the way they're taking over this area. Daly City's turning into another Manila. All they do is buy, buy, buy—houses, cars, stuff by the truckload. You know, there's a joke that the first three words their babies learn are 'Mama, Papa, and Serramonte.' " Serramonte was a large shopping mall south of San Francisco.

The roots of the resentment she voiced were clear to me. One of our largest immigrant groups today, the Filipinos are highly westernized and by and large better educated and more affluent than other recently arrived Asians—or many of their neighbors, black or white. Isabel Angeles, for all her bright, cheap clothing and excessive makeup, had behind her a tradition of industriousness and upward mobility that might help her to secure a better place in the world than Madeline Dawson could aspire to.

I wasn't going to allow Madeline's biases to interfere with my line of questioning. I said, "About Dragón not having shot your husband—"

"Hey, who knows? Or cares? The bastard's dead, and good riddance."

"Why good riddance?"

"The man was a pig. A pusher who cheated and gouged people—people like me who need the stuff to get through. You think I was always like this, lady? No way. I was a nice Irish Catholic girl from the Avenues when Reg got his hands on me. Turned me on to coke and a lot of other things when I was only thirteen. Liked his pussy young, Reg did. But then I got old—I'm all of nineteen now—and I needed more and more stuff just to keep going, and all of a sudden Reg didn't even *see* me anymore. Yeah, the man was a pig, and I'm glad he's dead."

"But you don't think Dragón killed him."

She sighed in exasperation. "I don't know what I think. It's just that I always supposed that when Reg got it it would be for something more personal than driving his car into a stupid shrine in a parking space. You know what I mean? But what does it matter who killed him, anyway?"

"It matters to Tommy Dragón, for one."

She dismissed the accused man's life with a flick of her hand. "Like I said, the Dragon's a killer. He might as well die for Reg's murder as for any of the others. In a way it'd be the one good thing Reg did for the world."

Perhaps in a certain primitive sense she was right, but her offhandedness made me uncomfortable. I changed the subject. "About the threats to Mrs. Angeles—which of the *Kabalyeros* would be behind them?"

"All of them. The guys in the gangs, they work together."

But I knew enough about the structure of street gangs—my degree in sociology from UC Berkeley hadn't been totally worthless—to be reasonably sure that wasn't so. There is usually one dominant personality, supported by two or three lieutenants; take away these leaders, and the followers become ineffectual, purposeless. If I could turn up enough evidence against the leaders of the *Kabalyeros* to have them arrested, the harassment would stop.

I asked, "Who took over the *Kabalyeros* after Dragón went to jail?"

"Hector Bulis."

It was a name that didn't appear on my list; Amor had claimed not to know who was the current head of the Filipino gang. "Where can I find him?"

"There's a fast-food joint over on Geneva, near the Cow Palace. Fat Robbie's. That's where the *Kabalyeros* hang out."

The second person I'd intended to talk with was the young man who had reportedly taken over the leadership of the Victors after Dawson's death, Jimmy Willis. Willis could generally be found at a bowling alley, also on Geneva Avenue near the Cow Palace. I thanked Madeline for taking the time to talk with me and headed for the Daly City line.

The first of the two establishments that I spotted was Fat Robbie's, a cinderblock-and-glass relic of the early sixties whose specialties appeared to be burgers and chicken-in-a-basket. I turned into a parking lot that was half-full of mostly shabby cars and left my MG beside one of the defunct drive-in speaker poles.

The interior of the restaurant took me back to my high school days: orange leatherette booths beside the plate glass windows; a long Formica counter with stools; laminated color pictures of disgusting-looking food on the wall above the pass-through counter from the kitchen. Instead of a jukebox there was a bank of video games along one wall. Three Filipino youths in jeans and denim jackets gathered around one called "Invader!" The *Kabalyeros*, I assumed.

I crossed to the counter with only a cursory glance at the trio, sat, and ordered coffee from a young waitress who looked to be Eurasian. The *Kabalyeros* didn't conceal their interest in me; they stared openly, and after a moment one of them said something that sounded like "tick-tick," and they all laughed nastily. Some sort of Tagalog obscenity, I supposed. I ignored them, sipping the dishwater-weak coffee, and after a bit they went back to their game.

I took out the paperback that I keep in my bag for protective coloration and pretended to read, listening to the few snatches of conversation that drifted over from the three. I caught the names of two: Sal and Hector—the latter presumably Bulis, the gang's leader. When I glanced covertly at him, I saw he was tallish and thin, with long hair caught back in a ponytail; his features were razor-sharp and slightly skewed, creating the impression of a perpetual sneer. The trio kept their voices low, and although I strained to hear, I could make out nothing of what they were saying. After about five minutes Hector turned away from the video machine. With a final glance at me he motioned to his companions, and they all left the restaurant.

I waited until they'd driven away in an old green Pontiac before I called the waitress over and showed her my identification. "The three men who just left," I said. "Is the tall one Hector Bulis?"

Her lips formed a little "O" as she stared at the ID. Finally she nodded. "May I talk with you about them?"

She glanced toward the pass-through to the kitchen. "My boss, he don't like me talking with the customers when I'm supposed to be working."

"Take a break. Just five minutes."

Now she looked nervously around the restaurant. "I shouldn't—"

I slipped a twenty-dollar bill from my wallet and showed it to her. "Just five minutes."

She still seemed edgy, but fear lost out to greed. "Okay, but I don't want anybody to see me talking to you. Go back to the restroom—it's through that door by the video games. I'll meet you there as soon as I can."

I got up and found the ladies' room. It was tiny, dimly lit, with a badly cracked mirror. The walls were covered with a mass of graffiti; some of it looked as if it had been painted over and had later worked its way back into view through the fading layers of enamel. The air in there was redolent of grease, cheap perfume, and stale cigarette and marijuana smoke. I leaned against the sink as I waited.

The young Eurasian woman appeared a few minutes later. "Bastard gave me a hard time," she said. "Tried to tell me I'd already taken my break."

"What's your name?"

"Anna Smith."

"Anna, the three men who just left—do they come in here often?"

"Uh-huh."

"Keep pretty much to themselves, don't they?"

"It's more like other people stay away from them." She hesitated. "They're from one of the gangs; you don't mess with them. That's why I wanted to talk with you back here."

"Have you ever heard them say anything about Tommy Dragón?"

"The Dragon? Sure. He's in jail; they say he was framed."

Of course they would claim that. "What about a Mrs. Angeles—Amorfina Angeles?"

". . . Not that one, no."

"What about trying to intimidate someone? Setting fires, going after someone with a gun?"

"Uh-uh. That's gang business; they keep it pretty close. But it wouldn't surprise me. Filipinos—I'm part Filipina myself, my mom met my dad when he was stationed at Subic Bay—they've got this saying, *kumukuló ang dugó*. It means 'the blood is boiling.' They can get pretty damn mad, 'specially the men. So stuff like what you said—sure they do it."

"Do you work on Fridays?"

"Yeah, two to ten."

"Did you see any of the *Kabalyeros* in here last Friday around six?" That was the time when Isabel had been accosted.

Anna Smith scrunched up her face in concentration. "Last Friday . . . oh, yeah, sure. That was when they had the big meeting, all of them."

"*All* of them?"

"Uh-huh. Started around five thirty, went on a couple of hours. My boss, he was worried something heavy was gonna go down, but the way it turned out, all he did was sell a lot of food."

"What was this meeting about?"

"Had to do with the Dragon, who was gonna be character witnesses at the trial, what they'd say."

The image of the three I'd seen earlier—or any of their ilk —as character witnesses was somewhat ludicrous, but I supposed in Tommy Dragón's position you took what you could get. "Are you sure they were all there?"

"Uh-huh."

"And no one at the meeting said anything about trying to keep Mrs. Angeles from testifying?"

"No. That lawyer the Dragon's got, he was there too."

Now that was odd. Why had Dragón's public defender chosen to meet with his witnesses in a public place? I could think of one good reason: he was afraid of them, didn't want them in his office. But what if the *Kabalyeros* had set the time and place—as an alibi for when Isabel was to be assaulted?

"I better get back to work," Anna Smith said. "Before the boss comes looking for me."

I gave her the twenty dollars. "Thanks for your time."

"Sure." Halfway out the door she paused, frowning. "I hope I didn't get any of the *Kabalyeros* in trouble."

"You didn't."

"Good. I kind of like them. I mean, they push dope and all, but these days, who doesn't?"

These days, who doesn't? I thought. *Good Lord. . . .*

The Starlight Lanes was an old-fashioned bowling alley girded by a rough cliff face and an auto dismantler's yard. The parking lot was crowded, so I left the MG around back by the garbage cans. Inside, the lanes were brightly lit and noisy with the sound of crashing pins, rumbling balls, shouts, and groans. I paused by the front counter and asked where I might find Jimmy Willis. The woman behind it directed me to a lane at the far end.

Bowling alleys—or lanes, as the new upscale bowler prefers to call them—are familiar territory to me. Up until a few years ago my favorite uncle Jim was a top player on the pro tour. The Starlight Lanes reminded me of the ones where Jim used to practice in San Diego—from the racks full of tired-looking rental shoes to the greasy-spoon coffeeshop smells to the molded plastic chairs and cigarette-burned scorekeeping consoles. I walked along, soaking up the ambience—some people would say the lack of it—until I came to lane 32 and spotted an agile young black man bowling alone. Jimmy Willis was a left-hander, and his ball hooked out until it hung on the edge of the channel, then hooked back with deadly precision. I waited in the spectator area, admiring his accuracy and graceful form. His concentration was so great that he didn't notice me until he'd finished the last frame and retrieved his ball.

"You're quite a bowler," I said. "What's your average?"

He gave me a long look before he replied, "Two hundred."

"Almost good enough to turn pro."

"That's what I'm looking to do."

Odd, for the head of a street gang that dealt in drugs and death. "You ever hear of Jim McCone?" I asked.

"Sure. Damned good in his day."

"He's my uncle."

"No kidding." Willis studied me again, now as if looking for a resemblance.

Rapport established, I showed him my ID and explained that I wanted to talk about Reg Dawson's murder. He frowned, hesitated, then nodded. "Okay, since you're Jim McCone's niece, but you'll have to buy me a beer."

"Deal."

Willis toweled off his ball, stowed it and his shoes in their bag, and led me to a typical smoke-filled, murkily lighted bowling alley bar. He took one of the booths while I fetched us a pair of Buds.

As I slid into the booth I said, "What can you tell me about the murder?"

"The way I see it, Dawson was asking for it."

So he and Dawson's wife were of a mind about that. "I can understand what you mean, but it seems strange, coming from you. I hear you were his friend, that you took over the Victors after his death."

"You heard wrong on both counts. Yeah, I was in the Victors, and when Dawson bought it, they tried to get me to take over. But by then I'd figured out—never mind how, doesn't matter—that I wanted out of that life. Ain't nothing in it but what happened to Benny Crespo and Dawson—or what's gonna happen to the Dragon. So I decided to put my hand to something with a future." He patted the bowling bag that sat on the banquette beside him. "Got a job here now—not much, but my bowling's free and I'm on my way."

"Good for you. What about Dragón—do you think he's guilty?"

Willis hesitated, looking thoughtful. "Why you ask?"

"Just wondering."

". . . Well, to tell you the truth, I never did believe the Dragon shot Reg."

"Who did, then?"

He shrugged.

I asked him if he'd heard about the *Kabalyeros* trying to intimidate the chief prosecution witness. When he nodded, I said, "They also threatened the life of her daughter last Friday."

He laughed mirthlessly. "Wish I could of seen that. Kind of surprises me, though. That lawyer of Dragón's, he found out what the *Kabalyeros* were up to, read them the riot act. Said they'd put Dragón in the gas chamber for sure. So they called it off."

"When was this?"

"Week, ten days ago."

Long before Isabel had been accosted. Before the dead dog and shooting incidents, too. "Are you sure?"

"It's what I hear. You know, in a way I'm surprised that they'd go after Mrs. Angeles at all."

"Why?"

"The Filipinos have this macho tradition. 'Specially when it comes to their women. They don't like them messed with, 'specially by non-Filipinos. So how come they'd turn around and mess with one of their own?"

"Well, her testimony *would* jeopardize the life of one of their fellow gang members. It's an extreme situation."

"Can't argue with that."

Jimmy Willis and I talked a bit more, but he couldn't—or wouldn't—offer any further information. I bought him a second beer, then went out to where I'd left my car.

And came face-to-face with Hector Bulis and the man called Sal.

Sal grabbed me by the arm, twisted it behind me, and forced me up against the latticework fence surrounding the garbage cans. The stench from them filled my nostrils; Sal's breath rivaled it in foulness. I struggled, but he got hold of my other arm and pinned me tighter. I looked around, saw no one, nothing but the cliff face and the high board fence of the auto dismantler's yard. Bulis approached, flicking open a switchblade, his twisty face intense. I stiffened, went very still, eyes on the knife.

Bulis placed the tip of the knife against my jawbone, then traced a line across my cheek. "Don't want to hurt you, bitch," he said. "You do what I say, I won't have to mess you up."

The Tagalog phrase that Anna Smith had translated for me—*kumukuló ang dugó*— flashed through my mind. *The blood is boiling.* I sensed Bulis's was—and dangerously high.

I wet my dry lips, tried to keep my voice from shaking as I said, "What do you want me to do?"

"We hear you're asking around about Dawson's murder, trying to prove the Dragon did it."

"That's not—"

"We want you to quit. Go back to your own part of town and leave our business alone."

"Whoever told you that is lying. I'm only trying to help the Angeles family."

"They wouldn't lie." He moved the knife's tip to the hollow at the base of my throat. I felt it pierce my skin—a mere pinprick, but frightening enough.

When I could speak, I did so slowly, phrasing my words carefully. "What I hear is that Dragón is innocent. And that the *Kabalyeros* aren't behind the harassment of the Angeleses—at least not for a week or ten days."

Bulis exchanged a look with his companion—quick, unreadable.

"Someone's trying to frame you," I added, "Just like they did Dragón."

Bulis continued to hold the knife to my throat, his hand firm. His gaze wavered, however, as if he was considering what I'd said. After a moment he asked, "All right—who?"

"I'm not sure, but I think I can find out."

He thought a bit longer, then let his arm drop and snapped the knife shut. "I'll give you till this time tomorrow," he said. Then he stuffed the knife into his pocket, motioned for Sal to let go of me, and the two quickly walked away.

I sagged against the latticework fence, feeling my throat where the knife had pricked it. It had bled a little, but the flow already was clotting. My knees were weak and my breath came fast, but I was too caught up in the possibilities to panic. There were plenty of them—and the most likely was the most unpleasant.

Kumukuló ang dugó. The blood is boiling. . . .

Two hours later I was back at the Angeles house on Omega Street. When Amor admitted me, the tension I'd felt in her earlier had drained. Her body sagged, as if the extra weight she carried had finally proved to be too much for her frail bones; the skin of her face looked flaccid, like melting putty; her eyes were sunken and vague. After she shut the door and motioned for me to sit, she sank into the recliner, expelling a sigh. The house was quiet—too quiet.

"I have a question for you," I said. "What does 'tick-tick' mean in Tagalog?"

Her eyes flickered with dull interest. *"Tiktík."* She corrected my pronunciation. "It's a word for detective."

Ever since Hector Bulis and Sal had accosted me I'd suspected as much.

"Where did you hear that?" Amor asked.

"One of the *Kabalyeros* said it when I went to Fat Robbie's earlier. Someone had told them I was a detective, probably described me. Whoever it was said I was trying to prove Tommy Dragón killed Reg Dawson."

"Why would—"

"More to the point, *who* would? At the time, only four people knew that I'm a detective."

She wet her lips, but remained silent.

"Amor, the night of the shooting, you were standing in your front window, watching for Isabel."

"Yes."

"Do you do that often?"

". . . Yes."

"Because Isabel is often late coming home. Because you're afraid she may have gotten into trouble."

"A mother worries—"

"Especially when she's given good cause. Isabel is running out of control, isn't she?"

"No, she—"

"Amor, when I spoke with Madeline Dawson, she said you were standing in the window watching for 'sweet Isabel, like always.' She didn't say 'sweet' in a pleasant way. Later, Jimmy Willis implied that your daughter is not . . . exactly a vulnerable young girl."

Amor's eyes sparked. "The Dawson woman is jealous."

"Of course she is. There's something else: when I asked the waitress at Fat Robbie's if she'd ever overheard the *Kabalyeros* discussing you, she said, 'No, not that one.' It didn't register at the time, but when I talked to her again a little while ago, she told me Isabel is the member of your family they discuss. They say she's wild, runs around with the men in the gangs. You know that, so does Alex. And so does Madeline Dawson. She just told me the first man Isabel became involved with was her husband."

Amor seemed to shrivel. She gripped the arms of the chair, white-knuckled.

"It's true, isn't it?" I asked more gently.

She lowered her eyes, nodding. When she spoke her voice was ragged. "I don't know what to do with her anymore. Ever since that Reg Dawson got to her, she's been different, not my girl at all."

"Is she on drugs?"

"Alex says no, but I'm not so sure."

I let it go; it didn't really matter. "When she came home earlier," I said, "Isabel seemed very interested in me. She asked questions, looked me over carefully enough to be able to describe me to the *Kabalyeros*. She was afraid of what I might find out. For instance, that she wasn't accosted by any men with guns last Friday."

"She was!"

"No, Amor. That was just a story, to make it look as if your life—and your children's—were in danger if you testified. In spite of what you said early on, you haven't wanted to testify against Tommy Dragón from the very beginning.

"When the *Kabalyeros* began harassing you a month ago, you saw that as the perfect excuse not to take the stand. But you didn't foresee that Dragón's lawyer would convince the gang to stop the harassment. When that happened, you and Isabel, and probably Alex, too, manufactured incidents—the shot-out window, the dead dog on the doorstep, the men with the guns—to make it look as if the harassment was still going on."

"Why would I? They're going to put me in jail."

"But at the time you didn't know they could do that—or that your employer would hire me. My investigating poses yet another danger to you and your family."

"This is . . . why would I do all that?"

"Because basically you're an honest woman, a good woman. You didn't want to testify because you knew Dragón didn't shoot Dawson. It's my guess you gave the police his name because it was the first one that came to mind."

"I had no reason to—"

"You had the best reason in the world: a mother's desire to protect her child."

She was silent, sunken eyes registering despair and defeat.

I kept on, even though I hated to inflict further pain on her. "The day he died, Dawson had let the word out that he was going to desecrate Benny's space. The person who shot him knew there would be fighting and confusion, counted on that as a cover. The killer hated Dawson—"

"Lots of people did."

"But only one person you'd want to protect so badly that you'd accuse an innocent man."

"Leave my mother alone. She's suffered enough on account of what I did."

I turned. Alex had come into the room so quietly I hadn't noticed. Now he moved midway between Amor and me, a Saturday night special clutched in his right hand.

The missing murder weapon.

I tensed, but one look at his face told me he didn't intend to use it. Instead he raised his arm and extended the gun, grip first.

"Take this," he said. "I never should of bought it. Never should of used it.

I hated Dawson on account of what he did to my sister. But killing him wasn't worth what we've all gone through since."

I glanced at Amor; tears were trickling down her face.

Alex said, "Mama, don't cry. I'm not worth it."

When she spoke, it was to me. "What will happen to him?"

"Nothing like what might have happened to Dragón; Alex is a juvenile. You, however—"

"I don't care about myself, only my children."

Maybe that was the trouble. She was the archetypal selfless mother: living only for her children, sheltering them from the consequences of their actions —and in the end doing them irreparable harm.

There were times when I felt thankful that I had no children. And there were times when I was thankful that Jack Stuart was a very good criminal lawyer. This was a time when I was thankful on both counts. I went to the phone, called Jack, and asked him to come over here. At least I could leave the Angeles family in good legal hands.

After he arrived, I went out into the gathering dusk. An old yellow VW was pulling out of Benny's space. I walked down there and stood on the curb. Nothing remained of the shrine to Benny Crespo. Nothing remained to show that blood had boiled and been shed here. It was merely a stretch of cracked asphalt, splotched with oil drippings, littered with the detritus of urban life. I stared at it for close to a minute, then turned away from the bleak landscape of Omega Street.

DOROTHY DAVIS's first crime novel was *The Judas Cat*, published in 1949. Since that time she achieved an enviable reputation for her ability to write novels and stories with *both* believable rural and urban settings. Her more than twenty novels include at least four that have been nominated for the Edgar Award and she was made a Grand Master of the Mystery Writers of America in 1984. Most critics consider *A Gentle Murderer* to be her best novel, and one of the best crime novels of the post-World War II era.

THE PUPPET

Dorothy Salisbury Davis

 Over the ring of the doorbell came the cry, "Help me, Julie . . . Let me in!"

Julie, out of bed before she was rightly awake, pulled on her robe and ran, barefoot, to the front of the shop. It was half-past one in the morning. She unbolted the door and opened it on the latch. Her upstairs neighbor, Rose Rodriguez, was shivering in a silvery dress that glowed in the stark Manhattan street light. Julie let her in, then bolted the door and lighted a lamp.

"I don't know where Juanita is. She's not in her bed. I thought maybe she comes to you?"

Julie shook her head. "Sit down while I get my slippers."

The chair creaked with its burden. In the years Julie Hayes had occupied the shop, the ground floor apartment on West 44th Street, Mrs. Rodriguez had put on weight. Her one child, Juanita, had grown from a string bean to puberty with a sudden promising beauty.

Mrs. Rodriguez pointed at the row of dolls when Julie returned. They sat on a table, their backs against the wall. "They are Juanita's, no?"

"We've been mending them," Julie said. "Now tell me what's with Juanita?"

"It's boys. I know it's boys."

You ought to know, Julie thought. It was apparent Mrs. Rodriguez had just returned from an evening out. Her husband wouldn't know about it. Juanita would. Julie was not a great hater, but she would have been hard put to find a kind word for the woman now twisting off the flashy rings from her fingers. "Where do you think she is? Let's start with that."

"She wants to go to her friend Elena's for supper. I say okay, but you be home by nine o'clock. The whole holiday weekend and she hasn't done her homework."

"*Did* she come home?"

"Julie . . ." The woman's face became a mask of contrition. "She has a very good father but not so good mother. You know?"

Julie ignored the ploy for sympathy. "Isn't it possible she tried to call you? To ask if she could stay overnight? And then stayed anyway when she couldn't reach you?"

"She knows better. Papa will not give permission. He will kill me. . . ." The woman began to sob.

"Stop that!" Julie shouted. "Let's call her friend's house right now."

"You know her number, Julie?"

"Don't you?"

"I don't even know her name except Elena."

"Then you can't do anything till morning. I can call the police. . . ."

"No. No police. They come and ask questions."

"Yeah."

Mrs. Rodriguez brushed away green tears. Her mascara was running. "You are right. She stays with Elena, I think. That's what I tell Papa if he looks and sees she's not in her bed. A wild man."

"First thing in the morning, call the school. Ask for the principal. Whoever you get, find out Elena's last name, her phone number. . . ."

The woman laid her hand on Julie's. "Please, will you call? Say it's for me, Señora Rodriguez. Say I don't speak very good English. That's the truth, no?"

"Mrs. Rodriguez . . ."

"Please, you call me Rose. We are friends, no?"

Julie could not go back to sleep. She listened for Juanita's father to come home from work, a tired, bemused man who moonlighted on a second job while his wife moonlighted in her fashion. Juanita had grown up a silent, angry child who beat her dolls and pulled off their arms and legs. Now she and Julie were putting them together again with glue and heavy thread, a

Christmas project for the really poor. It had taken Julie a long time to make her smile, then laugh, to make her see the dolls as little Juanitas. A lot of her own angry childhood had gone into the making.

Mr. Rodriguez came home. Julie waited for the explosion, the reverberations of which would run through the building. But none came. The woman would have persuaded him the child was asleep in her bed. Julie sat up and phoned the local precinct. The only complaints involving children were drug related: downtown bookings, parents contacted.

"How about the prostitutes—any young ones?" The wildest possibility.

"They're all young—and as old as Magdalene," the desk sergeant said. Then: "This wasn't a sweep night, Julie."

Nothing came of inquiries to the local hospitals.

Julie lay back and thought about when she had last seen the youngster. Late afternoon yesterday. Probably when she was coming home to ask permission to go to Elena's. What was she wearing besides the red, white, and green streamers? Julie couldn't remember. The Italian colors were for the Columbus Day Street Fair. Nor could she remember Juanita's ever mentioning Elena. She was only beginning to make friends. So, thank God for Elena. Sleep finally came.

The girl opened her eyes. She seemed to be dreaming of waking up, but she had to be still asleep. She was lying in a huge, strange bed under a blanket with her clothes on. The room was dark except for a patch of gray light in the ceiling. Curled up on her side, her thumb in her mouth, she stared at the light. It looked more like a sheet floating up there, but the flickering lights of a plane appeared and moved quickly out of sight again. She heard the roar go away. It was a skylight in the ceiling, something she had seen only in a movie.

She tried to wake up. She bit her thumb, and when it hurt she knew that she was already awake. Then she remembered what had happened to her before the sleep: the woman and a man in the dirty lobby of an old theater where she had gone to see the puppets. At the fair the woman had told her about them and promised to show her how they worked. She had wanted to learn how to make puppets and how to make them act. The woman said she was a natural. She and Julie might even use the dolls and make their own puppet show. But there weren't any puppets, and she knew the minute the door had closed behind her that she should never, never have gone there. The woman grabbed her and covered her mouth when she started to scream; the man held her legs and roped them together, then knocked them out from under her, sat on her, pinned her arm down, and must have stuck a needle in her. The place in the hollow of her arm hurt now when she touched it. She distinctly heard him say, "Five minutes." She tried to scratch and bite. The man swore at her and the woman said, "For Christ's sake, Danny, do you want her looking like a battered child?" Her memory stopped right there. Now the important thing was she had to go to the bathroom.

She inched her way to the edge of the bed in the direction she was facing. Something white stood on the floor a few feet from the bed—a bucket, she made out after a few seconds of study. She would have to use it, and maybe that was what it was there for. She crawled to it. It seemed safer to stay close to the floor. She wondered if her shoes were in the bed but didn't think so. She squatted over the bucket but nothing happened. While she waited she made out the shapes of some scary figures on the other side of the bed—a lot of chalky white people just standing. They seemed to be moving toward her. She tried to cry out, but couldn't, and her legs were shaking. She was sure she was going to fall. She managed not to, and the figures didn't come round the bed. They weren't even moving. Statues? If that was what they were, could one of them be the Blessed Virgin? "Hail Mary, full of grace, the Lord is with thee. . . ." She heard her own voice mumbling the prayer, then the beginning trickle of her water, then the gush, noisy in the pail.

She had just finished when the door opened behind her and sent a splash of light across the room. The man came in and lit a lamp on a table near the door.

"Figured out what that was for, did you? You're a smart girl."

She made no sound or move.

"Get back into bed and stay there till she brings your breakfast. I don't want you messing round the studio. Do you know what a studio is? It's where artists work."

If she ran for the door, what would happen? He was too close to it and she couldn't run. She couldn't even move. Only her heart bumped inside her.

"Did you hear me? Into bed!"

"No."

He grinned at her and took the hypodermic needle from his pocket.

She lunged, stumbling, toward the bed.

The guidance counselor, Dr. Alverez, sent Elena Cruz back to her classroom. Julie used the counselor's phone to call Mrs. Rodriguez and tell her the news was not good. "You'd better waken your husband and then call the police, nine one one. Juanita did not go to Elena's house at all last night. Elena was at her aunt's house for dinner. In other words, Juanita has been missing since you last saw her. You simply must call the police."

"Julie, please!" The woman's voice rose hysterically.

"I'll call you later," Julie said and hung up.

The counselor was watching Julie with an appraising eye. "You know, don't you, you're the best thing that ever happened to Juanita."

"Doesn't help much now, does it?"

"If there's anyone she'll get in touch with it's you."

"So if I don't hear from her, where is she? What's the worst possibility you can think of, doctor?"

The counselor gave an enormous sigh. "That she was abducted. But if she was, she must have set herself up for it willingly—the lie about dinner at Elena's."

"Her mother thinks it's all about boys," Julie said.

"I wish it were. Ridiculous of me to say that, but the boys are a lot more interested in Juanita than she is in the boys."

"Do you know what her home situation is like?"

Alverez nodded. "Her father works long hours. Whatever her mother does while he's away, Juanita's ashamed of it."

"She usually stops at my place on the way home if I'm there. Yesterday she didn't. I just happened to see her go by. I think she'd been to the street fair. If you'd ask her classmates whether anyone saw her—where and what time— it would be great. When I went out not long after I saw her, I found a flyer stuck in my mail drop. Now I wonder if she put it there. Maybe. You try to think of everything. This was about a rally of the West Side women to close up the porn shops in the neighborhood."

Alverez smiled. "Well, I can tell you this: If there's a budding feminist in the sixth grade, it's Juanita Rodriguez."

"Take a bite, honey, or I'll eat it. Didn't your mother ever say, 'If you don't eat it, I will'?"

Juanita did not answer. She was sitting at the table, the big woman between her and the door. It was daylight, but the room was lighted mostly by long tubes in the ceiling. There weren't any windows except the one in the roof. The man, Danny, was poking around among the statues and moving some boxes. There were paintings, too, one on a three-legged stand and others stacked on their sides. Danny wasn't doing anything, only moving things around. With his little eyes and skinny moustache he didn't look to her like an artist.

The woman broke off a piece of the Danish, touched Juanita's tight lips with it, and then ate it herself. Her fingernails were like dabs of blood, her mouth a red smear. Even her hair was red. She was as old as Mama, a lot older than Julie. Everybody would be looking for her, but where would they look? Papa would shout and whack her mother. Then he'd cry.

"Take some coffee, Juanita. It won't hurt you, I promise."

"You promised there were puppets." Her first words except for the "No" to the needle.

"We do make puppets."

The man gave a bark of laughter.

"Shut up, Danny. And you're not supposed to touch any of their things back there. It's in the agreement."

"Fuck the agreement."

"Don't you talk like that in front of her," the woman shouted.

"What in hell is going on with you, Dee?"

"Why don't you go out and look for what you're supposed to be looking for?"

"Because it's nine A.M. and nothing's open yet." He came out from among the statues and stopped at the table. "The lights in here are no damn good for us. We should've known that."

"Then get some that are! Honest to God, Danny, you're in New York City."

"Don't hassle me, Dee. You're the one jumped the gun, though I'm damned if I see why. Little Miss Perfect here." He caught a handful of Juanita's hair and pulled her head back—not roughly, but not gently either. He looked at her from her eyes to as far down as he could see and then let go. He poked his finger at the woman's face. "Just don't get too fond of her. She's a puppet, remember."

Julie, after several phone calls, reached an organizer of the antiporn rally. She promised an item in the *Our Beat* column and then told of the missing youngster. "It's a long shot, but if you were handing out flyers at the street fair yesterday, I wonder if you saw her."

"I wasn't there myself, but there was an incident at the fair that might have involved your young person. Let me give you the number of Sue Laughlin. You mustn't take her literally if she makes it sound like gang rape. That's just Sue."

A chorus of infant and toddler voices rang through Julie's conversation with Sue Laughlin. "I thought the girl was older—sixteen, maybe. And she did volunteer. Anyway—shut up, Jamie. Can't you see Mommy's on the phone?—anyway, she was handing out our flyers when this gang of young jocks started to tease her—'What's pornography, Juanita?' That sort of thing."

"Did they call her by name? It's important."

"How would I know her name if they hadn't? Then one of them snatched the flyers from her and they all clowned around throwing them into the air. And what did she do? She grabbed an umbrella from a concession stand and began thrashing the mischief out of them."

Gang rape, Julie thought.

"They ran off and the guy selling the umbrellas tried to make her buy the one she'd taken. I was going to say something, but a woman who'd been watching the whole thing said she'd buy the umbrella."

"Did you know the woman?"

"No. I don't think she's from the neighborhood. There were hundreds of people, you know."

Julie felt herself tighten up. "Did she speak to Juanita?"

"I couldn't say for sure. I just wasn't paying attention after that."

"Could you describe the woman?"

"A big, solid woman, well dressed but flashy, too much makeup, red hair . . ."

Julie reached Detective Russo at precinct headquarters with her bits of information. Dominic Russo and she were old friends so he could say frankly that he would give it what time he could, but from her parents' report the youngster sounded like a runaway. The case would go to Missing Persons within twenty-four hours. "We'll give out her description at roll call and put it on the bulletin board. But you know how many kids hit the streets every day."

"Yeah."

"Most of them come home in a day or two."

"Some don't ever. I'll keep in touch, Dom."

"Don't I know that," he said.

Julie went upstairs to see the Rodriguezes as soon as they got home. Juanita's father was sitting in the kitchen, his head in his hands. He looked up at her when she laid her hand on his shoulder. His eyes were wet. "Why she do this to us? Why?"

Julie, to reassure them of the girl's resourcefulness, told them how Juanita had confronted the boys who were taunting her. Mrs. Rodriguez turned and stormed at her husband, "Men are pigs. You're all pigs!" It ought to have been funny, Julie thought, but it wasn't.

Juanita sat on the bathroom stool in a silk robe that was much too big for her. She had taken a shower she hadn't wanted and washed her hair on the woman's command. She hadn't wanted to take off her clothes, but she was afraid the woman might make her, and might come into the bathroom with her. She hadn't done that. She only made Juanita hand out her jeans, jacket, and sweat shirt, her bra, panties, and socks. She hadn't seen her sneakers since they brought her here.

She knew now that this was a loft. The bathroom was fancy-new. So was the kitchen, which didn't have any doors. The living room ran all the way from the studio—the room with the big bed and the statues—to what must be the front of the building. Street noises seemed to come from there, and there must be a very big window with heavy curtains covering it. Threads of light showed at the top and at the floor. A Castro convertible bed, where they must have slept, was open. The woman, who said she must call her Dee, told her the big door was to the elevator and was kept locked. Juanita was pretty sure there had to be a fire escape. But where?

"Come out now, Juanita. I want to fix your hair."

"Could I have my clothes, please?"

"You'll get dressed later. Come on now."

She went out to where the woman motioned her into a chair in front of a mirror. "Can't I get dressed before he comes back?"

"First I want to do up your hair." Dee had a dryer in hand. "Little dark pom-poms might be nice. You could look Japanese. Like a geisha girl."

"Please. I hate this." Juanita tugged at the robe.

"Just be patient. You're going to have beautiful new clothes."

Dee blow-dried her hair to where she could work with it, making little round buns she fastened and then let loose, then fashioned again. "Very pretty, my little geisha."

Juanita's fear was getting bad again. She almost wished the man would come. They might have another fight, a long one. When her mother and father fought, she could run away and hide. Where could she run and hide here? She'd make a dash for the big window and pound on it. She would jump up and down. But people would point and laugh and wouldn't do anything. Unless the man came and tried to give her the needle and she fought him right there in the window. Maybe then.

"A penny for your thoughts." Dee smiled at her in the mirror and then looked at herself. "How I wish I was young like you again."

"Don't let him stick the needle in me anymore."

"Over my dead body."

Juanita felt a little more secure and tried once more, "Couldn't I have my clothes back now?"

"No, dear. I've already put them in the garbage disposal."

In the early afternoon, with the help of Vendor Licensing and Traffic Control, Detective Russo located the Greystone Puppets truck. It was impounded in the Twelfth Avenue lot for illegal parking overnight. According to the gatekeeper, the owner had arrived early that morning, but without enough money to pay both fine and storage. He was due back within the hour. Otherwise he'd owe the city another hundred dollars for storage. Julie took what money she had in the house and waited outdoors for the squad car to pick her up. Where she had used to carry a pocketful of coins for blind beggars and street musicians, she now carried dollar bills for the homeless.

She and the two precinct officers Russo had commandeered examined the truck. It was locked up tight, but that didn't mean much, given its condition. As one of the cops said, it was hard to tell what breed it was. They could see the skeleton of a stage set on a platform that probably rolled out onto the tailgate. There was a trunk marked COSTUMES and some painted scenery scaled to the stage. But no puppets.

Very soon a little man with a wisp of a moustache, hollow cheeks, and great melancholy eyes, came up lugging a duffel bag. He showed the cops his receipt from the city. "I had to hock my puppets. They're my kids! My goddam living."

"I'll help you if you can help me," Julie said. She didn't look as though she had much to help with, in sneakers and raincoat. But as soon as she started to describe Juanita she was in charge. She soon had the puppeteer wagging his head. He remembered the girl, all right. "She kept asking me questions—did I make the puppets myself, did I make them out of old dolls. Could she make them. She wanted to know where I was going next. 'Florida,' I says. 'I don't want them to catch cold.' When she saw I was putting her on—the saddest look I ever saw." Then he was jolted aware. "She's come up missing?"

"Since five o'clock last night."

"I was there on the street till ten. But listen: there was this woman I thought at first was the kid's mother. She was telling her about puppets. I was changing the act, see. I got three different acts. . . ."

Julie waited out his setting the scene. One of the cops activated a pocket recorder.

"Somewhere in there I got the idea this dame was a con artist. I don't mean I thought it exactly. It just crossed my mind. She was like playing to me too. That's what kept the youngster interested. She watched to see if I was interested. That kid's no fool. The redhead was telling about this old theater she was renovating and how she was collecting puppets that could make like singers. . . ."

"Where? Did she say where it was?"

"No, ma'am. Not to me, she didn't, and I'll tell you this, she knew about as much about puppets as I know about King Tut. But that's where I lost touch. I got a hand puppet that's my buddy. Whenever we get enough people around, Andy and I pass the hat. It's a living. I guess you could call it a living."

"What else about Juanita?"

He shrugged. "One minute they were there, gone the next. That's how it is when you're playing the street."

The police pressed him for a description of the redheaded woman. Then Julie asked him if he thought the theater she spoke about might be a real place.

"Could be."

"Nearby?"

Again he shrugged. Then: "I don't think that kid would go with her anyplace she couldn't walk to."

A buzzer signaled Danny's return. While the elevator groaned its way up, Juanita glanced toward the heavily draped window at the front of the loft. Dee clamped her fingers around the girl's wrist. "Don't you even think of it! Do you want to get killed?"

Juanita, still in the silken robe, gathered it tighter in front of her. It didn't have any buttons. She tried not to see herself in the mirror because it wasn't really her. Dee had made her up to look oriental. But she watched in the mirror for the elevator's arrival. When it stopped, Dee had to unlock the door to let Danny in. He took the key from her and locked it again.

"So?" Dee wanted to know.

He didn't answer. He came near and stared at Juanita in the mirror. He made a face like he was going to throw up. "What've you done to her? And what in hell is she doing out of the studio?"

"We needed a bath."

"Then *we* need another bath. She looks like a midget's whore."

"Fun-nee. Did you get what you went for?"

"No. The answer is no. Dee, she's supposed to look like an angel. That's why you fell in love with her."

"Oh, shut up."

"I got a contact. That's all I got and I'm going to go see him as soon as you and I straighten some things out."

"Danny, how much time do you think we have?"

"Maybe we don't have any. This town ought to be the best. But it's the worst yet. Get her inside there so we can talk."

Confined again in the studio, Juanita put her ear to the frame of the door, then to the keyhole. Then she lay down on the floor and tried to hear from under the door, but only the sound of their voices reached her, going away as though to the front of the building. A new sound startled her until she realized it was her stomach growling. She'd promised Dee she would eat. She knew Dee liked her. That's what made Danny mad. But there wasn't any food. Dee looked in the cupboards and the fridge. How could they live someplace with no food in the house? They didn't live here. It was like a hotel, only it was a loft they rented. Their suitcases were on the floor, open, with clothes falling out of them. They'd rented from an artist, which was why Danny wasn't supposed to touch anything in the studio.

She sat on the edge of a chair and wound her feet around its legs. The dressing gown smelled of perfume and sweat. She wished they'd start fighting again so she could hear them. If they didn't have any time, would they go away and leave her locked in this room with the bucket and the big bed? She hated beds more than most things. Her mother and father fought a lot about beds, and her mother had boyfriends she didn't think Juanita or Papa knew about. Papa didn't. She did. She knew that was why her mother let her go when she said she was going to Elena's. She had a date with a boyfriend. Juanita thought of the kids getting on her about the flyers—"What's pornography, Juanita? how come you know so much about it?" She knew it was dirty pictures, but she wasn't going to say it to them. She felt herself going sick again, scared. She tried to think of Julie. Julie would really try to find her. Maybe she'd find the puppet man. He could tell her about Dee. But what else? She hadn't seen Danny before she walked into the old building with the hand-painted sign on the door: PUPPET SHOW INSIDE. Julie walked a lot and she might find it.

Juanita began to walk then, too. Round and round the room she went, barefoot, the silk gown dragging the floor. Finally she entered the alcove where the statues stood around like people at a funeral. There were other things, half-finished bodies, heads. She recognized the smell of clay. Tools and brushes and tubes of paint lay on a table. There was a painting on a three-legged stand, and other paintings were stacked in racks. This was where Danny wasn't supposed to touch anything. She came on several camera cases then, and something rolled up with metal legs sticking out. There were two flat boxes with straps that were marked FILM. These things belonged to Danny, she felt sure, not to the artist. Danny said the light wasn't any good. He was going to take her picture, and he wanted her to look like an angel. That didn't sound like Danny. She'd have thought he would want her to look like a whore.

Julie was in luck when she reached the Actors Forum. A session had just ended. Nobody there knew much about puppets, but when she'd given the actors and apprentices the story, most of them volunteered to organize a street-by-street search of old West Side buildings in which a puppet theater might now be playing or where appropriate renovation might be under way. They would all go first to precinct headquarters and coordinate with the police. "Mind you," Julie cautioned, "the real puppeteer said the woman didn't know anything about puppets. It was probably a story made up to lure the youngster. She's eleven years old and she's pretty. What else can I tell you?"

"We'll find her, sister." Nuba Bradley, a tall, black actor who seemed to have grown three inches with the current hair style, bent almost in two to kiss her cheek.

Reggie Bauer hung back to talk to Julie while the others got under way. Slight, blond, and brittle, Reggie knew New York society from the Bowery to the bridge tables; these were where, it was said, he made enough money to support himself as an actor. "You don't think for a minute it's got anything to do with puppets, do you?"

Julie waited.

"Do you want my scenario?"

"Not if it's too far out. Of course, I want it."

"Kid porn."

"What does that mean?" She knew well enough. Or thought she did, but she hoped it wasn't so.

"Child pornography. The lady was shopping for innocence, the real thing. In the meantime, either she's got a partner for her or somebody's out there looking for an experienced young dude to match her up with."

Julie didn't question him on his expertise. She thought she knew how he came by it. Except that Reggie was gay. The thought must have shone through her eyes. He said, "A lot of it's faked, you know, especially the pleasure."

"How would they find a boy like that? Where?"

"Through somebody in the business. Somebody knows somebody who likes boys. A certain amount of trust is involved in the transaction."

"Oh, my God," Julie said. "Maybe I know someone myself."

Juanita stood beneath the skylight and turned around slowly. On tiptoe she could see what looked like the top of a barrel. Bringing one of the chairs to stand on, she could see that it was a water tower. She could see other buildings and a lot of sky. She could also see where water leaked in around the skylight. If she could get up there, she might be able to push the window out.

She went back to the door and listened. She couldn't hear anything except faraway car horns and the rumble of the city much as it sounded when she was home alone in the daytime. Maybe they'd both gone out. Maybe they'd already gone and left her. And left the camera and everything? She didn't think so. She wasn't going to let them photograph her without her clothes on. Not unless he used the needle again. This time she'd kick it out of his hand or kick him where she knew it would hurt most. "Over my dead body," Dee had said. But Dee was afraid of him too.

She took the painting off the three-legged stand. Even if she could step on the stand, it wouldn't be high enough. Again she listened at the door. They'd gone out to lunch, she decided, and Dee would bring back something for her. It had to be after lunchtime. As quietly as she could she pulled the table under the skylight. The stand just fit on top of it. The dressing gown made it hard for her to climb, and she knew it was going to get in her way if she got high enough to try to move the window. But it had pockets. She found a paint-smeared knife and a chisel, which she pocketed. She also took a hammer and tied it around her waist with the sash of the robe. She tried not to think of Danny, but in spite of herself she imagined him unlocking the door just as she stepped from the chair onto the table. She began to melt again with fear.

"No!" she cried aloud without meaning to. She waited. Nothing happened. She could not climb up on the stand. The ledge she wanted to step onto was too high. She pulled the chair up onto the table, but in doing it she nudged one of the legs of the stand and the whole thing clattered to the floor. Not a sound came from the other side of the door. This time, after she'd set up the stand and placed the chair beneath it, she boosted herself up without tumbling the works. She waited and listened. There were sounds she hadn't heard before in the building, noise like heat coming up in the pipes, machinery sounds that might be the elevator. But it never seemed to arrive. Her heartbeat was too loud to hear much else. She made it safely up onto the chair. She could see the twin towers of the Board of Trade Buildings. She was in lower Manhattan. SoHo. Of course: where the artists were. She got one foot sidewise onto the ledge and tested to see if it would hold her. It seemed to, but when she tried to lift the other foot the stand wobbled and collapsed. She missed the chair and fell and, flailing, brought the chair down after her. Before she knew whether or not she was hurt, Dee threw open the door and came running to her. Juanita tried to pull the robe close around her.

"I wouldn't've believed it! He was right, I shouldn't've left you alone. Let me look at your face." On her knees, Dee examined her face, touched her eyes, nose, lips. "Say ouch if it hurts."

Juanita determined not to say ouch no matter how much it hurt. She managed to loosen the hammer and tie the sash around her. Dee felt down her arms and pulled the robe open to see her middle. Juanita closed it again. She knew there would be bruises where she'd hit the table, but she didn't make a sound when Dee touched the sore spots.

Dee got to her feet and pulled the girl up. "You're lucky in more ways than one, you little fool. Let's put these things back where they were. I promise I won't tell Danny if you promise to do what you're told from now on. Promise me?" She gave the girl a shake.

Juanita was trying not to cry. She did hurt, but she forced a big smile and nodded what could be taken for a promise. She had lost the chisel on the way down, but she could feel the knife stuck deep in the pocket of the robe.

Julie stopped at the shop to see if any message had come through her service. Most of the calls pertained to business. She put them on hold. Several Women Against Pornography members had joined the neighborhood search. Mrs. Rodriguez had called twice. Julie ran upstairs. The woman had heard nothing. Her husband had gone to the police station to wait. There were a lot of *Perdidas* in her lamentation.

Julie walked the four blocks to Kevin Bourke's electrical shop on Eighth Avenue. Mr. Bourke was one of the first people she'd met after moving into the shop. He loaned a friend of hers some lamps to help decorate it. He had lived in the neighborhood all his life, he attended St. Malachy's where the Catholic actors went, supported the Irish Theater, and looked a bit like Sean O'Casey, whose plays he admired fervently. He had been in trouble when Julie met him, on the complaint of a boy who turned out later to have been a prostitute. Julie might not have been so direct if her mission had been less urgent.

Mr. Bourke looked at her sadly over the top of his rimless glasses. "I'll not waste your time asking why it was me you came to. Do you know how many years I've been in therapy to amend that fall from grace?"

"I wouldn't have come to you at all if I knew anyone else to go to."

"You're not alone, and I'd rather have you remember than most of those who do. Thank God, I'll soon be an old man."

Julie thought he already was.

"I wish I could help you, Julie, but I've not been hospitable to that kind of visitor for a long time."

"I understand and I'm sorry I came, Mr. Bourke."

Mercifully, a customer entered the shop and she could get away. She plunged out the door and almost collided with a street person who stepped back to admire the window he had cleaned of a car illegally parked at the curb. What could he see, she wondered, the windows all blacked out. She glanced back at the license plate—California. All that sunshine they wouldn't let in the windows.

Juanita ate. Ordinarily she loved Chinese food, but now she could hardly swallow. She had a plan. It came out of the daydreams she often made up about Julie and herself. Dee, she could see, was getting nervous. She walked back and forth waiting for Juanita to finish eating. She stopped and threw a lot of clothes that were lying about into one of the suitcases. She listened for the elevator. She looked at her watch. She was waiting to change Juanita's hairdo. The pom-poms had come undone when she tumbled off the table. Danny didn't want her to look like a geisha girl anyway. Dee wouldn't tell her what a geisha girl was. She knew what an angel was, but she didn't feel like one of them either.

Dee came close and looked at the plate. "Starved, weren't you?"

"Dee, I don't like Danny. Do you?"

The woman gave a surprised laugh. "Not always."

"Are you married to him?"

"We're partners. Does that answer your question?"

"You just live together, right?"

"Right. If you've had enough to eat, go sit in front of the mirror." Dee took the plate to the sink and scraped and rinsed it.

Juanita sat on the bench at the dressing table and drew the robe tightly around her. She watched Dee approach, drying her hands on a dish towel. "Why don't you split from him? I mean, everybody does it. My mother and father talk about it all the time."

"Stop talking so much and go wash your face. You got some dirt on your cheek."

The dirt was a sore spot. Juanita saw that her plan wasn't going to work, but she had to try anyway. She didn't have any other. "Dee, what if you and I ran away before he gets back? He's mean to you, too. I'll bet he beats up on you, right? Couldn't we go someplace and make a real puppet show?"

Dee folded her arms and looked down at her for a long time. "Don't you ever want to see your parents again?"

"Not really." She gave her shoulders a shrug.

"You're a conniving little bitch, Juanita. Did you think I'd fall for a line like that? Get up and take off the robe."

"No." The knife was in the pocket. "I don't want to take it off, please."

Dee came up behind her and tried to wrench the robe from her shoulders. Juanita clung to the lapels. But when she could hold on no longer, she wriggled round on the bench and swung at Dee with all her might. The red hair leaped off the woman's head and plopped on the floor like a bird's nest. Juanita jumped for the wig and ran with it to the front of the loft. She tried to get through the heavy curtains, but Dee was too close. She threw herself at the girl and brought her to the floor.

Julie was near despair when she got home. Reggie Bauer's scenario could be due entirely to his own aberration. Great. But if that were so, what to do next? Once more she checked in with her service. A call had come from Nuba Bradley of the Actors Forum. They had found a sign saying PUPPET SHOW INSIDE. A homeless person was incorporating the sign into his wind shelter. A building-by-building search was under way. Julie called Detective Russo. He confirmed the search and the discovery of a pair of sneakers that could belong to the missing subject. "You might as well know the worst," Russo summarized. "They're bringing in a squatter from the building across the way. He watched two people load something into a station wagon about eight o'clock last night. We'll try to improve his memory, but all there is so far—a black wagon. Even the windows looked black to him."

Julie phoned Kevin Bourke. The line was busy. She had left his place only ten minutes before and had not even taken off her coat. She ran back to and up Eighth Avenue. A cabbie pulled alongside her and tapped his horn. She signaled that she wanted him, but kept on running. She could see the black car at the curb outside Bourke's shop. Not a cop in sight, not even a meter maid.

Mr. Bourke stepped out of the shop with the customer, who looked at his watch and poked a cautionary finger at Bourke. He strode to the wagon and pushed the street person out of his way. When he drove off, the cabbie took over the spot.

"I tried to call you," Bourke said. "You'd have known what I meant."

"I got a bead on him," the cabbie said as Julie jumped in. The wagon turned left at the stoplight. The late afternoon traffic was building. On Ninth Avenue it was at a crawl. The wagon stayed near the middle lane; the cabbie, to be sure the car he followed didn't opt for the Lincoln Tunnel, kept to the fire lane himself.

Julie made a note of the California license number and asked the driver if he couldn't radio a message to the police.

"No, ma'am. I'm a gypsy. I don't have that intercom stuff. But don't you worry none, he ain't going to get away."

But he almost did get away, slipping into a tunnel lane and then spurting out of it instead of turning west. He ran the light and went free while the westbound traffic closed in ahead of Julie's cab.

"He sure drives California style," the driver said. "What're you after him for?"

"I'm pretty sure he helped kidnap an eleven-year-old girl."

The cabbie shot out on the orange light and within four blocks of progressive lights was headlights-to-back-bumper with the wagon. "I'll ram him if you want me to."

"For God's sake, no. I want to see where he's going."

At Fourteenth Street the wagon made a couple of starts in the wrong direction before taking off down Hudson. Now Julie was afraid he'd know the cab was following him. At Bleecker and Bethune he came to a full stop at the playground gate.

"Keep going," Julie said.

But the driver in the wagon rolled down his window and signaled. The cabbie stopped alongside him.

"How in hell do I get to Houston Street from here?" He pronounced it like a Texan.

"Follow me," the cabbie said, and then to Julie as he led the way through the Greenwich Village maze, "See my point?"

The cabbie crossed Houston, a one-way street going west at that point, and signaled the wagon. But the wagon turned east, the wrong way.

The cabbie swore and ran two lights to get back on Houston by way of Sixth Avenue where Houston was two-way by then. They kept their distance as the wagon slowed down at every intersection, the driver looking for his street. He turned in at Wooster. But Wooster, they discovered when they got there, was blocked this side of Prince Street. A movie shooting there? So where were the trailers, where were the cops? The cops loved movies. Julie overpaid the cabbie and took her chances on foot. She knew SoHo pretty well.

She soon spotted the black wagon parked tight against a high wire fence midblock. The driver was wriggling across the front seat to get out on the passenger side. He went to the back and unloaded a couple of high-wattage lamps and a reflector. Could be they were on rental from Mr. Bourke. The man started up the street with them on the opposite side to the crowd. Julie stayed on the crowd's side, but at the fringe. At last the distant wail of approaching police. Two things happened at once: the man set down the lamps and reflector and, ignoring the crowd, took out his keys to unlock a door, and the crowd let out a collective cry, "Look! Look!"

Julie looked. A woman was dancing nude in the third-floor picture window. Not dancing, but jumping up and down, flailing her arms, and not a woman. It was Juanita.

Julie plunged across the street, waving to the girl and calling out, "Juanita!"

Some of the crowd moved with and past her. Interpreting for themselves, they caught hold of the man, pushed him from one to another, and pulled at his clothes. The multilocked loft door swung open. The redheaded woman took a step into the street, then tried to retreat inside the building again. When no one else took hold of her, Julie lunged and grappled her to the ground. The crowd loved it. The police came finally, swinging their night-sticks to disperse the crowd.

Julie and Juanita rode home in the chief inspector's car after they had stopped at One Police Plaza, to swear out the necessary complaints. There were things Juanita would not or could not talk about—mostly her fear and what she'd imagined might happen to her, but she liked to tell the action parts, especially how, when Dee had chased and caught her, she clung to the front window drapes and brought them down on top of Dee and her. By the time Dee had found her wig, Juanita was dancing in the window. Oh, yes, she insisted, she *was* dancing.

In time, police across the country fleshed out the chronicle of Dee and Danny, a horror story. They would arrive in a city, sublet quarters, recruit local talent, film, and move on. They supplied a flourishing market in underground cassettes. The true horror was not only in their corruption of the innocent, but in the despair in which they left the corrupted. These unfortunates rarely went home again and almost never broke their silence on the street.

THE SCAR

Nancy Pickard

 The reason Jean Williams took her son to the Botanic Gardens every day they were in Wellington, New Zealand, was that her husband was in such a lousy mood that she wanted to get out of the hotel and far away from him.

"I'm taking Zach to the park," Jean announced on the second morning of Lyle's sulk. Lyle had acquired an upper respiratory infection while they were up north in Auckland, and that accounted for some of his mood. But the truth was that coming to New Zealand on this vacation was Jean's dream, not his; Lyle wanted to visit only Australia, and it would be another ten days before they flew there. New Zealand, he complained, was too expensive and too cold, and he hated driving on the "wrong" side of the road. "But it's so beautiful," Jean said. "So is Alaska," he griped, "and we wouldn't have to spend a fortune to get there."

Well, if he was going to pout, Jean decided, she'd take Zach and they'd explore on their own. There was no point in ruining the trip for all of them. So she said, with more enthusiasm than she really felt, "Let's go, Zach!"

"I wanna go to a playground," Zach informed her.

That was no surprise. Only four years old, Zachary wasn't big on museums, art galleries, and guided tours. Zach was big on swings and slides and "roundy-rounds." Jean felt locked up and closed in and wanted to spend the day outside anyway.

"Right, mate," she said, mimicking an Australian accent and making her little boy laugh.

"Right, mate!" Zach shouted, and off they went, holding hands.

The main entrance to the famous Wellington Botanic Gardens lay directly across from their hotel, but Jean followed the advice of a tour book and hired a taxi to drive them to the entrance at the top of the park.

"It's a long and beautiful walk down," the book said, *"but a long and exhausting walk up. In the middle, exactly where adults will want to sit down and take a breather, there's a charming playground the little ones will love."*

The guidebook was right on all counts.

"Two slides!" Zachary squealed when he saw the playground.

"Wow. Go for it, Sweetpea. I'll be on that bench under that big tree over there."

He raced at breakneck speed down the path toward the playground equipment while Jean held her breath, watching him. When he reached the first slide safely, without falling to his chubby bare knees, Jean walked over to the wooden bench and sat down.

Big tree, she thought, mocking herself. She peered up into its branches. *Some botanist I'd make. Big green tree. Maybe it's labeled.* She looked down at its roots, where a label did indeed inform her it was a *Metrosideros umbellata (myrtle) (rata)*. Rata was probably the Maori word for it, she guessed. The Maoris, Jean knew from her reading if not from ever actually having seen one, were the Polynesians who still inhabited New Zealand after more than a thousand years.

She dug out of her purse the paperback history of New Zealand she had brought with her to read while Zach played. Opening it, she glanced up again through the branches of the myrtle *(big green)* tree at the clear and sunny New Zealand sky. She sighed happily and then looked down and thumbed to the page where she had last stopped reading about the Maoris: *". . . tribe and family were all-important. Every aspect of life was bound together and ruled by principles such as* tapu *(sacredness),* mana *(spiritual authority), and* mekutu *(sorcery). . . ."*

"Mommy! Look at me, Mommy!"

Zachary waved to her from atop the tallest slide. Jean, who had been thirty-eight years old when she had him, her first and only child, felt her heart lurch at the sight of him, so high. But she only smiled and mouthed up at her son: "Wow." He waved furiously, all wrist action, then swooshed down, landing with a thump on his bottom instead of on his feet. Jean watched him decide whether to cry and run back to her, or to laugh and run back to the ladder. When he laughed, she relaxed and returned to her reading.

" '. . . the Maori,' wrote Captain James Cook in his journal, 'have some arts among them which they execute with great judgement (sic) and unwearied patience. . . .' "

"Look at me, Mommy!"

"I'm looking!"

She also looked around her at the other mothers and children. The women, in their sleeveless cotton blouses and their flowered cotton skirts that clung to their slim legs, were almost uniformly pretty and blond, but it was the New Zealand children who took Jean's breath away. So blond, so tanned in this summer month, so blue-eyed and milk-fed and gorgeously healthy looking. *Pakehas.* From her book Jean had learned that was the Maori word for the invading Europeans. *Maori,* on the other hand, meant "normal." She decided she'd never seen so many beautiful children all in one place. And the prettiest one of all was a little blond beauty swinging by herself.

Jean stared, unable to take her eyes from the child, who looked about Zach's age, and whose deeply tanned skin dramatically set off the blue of her almond eyes and her curly blond hair. When the beauty hopped down from the swing and ran toward the slide where Zachary played, Jean continued to stare.

"Angie!"

The little girl named Angie turned toward the woman calling her. At the sudden sight of the other side of the child's face, Jean gasped and then tried to hide her shock by coughing and looking quickly away. An appalling scar ran down the left side of that exquisite face. As the little girl ran toward the woman who had called to her, Jean glanced at her again, not wanting to stare but unable to look away.

The scar bisected the child's left cheek.

It started just below the outer edge of her left eye, curved under the eyeball, then cut back through the middle of the cheek, finally curving down and under her chin, below the outer edge of her mouth. The scar was deep and as startlingly pink as the hibiscus flowers in the park.

"Oddly enough," Jean told Lyle that night at dinner, "the scar didn't detract from her beauty. I know this sounds strange, but the poignancy of it, the, I don't know, the *sadness* of it, somehow enhanced her beauty. At least, for me."

"Car accident, do you think?"

"I hope so," Jean said.

Her husband looked startled. "What?"

"I mean, at least that might be an innocent explanation of how she got it."

"Oh, you mean, maybe it was—"

With a sharp nod of her head toward Zachary, Jean stopped Lyle from actually saying the words "child abuse," although that was what she herself feared. Still, Wellington wasn't Chicago, and New Zealand wasn't the United States. Her guidebooks called it a family-oriented country, for both pakeha and Maori.

As Jean ate her lamb chops and browned potatoes, she thought about the woman who had called the girl away from her play. Who was she to the girl? An older mother, like Jean herself? An aunt? A baby-sitter, perhaps, or maybe even a grandmother?

At the park, the woman, the only one there who had looked as old as Jean, had taken the child's hand and together they had walked away from the playground, heading back up the hill toward the top of the park. Jean had stared after them, feeling like weeping. She had glanced back toward the slide and was surprised to see that Zachary, too, was staring after the beautiful, scarred little girl.

Over dessert, she teased, "You liked her, didn't you, Zach?"

"I love her," the little boy said solemnly.

Lyle's sulk deepened at breakfast the next morning, mainly, it seemed to Jean, because he couldn't abide the British custom of serving cooked tomatoes along with the fried eggs. And the bacon wasn't real bacon at all, he complained, it was ham. And didn't the New Zealand newspapers realize there were other parts of the world besides the South Pacific?

"Zach wants to go to the park again," Jean said.

"Swings, Daddy!"

Lyle managed a smile for his son and then a rueful version of it for his wife, one that told her he knew he was being a grump but that he couldn't help it. "Have fun." He coughed a couple of times. "I'm going back to bed. This damned hotel's so expensive, I don't want to miss a minute of it."

"You might feel better if you got out."

"I'll feel better when I get out of New Zealand."

But he softened the cynicism by winking at his son.

The beautiful little girl with the scar was at the park again that day. Jean watched the child and her own son—the two outsiders—tentatively greet each other and then happily play together.

"I'm Zachary David Williams."

"I'm Angela Susan Jones."

"What happened to your face?"

"How come you talk so funny?"

"I'm a United States for American!"

"Race you to the slide, Zachary!"

Several times Jean tried to catch the eye of the woman who accompanied Angie, but she never succeeded in doing it. The woman, short, stouter, older, and more solemn-looking than the other mothers, kept her hands folded in her lap and her eyes on her charge. After a while Jean gave up the effort of making a friend for herself and pulled her book on the history of New Zealand out of her purse. Skipping the chapter on Maori art, in which she wasn't particularly interested, she turned quickly past pictures of wood carvings that looked like Alaskan totems and thumbed to the chapters about modern-day New Zealand.

". . . *Greek and Italian restaurants are enormously popular*. . . ."

She was happy that Zachary had found a pal. It was still an effort not to stare at Angie's face, but Jean noticed that the other people in the park rarely did, as if they were used to seeing the child there. Soon, lost in photographs of spectacular scenery, lulled by the music of her own child's screams and giggles, Jean nearly forgot about it herself.

"Mom."

She looked up into Zach's face.

"I'm cold, Mommy."

"Well, no wonder, look at the time! I've been lost in my book. Where'd your little friend go?"

"Angie went home."

Jean smiled tenderly to see the expression of loss in his eyes. "You have really made a good friend, all this long way from our own home, haven't you?"

"Come back tomorrow, Mommy?"

"Yes, I promise."

And they did return to the park every day they remained in Wellington, until it was time to leave for the fjords and glaciers of the south island.

But when they had to say good-bye to Angela for the last time, Zachary and his little friend couldn't seem to grasp that they would never see each other again. Jean knelt down on the ground beside them and explained over and over that Zachary and his mom and dad had to leave, and they wouldn't be able to come back to the park.

But Zach said, "We come tomorrow, Angie!"

"No, darling, we won't be able to do that."

"*Yes!*" He shouted at his mother. "*Park! Yes!*"

"Shh, Zachy, here's what we'll do." Jean grabbed her purse and took out a scrap of paper and a pen. "I'll write down our name and address and give it to Angie, so maybe someday she can write to you, okay?"

"We come to park," Zach said stubbornly.

Jean gave the scrap of paper to Angela, who grabbed it and stuffed it into the pocket of her little skirt. "Good-bye, Angie." Jean ached to kiss the child's scarred cheek; instead, she touched her fingers gently to the curly blond hair and then to the other, perfect, cheek. When Angie smiled, her wide, pretty mouth and her haunting almond eyes turned up sweetly at the corners.

"Angie!"

From her park bench, the woman called.

Angie hugged her friend, and then ran off, waving and shouting, *"See you! See you tomorrow, Zach!"*

Zach argued with his mother about anything and everything all the way down the path to the hotel. Finally his fury turned to tears. Then he cried so inconsolably, and for so long, that Jean began to worry and to feel grateful they were leaving so the separation of the two little friends wouldn't be any harder than it already was.

"Honestly, Lyle," Jean whispered to her husband that night in bed. Zach was asleep, and breathing noisily through his tear-clogged nose, in the single bed across the room from their double. "You'd think this was that Maori legend I read about, the one where Rangi and Papa were separated by Tane."

"Do I know these people?" Lyle whispered back.

"Rangi was sky father, Papa was earth mother, and Tane was their son, and they were all together in the primordial darkness. But Tane was also the god of the forests, and so he had to push his parents away from him in order to create night and day so that his forests could grow. The story was that Rangi the sky father was so grief stricken at being separated from Papa the earth mother that his tears filled her with oceans and lakes."

"So it's old Rangi's fault that we couldn't drive down here from Chicago?"

"I feel so sorry for Zach! I'll swear, trying to explain why he won't ever see Angie again is like trying to explain death to a four-year-old. He doesn't understand that it's permanent, and that she's gone forever from his life."

"I need that Tane fellow," Lyle muttered into his pillow, "to separate me permanently from New Zealand before this hotel separates me permanently from my money."

"Oh, good night, you!"

But Jean was wrong—the separation wasn't permanent.

When Zachary was ten, he received a postcard from Angela Susan Jones in Wellington, New Zealand. The front of the card had a photograph of the playground in the Botanic Gardens, and she'd circled the tallest slide with a red, indelible marker.

"Do you remember?" it said on the back. *"I put your address in a secret*

place and saved it all these years. Will you please, please, please write back to me?"

She had signed it, *"I still love you. Angie,"* and printed her address. Zachary wrote back.

When Zachary was twenty-four and in the second year of medical school at the University of Chicago, he announced to his parents the specialty he intended to pursue.

"I'll be a plastic surgeon," he said.

"Good, maybe you can take a few tucks in my wallet," his father joked. "It's feeling loose and flabby after putting you through med school."

But Jean, who had never before heard her son mention any special interest in plastic surgery, was surprised and a little puzzled by his decision.

During the last year of Zachary's medical residency, he told Lyle and Jean that "the little girl from Wellington" was coming to Chicago to stay with him for a visit.

"Do you remember her, Mom?"

"You've written to Angie all these years, honey?"

"Yeah, didn't I ever tell you?"

"No, but I should have guessed."

A day later, she called her son back.

"Zach, are you hoping to fix Angie's scar? Is that why she's coming? Is that why you decided to be a plastic surgeon?"

"Sure," he said, as if it were a foregone conclusion. "I'm going to take a look at it, and see what I can do."

"Does Angie know this?"

"Of course, Mom, we planned this together a long time ago. We've always known she'd come up here, and I'd become a doctor, and we'd fix her face."

"Zach, what caused that scar?"

"I don't know," he said matter-of-factly, "because Angie doesn't know. Her mother told her it happened when she was a baby, before she was adopted. She doesn't have any memory of it."

"Angie's adopted?"

An image flitted through Jean's mind, a memory of a silent woman of about Jean's age, sitting alone on a park bench, her hands folded in her lap, watching the little girl.

"You don't care, do you, Mom?"

"Of course not, honey."

But as Jean hung up the phone from talking to her son, she felt chilled and frightened by something she couldn't identify at first. And then she realized that it was this . . . obsession . . . there was no other word for it . . .

this *obsession* of his that unnerved her, this fixation on a little girl he'd met twenty-five years earlier. No, she corrected herself, this obsession of *theirs*, Zach's and Angie's, too.

"Since they were four years old!" she exclaimed to Lyle.

"So? It's romantic," he said. "I think it's nice."

"You do?"

"Sure. At least it's one good thing to come out of that awful trip to New Zealand. Relax."

But in spite of all of his newly acquired skill and the help of more experienced surgeons, Zachary was not able entirely to erase Angie's scar, and so at their wedding the guests whispered to one another about the faint disfiguring mark on her left cheek.

"She's beautiful anyway," most of them agreed, and she was. Angie was lovely, and so was the baby boy that was born to her several years later.

When Justin Jones-Williams was six months old, Angie called Jean and Lyle to say, "We're going home! Zach's taking time off! We want to go back to Wellington to see my family and show off Justin! Will you come, too?"

"Us? Go, too?" At seventy-five and seventy-four, Lyle and Jean were still quite healthy and active, but Jean was startled and a little frightened by this invitation. Could they possibly manage such a trip? "Oh," she said, stalling as she smiled into the phone, "you just want us to come along as baby-sitters."

"Of course we do!" Angie's laugh was so light and happy that it flooded Jean with memories of the first time she'd ever heard it making music with her own son's laughter. "Please, Jean?"

And so she went along, too, but without Lyle this time.

"I hated New Zealand," he said at the airport.

"No kidding," Jean murmured, and kissed him good-bye.

Through the endless flights, from Chicago to San Francisco, from Honolulu to Auckland, and then on down to Wellington, Jean took turns holding Justin, feeding him, playing with him, walking him in the aisles, cuddling him when he slept. And all the while she was filled with a terrible terror: What if Angie longed to remain with her family, what if Zachary decided to look for a medical post in New Zealand, what if the other grandparents wanted their share of the baby, *what if she had to go home without them?* Once, having those awful thoughts somewhere in the air between Honolulu and Auckland, when she was half-nutty with fatigue, Jean felt hysterical giggles bubble in her throat! And wouldn't *that* just confirm Lyle's worst opinions of New Zealand. She buried her lips in the baby's neck to hide her trembling mouth.

* * *

The house where Angie grew up and where her parents still lived was only a front yard away from the taxi stop where Jean and little Zach had been dropped off at the Botanic Gardens.

Well, of course, Jean thought, when she saw that. *It was fate, it was always fate.*

Rather than amusing her, however, the thought tired her. After two days on airplanes, Jean felt as if fate was wearing her out.

The Joneses' home was a two-story cottage built on a precipitous slope. It had a garage at street level but required walking a long flight of stairs down to reach the front door. The woman who answered their knock was the same short, stout, dark-haired woman of Jean's age who had accompanied Angie to the playground all those years ago. She turned out to be Miriam Jones, Angie's adoptive mother; her father was Malcolm Jones, a tall, blond, bandy-legged man who was a retired government worker. Jean was weary enough to be nonplussed at the sight of the lines around Miriam's mouth and the age freckles on Miriam's hands; it was one of those moments when Jean was caught off guard by the shock of the passing of her own years.

"*What* a lovely boy," Miriam and Malcolm said of their grandson. But neither of them took him—or Angie—into their arms to welcome them home. At her first glimpse of her daughter's mended cheek, Miriam Jones murmured, "Well, I see they didn't get it all, did they?" And Malcolm looked at his son-in-law and then said to his wife, "Thought she was fine as she was, didn't we?"

Tears sprang to Jean's eyes in defense of her son and out of hurt for Angie, but she also felt a rush of joy of which she was mightily ashamed. These were not warm, affectionate parents to whom a daughter might long to return.

Fools, Jean thought, and smiled happily at them.

That evening after Miriam served lamb stew, cooked carrots, and mashed potatoes, she offered coffee to the Americans, along with a meringue and fruit dessert called a pavlova. Jean accepted a glass of sweet sherry, instead, and proceeded nearly to drop off to sleep in a rocking chair, cradling Justin. She could barely hold her jet-lagged eyes open; it was all she could do to pick up snatches of the conversation, and even they seemed only dialogue in a funny kind of surrealistic dream . . .

". . . While I'm here, don't want to hurt you or Father . . . find my birth parents . . ."

". . . Can't imagine why you . . ."

". . . Never knew, did we, Malcolm? Except what the social welfare people said . . ."

". . . What's the good, really . . ."

"In the U.S., you'd write to the . . ."

"Now that we have Justin, I think we ought to know . . ."

". . . Not always good to know . . ."

"*Why? Why not?*"

Jean's eyes flew open at the uncharacteristically sharp sound of her daughter-in-law's voice. She was disturbed to see that Angie's face was flushed, making her scar more pinkly visible. Jean tried to shift a bit, to ease her stiffness without waking the baby, but when the rocking chair creaked loudly, drawing the others' attention, she settled back quietly, if uncomfortably. What was going on here? What had she missed by dozing off? Why was Zachary looking at Angie with such a worried expression?

"Tell me what you remember," Angie half pleaded, half demanded of her parents. "If you don't, I shall have to make inquiries that will take such time and trouble, and . . ."

"All right!" Miriam Jones raised both of her hands in an exasperated gesture of surrender. "But there's so little we can tell you! The names of your biological parents were kept secret, but I do think the social worker told us you were born in Te Kapura."

Angie touched her cheek. "Did they tell you about this?"

"No." The mother looked straightforwardly at her daughter. "Except to say that you had not received any medical care at the time it happened, so it had never even been stitched by a doctor. When we got you, the wound was still raw, but healing." Jean wondered if she only imagined that Miriam's glance slid away from her daughter for a moment as she added, "They didn't tell us anything else about you. And we didn't ask. We were older than most adoptive parents, and you were hard to place." Jean flinched inwardly, for Angie's sake. But then her heart warmed to Miriam when the other woman looked up at her adopted daughter and said with a formal but moving simplicity, "We wanted you so. We have never regretted our decision to take you. We hope you don't regret it either."

"Mother." Angie looked as if she longed to rush to Miriam's side, but her mother's reserve kept the daughter pinned to her chair. "Of course I don't. I'm so grateful." Angie, who was so easily and openly demonstrative with her American family, cleared her throat and said awkwardly, "I love you both."

Malcolm shifted his weight on the sofa.

"Well, now you'd best forget all about it," he advised.

"Yes, it's done now, isn't it?" his wife agreed.

But if they thought they would deflect their daughter and son-in-law with a taste of the truth, they misjudged the young couple. Jean thought they should have known better than to underestimate Angie's and Zach's tenacity when those two became obsessed about something!

"What town did you say?" Angie asked.

Her mother sighed. "Te Kapura."

"Do you want to go tomorrow?" Zach asked Angie.

"Yes." She turned to her mother-in-law. "You, too, Jean?"

"No," Jean said, feeling they needed time alone. "I'll stay here and baby-sit with Justin." Jean smiled at her son. "Maybe I'll take him to the playground, and he'll meet his future wife."

"I think we ought to take him with us," Zach said.

"Yes, let's," his wife said.

Jean saw Miriam and Malcolm exchange glances. They noticed her observing them and for a moment all three grandparents were united in a strange bond that felt to Jean like complicity. Was she voicing a shared fear, Jean wondered, when she said, attempting a light tone:

"Well, do bring our baby back."

But Jean did go, because Justin—who was spoiled by the airline flights where the adults gave him anything he wanted just to keep him happy—wailed at being dragged from her arms after she gave him his bottle the next morning.

"You'd better come, Mom," Zach said.

"Please," Angie pleaded. "I don't think I can cope with this day and with him, too."

Jean pretended to give in gracefully, as if she were sacrificing a perfectly lovely day on her own in Wellington, but she'd go with them if they *insisted*.

"Well, all right," she said happily.

Although she said nothing about it to anyone, she felt a sense of relief at going along with them that wasn't altogether connected to her joy at spending the day with her grandson.

Te Kapura, they learned from a map, was twenty-five miles inland, north of Wellington along winding country roads. Angie drove, as she was the only one of them who was accustomed to the British way, while Jean sat in the front narrating the trip from the same old paperback history book that she'd brought to New Zealand the first time, and Zach played with Justin in the back. Jean finally gave up the reading, however, when it became impossible to make herself heard over the squeals and giggles.

"Angie," she said to her daughter-in-law. "How are you going to go about this search?"

"Well," Angie said, "I suppose we'll just knock on doors, won't we?" Only twenty-four hours back in New Zealand and Angie's accent was already stronger, Jean noticed; she had also retrieved the British habit of turning statements into interrogatories. "If the town's as tiny as most of these villages are, they'll surely remember a baby with this, won't they?" She twitched her own scarred cheek.

"I'm afraid it's a needle in a haystack," Jean warned.

But Angie, pretty, persistent Angie, only smiled. "You forget, New Zealand is a very small haystack, small enough to examine every straw, if we have to."

Jean reached over her seat to pat the baby, and sighed. "And knowing your mother and father, Justin, no doubt they'll do just that."

Zach and Angie, who had heard her, both burst out laughing.

Te Kapura was a tiny haystack, indeed.

Five little houses along a sunny mountain road.

Nobody was home at the first two. At the third one, they found a woman with three babies, but she was too young and too new to the village to remember. But at the fourth house, an old man was waiting for them as they walked up to his front door.

He had the same blond, thin, bandy-legged look as Angie's father, Malcolm, but there was a furtive amusement in this old man's smile, as if he knew a private, rather nasty joke.

"You'll be looking for someone, won't you?" he said in a wheezy, whispery voice. "Three strangers and a baby walking up our road, they must be looking for something."

"I'm looking for my parents," Angie said, and then she told him she'd been born here, and the year. "Did you live here then? I have this scar . . . do you see it . . . so there may have been an accident of some sort. Do you remember anything at all? Can you help me to find my birth family?"

The bony old man leaned toward her to examine the scar, and a sly look came into his eyes. He started to touch it, but Angie drew back sharply from his finger. That only seemed to amuse him more. "You'll be wanting to inquire across the way at the widow's house, won't you?" he said. "That'll be the ticket, now won't it?"

He cackled as if at a joke they didn't get.

Angie, Zach, Jean, and even the baby turned their heads to look at the tiny blue house that stood by itself across the road.

"Who lives there?" Zach asked.

"The widow," he said.

"What's her name?" Angie asked.

He didn't reply, but only stared openly at Angie's cheek.

"Good day," Angie murmured to him. "Thank you."

"Good day, is it?" he cackled. "Thank me, will you? We'll see about that, won't we?" His eerie laughter sent shivers down Jean's spine, but it made the baby laugh. They started walking across the road. The more Justin laughed, the louder the old man cackled, and then the more the baby screamed with delight, until the air of Te Kapura was filled with the loud, strange sound of their duet. Angie, with a desperate glance, implored Jean to quiet the baby. She tried, bouncing him and trying to distract him, until he just as suddenly burst into tears.

"Oh, dear," Angie said, looking near tears herself. Clearly, this return to her native country, to her adoptive parents, and maybe—today—even to her roots, was beginning to take a heavy emotional toll on her. She lifted her son from Jean's arms, and said, seemingly as much for herself as for the boy, "Poor baby, please, please, please, poor baby, it's all right, Mama's here. . . ."

Fate, Jean thought later, of course it was fate, and of course the widow would open the door to the little blue house just at the moment that Angie said those words.

Mama's here.

The woman standing in the doorway looked even older than the cracked old man across the street. She had beautiful silver hair that hung to her waist and plump brown features and the stillest face that Jean had ever seen, a face that looked as if it had been carved from a native tree and then aged for generations. As if by some unspoken accord, Zach took Justin back from Angie, and he and Jean hung back, while Angie walked slowly, and then ever more quickly forward until she was nearly running up to the old woman in the door. Breathless, the lovely young blond pakeha woman stood before the old brown Maori one.

Angie lifted her hair off her scarred cheek.

The old woman raised both of her hands to touch the scar.

"I am Te Po," she said. "I am your grandmother."

A beautiful and bored Maori girl named Te Anamarie, from the village of Te Kapura. Who met a lost and wandering, beautiful pakeha boy named Joseph. A baby girl. A tragic accident, only dimly remembered, in the birthing. And Joseph, the father, stole his baby from Te Anamarie and from her mother Te Po, and the villagers of Te Kapura never saw the father or the child again.

That was the haunting story the old woman told.

"He turned me over for adoption," Angie said.

"My child," the old woman said.

"I'm here," Angie whispered to her grandmother. "What was my Maori name?"

But the old woman shrugged off the question, as if she didn't remember, or it didn't matter now.

"Please," the old grandmother said, "let me play with my great-grandson for a while alone. Let me imagine that you were never taken from us, that he will always be able to visit me. Let me feed him once, and change him, and play with him. Let me sing the old Maori songs to my great-grandson, this once, let me tell him of his ancestors and his gods. Please, my granddaughter, give me this small favor to make up for all the tears of all these many years. I will tell him of the canoes that brought us, of the flax that clothed us and the fish that fed us. I will sing to him of maru and tapu and the beginning of time. Let me tell him of the land we shared, of the feasts, of the wars, even of the eating of the flesh of one another. I will tell him of your mother, who did not outlive her grief, of his grandmother, and my mother before us all, and her mother before. All of his life he will live among pakehas, it is the way of the world, but for this small moment in never-ending time, let me sing to him of his other world. Go in your car and drive. I am his great-grandmother who values him above all others. He is my beloved child whom I will never see again, and I must have this time alone with my great-grandson before I die. Please. I ask you in the name of your mother who never held you. Leave us. Go."

"Did I do the right thing?" Angie asked the others anxiously, a few minutes later, outside the blue house. "How could I say no to her?"

"Of course you couldn't," Jean assured her.

"No way," Zach agreed, though Jean noticed that he kept glancing back at the tiny blue house. "She's your grandmother, after all. He'll be fine. But what'll we do now to kill an hour?"

"Let's take a walk," Angie said. "And let me get used to the wonderful, incredible idea of being part Maori. This is what my parents were afraid I'd discover! As if I could ever be ashamed of it! My mother was Maori! My curly hair . . ."

"The shape of your eyes . . ."

"And I'm not as fair as most New Zealand women."

"You two go on without me," Jean suddenly said as the young couple started walking down the side of the road. "I'll stay here, maybe find a rock to sit upon. You need time to be together, and I need time . . . to be alone, I think."

Jean saw that it relieved her son to hear her say that she would stay behind. The old woman was Angie's blood relative, yes, but she was still a stranger to them.

Jean waved them off with a kiss.

Across the road, the old man was still out on his porch, hanging on to a railing, and staring across at the little blue house almost as if he were waiting for something to happen. He noticed Jean, and waved her toward him.

She shook her head, and walked in the opposite direction.

The rock she finally found was a boulder in the ditch beside the road.

There, in the sun, she pulled out of her purse the old history book she had been reading aloud to the kids, and turned to the section on Maori culture.

"*. . . a tribal society,*" she read, "*that nearly became extinct in the 1800s, following the depredations of the white man's diseases, of the introduction of his animals, particularly the rabbit that became the scourge of the native agriculture . . .*"

The sun was so warm, and Jean was seventy-four years old, and exhausted by this incredible, emotional journey into her daughter-in-law's past and all of their hearts. She tried mightily to keep her eyes open against the glare, wanting to learn more about the Maoris, out of respect for the old woman and love for Angie and Justin.

"*. . . after near decimation, resurgence of Maori population and a shift by the younger generation to the urban centers . . . harder on the older generation to whom the loss of their ancient ways was a bitter pill to swallow . . .*"

So sleepy, so warm, and her eyes were closing. Besides, she remembered, vaguely, having read this same chapter more than thirty years before. She turned the page to a chapter about Maori art, which she suspected she had skipped the first time.

"*. . . effort to renew Maori crafts and customs, including wood carving . . .*"

A monstrous face stared out at her from the page, a face with its huge tongue stuck out, a face on which ceremonial lines were deeply etched. "Boo," Jean said to the scary face, and then she laughed to herself.

"*. . . the custom of tattooing in which a straightedge blade is used to carve the lines deeper into the face and breasts of women, the face and buttocks of men, thereby to inject the die more deeply and to give the design more the look of carving than of the tattooing to which Western eyes are more accustomed . . .*"

Something about that paragraph, Jean thought. *Read that paragraph again. Tattooing. Straightedge blade. Deep grooves.* Her glance shifted to the carved wooden face on the other page. Some of the carved lines—meant to represent tattooing?—started below the figure's eyes and then curved back, bisecting the cheek, and running down below the chin. . . .

Jean screamed and leaped to her feet.

And then the wailing started, a loud, dirgelike wailing, a woman's voice coming from the tiny blue house. And the old man across the way began to cackle again and to watch Jean running down the road from the rock. Oh, but she wasn't young enough, she wasn't forty-two now, she was seventy-four, and her breath was coming hard and painfully, and she was so frightened, so frightened, and she wanted to scream and scream, to cry out for Justin to crawl away, to crawl down the dirt road to her . . . Justin, Justin, baby, baby . . . And the old man called to her, "It's the call of mourning for the dead, which only the women can sing, and she will put on her black dress of mourning." He cackled and cackled, a crazy old pakeha watching Jean stumble down the road toward the tiny blue house. "Te Po, her name, means the endless night before the birth of the Gods, did you know that, did you know that?"

Her heart was beating so unmercifully, oh, dear God, she would have a heart attack, she would die on this road before she reached the baby and the other old woman, the old woman like a carving, like a carving, like a tattooed carving. . . .

"No . . . !"

Jean flung herself into the blue house. Blinded by the sudden plunge into dimness, she began to sob helplessly. *No, no, no, no, no.* Then she could see the old woman, Te Po, dressed all in black as the old man had predicted, a straightedge knife raised over the naked baby boy who lay crying on the floor.

Jean threw herself at Te Po.

Both old women fell to the floor near the baby.

The knife sliced through soft, soft skin, carving its ancient tattoo.

In nearly thirty years, the myrtle tree *(Metrosideros umbellata, rata)* beside the bench in the playground had grown magnificently.

"Hello, tree," Jean murmured to it. "Big green tree."

Seated there in its shade, Jean watched Zachary put Justin on his lap at the top of the tallest slide.

"Mom!" Zach called out to her. "Watch us!"

"I'm watching!"

They whooshed down from the top of the tallest slide, down to the bottom, where Angie waited with open arms to embrace them both.

Jean smiled and turned her left arm over to expose her wound to the healing warmth of the sun.

MURDER WITHOUT A TEXT

Amanda Cross

 At the time of Professor Beatrice Sterling's arraignment, she had never set foot in a criminal court. As a juror, a duty she performed regularly at the close of whatever academic year she was called, she had always asked to serve in the civil division. She felt too far removed from the world of criminals, and, because of her age (and this was true even when she was younger, referring as it did more to the times in which she had been born than to the years she had lived), too distanced from the ambience of the criminal to judge him (it was almost always a him) fairly. She was, in short, a woman of tender conscience and unsullied reputation.

All that was before she was arrested for murder.

Like most middle-class dwellers in Manhattan, therefore, she had never been through the system, never been treated like the felon the DA's office was claiming her to be. It is a sad truth that those engaged in activity they know to be criminal, shoddy business practices, drug dealing, protection rackets, contract killings, have quicker access to the better criminal lawyers. Those unlikely to be accused of anything more serious than jaywalking often know only the lawyer who made their will or, at best, some pleasant member of a legal firm as distant from the defense of felons as from the legal intricacies of medieval England. Beatrice Sterling's lawyer was a partner in a corporate law firm; long married to a woman who had gone to school with Beatrice, he had some time ago agreed to make her will as a favor to his wife. His usual practice dealt with the mergers or takeovers of large companies; he had never even proffered legal advice to someone getting a divorce, let alone accused of murder. There was not even a member of his firm knowledgeable about how the criminal system worked at the lower end of Manhattan, next door though it might have been to where their elegant law firm had its being. The trouble was, until her arraignment, neither Beatrice nor her sister considered any other lawyer. It is always possible that with the best legal advice in the world, Beatrice would still have been remanded, but as it happened, she never had any chance of escaping rides to and from Riker's Island in a bus reinforced with mesh wiring, and incarceration in a cell with other women, mostly drug dealers and prostitutes. By that time Beatrice was alternately numb or seized with such rage against the young woman she was supposed to have murdered that her guilt seemed, even to her unhappy corporate counsel, likely.

Professor Beatrice Sterling was accused of having murdered a college senior, a student in a class Beatrice had been teaching at the time the young woman was found bludgeoned to death in her dormitory room. The young woman had hated Beatrice; Beatrice had hated the young woman and, in fact, every young woman in that particular class. She would gladly, as she had unfortunately mentioned to a few dozen people, have watched every one of her students whipped out of town and tarred and feathered as well. She had, however, insisted that she had not committed murder or even laid a finger on the dead girl. This counted for little against the evidence of the others in the class who claimed, repeatedly and with conviction, that Beatrice had hated them all and was clearly not only vicious but capable of murder. The police carried out a careful investigation, putting their most reliable and experienced homicide detectives on the case. These, a man and a woman, had decided that they had a better than even case against the lady professor, and, since the case might become high profile, got an arrest warrant and went to her apartment to arrest her and bring her into the precinct.

It is possible, even at this stage, to avoid being sent to jail, but not if the charge is murder in the second degree (first degree murder is reserved for those who kill policepersons). Those accused of minor misdemeanors are issued a Desk Appearance Ticket and ordered to appear in court some three or four weeks hence. (Sometimes they do, sometimes they don't, but such a choice was not offered to Beatrice, who would certainly have appeared anytime she was ordered to). She was allowed one phone call, which she made to her sister to ask for a lawyer, a wasted call since the sister, whose name was

Cynthia Sterling, had already called the corporate lawyer husband of Beatrice's school friend. Beatrice was told by the woman detective that it could be anywhere from twenty-four to seventy-two hours until her arraignment and that probably no lawyer could get to her until a half hour before that occurred. Men who go through the system are held during this period in pens behind the courtrooms. Since there are, in the Manhattan criminal system, no pens for women, Beatrice was held in a cell in the precinct. The system happened at that time to be more than usually backed up—and it was usually backed up—so she was not taken directly to Central Booking at One Police Plaza, police headquarters for all the boroughs and Central Booking for Manhattan, until two days had passed.

Neither Beatrice nor her sister Cynthia had ever married, and a more unlikely pair to become caught in the criminal system could not easily be imagined. As Beatrice in jail alternated between numbness and rage, weeping and cold anger, Cynthia came slowly, far too slowly as she later accused herself, to the conclusion that what she needed was help from someone who understood the criminal system. Beatrice's school friend's husband was useless: less than useless, because he did not know how little he knew. A knowledgeable lawyer could not now save Beatrice from her present incarceration and all the shame and humiliation connected with it; but he or she might be able to offer some worthwhile, perhaps even practical, advice.

We all know more people than we at first realize. Cynthia could have sworn that she knew no one connected with law enforcement or criminal defense even four times removed. She forced herself to sit quietly, and upright, in a chair, calming herself in the manner she had read of as recommended for those undertaking meditation in order to lower their blood pressure. She sat with her feet flat on the floor, her back straight to allow a direct line from the top of her head to the base of her spine, and in this position she repeated, as she thought she remembered from her reading, a single word. Any one-syllable word, if simple relaxation as opposed to religious experience were the aim, would suffice. She chose, not without some sense of irony, the word "law." Faith in law was what, above all, she needed. Slowly repeating this word with her eyes closed and her breathing regular, she bethought herself, as though the word had floated to her from outer space, of Angela Epstein.

Cynthia, after continuing her slow breathing and word repetition for a few seconds out of gratitude, contemplated the wonders of Angela Epstein. She had come to Cynthia's office only a week or two ago to say hello. Could fate, were there any such thing, have whispered in her ear? Cynthia was the dean in charge of finances at a large, urban college quite different from the elite suburban institution in which Beatrice taught. In that capacity, Cynthia had, in the past, been able to put Angela Epstein in the way of fellowship aid, and

Angela, unlike the greater number of her kind, had continued to be grateful. Finding herself in the area of her old college, she had stopped in to greet Cynthia, to thank her for her past help, and to tell Cynthia about her present life. What Angela did—it was something in the investment line—Cynthia could not precisely remember, but a sentence of Angela's echoed, like the voice of a guardian angel in a legend, in Cynthia's postmeditation ears: "I'm living with a wonderful guy; he's a public defender, and he loves what he does. It's great to live with someone who loves what he does, and who does good things for people caught up in New York's criminal system; between us, we can afford a loft in Manhattan."

From Information, Cynthia got the number of Angela Epstein. Here, as it was night, she got a message machine. She left as passionate a request for Angela to call back as she could muster; indeed, passion quivered in every syllable. But if Angela and lover had retired at midnight, they might not return her call until morning, perhaps not until they returned from work the next day. Cynthia decided—rather, she was seized by a determination—to go and visit Angela herself at that very moment. Perhaps she would not get in; perhaps she would be mugged in the attempt. But with Beatrice behind bars, any action seemed better than no action. She pictured herself banging on the door of their loft until allowed entrance and the chance to plead. She dressed hurriedly, descended to the street, commandeered a taxi, and told the driver to take her to the Lower East Side, insisting over his protests that that was indeed where she wanted to go.

"This time of night, you gotta be outta your mind."

It occurred to Cynthia, even in the midst of her distracted determination, that she had not been driven by an old-fashioned cabdriver for a very long time indeed. He was American, old, shaggy, and wonderfully soothing.

"I have to go now," she said. "Please. Take me."

"It's your funeral, literally. I'm telling you. I wouldn't be out on the streets myself this time of night, except it's my nephew's cab; my nephew's having a baby in the hospital with his wife. It takes two to have a baby these days, I mean to have it, not to start it, if you see what I mean. Me, I drive only by day."

"I see," Cynthia said, blessing him for beginning to drive.

"He's working his way through law school, drives a cab at night. These days, in this city, you don't need to be a lawyer, you need to hire one, and a doctor too while you're at it, I tell him. So he's crazy, so you're crazy. You're not buying drugs, I hope?"

Cynthia assured him that she was not. Was meditation like prayer? Was it answered like prayer? First the name had come to her, then this wonderful cabdriver. Could another miracle happen, that they would hear her pounding on the door and let her in and listen to her story?

Another miracle happened, though not quite that way. As she emerged from the taxi, a couple approached her. They looked at her oddly; she was not, it was to be assumed, a usual type to be seen in this neighborhood at this hour. The couple had also emerged from a taxi, even now departing.

"Dean Sterling!" someone shouted. It was Angela Epstein. "What on earth are you doing here?"

"I'm looking for you," Cynthia said, suddenly unbelievably tired, worn out by all the sudden good fortune that had come her way.

"So ya gonna pay me, or ya forgot and left your purse at home?"

Cynthia came to her senses, apologizing to the cabdriver and the astonished young couple. She reached into her purse and gave the cabdriver a large bill. "For you and your nephew and the baby," she said. "You are wonderful."

"You too," he shouted, taking off with a screech of tires. Cynthia had meant to beg him to return, but she merely shrugged. It was Angela Epstein's young man upon whom she now turned her full attention.

"You are a public defender, you understand the criminal system?" she said, as though he might deny it and turn out to be something wholly useless.

"Yes," he said, taking her arm. "Are you in trouble? Why don't we go upstairs and talk about it?" Over her head, for he was a tall young man, he gave Angela a quizzical look; she made soothing gestures and rushed ahead to open the building door, peering about to see that there were no dangerous types lurking.

"I'm afraid I don't even know your name," Cynthia said.

"My name's Leo," he said. "Leo Fansler. What's yours?"

"Cynthia Sterling. My sister Beatrice Sterling is in jail, accused of murder. And I'm afraid they won't even let her out on bail; that seemed to be the only coherent statement I could get out of the lawyer I called. Will you help us?"

"I'll try," Leo Fansler said.

They got her settled on the couch with a cup of tea and a blanket over her legs because the loft was chilly. Besides, they wanted to do all the easy things they could think of to help her. She had always appeared to Angela as a woman of such power and efficiency, but she now looked the very picture of distraction and disarray, rather—Leo later said to Angela—like the White Queen. (Leo had to explain who the White Queen was. "You've read everything," Angela lovingly accused him. "Not really," he answered. "I just lived for a time with a literary aunt.")

At last Cynthia managed to tell Leo, in answer to his questions, with what her sister was charged, when she had been arrested, whether or not the detectives had had a warrant, and whether she had yet been arraigned. He tried, as gently as possible, to keep her from telling him the whole story from the very beginning. "Not yet," he said. "I'll find out from your sister; I'll talk to her. I'll get the whole story, believe me. But right now all I want to know is where she is, and what's already happened in court."

Cynthia made a noble attempt to be as coherent as possible. To her infinite relief, Leo understood her, interpreted her vague answers, knew what to do.

"Do you know when the arraignment is?" he asked. "Did they tell you, or her?"

"Probably tomorrow, but they can't be sure."

"Okay. I'll be there," Leo said. "Her lawyer will try for bail at the arraignment, but probably won't get it. The chances are she'll be remanded, and we'll try again; we may do better upstairs at the felony arraignment. But if she does get bail for a murder charge, it may be in the neighborhood of a million dollars. Can you raise that much? There are bondsmen. . . ."

"I'll raise it," Cynthia said. "The lawyer already spoke to me about that. The one who doesn't know anything. I think he talked about money because that's all he knows anything about. We'll mortgage our apartment. It's very valuable. It's worth over a million now, though it wasn't when we moved in thirty years ago."

"It takes a while to get a mortgage, even a loan," Leo said, more to himself than her. "I'm going to call you a taxi now; the company will send one if we offer double. Otherwise they avoid this neighborhood at night. You go home and try to get some rest. Meet me in the public defender's office on Centre Street across from the courthouse tomorrow morning at nine. Can you manage that?"

"I could take her," Angela said. "I could be late to work."

"I'll find it," Cynthia said. "Please, you've done enough. I'll meet you there."

"Get off the subway at Chambers Street. Then ask someone the way. Don't take a taxi; you'll be stuck in traffic for hours."

"I'll be there," Cynthia said. "Poor Beatrice. I'll be there. You will let me convince you she's innocent."

"Tomorrow, or maybe even later. The important thing is, you've got someone on your side who knows the system. That's all you have to think about right now. I'm going to try to get you another lawyer for the trial. I know it's impossible, but try not to worry too much."

Cynthia arrived at the public defender's office at nine o'clock. She saw no reason to tell Leo, who came out to the reception desk to meet her, that she had set out at seven, and wandered around the confusing streets of lower Manhattan for at least an hour, until a truck driver finally gave her proper directions. Leo led her off to his office, hung up her coat, sat her down, and tried to tell her what had happened so far.

"Where is Beatrice now?" Cynthia asked, before he began.

"Probably on her way in from Central Booking. We haven't much time, so you must listen."

"I am listening," Cynthia said, drawing together all her powers of attention. The time for action had come.

"All right," Leo said. "She was arrested and taken to your precinct, where pedigree information, name, address, and so on, are taken, and a warrant check is made, that is, to see if she is wanted on any other cases. I know, I know, but we're talking about the system here, not your sister. As you'll see when we go to court, most of those arrested have records, and quite a number do not have an address, so she's ahead on that count. The detectives will have questioned your sister extensively, and we can only pray she had the sense not to say anything at all. Any statement she made upon arrest can and will be read out at her arraignment."

"It all seems very unfair," Cynthia said, "taking advantage of people when they're upset."

"That's exactly the point. And even hardened criminals rarely know enough to shut up. I don't know how long she was held in the precinct—I'll find out—but it was as long as they had to wait before Central Booking was ready to process more bodies." Leo ignored the fact that Cynthia had closed her eyes and gone white. He kept on talking to bring her around. "Her prints were then faxed to Albany, where they are matched by computer against all other prints in the state. The result is a rap sheet, which in your sister's case will be encouragingly blank. I assume she has no record." He looked at Cynthia, who nodded certainly. "That's good news for our side when it comes to pleading for bail," Leo said.

"The reason she's now in jail is because the system was backed up; they had to go to the DA's office for a complaint to be drawn up, and because she had to be interviewed by the Criminal Justice Agency." Leo noticed that Cynthia was beginning to look faint. "Hold on," he said. "We're almost finished with this part. She's got a CJA sheet—for Criminal Justice Agency," he added, as faintness was now joined by bewilderment. "Everyone in court, the judge, the DA, your sister's lawyer, will use that sheet. It gives her years at her address, her employment, length of employment, and so on. That's going to help your sister, because she's obviously been a responsible member of the community with a good employment record and a steady address. We're waiting now until all these papers reach the court. We'll try for bail at the arraignment, but don't be hopeful. On a murder charge like this, she'll almost certainly be remanded at arraignment."

"Will you be at the arraignment arguing for her bail?"

"I can't be," Leo said. "She's not eligible for legal aid. But I've got her a lawyer, a woman I went to law school with. She's first-rate, she has worked for the DA, she knows what she's doing, she's smart, and above all, she'll understand where your sister's coming from. She's already gone to the court to be ready to meet with your sister when she's brought in from Central Booking to the arraignment. That's the whole story. Are you okay for now?"

"Will they put her in a cell when she gets here?"

"No. Women aren't put into pens. She'll sit on a bench with other women prisoners at the front of the courtroom. She'll go into a booth there to talk to her lawyer. We're going over there now; you'll see the setup."

"Will she see me?"

"Yes. But you mustn't try to talk to her or to reach her. Sally, that's her lawyer, will tell her about what you've done so far, including finding me. Ready? Here's your coat. Let's go."

"Don't you need a coat?"

Leo shook his head. Nothing, he thought, would keep a woman from noticing he didn't wear a coat racing around the courts; no man would ever notice it. It had something to do with female nurturing, Angela would say.

"Do you think you could walk down six flights," he asked, "because the elevators take forever? Good. We're off."

There was a lot happening at the court. Cynthia saw the judge, the DAs, and men in white shirts with guns who Leo said were court officers; they carried the papers between the lawyers and the judge. When Beatrice was brought in front of the judge, holding her hands behind her, Cynthia thought she would weep and never stop. She couldn't hear what any of them said, except for the DA who spoke loud and clear: "The people are serving statement notice. Defendant said: 'I didn't kill her. I loathed her but I didn't kill her. I couldn't kill anyone.' No other notices."

Cynthia looked with agony at Leo.

"Never mind. Not exactly inculpatory. It's always better to shut up, but a protest of innocence is not the worst. Listen now; Sally's asking for bail. The DA asked that she be remanded—sent to jail while awaiting trial. Sally's answering."

"With all due respect, your honor, the ADA's position, while predictable, takes no account of my client's position in the community. The case is not strong against my client; the major evidence is circumstantial. We have every intention of fighting this case. My client not only has no record, but is a long-honored professor in a well-established and well-known institution of higher education. She has been a member of the community and has lived at the same address for many years. There can be no question of my client's returning. We ask that bail be set sufficient to insure that return, but not excessive. My client is a woman in her late fifties who is innocent and intends to prove it." There was more, but Cynthia seemed unable any longer to listen. Leo had said there was little hope for bail at this point. She tried to send thought waves of encouragement and support to Beatrice, but the sight of her back with her hands held together behind her was devastating.

The judge spoke with—Cynthia might have felt under other circumstances—admirable clarity. "The defendant is remanded. Adjourned to AP–17, January sixth, for grand jury action."

That was that. Beatrice was led away, and Cynthia wept.

"It won't be too long," Leo said, trying to find some words of comfort. "The law does not allow anyone to be kept more than one hundred forty-four hours after arrest without an indictment. And now she has a lawyer who knows what she's doing, and who will, with any luck, get bail for her after her felony arraignment upstairs. You go home and try to be ready to raise it. At least a million; that's a guess, but probably a good one. Can you get home all right?" Cynthia looked at where Beatrice had been, but she was gone. She saw the booths, like confessionals, she thought, where Beatrice might have talked to her lawyer before Leo had brought her. But Leo hurried her out; he was already late for another hearing in another court.

Later Leo and Sally met for lunch in a Chinese restaurant on Mulberry Street. Sally was not encouraging. "Am I sure she didn't do it? No, I'm not sure, so what is a jury going to make of her? Talk about reasonable doubt: I'd have less doubt if I saw the cat licking its lips before an empty birdcage. Leo, my love, my treasure, take my advice: start thinking about a plea in this case. She'll get eight and a third to twenty-five if she's maxed out on a manslaughter plea, with parole after eight and a third. Otherwise, we're talking fifteen to life. Think of Jean Harris."

"Jean Harris shot her lover."

"That's more excusable than bludgeoning to death a twenty-year-old girl."

"What happened exactly?"

"According to the DA? The girl was found dead in her dormitory room on a Saturday night. The dormitory was close to empty, and no one saw anything, except some boy on his way out who saw an old lady, and picked Professor B out of a lineup. A hell of a lot of good her corporate lawyer did her there. Professor B says she was home; sister away at some institutional revel. Every one of the girl's friends has testified that Professor B hated her, though only slightly more than she hated the other girls in her seminar. Something to do with women's studies, more's the pity."

"That's all the DA's got?"

"An eyewitness, a lack of other suspects, and Professor B's prints all over the girl's notebook. Even Daphne's friends admit she went rather far in goading the old lady, but that hardly excuses murder. It's not as though we're dealing with the battered woman's syndrome here. That's how it is, Leo. We'll have to plead her out."

* * *

"Thanks for agreeing to a Japanese restaurant," Leo said. "I know it's not your thing. I needed some raw fish: brain food. Also you like the martinis here; I think you better have two before I start on my story."

Kate Fansler sipped from the one she had already ordered and contemplated Leo. He had said he wanted advice; the question was, about what? Kate considered the role of aunt far superior to that of parent, which did not alter the fact that the young made her nervous. This advice, however, turned out not to be about the young.

"It doesn't sound like a very strong case against her," Kate said, when Leo had told her the story and consumed several yellowback somethings; he went on to eel.

"It's not; but it's the sort of case they'll win. They'll bring on all the girl's friends, and what's on Beatrice's side? A devoted sister, and all the stereotypes in the world to tell you she had a fit of frantic jealousy and knocked the girl's head in."

"You sound rather involved."

"I'm always involved; that's why I'm so good at what I do, and why it's interesting. I also know how to get uninvolved at five o'clock and go home, unlike high-class lawyers."

"So Sally's arguments have a certain cogency."

"Naturally. That's the trouble. It's a little early to tell, but it looks to me like either she cops or, as my clients say, she'll blow trial and get a life term. As far as I can see it's a dilemma with only one way out. Find the real killer. Right up your alley, I rather thought."

Kate, who had decided on only one martini, waved for the waiter and ordered another. "I've known you so long," she said, "that I'm not going to exchange debating points. We can both take it as said. If I wanted to talk with your murderer, would I have to go out to Riker's Island?"

"No. Anyway, I'm pretty sure Sally will get bail after the indictment, if we have any luck at all with the judge. There's every reason not to keep the old gal in jail, and Sally can be very persuasive. In which case you can visit her in the apartment they have just mortgaged to get the bail."

"Leo, I want one thing perfectly clear. . . ."

"As you said, dear Aunt Kate, we know the debating points. Just talk to the elderly sisters, together, separately, and let me know what you decide. End of discussion, unless of course, you decide they're innocent and I can help."

"I thought it was just one of them?"

"It is; but Cynthia's the one I met first, so I sort of think of them as a pair. I've never met Beatrice; just caught sight of her with the other women prisoners at the arraignment. But I have met Cynthia, I've heard Angela on Cynthia, and I'm not ready to believe that Cynthia's sister could have murdered anyone."

* * *

Leo had told Kate that for a woman of Professor Beatrice Sterling's background, experience of the criminal system would be a nightmare; indeed, Beatrice, as she asked Kate to call her, had the look of someone who has seen horrors. They were meeting in the sisters' apartment after bail had been granted. Cynthia, now that Beatrice was home, was clearly taking the tack that a good dose of normality was what was needed, and she was providing it, with a kind of courageous pretense at cooperation from Beatrice that touched Kate, who allowed a certain amount of desultory chatter to go on while she reviewed the facts in her mind.

Burglary had always been a possibility, but it was considered an unlikely one. The victim's wallet had not been taken, though the cash, if any, had. Her college ID, credit cards, and a bank card remained. Pictures that had been in the wallet had been vigorously torn apart and scattered over the body. Her college friends, although they knew the most intimate facts of her life as was usual these days, did not know how much money she usually carried or if anything else was missing from her wallet. She had been bludgeoned with a tennis award, a metal statue of a young woman swinging a racket that had been heavily weighted at the base. The assailant had worn gloves. What had doomed Beatrice was not so much these facts, not even the identification by the young man (though this was crushing), but the record of deep dislike between the victim and the accused that no one, not even the accused, denied. Motive is not enough for a conviction, but, as Leo had put it, the grounds for reasonable doubt were also, given the likely testimony of the victim's friends, slim. Kate put down her teacup and began to speak of what faced them.

"You are our last hope," Cynthia said, before Kate could begin.

"If that is true," Kate answered, looking directly into the eyes of first one and then the other, "then you are going to have to put up with my endless questions, and with retelling your story until you think even jail would be preferable. Now, let's start at the beginning, with a description of this seminar itself. How did you come to teach it, were these students you had known before, what was the subject? I want every detail you can think of, and then some. Start at the beginning."

Beatrice took a deep breath, and kept her eyes on her hands folded in her lap. "I didn't know those particular students at all," she said, "and I didn't particularly want to teach that seminar. For two reasons," she added, catching Kate's "Why?" before it was spoken. "It was in women's studies, which I have never taught. I'm a feminist, but my field is early Christian history, and I have not much expertise about contemporary feminist scholarship. The seminar was for writing honors theses in women's studies, which meant there were no texts; in addition, the students were all doing subjects in sociology or political science or anthropology, and I know little of these fields beyond their relation to my own rather ancient interests. I had worked hard, and under some unpleasant opposition, to help establish women's studies at our college, so I had little excuse not to take my turn in directing this seminar; in any case, there was no one else available. There were twelve students, all seniors, and yes, it did occur to me to relate it to the Last Supper, which I mention only because you will then understand what the seminar invoked in me." A sigh escaped, but Beatrice, with an encouraging pat from Cynthia, continued.

"The young are rude today; anyone who teaches undergraduates can tell you that. They are not so much aggressively rude as inconsiderate, as though no perspective but theirs existed. The odd part of this is that the most radical students, those who talk of little but the poor and the racially oppressed, are, if anything, ruder than the others, courtesy being beneath them. Forgive me if I rant a bit, but you wanted to hear all this.

"The point is, they hated me on sight and I them. Well, that's an exaggeration. But when I tried to suggest what seemed to me minimal scholarly standards, they sneered. Quite literally, they sneered. I talked this over with the head of women's studies, and she admitted that they are known to be an unruly bunch, and that they had not wanted me for their seminar, but she couldn't do anything except cheer me on. They spoke about early feminists, like me, as though we were a bunch of co-opted creeps; worst of all, they never talked to me or asked me anything; they addressed each other, turning their backs on me. You're a teacher, so perhaps this will sound less silly to you than to the police. It was the kind of rudeness that is close to rape. Or murder. Oh, don't think I don't usually run quite successful classes; I do. Students like me. Of course, my students are self-selected: they're interested in the subject, which they elect to take. But even when I teach a required history survey, I do well. I'm not as intimate with the students as some of the younger teachers, and I regret that, but I grew up in a different time, and it seems best to be oneself and not pretend to feelings one doesn't have. Do you agree?"

Kate nodded her agreement.

"The dead girl—they called each other only by their first names, and hers was Daphne, but I remembered *her* last name (which the police found suspicious) because it was Potter-Jones, and that sounded to me like something out of a drama from the BBC—she was the rudest of the lot and was writing on prostitutes, or, as they insisted on calling them, sex-workers. I should add that all their subjects were enormous, totally unsuitable to undergraduates, and entirely composed of oral history. All history, all previously published research, was lies. They would talk to real sex-workers, real homeless women, real victims of botched abortions, that sort of thing. When I suggested some academic research, they positively snorted. Daphne said that being a sex-worker was exactly like being a secretary—they were equally humiliating jobs —but at least we might try to see that sex-workers got fringe benefits. My only private conversation, if you can call it that—they never, any of them, came to my office hours or consulted me for a minute—was with Daphne. She had been advised at a seminar to pretend to be a sex-worker and try to get into a 'house' so that she might meet some prostitutes; she had, not surprisingly to me but apparently to her and all the others, found it difficult to get prostitutes to talk to her. I took her aside at the end of the class and told her I thought that might be rather dangerous. She laughed, and said she had told her mother, who thought it was a great idea. I know all this may sound exaggerated or even the wanderings of a demented person, but this is, I promise you, a straightforward rendition of my experience. I have spared you some details, considering them repetitive. No doubt you get the picture. It occurred to me, when I was in Riker's Island, that perhaps I might now be of some interest to the members of the seminar, except of course that they thought I had murdered their friend, so I failed to interest them even as an accused murderer. Cynthia thought I oughtn't to mention that, but my view is if, knowing it all, you can't believe me, I might as well plead to manslaughter as my young but clearly smart lawyer urges."

Kate did not break for some minutes the silence that fell upon them. She was trying to order her perceptions, to analyze her responses. Could the hate Beatrice felt have driven her to violence? Kate put that thought temporarily on hold. "Tell me about the night of the murder," she said. "You were here the whole time alone. Is that the whole truth?"

"All of it. The irony is, Cynthia tried to persuade me to go with her to the party, which she thought might be better than most. I almost went, but I had papers to correct, and in the end I stayed home, thereby sacrificing my perfect alibi. Do you think the moral is: always accept invitations?"

"When did you last see Daphne?"

"I last saw them all the day before, at the meeting of the seminar. I think they had been told that I would give them a grade, and that attendance would count. The director was probably trying to help me, but that of course only increased their resentment, which increased mine. I don't want to exaggerate, but at the same time you should know that this was the worst teaching experience I have ever had."

"Were you shocked when that young man picked you out of the lineup?"

"At the time, yes, shocked and horrified. But soon after it all began to seem like a Kafka novel; I wasn't guilty, but that didn't matter. They would arrange it all so that I was condemned. And they had found my fingerprints on Daphne's notebook; it was like mine, and I had picked it up by mistake at the last seminar. Daphne always sat next to me, I never knew why, but I supposed because from there, as I was at the head of the table, she could most readily turn her back to me and address her comrades. I had opened her notebook before I saw my mistake; I've no doubt I left my fingerprints all over it. But that also told against me. You might as well hear the worst. Before I was arrested, I would have told you that I was incapable of bludgeoning anyone to death. Now, I think I am quite capable of it."

Some days later Kate summoned Leo to dinner, requesting that he bring along Beatrice's lawyer; they met this time in an Italian restaurant: Kate's tolerance for watching Leo consume raw fish had its limits. Sally had clearly come prepared for Kate's admission that any defense would be quixotic, if not fatal.

"I'm not so sure," Kate told her. "There's nothing easy about this case. Beatrice's reaction to this seminar was unquestionably excessive; on the other hand, had murder not occurred, she would probably have forgotten the whole thing by now. No doubt her words would seem extreme to anyone who had not labored long in the academic vineyards; I'll only mention that when Beatrice took up teaching, she saw respect for the scholar as one of the perks of the job; she has, in addition, risked much and undergone considerable pain as an early feminist. To her, it seems as though all this has become less than nothing. Add that to what may well be a period of personal depression, and you have this reaction. Do we also have murder? I don't think so, and for three reasons.

"First, I think the last thing Beatrice would do would be to go to that girl's room under any pretense whatsoever; Beatrice claims never to have entered a dormitory and I believe her. I know, so far nothing counts that much with you"—Kate held up a cautioning hand to Sally—"but I have two other reasons, both of them, I think, persuasive. One, I purchased a cheap gray wig, donned some rather raggy clothes, and wandered into the dorm where Beatrice was supposedly spotted. I'm prepared to stand in a line and see if that young man or anyone else picks me out: to youth one gray-haired, frumpish woman looks very like another. Doffing my wig, donning my usual dress, I returned to the dormitory half an hour later; needless to say, no one recognized me. I was there this time to interview Daphne's roommate, who was also in the seminar. She told me how close she and Daphne were—they even looked alike—and how devastated she was. She, it turned out, was writing on the homeless and had had almost as much difficulty in interviewing her subjects as had Daphne. Her animus against Beatrice was pronounced, but that was hardly surprising. I asked how her paper was going; she had gotten an extension under the circumstances, but had, in fact, found only one homeless woman to interview. She told me about her. No, don't interrupt. Good pasta, isn't it?

"I tried to find this homeless woman and failed, but I did get a description. I would suggest that when you find her, she and some others similarly dressed be put in the lineup with Beatrice to let that young man reconsider. No, that isn't my clincher. Here's my clincher." Kate took a sip of wine and sat back for a moment.

"I noticed that Daphne had a MasterCard, an American Express card, and no VISA card. Now that's perfectly possible, not all of us carry every card, but I was, as you know, grasping at straws, or at least thinnish reeds. Nudged by me, the police arranged to see every credit card bill that came in after Daphne's death. That merely seemed like another crazy idea of the lady detective, until yesterday. The VISA bill came in yesterday. Here it is." Kate passed it to Sally; Leo looked at it too. "See anything of interest?" Kate asked.

"Yes," Sally said. "There's a charge during the days when Beatrice was in Riker's Island; two, in fact. But these charges aren't always recorded on the day they're charged."

"Those from supermarkets are," Kate said. "I've checked with this particular supermarket, which is in a shopping center near the college; Beatrice never goes there, since she lives in the city, but it's also doubtful that Daphne did; she was, in any case, dead at the time of this charge."

"Let me be sure I have this right," Leo said, as Sally continued to stare at the bill. "You're saying Daphne's roommate's homeless interviewee killed Daphne, tore up the pictures in anger, perhaps mistook Daphne for her roommate or was too full of rage to care, stole the cash and one credit card that she later used to buy food at a supermarket. The police will have to find her, that's for sure."

"I think if the police put their minds to it, they'll find more evidence still. What *you've* got to do, Sally, after you've got the charges against Beatrice dismissed, is take up the defense of the homeless woman. I'll pay the legal costs. Given one of those uppity girls questioning and patronizing her, and probably inviting her once or twice to their comfy dormitory room, I should think you'd get her a suspended sentence at the very least. Extreme provocation."

"Please God she hasn't got previous convictions," Sally said.

"I doubt it," Kate said. "It could well take an undergraduate to send even the most benign homeless person over the edge. The trouble with the police," she added sanctimoniously, "is that they've never tried to teach a class without a text. One can do nothing without the proper equipment, as they should be the first to understand. I have urged Beatrice to write a calm letter to the director of women's studies suggesting an entire revamping of the senior thesis seminar. They must require texts. Under the circumstances, it seems the least they can do.

"More wine?"

DISCARDS

Faye Kellerman

 Because he'd hung around long enough, Malibu Mike wasn't considered a bum but a fixture. All of us locals had known him, had accustomed ourselves to his stale smell, his impromptu orations and wild hand gesticulations. Malibu preaching from his spot—a bus bench next to a garbage bin, perfect for foraging. With a man that weatherbeaten, it had been hard to assign him an age, but the police had estimated he'd been between seventy and ninety when he died—a decent stay on the planet.

Originally they'd thought Malibu had died from exposure. The winter has been a chilly one, a new arctic front eating through the god-awful myth that Southern California is bathed in continual sunshine. Winds churned the tides gray-green, charcoal clouds blanketed the shoreline. The night before last had been cruel. But Malibu had been protected under layers and layers of clothing—a barrier that kept his body insulated from the low of forty degrees.

Malibu had always dressed in layers even when the mercury grazed the hundred-degree mark. That fact was driven home when the obituary in the

Malibu *Crier* announced his weight as 126. I'd always thought of him as chunky, but now I realized it had been the clothes.

I put down the newspaper and turned up the knob on my kerosene heater. Rubbing my hands together, I looked out the window of my trailer. Although it was gray, rain wasn't part of the forecast and that was good. My roof was still pocked with leaks that I was planning to fix today. But then the phone rang. I didn't recognize the woman's voice on the other end, but she must have heard about me from someone I knew a long time ago. She asked for *Detective* Darling.

"Former detective," I corrected her. "This is Andrea Darling. Who am I talking to?"

A throat cleared. She sounded in the range of middle-aged to elderly. "Well, you don't know me personally. I am a friend of Greta Berstat."

A pause allowing me to acknowledge recognition. She was going to wait a long time.

"Greta Berstat," she repeated. "You were the detective on her burglary? You found the men who had taken her sterling flatware and the candlesticks and the tea set?"

The bell went off and I remembered Greta Berstat. When I'd been with LAPD, my primary detail was grand theft auto. Greta's case had come my way during a brief rotation through burglary.

"Greta gave you my phone number?" I inquired.

"Not exactly," the woman explained. "You see, I'm a local resident and I found your name in the Malibu Directory—the one put out by the Chamber of Commerce? You were listed under Investigation right between Interior Design and Jewelers."

I laughed to myself. "What can I do for you Ms. . . ."

"Mrs. Pollack," the woman answered. "Deirdre Pollack. Greta was over at my house when I was looking through the phone book. When she saw your name, her eyes grew wide and my-oh-my did she sing your praises, Detective Darling."

I didn't correct her this time. "Glad to have made a fan. How can I help you, Mrs. Pollack?"

"Deirdre, please."

"Deirdre it is. What's up?"

Deirdre hemmed and hawed. Finally, she said, "Well, I have a little bit of a problem."

I said, "Does this problem have a story behind it?"

"I'm afraid it does."

"Perhaps it would be best if we met in person?"

"Yes, perhaps it would be best."

"Give me your address," I said. "If you're local, I can probably make it down within the hour."

"An hour?" Deirdre said. "Well, that would be simply lovely!"

From Deirdre's living room I had a one-eighty-degree view of the coastline. The tides ripped relentlessly away at the rocks ninety feet below. You could hear the surf even this far up, the steady whoosh of water advancing and retreating. Deirdre's estate took up three landscaped acres, but the house, instead of being centered on the property, was perched on the edge of the bluff. She'd furnished the place warmly—plants and overstuffed chairs and lots of maritime knickknacks.

I settled into a chintz wing chair; Deirdre was positioned opposite me on a loveseat. She insisted on making me a cup of coffee, and while she did I took a moment to observe her.

She must have been in her late seventies, her face scored with hundreds of wrinkles. She was short with a loose turkey wattle under her chin, her cheeks were heavily rouged, her thin lips painted bright red. She had flaming red hair and false eyelashes that hooded blue eyes turned milky from cataracts. She had a tentative manner, yet her voice was firm and pleasant. Her smile seemed genuine even if her teeth weren't. She wore a pink suit, a white blouse, and orthopedic shoes.

"You're a lot younger than I expected," Deirdre said, handing me a china cup.

I smiled and sipped. I'm thirty-eight and have been told I look a lot younger. But to a woman Deirdre's age, thirty-eight still could be younger than expected.

"Are you married, Detective?" Deirdre asked.

"Not at the moment." I smiled.

"I was married for forty-seven years." Deirdre sighed. "Mr. Pollack passed away six years ago. I miss him."

"I'm sure you do." I put my cup down. "Children?"

"Two. A boy and a girl. Both are doing well. They visit quite often."

"That's nice," I said. "So . . . you live by yourself."

"Well, yes and no," she answered. "I sleep alone but I have daily help. One woman for weekdays, another for weekends."

I looked around the house. We seemed to be alone and it was ten o'clock Tuesday morning. "Your helper didn't show up today?"

"That's the little problem I wanted to tell you about."

I took out my notebook and pen. "We can start now if you're ready."

"Well, the story involves my helper," Deirdre said. "My housekeeper. Martina Cruz . . . that's her name."

I wrote down the name.

"Martina's worked for me for twelve years," Deirdre said. "I've become quite dependent on her. Not just to give me pills and clean up the house. But we've become good friends. Twelve years is a long time to work for someone."

I agreed, thinking: twelve years was a long time to do anything.

Deirdre went on. "Martina lives far away from Malibu, far away from me. But she has never missed a day in all those years without calling me first. Martina is very responsible. I respect her and trust her. That's why I'm puzzled even though Greta thinks I'm being naïve. Maybe I am being naïve, but I'd rather think better of people than to be so cynical."

"Do you think something happened to her?" I said.

"I'm not sure." Deirdre bit her lip. "I'll relate the story and maybe you can offer a suggestion."

I told her to take her time.

Deirdre said. "Well, like many old women, I've acquired things over the years. I tell my children to take whatever they want but there always seem to be leftover items. Discards. Old flower pots, used cookware, out-of-date clothing and shoes and hats. My children don't want those kinds of things. So if I find something I no longer need, I usually give it to Martina.

"Last week, I was cleaning out my closets. Martina was helping me." She sighed. "I gave her a pile of old clothes to take home. I remember it well because I asked her how in the world she'd be able to carry all those items on the bus. She just laughed. And oh, how she thanked me. Such a sweet girl . . . twelve years she worked for me."

I nodded, pen poised at my pad.

"I feel so silly about this," Deirdre said. "One of the robes I gave her . . . it was Mr. Pollack's old robe, actually. I threw out most of his things after he died. It was hard for me to look at them. I couldn't imagine why I had kept his shredded old robe."

She looked down at her lap.

"Not more than fifteen minutes after Martina left, I realized why I hadn't given the robe away. I kept my diamond ring in one of the pockets. I have three different diamond rings—two of which I keep in a vault. But it's ridiculous to have rings and always keep them in a vault. So this one—the smallest of the three—I kept at home, wrapped in an old sock and placed in the left pocket of Mr. Pollack's robe. I hadn't worn any of my rings in ages, and being old, I guess it simply slipped my mind.

"I waited until Martina arrived home and phoned her just as she walked through her door. I told her what I had done and she looked in the pockets of the robe and announced she had the ring. I was *thrilled*—delighted that nothing had happened to it. But I was also extremely pleased by Martina's honesty. She said she would return the ring to me on Monday. I realize now that I should have called my son and asked him to pick it up right at that moment, but I didn't want to insult her."

"I understand."

"Do you?" Deirdre said, grabbing my hand. "Do you think I'm foolish for trusting someone who has worked for me for twelve years?"

Wonderfully foolish. "You didn't want to insult her," I said, using her words.

"Exactly," Deirdre answered. "By now you must have figured out the problem. It is now Tuesday. I still don't have my diamond and I can't get hold of Martina."

"Is her phone disconnected?" I asked.

"No. It just rings and rings and no one answers it."

"Why don't you just send your son down now?"

"Because . . ." She sighed. "Because I don't want him to think of his mother as an old fool. Can you go down for me? I'll pay you for your time. I can afford it."

I shrugged. "Sure."

"Wonderful!" Deirdre exclaimed. "Oh, thank you so much."

I gave her my rates and they were fine with her. She handed me a piece of paper inked with Martina's name, address, and phone number. I didn't know the exact location of the house, but I knew the area. I thanked her for the information, then said, "Deirdre, if it looks like Martina took off with the ring, would you like me to inform the police for you?"

"No!" she said adamantly.

"Why not?" I asked.

"Even if Martina took the ring, I wouldn't want to see her in jail. We have too many years together for me to do that."

"You can be my boss anytime," I said.

"Why?" Deirdre asked. "Do you do housekeeping too?"

I informed her that I was a terrible housekeeper. As I left, she looked both grateful and confused.

Martina Cruz lived on Highland Avenue south of Washington—a street lined by small houses tattooed with graffiti. The address on the paper was a wood-sided white bungalow with a tar paper roof. The front lawn—mowed but devoid of shrubs—was bisected by a cracked red plaster walkway. There was a two-step hop onto a porch whose decking was wet and rotted. The screen door was locked, but a head-size hole had been cut through the mesh. I knocked through the hole but no one answered. I turned the knob and, to my surprise, the door yielded, screen and all.

I called out a "hello," and when no one answered, I walked into the living room—an eight-by-ten rectangle filled with hand-me-down furnishings. The sofa fabric, once gold, had faded to dull mustard. Two mismatched chairs were positioned opposite it. There was a scarred dining table off the living room, its centerpiece a black-and-white TV with rabbit ears. Encircling the table were six folding chairs. The kitchen was tiny, but the counters were clean, the food in the refrigerator still fresh. The trash hadn't been taken out in a while. It was brimming over with Corona beer bottles.

I went into the sole bedroom. A full-size mattress lay on the floor. No closets. Clothing was neatly arranged in boxes—some filled with little-girl garments, others stuffed with adult apparel. I quickly sifted through the piles, trying to find Mr. Pollack's robe.

I didn't find it—no surprise. Picking up a corner of the mattress, I peered underneath but didn't see anything. I poked around a little longer, then checked out the backyard—a dirt lot holding a rusted swing set and some deflated rubber balls.

I went around to the front and decided to question the neighbors. The house on the immediate left was occupied by a diminutive, thickset Latina matron. She was dressed in a floral print muumuu and her hair was tied in a bun. I asked her if she'd seen Martina lately, and she pretended not to understand me. My Spanish, though far from perfect, was understandable, so it seemed as if we had a little communication gap. Nothing that couldn't be overcome by a ten-dollar bill.

After I gave her the money, the woman informed me her name was Alicia and she hadn't seen Martina, Martina's husband, or their two little girls for a few days. But the lights had been on last night, loud music booming out of the windows.

"Does Martina have any relatives?" I asked Alicia in Spanish.

"Ella tiene una hermana pero no sé a donde vive."

Martina had a sister but Alicia didn't know where she lived. Probing further, I found out the sister's name—Yolanda Flores. And I also learned that the little girls went to a small parochial school run by the *Iglesia Evangélica* near Western Avenue. I knew the church she was talking about.

Most people think of Hispanics as always being Catholic. But I knew from past work that Evangelical Christianity had taken a strong foothold in Central and South America. Maybe I could locate Martina or the sister, Yolanda, through the church directory. I thanked Alicia and went on my way.

The Pentecostal Church of Christ sat on a quiet avenue—an aqua-blue stucco building that looked more like an apartment complex than a house of worship. About twenty-five primary-grade children were playing in an outdoor parking lot, the perimeters defined by a cyclone fence. The kids wore green-and-red uniforms and looked like moving Christmas tree ornaments.

I went through the gate, dodging racing children, and walked into the main sanctuary. The chapel wasn't large—around twenty by thirty—but the high ceiling made it feel spacious. There were three distinct seating areas— the Pentecostal triad: married women on the right, married men on the left, and mixed young singles in the middle. The pews faced a stage that held a thronelike chair upholstered in red velvet. In front of the throne was a lectern sandwiched between two giant urns sprouting plastic flowers. Off to the side were several electric guitars and a drum set, the name *Revelación* taped on the bass drum. I heard footsteps from behind and turned around.

The man looked to be in his early thirties with thick dark straight hair and bright green eyes. His face held a hint of Aztec warrior—broad nose, strong cheekbones and chin. Dressed in casual clothing, he was tall and muscular, and I was acutely aware of his male presence. I asked him where I might find the pastor and was surprised when he announced that he was the very person. I'd expected someone older.

I stated my business, his eyes never leaving mine as I spoke. When I finished, he stared at me for a long time before telling me his name—Pastor Alfredo Gomez. His English was unaccented.

"Martina's a good girl," Gomez said. "She would never take anything that didn't belong to her. Some problem probably came up. I'm sure everything will work out and your *patrona* will get her ring back."

"What kind of problem?"

The pastor shrugged.

"Immigration problems?" I probed.

Another shrug.

"You don't seem concerned by her disappearance."

He gave me a cryptic smile.

"Can you tell me one thing?" I asked. "Are her children safe?"

"I believe they're in school," Gomez said.

"Oh." I brightened. "Did Martina bring them in?"

"No." Gomez frowned. "No, she didn't. Her sister brought them in today. But that's not unusual."

"You haven't seen Martina today?"

Gomez shook his head. I thought he was telling me the truth, but maybe he wasn't. Maybe the woman was hiding from the INS. Still, after twelve years, you'd think she'd have applied for amnesty. And then there was the obvious alternative. Martina had taken the ring and was hiding out somewhere.

"Do you have Martina's husband's work number? I'd like to talk with him."

"José works construction," Gomez said. "I have no idea what crew he's on or where he is."

"What about Martina's sister, Yolanda Flores?" I said. "Do you have her phone number?"

The pastor paused.

"I'm not from the INS." I fished around inside my wallet and came up with my private investigator's license.

He glanced at it. "This doesn't mean anything."

"Yeah, that's true," I put my ID back in my purse. "Just trying to gain some trust. Look, Pastor, my client is really worried about Martina. She doesn't give a hoot about the ring. She specifically told me *not* to call the police even if Martina took the ring—"

Gomez stiffened and said, "Martina wouldn't do that."

"Okay. Then help us both out, Pastor. Martina might be in some real trouble. Maybe her sister knows something."

Silently, Gomez weighed the pros and cons of trusting me. I must have looked sincere because he told me to wait a moment, then came back with Yolanda's work number.

"You won't regret this," I assured him.

"I hope I don't," Gomez said.

I thanked him again, taking a final gander at those beautiful green eyes before I slipped out the door.

I found a pay booth around the corner, slipped a quarter in the slot, and waited. An accented voice whispered hello.

Using my workable Spanish, I asked for Yolanda Flores. Speaking English, the woman informed me that she was Yolanda. In the background I heard the wail of a baby.

"I'm sorry if this is a bad time," I apologized. "I'm looking for your sister."

There was a long pause at the other end of the line.

Quickly, I said, "I'm not from *inmigración*. I was hired by Mrs. Deirdre Pollack to find Martina and was given your work number by Pastor Gomez. Martina hasn't shown up for work in two days and Mrs. Pollack is worried about her."

More silence. If I hadn't heard the same baby crying, I would have thought she'd hung up the phone.

"You work for Missy Deirdre?" Yolanda asked.

"Yes," I said. "She's very worried about your sister. Martina hasn't shown up for work. Is your sister okay?"

Yolanda's voice cracked. "Es no good. Monday *en la tarde,* Martina husband call me. He tell me she don' work for Missy Deirdre and she have new job. He tell me to pick up her girls cause Martina work late. So I pick up the girls from the school and take them with me.

"Later, I try to call her, she's not *home*. I call and call but no one answers.

I don' talk to José, I don' talk to no one. I take the girls to school this morning. Then José, he call me again."

"When?"

"About two hour. He ask me to take girls. I say jes, but where is Martina? He tell me she has to sleep in the house where she work. I don' believe him."

It was my turn not to answer right away. Yolanda must have been bouncing the baby or something because the squalling had stopped.

"You took the children yesterday?" I asked.

"I take her children, jes. I no mind takin' the kids but I want to talk to Martina. And José . . . he don' give me the new work number. I call Martina's house, no one answer. I goin' to call Missy Deirdre and ask if Martina don' work there no more. *Ahorita,* you tell me Missy Deirdre call *you.* I . . . scared."

"Yolanda, where can I find José?"

"He works *construcción.* I don' know where. Mebbe he goes home after work and don' answer the phone. You can go to Martina's house tonight?"

"Yes, I'll do that," I said. "I'll give you my phone number, you give me yours. If you find out anything, call me. If I find out something, I'll call you. Okay?"

"Okay."

We exchanged numbers, then said good-bye. My next call was to Deirdre Pollack. I told her about my conversation with Yolanda. Deirdre was sure that Martina hadn't taken a new job. First of all, Martina would never just leave her flat. Secondly, Martina would never leave her children to work as a sleep-in housekeeper.

I wasn't so sure. Maybe Martina had fled with the ring and was lying low in some private home. But I kept my thoughts private and told Deirdre my intention to check out Martina's house tonight. She told me to be careful. I thanked her and said I'd watch my step.

At night, Martina's neighborhood was the mean streets, the sidewalks supporting pimps and prostitutes, pushers and buyers. Every half hour or so, the homeboys cruised by in souped-up low riders, their ghetto blasters pumping out body-rattling bass vibrations. I was glad I had my Colt .38 with me, but at the same time I wished it were a Browning Pump.

I sat in my truck, waiting for some sign of life at Martina's place, and my patience was rewarded two hours later. A Ford pickup parked in front of the framed house, and out came four dark-complexioned males dressed nearly identically: jeans, dark windbreakers zipped up to the neck, and hats. Three of them wore ratty baseball caps; the biggest and fattest wore a bright white painter's cap. Big-and-Fat was shouting and singing. I couldn't understand his Spanish—his speech was too rapid for my ear—but the words I could pick up seemed slurred. The other three men were holding six-packs of beer. From the way all of them acted, the six-packs were not their first of the evening.

They went inside. I slipped my gun into my purse and got out of my truck, walking up to the door. I knocked. My luck: Big-and-Fat answered. Up close he was nutmeg-brown with fleshy cheeks and thick lips. His teeth were rotten and he smelled of sweat and beer.

"I'm looking for Martina Cruz," I said in Spanish.

Big-and-Fat stared at me—at my *Anglo* face. He told me in English that she wasn't home.

"Can I speak to José?"

"He's no home, too."

"I saw him come in." It wasn't really a lie, more of an educated guess. Maybe one of the four men was José.

Big-and-Fat stared at me, then broke into a contemptuous grin. "I say he no home."

I heard Spanish in the background, a male voice calling out the name José. I peered around Big-and-Fat's shoulders, trying to peek inside, but he stepped forward, making me back up. His expression was becoming increasingly hostile, and I always make it a point not to provoke drunk men who outweigh me.

"I'm going," I announced with a smile.

"Pasqual," someone said. A thinner version of Big-and-Fat stepped onto the porch. "Pasqual, *qué pasó?*"

Opportunity knocked. I took advantage.

"I'm looking for José Cruz," I said as I kept walking backward. "I've been hired to look for Martin—"

The thinner man blanched.

"Go away!" Pasqual thundered out. "Go or I kill you!"

I didn't stick around to see if he'd make good on his threat.

The morning paper stated that Malibu Mike, having expired from natural causes, was still in deep freeze, waiting for a relative to claim his body. He'd died buried under tiers of clothing, his feet wrapped in three pairs of socks stuffed into size twelve mismatched shoes. Two pairs of gloves had covered his hands, and three scarves had been wrapped around his neck. A Dodgers' cap was perched atop a ski hat that cradled Malibu's head. In all those layers, there was not one single piece of ID to let us know who he really was. After all these years, I thought he deserved a decent burial, and I guess I wasn't the only one who felt that way. The locals were taking up a collection to have him cremated. Maybe a small service, too—a few words of remembrance, then his ashes would be mixed with the tides.

I thought Malibu might have liked that. I took a twenty from my wallet and began to search the trailer for a clean envelope and a stamp. I found what I was looking for and was addressing the envelope when Yolanda Flores called me.

"Dey find her," she said, choking back sobs. "She *dead.* The police find her in a trash can. She beat to death. Es *horrible!*"

"Yolanda, I'm so sorry." I really was. "I wish I could do something for you."

"You wan' do somethin' for me?" Yolanda said. "You find out what happen to my sister."

Generally I like to be paid for my services, but my mind flashed to little dresses in cardboard boxes. I knew what it was like to live without a mother. Besides, I was still fuming over last night's encounter with Pasqual.

"I'll look into it for you," I said.

There was a silence across the line.

"Yolanda?"

"I still here," she said. "I . . . surprise you help me."

"No problem."

"Thank you." She started to cry. "Thank you very much. I pay you—"

"Forget it."

"No, I work for you on weekends—"

"Yolanda, I live in a trailer and couldn't find anything if you cleaned up my place. Forget about paying me. Let's get back to your sister. Tell me about José. Martina and him get along?"

There was a very long pause. Yolanda finally said, "José no good. He and his brothers."

"Is Pasqual one of José's brothers?"

"How you know?"

I told her about my visit with Pasqual the night before, about Big-and-Fat's threat. "Has he ever killed anyone before?"

"I don' know. He drink and fight. I don' know if he kill anyone when he's drunk."

"Did you ever see Pasqual beating Martina?"

"No," Yolanda said. "I never see that."

"What about José?"

Another moment of silence.

Yolanda said, "He slap her mebbe one or two time. I tell her to leave him but she say no 'cause of the girls."

"Do you think José could kill Martina?"

Yolanda said, "He slap her when he drink. But I don' think he would kill her to kill her."

"He wouldn't do it on purpose."

"Essackly."

"Yolanda, would José kill Martina for money?"

"No," she said firmly. "He's *Evangélico*. A bad *Evangélico*, but not *el diablo.*"

"He wouldn't do it for *lots* of money?"

"No, he don' kill her for money."

I said, "What about Pasqual?"

"I don' think so."

"Martina have any *enemigos*?"

"*Nunca persona!*" Yolanda said. "No one want to hurt her. She like sugar. Es so *terrible!*"

She began to cry. I didn't want to question her over the phone. A face-to-face meeting would be better. I asked her when was the funeral service.

"Tonight. *En la iglesia a las ocho.* After the *culto funeral*, we go to ce-menterio. You wan' come?"

"Yes, I think that might be best." I told her I knew the address of the church and would meet her eight o'clock sharp.

I was unnerved by what I had to do next: break the bad news to Deirdre Pollack. The old woman took it relatively well, never even asked about the ring. When I told her I'd volunteered to look into Martina's death, she offered to pay me. I told her that wasn't necessary, but when she insisted, I didn't refuse.

I got to the church by eight, then realized I didn't know Yolanda from Adam. But she picked me out in a snap. Not a plethora of five-foot-eight, blond, blue-eyed Salvadoran women.

Yolanda was petite, barely five feet and maybe ninety pounds tops. She had yards of long brown hair—Evangelical women don't cut their tresses—and big brown eyes moistened with tears. She took my hand, squeezed it tightly, and thanked me for coming.

The church was filled to capacity, the masses adding warmth to the un-heated chapel. In front of the stage was a table laden with broth, hot choco-late, and plates of bread. Yolanda asked me if I wanted anything to eat and I declined.

We sat in the first row of the married women's section. I glanced at the men's area and noticed Pasqual with his cronies. I asked Yolanda to point out José: the man who had come to the door with Pasqual. The other two men were also brothers. José's eyes were swollen and bright red. Crying or post-alcohol intoxication?

I studied him further. He'd been stuffed into an ill-fitting black suit, his dark hair slicked back with grease. All the brothers wore dark suits. José looked nervous, but the others seemed almost jocular.

Pasqual caught me staring, and his expression immediately darkened, his eyes bearing down on me. I felt needles down my spine as he began to rise, but luckily the service started and he sank back into his seat.

Pastor Gomez came to the dais and spoke about what a wonderful wife and mother Martina had been. As he talked, the women around me began to let out soft, muted sobs. I did manage to sneak a couple of sidelong glances at the brothers. I met up with Pasqual's dark stare once again.

When the pastor had finished speaking, he gave the audience directions to the cemetery. Pasqual hadn't forgotten about my presence, but I was too quick for him, making a beeline for the pastor. I managed to snare Gomez before Pasqual could get to me. The fat slob backed off when the pastor pulled me into a corner.

"What happened?" I asked.

Gomez looked down. "I wish I knew."

"Do the police—"

"Police!" The pastor spat. "They don't care about a dead Hispanic girl. One less flea in their country. I was wearing my work clothes when I got the call this morning. I'd been doing some plumbing and I guess they thought I was a wetback who didn't understand English." His eyes held pain. "They joked about her. They said it was a shame to let such a wonderful body go to waste!"

"That stinks."

"Yes, it stinks." Gomez shook his head. "So you see I don't expect much from the police."

"I'm looking into her death."

Gomez stared at me. "Who's paying you to do it?"

"Not Yolanda," I said.

"Martina's *patrona*. She wants her ring."

"I think she wants justice for Martina."

The pastor blushed from embarrassment.

I said, "I would have done it gratis. I've got some suspicions." I filled him in on my encounter with Pasqual.

Gomez thought a moment. "Pasqual drinks even though the church forbids alcohol. Pasqual's not a bad person. Maybe you made him feel threatened."

"Maybe I did."

"I'll talk to him," Gomez said. "Calm him down. But I don't think you should come to the *cementerio* with us. Now's not the time for accusations."

I agreed. He excused himself as another parishioner approached and suddenly I was alone. Luckily, Pasqual had gone somewhere else. I met up with Yolanda, explaining my reason for not going to the cemetery. She understood.

We walked out to the school yard, into a cold misty night. José and his brothers had already taken off their ties and replaced their suit jackets with warmer windbreakers. Pasqual took a deep swig from a bottle inside a paper bag, then passed the bag to one of his brothers.

"Look at them!" Yolanda said with disgust. "They no even wait till after the funeral. They nothing but *cholos*. Es terrible!"

I glanced at José and his brothers. Something was bothering me and it took a minute or two before it came to me. Three of them—including José— were wearing old baseball caps. Pasqual was the only one wearing a painter's cap.

I don't know why, but I found that odd. Then something familiar began to come up from the subconscious, and I knew I'd better start phoning up bus drivers. From behind me came a gentle tap on my shoulder. I turned around.

Pastor Gomez said, "Thank you for coming, Ms. Darling."

I nodded. "I'm sorry I never met Martina. From what I've heard, she seemed to be a good person."

"She was." Gomez bowed his head. "I appreciate your help and I wish you peace."

Then he turned and walked away. I'd probably never see him again and I felt a little bad about that.

I tailed José the next morning. He and his brothers were part of a crew framing a house in the Hollywood Hills. I kept watch from a quarter block away, my truck partly hidden by the overhanging boughs of a eucalyptus. I was trying to figure out how to get José alone, and then I got a big break. The roach wagon pulled in and José was elected by his brothers to pick up lunch.

I got out of my truck, intercepted him as he carried an armful of burritos, and stuck my .38 in his side, telling him if he said a word, I'd pull the trigger. My Spanish must have been very clear, because he was as mute as Dopey.

After I got him into the cabin of my truck, I took the gun out of his ribs and held it in my lap.

I said, "What happened to Martina?"

"I don' know."

"You're lying," I said. "You killed her."

"I don' kill her!" José was shaking hard. *"Yo juro!* I don' kill her!"

"Who did?"

"I don' know!"

"You killed her for the ring, didn't you, José?" As I spoke, I saw him shrink. "Martina would never tell you she had the ring: she knew you would *take* it from her. But *you* must have found out. You asked her about the ring and she said she didn't have any ring, right?"

José didn't answer.

I repeated the accusation in *español*, but he still didn't respond. I went on.

"You didn't know what to do, did you, José? So you waited and waited and finally, Monday morning, you told your brothers about the ring. But by *that* time, Martina and the ring had already taken the bus to work."

"All we wan' do is talk to her!" José insisted. "Nothin' was esuppose to happen."

"What wasn't supposed to happen?" I asked.

José opened his mouth, then shut it again.

I continued. "Pasqual has a truck—a Ford pickup." I read him the license number. "You and your brothers decided to meet up with her. A truck can go a lot faster than a bus. When the bus made a stop, two of you got on it and made Martina get off."

José shook his head.

"I called the bus company," I said. "The driver remembered you and your brother—two men making this woman carrying a big bag get off at the stop behind the big garbage bin. The driver even asked if she was okay. But Martina didn't want to get you in trouble and said *todo está bien*—everything was fine. But everything wasn't fine, was it?"

Tears welled up in José's eyes.

"You tried to force her in the truck, but she fought, didn't she?"

José remained mute.

"But you did get her in Pasqual's truck," I said. "Only you forgot something. When she fought, she must have knocked off Pasqual's Dodgers' cap. He didn't know it was gone until later, did he?"

José jerked his head up. "How you know?"

"How do I know? I *have* that cap, José." Not exactly true, but close enough. "Now, why don't you tell me what happened?"

José thought a long time. Then he said, "It was assident. Pasqual no mean to hurt her bad. Just get her to talk. She no have ring when we take her off the bus."

"Not in her bag—*su bolsa?*"

"*Ella no tiena niuna bolsa.* She no have bags. She tell us she left ring at home. So we took her home, but she don' fin' the ring. That make me mad. I *saw* her with ring. No good for a wife to *lie* to husband." His eyes filled with rage, his nostrils flared. "No good! A wife must always tell husband the truth!"

"So you killed her," I said.

José said, "Pasqual . . . he did it. It was assident!"

I shook my head in disgust. I sat there in my truck, off guard and full of indignation. I didn't even hear him until it was too late. The driver's door jerked open and the gun flew out of my lap. I felt as if I'd been wrenched from my mother's bosom. Pasqual dragged me to the ground, his face looming over me, his complexion florid and furious. He drew back his fist and aimed it at my jaw.

I rolled my head to one side and his hand hit the ground. Pasqual yelled but not as loud as José did, shouting at his brother to *stop*. Then I heard the click of the hammer. Pasqual heard it too and released me immediately. By now, a crowd had gathered. Gun in hand, José looked at me, seemed to speak English for my benefit.

"You kill Martina!" José screamed out to Pasqual. "I'm going to kill you!"

Pasqual looked genuinely confused. He spoke in Spanish. "*You* killed her, you little shit! You beat her to death when we couldn't find the ring!"

José looked at me, his expression saying: do you understand this? Something in my eye must have told him I did. I told him to put the gun down. Instead, he turned his back on me and focused his eyes on Pasqual. "You lie. You get drunk, you kill Martina!"

In Spanish, Pasqual said, "I tried to stop you, you *asshole*!"

"You lie!" José said. And then he pulled the trigger.

I charged him before he could squeeze another bullet out of the chamber, but the damage had been done. Pasqual was already dead when the sirens pulled up.

The two other brothers backed José's story. They'd come to confront Martina about the ring. She told them she had left it at home. But when they returned to the house and the ring wasn't around, Pasqual, in his drunken rage, beat Martina to death and dumped her body in the trash.

José will be charged with second degree murder for Pasqual, and maybe a good lawyer'll be able to bargain it down to manslaughter. But I remembered a murderous look in José's eyes after he'd stated that Martina had lied to him. If I were the prosecutor, I'd be going after José with charges of manslaughter on Martina, Murder One on Pasqual. But that's not how the system works. Anyway, my verdict—rightly or wrongly—wouldn't bring Martina back to life.

I called Mrs. Pollack after it was all over. Through her tears, she wished she'd never remembered the ring. It wasn't her fault but she still felt responsible. There was a small consolation. I was pretty sure I knew where the ring was.

I'm not too bad at guesses—like the one about Pasqual losing his hat in a struggle. That simple snapshot in my mind of the brothers at the church—three with beat-up Dodgers' caps, the fourth wearing a *new* painter's cap. Something off kilter.

So my hunch had been correct. Pasqual had once owned a Dodgers' cap. Where had it gone? Same place as Mr. Pollack's robe. Martina had packed the robe in her bag Monday morning. When she was forced off the bus by

José and his brothers, I pictured her quickly dumping the bag in a garbage bin at the bus stop, hoping to retrieve it later. She never got that chance.

As for the ring, it was right where I thought it would be: among the discards that had shrouded Malibu Mike the night he died. The Dodgers' cap on Malibu's head got me thinking in the right direction. If Malibu *had* found Pasqual's cap, maybe he found the other bag left behind by Martina. After all, that bin had been his spot.

Good old Malibu. One of his layers had been a grimy old robe. Wedged into the corner of its pocket, a diamond ring. Had Malibu not died that Monday, José might have been a free man today.

Mrs. Pollack didn't feel right about keeping the ring, so she offered it to Yolanda Flores. Yolanda was appreciative of such generosity, but she refused the gift, saying the ring was cursed. Mrs. Pollack didn't take offense; Yolanda was a woman with pride. Finally, after a lot of consideration, Mrs. Pollack gave the ring to the burial committee for Malibu Mike. Malibu never lived wealthy, but he sure went out in high style.

LADY ANTONIA FRASER, a London resident, is the widely heralded author of several best-selling biographies of notable British figures, including *Mary, Queen of Scots; Royal Charles;* and *Cromwell.* To millions of mystery readers she is known as the creator of Jemima Shore, television interviewer and capable detector of criminals. Ms. Shore has appeared in more than ten adventures to date, including *A Splash of Red, The Wild Island,* and *Oxford Blood,* as well as in a collection of stories, *Jemima Shore's First Case.*

GETTING TO KNOW YOU

Antonia Fraser

 The moment the door was shut behind her, the man put the security chain across it. Then he ordered Jemima Shore to take her clothes off. All of her clothes.

"But you can leave your shoes on, if you like. They're pretty."

Jemima found that the sheer unreality of the situation prevented her from taking in what he was saying. She could hear the words, all right; the man was standing right beside her, his breath on her cheek—although he was not in fact breathing particularly heavily. They were about the same height: his eyes, very widely set, the color of glossy chestnuts, were level with hers.

The man's hair was dark, very thick, and quite long and shaggy; they were so close that she could see one or two silver threads in the dark mass. He had a moustache, sideburns, and soft dark down on his cheeks; that was what gave him a Mediterranean look. His accent, however, faint but discernible, she could not place. He wore a clean white T-shirt with some kind of logo on it, and jeans. The broad shoulders and the heavy arms revealed by the con-tours of the T-shirt gave an impression of considerable physical strength. In spite of his calm breathing, Jemima was aware that he was sweating slightly.

She was carrying a large green Chanel-type handbag of quilted leather slung over her shoulder by two gilt chains. The man took the bag from her and put it carefully on the king-size bed that dominated the hotel room. The curtains were drawn and the lamp by the bed was lit, although it was in fact only eleven o'clock in the morning.

The man repeated his command: "Take off your clothes." He added "I want to get to know you."

It was idiotic, thought Jemima: the previous television program she had worked on had actually been about rape. During that period she had spoken to at least a dozen victims—of widely differing ages—on the subject. The words she had heard most frequently went something like this: "You just don't understand what it's like. . . . Helplessness . . . If it's never happened to you . . . Until it's happened to you . . ."

Naturally, she had never sought to argue the point. Her intention, as an investigative television reporter, had been to present her evidence as sympathetically but candidly as possible in order to illustrate just that gulf: between sufferers and the rest, however well intentioned. The program about rape had been the last in a series of which the overall title had been *Twice Punished:* it had concentrated on the tragic social aftereffects of certain crimes.

"Helplessness . . . You just don't understand. . . . Until it happens to you." Now it seemed Jemima was going to find out for herself the truth of those sad, despairing cries. Rather too late for her program. Ironically enough. And she had a feeling she was going to need all the sense of irony (or detachment) she could hang on to in the present situation. And then something more.

"Take off your clothes," the man said for the third time. "I want to get to know you." He was still not hurried or breathing heavily; only the slight perspiration on his upper lip betrayed any kind of agitation. Jemima now guessed him to be Moroccan or Algerian, maybe even Turkish; his actual use of English was more or less perfect.

"Who are you? And where is Clemency Vane? I have come to interview Clemency Vane." Jemima decided the best course was to ignore the ludicrous, frightening command altogether and attempt in some way to gain a mastery of the situation. She was glad to find that her own voice was absolutely steady even if she, unlike the man himself, was panting a little. She found that she was also able to manage a small, sweet, composed smile, the one the viewers loved, because Jemima generally went to demolish the recipient of that sweet smile—some pompous political leader perhaps—politely but totally.

"Clemmie"—he accented the last syllable just slightly—"is not here. I have come instead. Now you will take off your clothes, please. Or . . ." He paused as if to consider the situation in a rational manner. "I could perhaps take them off for you. But you would probably prefer to do it yourself."

The man bent forward and undid the loose drawstring tie at the neck of Jemima's cream-colored jersey dress. His hands, like his shoulders, were large and muscular; they were covered with dark hair; the nails, Jemima noticed automatically, were very clean, as if scrubbed, and well kept. He undid the first pearl button and made as if to touch the second; then he drew back.

This is where I scream, thought Jemima. *Argument stops here. There must be somebody in earshot in this damn barn of a hotel.*

"Don't touch me, please," she said aloud. "And I must tell you that whoever you are, my camera crew are due to arrive in this room in exactly one minute; they took the next lift."

"Oh, don't be frightened." The man ignored her remark about the camera crew, which was in itself a worrying sign—since it was in fact quite untrue. Jemima doubted whether at this precise moment anyone in the world knew exactly where she was, not even Cherry, her faithful P.A. at Megalith Television.

"I'm not going to hurt you," he said. "Even if you scream"—he had clearly read her mind—"I shall not hurt you, only silence you with this." For the first time Jemima realized the man was carrying a large white scarf or cloth on his arm. "But please do not scream. There would be no point, I think, since both the rooms near us are empty, and the maid is far away."

The man hesitated, then he led Jemima quite gently but firmly in the direction of the large bed. They both sat down. That brought her—possibly —within reach of her green handbag; but what kind of weapon was a soft quilted-leather handbag, however large? The man gazed at her earnestly with those wide-apart brown eyes.

"I have seen you on television, Jemima, I think you're very beautiful, and you're intelligent too. I like that very much. You'll find I really appreciate your intelligence when we get to know each other better. Women should cultivate their intelligence so as to be of interest to men. How can a stupid woman be of any interest to a man? Education is very important for women. In order to help their man."

Now that the man was talking, almost rattling along, poking his face close to hers, talking at manic speed but not attempting otherwise to touch her or her clothing in any way, the best plan seemed to be to keep him at it.

The education of women! A bizarre subject to discuss, perhaps, under the present circumstances, but one on which Jemima did at least have strong views—if not precisely these views.

"You're absolutely right," she agreed, her tone still resolutely equable, resisting the temptation to adjust the loose tie and button of her dress.

On the subject of education, would it be a good plan or a very bad plan— to reintroduce the subject of Clemency Vane? Her captor—for such he was —either knew her or knew of her. As it was, one could indeed fruitfully talk about the education of Clemency Vane and at some length, in view of what had happened to her following that education. Had the missing Clemency been actually present in the hotel room where she promised to be, Jemima herself would have shot off some pertinent questions on the subject: even if she would have recorded the answers in her own well-trained memory (and not as yet with a camera crew). Clemency had asked for her to take no notes and certainly not use a tape recorder at these preliminary interviews. And Jemima, who at this stage was committed to nothing, Clemency having made all the running herself, had nothing to lose by agreeing to her terms.

Clemency Vane was a convicted criminal who had recently been released from prison, where she had spent something over five years on a charge of drug dealing. It was an odd case. Nobody seemed to know quite where all the money had gone: some really large sums had vanished. Jemima remembered that the original sentence had been for eight years and that Clemency had been released for good behavior: it had certainly been a strong sentence for a first offender. On the other hand the proved details of Clemency Vane's drug dealing were pretty strong too. And it was undeniably dealing: no question of a desperate addict merely trying to service her own expensive habit. Quite apart from the fact that she had pleaded "guilty."

The oddness lay in the hint of political background to it all, a hint that mysteriously and totally disappeared when the case came to be tried and the "guilty" plea was entered. What was the country concerned? Jemima tried to remember. Red Clemmie? Blue Clemmie? *Green* Clemmie? Not the latter presumably in view of the drug dealing. Since none of this had finally been proffered by the defense at her trial, temporarily the name of the country eluded her, which was ridiculous. But she would have reminded herself of all the details of the case beforehand if Clemency Vane's summons to an interview in the anonymous barn of a West London hotel had not come so peremptorily to her this morning. That had altered their previous more-long-term arrangements.

"No, it can't wait. I thought it could when I spoke to you originally. But now it can't."

Santangela. That was it. Santangela: one of those little states, whose precise connection with drug traffic, antidrug traffic measures, nationalism, and anti-imperialism was so difficult to establish even for those who were keenly interested. Which most Britons, and Jemima was no exception, frankly were not. That was the hint of political background that had come and then mysteriously gone away. After all, shortly after Clemency Vane was imprisoned, there was a successful revolution in Santangela in any case; so the whole situation had changed. Santangela: where exactly was the place? Latin America? Central America? South America? It was ridiculous to be so ignorant about sheer geography, which was after all a matter of fact. But then that was Europe-centered Britain—including Jemima Shore—for you.

Jemima looked at the man again. Not a Moroccan, an Algerian, or a Turk, then, but a Santangelino? If that was what its nationals were called, as she seemed to remember they were. More vagueness, she ruefully admitted. All the same, for the first time her gaze was inquisitive, not challenging and self-protective. A Santangelino. Somehow connected to Clemency Vane's drug charge, once deemed in some way political, then all of a sudden quite apolitical, just criminal. What she was not yet in any way clear about as yet was exactly how Clemency and her drugs fitted into Jemima's current series. She had been wondering that ever since Clemency Vane had made the first contact. But there seemed plenty of time to find out.

Jemima's new series—very much at the planning stage—was tentatively entitled *For the Love of the Cause*. It concerned the rival claims of public campaigning and private life. She had already made various soundings concerning it and had had one or two preliminary interviews with dedicated campaigners of various sorts—including one with a man who, very much against Jemima's own beliefs, wanted to bring back capital punishment but whose wife opposed him. To her irritation, she was failing to turn up sufficient numbers of "strong women" who fitted this particular bill; they existed, all right, but preferred to keep their private lives and/or disputes to themselves. Jemima sympathized, of course, but remained professionally irritated. . . .

Then Clemency Vane telephoned out of the blue. Jemima herself would certainly never have thought of a reformed—one hoped—drug dealer in connection with this series. Yet Clemency's original call, fielded by Cherry, indicated that this area of conflict was what she wished to discuss. Various other calls followed, guarded conversations, all on the telephone, with Jemima herself, with no direct information offered absolutely pertinent to the program, yet a good deal of talk about the principles involved. Love and duty, their rival demands, and so forth.

They had met only once; as now, in a hotel, an anonymous block in a different part of London; as now, the summons had come suddenly, giving Jemima little time to prepare.

"I can get away now," Clemency Vane had said. "Please come." And Jemima, to the sound of a few protests about work load from Cherry, had gone.

For Clemency Vane's appearance, Jemima had been dependent on the numerous newspaper and television news images: the strong features, particularly the nose, which might be described kindly as patrician, otherwise as beaky; the circular tinted glasses that added a somewhat owlish look; and the pretty, softening halo of blond curly hair at her trial. In fact Clemency was darker than Jemima had expected, or perhaps the blond hair had been allowed to darken in prison; as it was, her hair, also much straighter, was scraped back, and her face behind the circular tinted glasses—they at least were familiar—virtually devoid of makeup. You got the impression of someone deliberately rendering herself unattractive, or at least unappealing; gone was the feminine softness of the prisoner on trial.

At the same time Clemency was quite tiny physically; that, along with her cultivatedly plain appearance, was another surprise. Well, you never really knew about people from their newspaper photographs, did you? That was one certain rule. Even television could be oddly delusive about size and scale.

It was still a strong face, despite the unexpectedly small scale of it all. A strong face: and a strong character too, judging from the evidence yielded up by the trial.

"I need to find out about you," Clemency had said at this meeting. She spoke quite abruptly, dragging on her cigarette. She had smoked throughout the interview, stubbing out each cigarette with fury when it was about halfway finished. "I need to know if I can trust you." Her attitude was certainly not conciliatory: defiant if anything. But she was also nervous.

"As it happens, you can trust me." Jemima was prepared to be patient. "But I hope you will find that for yourself. With time. That's the best way. I'm in no hurry about this series: we've only just started to research it, as a matter of fact. *For the Love of the Cause*. It's a fascinating topic but a tricky one. I need to get exactly the right people—"

"That piece in the paper—the woman spy in love with an Israeli—"

"Ah, you saw that. I wondered. Premature, I'm afraid. She won't talk to us. Too much conflict already about what she did for love—"

"I, too, did it for love," Clemency said, interrupting her. "You could say that I, too, gave up everything for love." She was busy stubbing out yet another of those wretched cigarettes, and she did not look at Jemima as she spoke.

"You mean there was a man involved?" Jemima spoke tentatively. Clemency's nervousness was perhaps not surprising under the circumstances but quite marked all the same, including this sudden out-of-the-blue request for a face-to-face interview. She had no wish to frighten her off at this stage.

"Correct. There was a man." Clemency pulled on her cigarette with increasing ferocity and then once again stubbed it out.

"That didn't come out at the trial."

"I didn't want it to. I pleaded 'guilty' and that was that."

"Is he still involved? Or rather, are you still involved with him? You were in prison a long time. Or is it over? Is it this love-versus-duty question of the woman spy and the Israeli you mentioned when you first contacted me? Is that what we might talk about on the program?"

Jemima realized too late that she had posed too many questions too quickly. An obstinate closed expression on Clemency Vane's face warned her of her mistake.

"I don't want to say anything more at the moment. You must understand: there are problems." And Clemency declined to explain any further, sharply and inexorably. That was all Jemima was left with—until the summons this morning.

So there was a man involved. And this was him? Was Jemima now looking at the man for whom Clemency—product of a privileged education, showered with worldly advantages by her doting parents, clever enough to achieve university, achieve anything she wished, in truth—had thrown it all away? Infatuation was a fascinating subject. One woman's infatuation was another woman's poison. . . . Take this man. Very strong physically, perhaps—she hoped not to find out—and certainly quite handsome . . . this was the man for whom a privileged English girl had wasted five years of her life. This Santangelino without even a name . . .

"My name is Alberto," he said to her with a smile—his first smile, and that might be a good sign, might it not? Once again, however, he had apparently read her thoughts—not such a good sign, that.

"First of all you will take off all these clothes. Even the shoes now. Then we will know each other better. And perhaps we will love each other." Alberto put both his big hands on her shoulders as though he were measuring her for something.

"Shouldn't we get to know each other first?" Jemima spoke in the most reasonable tone she could muster. She must at all costs, she knew from studying such things, humor him: she must not arouse his violence, his hostility, give him that psychological impetus he needed to transform the situation from polite parleying to physical action. It was the feeling of helplessness that was so terrible, just as she had been told so many times.

And perhaps we will love each other. For God's sake, it wasn't the stripping that mattered! Jemima had a beautiful body, or at least had been assured of it enough times to lack self-consciousness on the subject. She had no particular feeling about nudity and privacy either, sunbathing topless or even naked when it seemed right without giving much thought to the subject. The exposure of her body, however disagreeable the demand in this secret claustrophobic context, was not the point. But to love each other!

How near, for example, was the hotel telephone? Looking round, she saw the telephone was on the far side of the bed. Her eye then fell on an ashtray with stubs in it. That gave her an inspiration. It was worth a try: even for a dedicated nonsmoker like herself.

"Could you let me have a cigarette first, please? Then I promise . . ."

Alberto hesitated. Finally he said: "I have no cigarettes."

Jemima gazed again at the stubs. Half-smoked. In spite of herself, she found she was trembling. And her voice shook when she spoke. She had not realized before how much she had been counting—subconsciously—on Clemency's arrival to interrupt them, somehow save her. Clemency Vane was after all the one person in the world who really did know where she was.

Jemima looked at the bathroom door. It was closed. She had not really thought about it, but now the blank door had a sinister look. "What's happening here? Is she—wait a minute—is she *still* here? Is this a plot?"

Alberto smiled again. Jemima, her fear rising, decided that his smile was not after all a good sign.

"A plot? Yes, you could call it that," he said. "A plot to get to know you. You thought it was your plot with your silly program about love and duty— even an intelligent woman like you, with your fine education, can be a little silly sometimes. But it was not your plot. It was our plot!"

"Clemency knows about this," exclaimed Jemima. "Well, she must. How else did you know I was coming? Listen, Clemency's here. That's what you're saying."

"Don't you understand? Clemency would do anything for me. She's my woman. The drugs, everything, prison, that was all for me. And now she has brought you here for me. She set you up for me.

"Clemmie told me to come here," he went on with that strange horrible exhilaration. "She laughed, yes, she laughed at you, for thinking that she would take part in your stupid program."

He was becoming vehement again but apparently unaware of what he was doing as the grip on her arm tightened.

"I'm a strong man, you see, the kind of man women love; women love to support and help men like me. Clemency knew that. 'Strong man,' she said, 'you get to know Jemima Shore then, if you want, get to know Jemima Shore if you like, because during all those years you never knew anything really about me. And now you never will. Poor Alberto, you will never know me.' "

Alberto's hand loosened again, and his voice too had changed subtly as though he were imitating Clemency herself. Her abrupt rather scornful tones. There was a silence between them.

You will never know me. But it was Alberto who had said that, quoting Clemency, not Jemima. It was Alberto himself, imitating Clemency.

"She did do it all for me, didn't she?" He was questioning Jemima now; there was something pathetic about him, despite his fierceness and the strong hands that still held her prisoner.

But then that temporary glimpse of something pathetic was quite gone. Alberto started to pull at Jemima's clothes. The beige jersey dress came off quite easily, or would have done so, but the very violence of his actions hindered him, those scrubbed strong hands seemingly frustrated by his own haste.

I must not struggle, thought Jemima desperately, *I must not even scream. I know what to do, I must be passive, I must endure, I must survive. Otherwise he'll kill me.* Now she was in her silk petticoat and the man was panting horribly, sweating much more. He began to talk, gabble: "Women, you like this, this is what you really want, bitches, traitors. . . ." He talked on, and then half hissed, half shouted at her: "You I'm really going to possess—"

In spite of herself Jemima lost control. The careful passivity went. She began to struggle in Alberto's grip, to shout at him.

"Even if you killed me"—*having raped me* was the unspoken phrase, for still she did not wish to pronounce the words, in spite of everything—"even if you killed me, and especially if you killed me, you would not get to know me. You would not possess me."

Alberto stopped. He still held her. Now they were both sweating, panting.

"She said that, Clemency." But before Alberto spoke the words, Jemima knew the truth, understood suddenly and clearly what had been implicit all the time. What had been done for love. Once long ago. And once only recently.

"Alberto—" She spoke more strongly now. "Release me. Then let me go into the bathroom."

"No. It's not right." Some of the power was waning in him, the passion. Jemima felt it. Her own increased.

"She's there. Clemmie," he added in a low voice.

"I—I want to see her," said Jemima.

"There's nothing you can do."

"You must let me go in there. There may be something I can do."

Alberto shook his head. "It's too late," he said.

"Listen, for God's sake—"

"It's too late. It was already too late when you arrived here." Now the force she had felt in him was totally extinguished. She was in command. In command as Clemency Vane had once been—had been until the very end.

"I followed her here," he went on. "I knew she was stealing out to come and see you. I pleaded with her when I got here. I knew she was trying to leave me, that she was getting frightened of what I might do to her. She found me so violent, so demanding after she came out of prison. She said sex didn't interest her. She never ever wanted to make love with me. She said I bored her."

Alberto began to sob convulsively.

"Then when I pressed her more, she said she never loved me in the first place. She did it all for the cause. Yet I helped her. I protected her. She wouldn't listen. The money was needed then, she said, so she did what she had to do. Now it was not. Santangela was safe. And she would tell the world why she did it all—not for me, but for the country, the cause."

He sobbed more terribly.

For love. Clemency's words came back to her. *You could say indeed that I gave up everything for love.* Dry, wry, defiant words. But for love of the cause, not the man.

Jemima jumped up and Alberto did not even try to stop her. She pulled on her dress and he made no move to stop that either. She went into the little clean white hotel bathroom, saw the shower, the bright pristine towels on the rail, not very big towels and an unremarkable beige color—it was that kind of hotel. All the towels were clean and untouched except one: that was the towel draped inadequately over the body of Clemency Vane lying in the bath.

The towel left her face exposed, or perhaps Alberto had not wished to cover it. Certainly he had not closed Clemency's eyes: they stared at Jemima, sightless and bulging, above the purpled discoloration of her face, the mouth, and the tongue. There was no sign of what Alberto had used to strangle her —but the memory of his strong, black-haired, well-tended, well-scrubbed-afterward, muscular hands came back to her. The hands that had held her, Jemima. And tried to know her, as in the end they had never known Clemency Vane.

"I told you it was too late," Alberto said from the bedroom. He had not moved. "You can go away now," he added, in a remote voice as though the subject no longer interested him. "I shan't harm you. Go. It's nothing to do with you anymore."

Much later, back at the Megalith office about seven o'clock, Cherry said to Jemima with that cheerfulness she maintained even toward the end of the office day: "Where were you this morning? There were quite a few calls. You left a message saying you were out seeing that woman, what's her name, the drug runner who did it all for love, the persistent one who kept ringing up about the new program. But you never left me a number. Did you see her?"

"I saw her," said Jemima. Later she would tell Cherry, of course, as she told her everything, and later still everyone would probably know. But not just now.

"Was there anything in it for the program?" inquired Cherry. "She was so sure she could help us."

"No, after all, nothing in it for the program."

"Ah, well," said Cherry comfortably. "You never really know about people, do you?"

Jemima Shore agreed.

Like Marcia Muller, **JULIE SMITH** is a California-based writer (Berkeley) and has given us three splendid series detectives—Rebecca Schwartz, a lawyer with clients in deep trouble; Skip Langdon, an officer with the New Orleans Police Department; and Paul McDonald, a mystery writer with considerable personal experience in things criminous. The fact that Ms. Smith is a former journalist may help account for the rugged realism of her writing.

A MATCH MADE IN HELL

Julie Smith

 Cursing the inventors of pantyhose, June weddings, and Southern tradition, Skip took the arm of the freckle-faced young usher and walked down the damn aisle. Her pantyhose swished as her thighs touched. The skinny little usher made her feel like a freak. He was about five six; Skip was six feet and Junoesque. (Or that was one way to put it; other ways were less polite.)

"Aren't you Skip Langdon? I remember you from Icebreakers."

Icebreakers. Seventh-grade subscription dances. The kid's face at twelve popped into focus: "Rhett Buchanan—not again!"

The usher giggled and dropped her off. They had been a terrible mismatch as junior high dancing partners and they still were. As far as Skip was concerned, she was mismatched with everyone and everything in New Orleans— maybe she'd come back to "work out" something. Who knew? It was a weird thing; she knew she didn't fit in, had never fit in, probably never would fit in, but when she'd decided to become a cop, she also knew she had to do it in New Orleans. She didn't know why, it was just that way.

The success of the exercise had yet to be determined. Uptown New Orleans, where Skip had grown up despite her daddy's Mississippi beginnings, seemed to her as ingrown—and as stifling—as any town in West Virginia. But it looked as if once you'd graduated from McGehee's and pledged Kappa, you were part of the equation even if you were a six-foot female cop from Mars—one of the gang whether you liked it or not. Frequently she hated it—at the moment, for instance.

The congregation stood for the wedding march. Clouds of clashing floral perfumes engulfed Skip, and she felt her left shoe begin to rub a blister on her heel. The soft gray pumps were new, to go with the lilac suit she'd probably never wear again.

The bride, darling Weezee Rounsaville, flashed thousands of dollars of wondrous white at her admirers. Skip knew for a fact from Alison Gaillard, who had made her come to this carnival of silliness in the first place, that Weezee's daddy had practically gone into hock to pay for his little girl's "cosmetic dentistry"; the standard straightening wasn't good enough for a future queen of Comus.

But the investment had paid off handsomely. Mardi Gras queens were a dime a dozen; marrying Aubrey Delacroix was a stellar achievement. Aubrey had dark, Creole good looks and several million dollars.

As for the bride, darling Weezee looked like an anemic angel—the white wispy hair, milk-white skin, and pouty lips style of beauty. Absolutely ethereal in ivory satin. *If that train were any longer,* Skip thought, *they'd have to call it the Chattanooga Choo-Choo.*

The congregation sat. The minister mentioned why they were there: "To join together," etc., etc.

Damn! There was her egregious brother Conrad, king of the "suppies" (Southern Urban Pains in the butt). This was his sort of thing, not hers. What was she *doing* here? Pleasing Alison Gaillard, that was what—it had become almost a career with her.

"If any of you," intoned the minister, "can show just cause why they may not lawfully be married, speak now; or else forever hold your peace."

That part tended to wake Skip up. She always sat up straighter, half wishing for someone to accept the invitation and liven up the proceedings.

Something banged at the rear of the sanctuary. Before she had time to turn, something else banged at the front. A figure burst from a door to the left, a man dressed in black, watch cap on head, stocking over face. He was holding a metal object at his side—a handgun? Automatically, she reached for her purse, her .38. But . . . damn! She hadn't brought it. It wouldn't fit into the leather envelope Alison had talked her into. Never again! Never, never never! Shit!

She ground her teeth in agony, watching the man raise the gun.

"I can show just cause." The voice came not from him, but from the rear of the church. "The groom's dead."

The man in black fired, fired again. Skip couldn't tell if Aubrey was hit. The best man, standing next to him, lifted off his feet and fell against him, knocking him backward, blood gushing onto his white shirt.

Over Weezee's screams, the bridesmaids' screams, all the screams in Creole hell, the voice from the rear spoke again. "Everyone stay where you are. Anybody move and I waste the place."

Skip turned. The man in the back also was dressed in black, also wore a stocking. He was pointing an Uzi. The shooter joined him. "Count to ten," said the speaker, and they were out the door.

Skip was halfway down the aisle before a round of gunfire tore through the heavy air of the afternoon. A warning. Now the aisle was filling up. Should she try to get to the victims? No. A doctor would go, maybe half a dozen. That was the kind of crowd it was.

"Police! Let me through! Police!"

She might as well have been reciting "Hail Marys" for all the good it did her.

Alison Gaillard caught up with her, tugged at her elbow. She had on a peach-colored dress and straw hat with matching floaty band, like some caricature of a Southern belle in a rum ad—*Try some of this in your Scorpion. Talk about deadly!* Except the woman in the ad would be running barefoot on a beach instead of teetering on heels that were more like stilts. And she wouldn't have tears welling in her china-blues. "Oh, Skippy, not *Aubrey!*"

Oh, Alison, not this crap!

Skip thought it. But she said, "Get me through this crowd, will you?"

Alison had the right shoes for it. Some might have kicked ass; Alison wasted insteps. Sailing past the injured, Skip finally made it outside. It was June 30, last chance for a June wedding, but the weather was more like August. Humid and still. Air you practically had to swim through. She felt her suit wilt as she ran to the curb, getting there just in time to watch a gray car turn the corner.

A maverick breeze caught Alison's hatband; it fluttered artistically. "Nobody ever thought Buddy Carothers *meant* it. I mean, *everybody* says they're gon' kill their girl friend's new flame."

"Alison, hold it. Weezee dumped someone for Aubrey?"

"There was a big scene at the Twelfth Night Revelers—didn't you hear about it?"

Skip shook her head. The revelers held their ball on the night in question, which meant the big scene would have been almost six months earlier. Plenty of time for tempers to cool.

"Buddy said he'd kill Aubrey on his wedding day. Who knew he *meant* it?"

Skip heard sirens. Good. Someone had thought to call the police. But for the moment she was the sole representative thereof. She went back inside, made her way to the front and found Aubrey well, standing outside a small crowd shaking their heads around the fallen best man. Three doctors had tried to help him. They told her, in that Southern way that simultaneously celebrates euphemism and false piety, that there was "nothing they could do for him."

They also told her he was Aubrey's father Noel, the Delacroix patriarch and head of the shipping company the family had founded.

She called homicide and returned quickly to help the uniformed officers who'd be the first to arrive. Since it was a Saturday, it was a while before the detectives came—when they did there was good news and bad news. The two who turned up were Joe Tarantino, a prince of a guy in Skip's book, and Frank O'Rourke, who had personal problems and liked to make Skip his personal scapegoat.

"Hey, Skip," said Joe. "You a witness?"

"Hello, Langdon," said Frank. "Tried Weight Watchers yet?"

She gave them her Buddy Carothers gossip, made herself useful taking statements, and in the end succeeded in behaving in so puppylike a fashion that Joe asked if she wanted to take a ride over to Buddy's.

O'Rourke was outraged: "She can't investigate. She's a witness!"

Joe only shrugged. "So maybe she can ID the guy."

Buddy lived in half a double shotgun up near Carrollton. A small gray car parked outside could have been the one Skip had seen at the church. But Buddy didn't answer the door. It opened when Frank tried it. The three looked at each other and shrugged, all knowing they shouldn't enter, all agreeing they were going to.

It was clammy and dark inside. They built these old places to stay cool no matter how hot it got, and the AC was on as well. Skip shivered.

There was no one in the living room. All was quiet. But they found a heavy-breathing lump under a sour sheet on the bed. Beer bottles were everywhere, and a half-drunk bottle of bourbon on the floor hadn't been reclosed. The bedroom reeked. A .38 lay on a nearby dresser. Skip sniffed the barrel. Recently fired.

Stuffed into Buddy's closet, thrown on the floor in a heap, were one pair of black jeans, one black turtleneck, and half a pair of pantyhose, all slightly sweat-soaked. They'd stink when they dried out, but not as much as the rest of the setup, Skip thought. She didn't like the open door.

The lump didn't move, didn't hear a thing, or else Buddy had taken acting lessons. The two men finally shook him awake enough to read him his rights.

Buddy's story was that he'd been drunk for two days because the woman he loved was getting married. He didn't own a .38 or a black outfit. He'd had a visitor the day before, a Jehovah's Witness, maybe—something like that;

he'd opened the door, talked to the person, and closed it, maybe locking it, maybe not.

Skip could almost buy the case against him. Buddy had done the shooting, with the accomplice doing the talking because Buddy's voice was known. The accomplice had dropped Buddy off and driven away in the gray car. Buddy had faked the whole drunk number, even down to his blood alcohol level, just by drinking fast. He might have even had a heat on at the church, which would explain his poor marksmanship.

But if he hadn't really been drunk—if the binge was a cover—then why leave the evidence lying around? And was there some other reason the accomplice had done the talking? Perhaps because the shooter was a woman?

It wasn't her problem; it was homicide's. The next thing she knew about it was what *The Times-Picayune* said in the morning: Buddy'd been booked. What the hell. If he was innocent, it would come out. It just wasn't her problem.

It had rained that night and the weather was fresher. It was 7:00 A.M. on a beautiful summer day and she had the only walking beat in the city, one of the most gorgeous urban walks in the country. V.C.D. was her district, the Vieux Carré to other New Orleanians—the French Quarter to people "from away."

Louis Two-Nose caught her on Bourbon, just above Canal, and dragged her over to Iberville where no one could see them. "Whereyat, Skip?"

"How you makin' it, Louis?" She didn't know how old he was. Fifty, maybe; or maybe thirty-five. A complex design covered his face, pinky-red, going to purple on his namesake honker. Today he wore a Band-Aid on his forehead, probably from a fall. He needed dental work and about a barrel of leafy green vegetables. And a month at the Betty Ford Center. He spoke in the Bronx-sounding patois uptown people call "yat." Killer fumes came with the words.

"I heard somepn' I thought you could use. Dey got da wrong man on da church murda."

"What makes you say that?"

"A conversation I heard."

Skip waited.

"You interested?"

She shrugged.

"I heard dese two guys settin' up da hit."

"What two guys?"

He looked astonished. "I don' know. I never seen 'em before."

"What'd they look like, Louis?"

"One black, one white."

She waited.

"Couldn't look at 'em close. Didn't want 'em to know I was listenin'."

"How do you know the white guy wasn't the one we got?"

"Well, he was da ex, right? You wouldn't hafta hire him to hit his own woman. Don' make sense."

"So the black guy was hiring the white guy."

Louis nodded.

"Louis, I'm losing my patience. What'd he say?"

"He was drawin' da church. Talkin' about a side door where da white dude could come in, and how his partner could come in t'ru the front and cover da congregation. Dem was da words caught my attention—'cover da congregation.' Ya don' hear dat kinda talk every day."

"Damn you, Louis! Why didn't you call me then? Did you ever think of trying to stop the thing?"

"I didn' know dey was settin' up a hit. For all I knew dey was actors in a play."

"Okay, okay."

"See, I only caught on after I heard about it."

"Louis, you know what this means, don't you?"

"Skip, it's a good tip—ain't it a good tip? Come on, Skip . . . it's worth somepn', ain't it? Gotta be worth *somepn'.*" Desperation was coming out of his pores along with last night's Thunderbird.

"Not yet it's not. Come on, Louis."

She took him to Joe Tarantino in homicide and left him there, first slipping him a couple of bucks for when they let him go. Joe would him show him pictures of white dudes and black dudes and also arrange a lineup with Buddy in it. Louis would be sorry he'd ever brought up the subject. *Oh, well,* Skip thought—*I'll give him a few more bucks tomorrow.*

She went back to her district and called Joe at 3:00 P.M., when her working day was over. Louis hadn't recognized anyone and Joe was sorry, but he and Frank just couldn't buy Louis's story—he knew Skip knew Buddy, maybe was a friend of his, but they thought it was a good bust.

Well, hell. It was her problem now—Louis Two-Nose might be a drunk, and an unreliable one, but he had neither the brains nor the initiative to make up a story like that.

She traded her uniform for the lilac suit and headed for the Delacroix place, cursing Louis's oversized proboscis and the messes he stuck it into.

The Delacroix family lived on Audubon Place, a short ribbon of elegance that had never had a moment's competition for *the* street, in its way as glaring an anachronism as New York's Gramercy Park—it was a private street, with a guard and a gatehouse.

Everyone who'd ever curried a moment's favor with the Delacroix would be there today, expressing sympathy and drinking. Skip knew her name would get her in; her father the social climber was family doctor to half the old families in town. But once there and asking questions, she might get thrown out—it had happened before.

Fortunately, Alison was there. Nobody was going to mess with Skip with her sponsor around. Alison had been one of her Kappa sisters during her brief and unsuccessful tour of Sophie Newcomb. They'd barely spoken then, but now that Skip was back in town and so delicious an oddity as an officer of the law, Alison couldn't be stopped.

She was determined to show Skip off. Or save her soul. Or maybe make a lady out of her. Skip couldn't begin to figure it out. All she knew was, Alison was always getting her invited to things—like Weezee Rounsaville's wedding —and making her go.

And why was Skip such a wimp she couldn't say no to some uptown version of a Jewish mother? Because Alison was a truly great source of information.

Not all criminals came from the lower echelons, as Skip had learned quite early in her career. She was the department expert on the uptown crowd and she owed her expertise largely to Alison. (And, she admitted grudgingly, to her dork of a brother, though his payoff was cheaper—he thought she fixed his parking tickets. What she really did was pay them herself and put in for informants' fees.)

"Love that suit, Skippy. Did Buddy confess or anything?"

Skip smiled. "I'm surprised you don't know, Gossip Goddess." Quickly, so Alison wouldn't press her, she changed the subject. "Listen, I know Aubrey and his mother, but they might not remember me. Could you reintroduce me?"

"I don't see Aubrey—come to think of it, I don't see Weezee either. Maybe they're having a private moment of grief." Her eyebrow went up and so did the corners of her mouth. "There's Clarice over there."

Aubrey's mother was tall, thin, nervous. She looked self-absorbed and unfriendly. Closer, Skip saw that her eyes were bright angry dots, periods punctuating a face in which all the lines pointed downward. Skip doubted if she'd smiled twice in her life. She wondered about the anger in her eyes—it could have been there because Clarice had just lost her husband, because Aubrey had taken a few minutes off, any number of things. Skip thought it was simply her habit. Clarice stared at her as if she were a maggot, perhaps a potato bug—something loathsome you could squash.

"You're Don Langdon's daughter, aren't you?"

Skip nodded. "I don't know if you know I'm with the police department now. I wonder if we could talk a moment?"

"I really don't think that would be appropriate."

"Aubrey may still be in danger."

Skip thought fear flickered on her face, but maybe it was just calculation. "Frankly, I don't see how. You people have made an arrest, haven't you?" Her voice was belligerent.

"We want to be sure we have the right man."

"Are you implying my son has enemies?"

He certainly has at least one. "Of course not. We're just completing our investigation."

"I really think you'd better leave."

"Could I talk to Aubrey first?"

"I think you'd better just go. Alison, dear, would you escort Miss Langdon?"

"But, Clarice—"

"Get this woman out of my house."

So much for Skip's fantasies of protection. As Clarice turned away, Alison only sighed. "Tarantula-woman strikes again. Sorry you had to be the victim, but if it's any comfort, you won't be the only one. She usually gets two or three a day."

"You know what just occurred to me? Aubrey isn't dead and his dad is."

"Well now, that *is* a brilliant deduction."

"Maybe she's not a tarantula—maybe she's a black widow."

Alison laughed. "Had him killed for his money? What's the point? To run away with her lover? Who'd have Clarice?"

Skip's mind was reeling, contemplating its own stupidity. Aubrey might or might not have had enemies, but rich, powerful Noel Delacroix was bound to have had dozens—perhaps some in his own family. She wished she knew who stood to inherit.

"Is Aubrey an only child?"

"Why, no." Alison looked as if she'd just realized she'd been as obtuse as Skip. "There's Gina. She's about our age. Where in hell *is* Gina? And where was she yesterday?"

"Who?"

"Aubrey's sister Gina. Comes from Regina." She pronounced both words with long "I's." "Isn't it obscene? She had a bad drug problem a few years ago. Dropped out of school, I think. I haven't seen her in years. Come to think of it, none of the Delacroix ever mentions her."

They were nearly at the door now. "Who'd know the story on Gina?"

"Cammy, I guess—the maid." Alison snapped her fingers. "Tante Adelle and Tante Tay-Tay. Great-aunts—Noel's father's sisters." Her head swiveled. "They were here a while ago. . . ."

The two aunts lived in a house on Prytania. Adelle was a widow and Tay-Tay a "maiden lady," if such females still existed. They were napping when

Skip arrived, having probably had a drop or two at their late nephew's. She was let in by a maid who acted the perfect hostess while the aunts pulled themselves together. But Skip declined her offer to sit, preferring to prowl, looking at pictures and books.

Adelle appeared first, still smoothing a hastily donned knit skirt over the mono-buttock a girdle makes. She stood erect, had shoulder-length black hair with a white streak in it. Her mouth was a little tight for Skip's taste.

"Adelle Gibert," she said. "You're Don Langdon's daughter, aren't you?"

Once Skip had hated to admit it, had longed to be known for herself and not her family, but that wasn't the way New Orleans was made.

"Sit down," said Adelle. "I hear Tay-Tay." So did Skip—unless a rhino was charging; lampshades shook as the floor vibrated. Tay-Tay entered the room with the air of one who owns the parish, possibly the state; someone used to authority. Skip had a flash: retired schoolteacher.

She was a large lady—gray-haired, deep-bosomed, grandmotherly, wearing shorts that showed varicose veins and a T-shirt that couldn't quite do its work —she had a solid line of bust to go with Adelle's mono-butt. She looked as if she could give a flying flirt.

"Octavia Delacroix." Without further ceremony, she plopped into a needlework rocker. "How can we help?"

"I was wondering about Aubrey's sister."

Adelle's eyebrows went up. "Gina? *Gina?*" Horrified.

Tay-Tay was placid. "Poor little Gina. What about her?"

"I wondered if you know where she is."

Adelle sat in censorious silence. Tay-Tay smiled. "Well, I guess we're gon' be awhile. Something cool, Miss Langdon? Or should I say Officer?"

"How about Skip?"

"And you must call me Tay-Tay. Or Tante Tay-Tay if you like. Everyone else does." Skip felt engulfed by the warmth of her. She'd probably taught first or second grade, let the kids crawl up in her lap. "I'll speak to Leeanna."

When she had left, Adelle said, "Gina's a very lovely girl, Miss Langdon. I can't think where you're going with this."

Tay-Tay's heavy step announced her return. She said, "I guess you noticed she wasn't at the wedding. You think she could have been one of those black figures . . . that's it, isn't it?"

"I have to ask, that's all."

"Well, she wasn't. She's not even in town. Gina's estranged from the family. Her daddy never had a moment's time for her after he found out she had a drug problem. Threw her out of the house when she was eighteen."

"Tay-Tay!"

"Adelle, she's gon' find out anyway. Might as well be from somebody that loves Gina." She turned back to Skip. "Who wouldn't take drugs with those two for parents?"

"I've met Clarice."

"Well, Noel was . . . a Delacroix. Staunch churchmen, the whole lot of them."

A little too staunch, Skip gathered.

"Anyway, next thing you know Gina got pregnant and he still refused to help her. Even when the baby was born. The good news is, she quit using, for the baby's sake." She smiled. "Darlin' little Heather. Cutest thing old Tante Tay-Tay ever saw in her life."

Adelle said, "We tried to help her, but Noel found out."

"Is she disinherited? Do people still do that?"

Leeanna arrived with a tray of iced tea. Overhearing, she snorted. Adelle's lips drew together again.

But Tay-Tay laughed. "Well, it's pretty hard, in this state, but it can be done. You're looking at two of the only . . ."

"Tay-Tay, I beg you!"

"Adelle, for heaven's sake. Everybody knows the story. What are you being so silly about?"

Skip made her face a polite blank.

"Adelle tells it herself at parties—or used to before everyone in New Orleans had heard it three times. You know about forced heirship?"

Skip shook her head, mystified.

"Well, Louisiana's the only state in the union that's got it—you can't cut a child completely out of the will, except in twelve very unusual circumstances. Or let's say eleven of those and one that's all too usual. Which is how Adelle got caught. When she was fifteen—a minor, you see—she ran away and got married."

Adelle said, "Damn the Delacroix and all they stand for!"

"Hear, hear!" said Tay-Tay, raising her iced tea glass. Skip suspected she was still a little high from whatever she'd been drinking at the wake. "They don't even cut their wives in any more than they have to. The bulk of Noel's estate will go to Aubrey, you watch. Clarice will get a house—though certainly not the one on Audubon Place—and just enough to live on, and Gina will get the fourth required by law. A bitter pill for Noel—she wouldn't even get that if it weren't for us. We've schooled the girl very carefully in the art of forced heirship—we're experts. She always made sure she contacted him at least once every two years—if she hadn't, she could have been disinherited. That's one of the twelve ways, and incidentally one of the three our father got us on."

"Both of you are disinherited?"

"Absolutely. And all because of our dear brother Charles. Now deceased."

Tay-Tay looked delighted about that. "You see he was the one who told Daddy he could do it and how—he was the lawyer in the family."

"And the one who stood to get the entire estate."

Adelle sniffed. "That's what Daddy wanted anyway. The name male chauvinist was invented for Delacroix."

Tay-Tay was enjoying herself. "They got me two ways, but one of them was fraudulent. A child can be disinherited if he hits a parent. Daddy and Charles claimed I hit Daddy when he told Adelle he was going to do it to her —but really, I only threw a vase. Anyway, after it all happened we never spoke to either of them again. Not even knowing *that* was one of the twelve grounds."

"What are the other grounds?" Skip knew, as did everyone in Louisiana, that the state's famous Napoleonic Code was eccentric, but this was such a preposterous twist she was fascinated.

"Oh, what are they, Adelle?"

Adelle held her tongue.

"Let's see," said Tay-Tay. "Refusing to ransom a parent is one. And accusing a parent of a capital crime. Except high treason, that is, because that's your duty. My personal favorite is refusing to take care of a parent who's become insane. How would you prove he was competent to make a will?" She turned serious. "I'm sorry. It isn't funny—I'm just used to it. To get back to our lovely family, Adelle has a little money from her late husband and I have my pension, but we've had to depend on Noel's good nature for a house to live in."

Adelle snorted. "His whims, you mean. Clarice bullied Noel into giving us this one *only* because it would have looked bad if we'd had to find a hovel somewhere."

"He didn't give it to us, Adelle."

"He *let* us live here. So that's why we couldn't help Gina, have her come live with us, when she needed it. He wouldn't permit it."

"Do you have her address?"

Adelle thought they shouldn't give it to her, but Tay-Tay prevailed. Softly, on the way out, she apologized for her sister's coldness: "She's just upset about Aubrey. The wedding being ruined and all."

Gina lived in Baton Rouge and worked at a drug abuse counseling center. Skip caught her at home, her eyes red, her hair slightly dirty. She didn't look as if she'd slept.

Skip made sympathy sounds.

Gina blew her nose. "I'm crying because I couldn't go to my own father's house today. The day after he died."

"You were forbidden to?"

"No. I couldn't bring myself to. Mama's Catholic too. They both thought I was a sinner that couldn't be forgiven."

And a social embarrassment.

The apartment was tiny, furnished with Goodwill bargains, every surface covered with the toys, clothes, and supplies of a five-year-old. Heather herself was watching an old black-and-white TV, there being barely any room in the place to do anything else.

"I gather you weren't at the wedding either. Why not just defy your parents and go?"

That started a fresh flood of tears: "Aubrey didn't invite me." She shrugged. "He did what Daddy wanted."

Skip was trying to figure out what could make a man like Noel tick—a man so heartless, so rigid, so out of sync with contemporary mores, when Gina said: "It's a Delacroix tradition. Hating women."

There was a bitter edge to her voice. "They even gave me a name that sounds like vagina. 'Generic female here; don't bother naming it.' Have you met my mother?"

"Yes."

"My grandmother was just like her. Their mothers are bitches, they marry more bitches, and they keep on hating women. But they're so mired in Catholic tradition they never admit to themselves what their wives are. To them all women are either Mary or Mary Magdalene. And Mary is *never* a bitch. So they spend their lives getting pushed around by these female storm troopers and pretend they're in control by being tyrants about money."

"You seem to have thought this out."

"You would have, too, in my shoes. I don't think you could possibly know how pathological my family is."

Skip thought of her own family. "I don't know—"

"Look at this." Gina handed her a letter:

Dear Regina,

This is to let you know that on July 1, 1990, the Louisiana law on forced heirship will change. On that day and afterward, children twenty-three and over can be disinherited. Enclosed please find a copy of the will I will sign that day.

"My God!"

"My daddy was a real sweetheart, wasn't he? It wasn't enough to do it, he had to make damn sure I knew about it."

"He was killed June 30."

"I guess that makes me an heiress, huh? Now I can move to a real house and go back to school." She blew her nose. "Ain't life grand?"

Her lips moved a little, to no apparent end. Skip thought she'd tried a smile but just couldn't manage it.

"Gina, I have to ask you. Where were you Saturday afternoon?"

"Drowning my sorrows."

You and Buddy Carothers.

"I was with a girl friend, Alicia Ravenel, and we were in a bar called The Glass Menagerie. I think quite a few people would remember. I was making a spectacle of myself."

Skip stayed late in Baton Rouge, visiting The Glass Menagerie (drinks in glasses animal-shaped), and calling on Alicia Ravenel.

The alibi checked out.

The case against Buddy Carothers was looking better. But if he did it, where did the black man come in? Had he been the man with the Uzi? He hadn't had a black accent. And Louis Two-Nose had been very clear about it: the black man had been the one doing the hiring, and he'd hired two men, the one in the bar and "his partner," who'd cover the congregation. Had Buddy sent a friend to hire a thug for him? Had Gina?

Skip called all the numbers in Buddy's address book and even consulted her least favorite source, her brother Conrad, who knew everyone even a little bit socially important. No one had ever seen Buddy speak with any black person who wasn't a servant or a bellman. The reason they could be so sure was he was a notorious racist.

As always in these situations, Skip wished she'd gotten it together and learned to meditate. She felt the need to focus her mind. She couldn't see how Noel's timely death (considering his letter) could be a coincidence. But if Gina had had him killed, why show Skip the letter? And who *was* the black man? She knew only two black people involved with the Delacroix family— Noel's maid Cammy and Leeanna; but there must be others.

She phoned Alicia Ravenel, Gina's boss, and friends of Gina's whose names she'd gotten from Alicia. She also called Alison, who made a few calls of her own. That afternoon she found herself visiting a man named Raybon Broussard.

After that, she dropped in on the aunts. This time they both wore white slacks, Adelle's elegant, Tay-Tay's the sloppy kind with drawstring waist. Adelle had pulled her hair back against the heat; she looked younger and a little vulnerable. Tay-Tay worked on a needlepoint pillow.

"I talked to Raybon today."

Tay-Tay looked up in alarm. "Oh, no! Leeanna—"

Adelle said, "I'll send her to the store."

When she returned, Skip saw that her color had gone. Raybon was Leeanna's son.

"He's sweating," said Skip, "and not because his AC's on the blink. He's one of the most scared young men I've seen lately."

"Has something gone wrong with his parole? I don't think I can take it if that boy has to go back to prison." Tay-Tay looked ready to cry. "There's no harm in Raybon, no harm at all."

"Armed robbery—"

"He was just a baby. Why, he's still a baby—won't be twenty-one till January."

Adelle said, "Tay-Tay never forgets his birthday. I sometimes think she loves Raybon better than Gina."

"That's not true, Adelle, and you know it. I love all my children just the same."

Skip was sure she'd been right about Tay-Tay—she *had* to have been a teacher. "He must love you too," she said. "He's trying really hard to protect you. But it's not going to work. I have the name of the man he sent you to."

She didn't, though. Not yet. Raybon had been a challenge. He was frightened, all right, which was how she knew she was on the right track. But fear didn't loosen his tongue any. She'd had to tell him Tay-Tay had already confessed to get him talking—and then he'd only said one thing and it wasn't enough for an arrest. But she was hoping hard.

"*What* on God's earth are you talking about?"

"He says it wasn't you who called him."

Adelle started to speak: "I had to tell him it was for Tay-Tay."

Skip stopped her. "Not yet. I have to Mirandize you."

Adelle nodded stoically. Her color was better; she'd probably gotten a jolt of adrenaline.

"What's happening?" Tay-Tay was panicked, looked as if her world was falling apart. And it was, thought Skip, feeling for her. When she'd read Adelle her rights, Skip asked if she wanted to waive them.

"Oh, hell, yes. I want to talk, and I don't want some stuffy lawyer in here clamming me up."

She might be a murderer, but Skip liked her spirit. She saw now that Adelle was no stiff-lipped Sunday school teacher; she'd seemed uptight because she'd been under the biggest stress of her life.

"Adelle, no."

"Hush up, Tay-Tay. Don't you see what she's doing? She's blackmailing me. If I talk, Raybon gets off."

Skip said, "I can't make any deals."

"But this way you won't take him to some horrible interrogation room and badger him, will you? Because I'm going to give you what you need, and tell you flat-out that he didn't have the least idea what it was all about. He just gave me a name, that's all. Wouldn't take a penny for it. Thought he was doing a favor for Tay-Tay. That's how I got him to cooperate."

She spoke directly to Skip, avoiding her sister's eye. "Gina called in tears about the letter—absolutely hysterical, poor little baby. Anyway, Tay-Tay wasn't home and I made up my mind not to tell her about it. I just made my plans. I told Raybon Tay-Tay had a problem and I wanted to solve it for her. I asked him to give me the name of a very bad man, someone from prison. I think he thought I wanted to scare somebody because he didn't give me a murderer. But his friend knew some Italians. I had to pay him five thousand dollars for the introduction; the Italians cost twenty apiece. Did you know it was so cheap to hire hit men?"

"That's all the money you have in the world!" Skip noticed Tay-Tay had changed the subject, unable yet to face what had happened.

"Gina will help me. I know she will."

She was getting a glazed look now. But Tay-Tay was snapping back to reality, taking it in.

"Adelle, murder. You did murder!"

"Poor little Heather—my heart just sank every time I saw that child in that tiny little crackerbox." Her bland face wore a look Skip had seen in court: a judge pronouncing sentence. "Somebody had to get this family back on track."

"But the wedding—why poor Aubrey's wedding?"

For the first time Adelle smiled. "I thought we needed a ritual murder."

Horror replaced the shock on Tay-Tay's gentle face. She spoke as if explaining it to herself. "You're crazy, Adelle. You're really mad."

"That's right, little sister. I'm really mad. But not crazy-mad." She paused and took a breath for maximum volume. "I'm *furious!*"

Skip thought little Heather probably heard her aunt up in Baton Rouge.

THEFT OF THE POET

Barbara Wilson

 It started gradually. Here and there on London streets new blue plaques that might have been placed there by the authorities, if the authorities had been reasonably literate, and unreasonably feminist, began to appear. At 22 Hyde Park Gate the enamel plaque stating that Leslie Stephen, the noted biographer, had lived here was joined by a new metal plate, much the same size and much the same color, which informed the passerby that this was where writer Virginia Woolf and painter Vanessa Bell had spent their childhoods. Over in Primrose Hill the plaque that read that Yeats had once been resident in this house was joined by a shiny new medallion gravely informing us that Sylvia Plath had written the poems in *Ariel* here before committing suicide in 1963.

Above the blue plaque at 106 Hallam Street, the birthplace of Dante Gabriel Rossetti, another one appeared to emphasize that poet Christina Rossetti had lived here as well. The plate at 20 Maresfield Gardens, which recorded that Sigmund Freud had passed the last year of his life here, was joined by a new one telling us that Anna Freud had passed forty-two years at this address. A medallion to Jane Carlyle, letter writer, joined that of her famous husband Thomas at 24 Cheyne Row, and a plaque telling us about

Fanny Burney, author of *Evelina* and other novels, appeared above that describing Sir Isaac Newton's dates and accomplishments on the outside of a library in St. Martin's Street.

The appearance of these blue plaques was at first noted sympathetically, if condescendingly, by the liberal newspapers and a certain brave editor at *The Guardian* was bold enough to suggest that it was high time more women writers who had clearly achieved "a certain stature" be recognized. The editor thus managed to give tacit approval to the choice of authors awarded blue plaques and to suggest that the perpetrators had gone quite far enough. "We wouldn't want blue plaques on every house in London, after all."

But the plaquing continued, heedless of *The Guardian*'s pointed admonition, to the growing excitement of many and the consternation of quite a few. Who was responsible and how long would it go on? Would the authorities leave the plaques up or bother to remove them? Apparently they had been manufactured out of a lighter metal than the original plaques, but instead of being bolted to the buildings, they had been affixed with Super Glue. Some residents of the buildings were delighted; other inhabitants, in a conservative rage, defaced the medallions immediately.

The next blue plaques to go up were placed on houses previously unrecognized as having been the homes of women worth remembering and honoring. A plaque appeared outside the house in Maida Vale where authors Winifred Holtby and Vera Brittain had shared a flat for several years. A similar plaque commemorating the relationship of poets H.D. and Bryher appeared in Knightsbridge. Mary Seacole, a Victorian black woman who had traveled widely as a businesswoman, gold prospector, and nurse in the Crimean War and who had written an autobiography about her life, was honored on the wall of 26 Upper George Street off Portman Square, as was Constance Markievicz, many times imprisoned Irish Republican, who was the first woman elected as a member of the British Parliament (though she refused to take her seat in protest over the Irish situation), and who was born in Westminster on Buckingham Street. Of course, my friends in the progressive backwater of East Dulwich were delighted when Louise Michel, the French Revolutionary Socialist and Communard, was honored with a plaque, and those of us who are interested in printing and publishing were quite thrilled when a plaque appeared at 9 Great Coram Street, home in the 1860s to Victoria Printers, which Emily Faithfull set up in order to train women as printers and where she published Britain's first feminist periodical.

The list could go on and on, and it did. You would have thought the authorities would be pleased. New tourists flocked to obscure neighborhoods, guidebooks to the new sites proliferated, tours were organized; handwritten notes appeared on walls suggesting plaques; letters to the editor demanded to know why certain women hadn't been honored. Other letters criticized the manner in which only bourgeois individuals were elevated and suggested monuments to large historical events, such as Epping Forest, where Boudicca, the leader of the Celts, fought her last battle with the Romans in A.D. 62, or the Parliament Street Post Office, where Emily Wilding Davison set fire to a letter box in 1911, the first suffragist attempt at arson to draw attention to the struggle for women's rights. One enterprising and radical artist even sent the newspapers a sketch for a "Monument of Glass" to be placed on a busy shopping street in Knightsbridge, to commemorate the day of March 4, 1912, when a hundred suffragists walked down the street, smashing every plate glass window they passed.

The Tory and gutter papers were naturally appalled by such ideas and called for Thatcher (whom no one had thought to plaquate) to put a stop to the desecration of London buildings and streets. Vigilant foot patrols were called for and severe penalties for vandalization were demanded.

This then was the atmosphere in which the news suddenly surfaced that the grave of a famous woman poet had been opened and her bones had gone missing.

As it happened, the small village in Dorset where the poet had been buried was also the home of a friend of mine, Andrea Addlepoot, once a writer of very successful feminist mysteries, back when feminist mysteries had been popular, and now an obsessive gardener and letter writer. It was she who first described the theft to me in detail, the theft that the London papers had hysterically headlined: POET'S GRAVE VANDALIZED.

My dear Cassandra,

By now you have no doubt heard that Francine Crofts "Putter" is no longer resting eternally in the small churchyard opposite my humble country cottage. My first thought, heretically, was that I would not miss her—meaning that I would not miss the hordes of visitors, primarily women, primarily Young American Women, who had made the pilgrimage to her grave since her death. I would not miss how they trampled over my tender flowers, nor pelted me with questions. As if I had known the woman. As if anyone in the village had known the woman.

And yet it is still quite shocking, and everyone here is in an uproar over it.

You of course realize that the theft is not an isolated action but only the latest in a series of "terrorist acts" (I quote Peter Putter, the late poet's husband) perpetrated on the grave, and most likely not totally unrelated to the unchecked rememorializing of London and surrounding areas. (Discreet plaquing is one thing, but I really could not condone the defacing of Jane Austen's grave in Winchester Cathedral. Surely "In

Memory of Jane Austen, youngest daughter of the late Reverend George Austen, formerly Rector of Steventon," says everything necessary. There was no reason on earth to stencil onto the stone the words "Author of *Pride and Prejudice* and other novels.")

These "terrorist acts" consisted of the last name, "Putter," in raised lead lettering, being three times chipped off from the headstone. The headstone was repaired twice but the third time Mr. Putter removed the headstone indefinitely from the grave site. That was over a year ago and it has not been reerected, which, despite what you might think, has not made my life any easier. I cannot count the number of times that sincere young women have approached me as I stood pruning my roses and beseeched me, most often in flat American accents, to show them the unmarked grave of Francine Crofts.

Never Francine Putter or Francine Crofts Putter.

For Francine Crofts *was* her name, you know, even if at one time she had been rather pathetically eager to be married to the upcoming young writer Peter Putter and had put aside her own poetry to type his manuscripts. Francine Crofts is the name the world knows her by. And, of course, that's what Putter cannot stand.

I know him, you must realize. Although his boyhood was long, long over by the time I moved here (after the enormous financial success, you recall, of *Murder at Greenham Common*), his parents Margery and Andrew and sister Jane Fitzwater—the widow who runs the local tearoom, and who has a penchant for telling anyone who will listen what a shrew Francine was and what a saint dear Peter—still live in the large house down the road that Peter bought for them. This little village represents roots for Peter, and sometimes you'll see him with one or another young girlfriend down at the pub getting pissed. When he's really in his cups he'll sometimes go all weepy, telling everyone what a raw deal he's getting from the world about Francine. It wasn't his fault she died. He really did love her. She wasn't planning to get a divorce. They were soul mates.

It's enough to make you vomit. Everybody knows what a cad he was, how it was his desertion of her that inspired Francine's greatest poetry and the realization that he wasn't coming back that led to her death. It's hard to see now what she saw in Putter, but, after all, he was younger then, and so was she. So were we all.

But Cassandra, I'm rambling. You know all this, I'm sure, and I'm equally sure you take as large an interest in the disappearance of Francine's bones as I do. Why not think about paying me a visit for a few days? Bring your translating work, I'll cook you marvelous meals, and together we'll see—for old times' sake—whether we can get to the bottom of this.

When I arrived at Andrea's cottage by car the next day, she was out in her front garden chatting with journalists. As usual she was wearing jeans and tall boots and a safari hat. In spite of her disdain for Americans, she was secretly flattered when anyone mentioned that she, rangy and weathered, looked a bit like the Marlboro man. At the moment she was busy giving quotes to the journos in her usual deep, measured tones:

"Peter Putter is an insecure, insignificant man and writer who has never produced anything of literary value himself, and could not stand the idea that his wife was a genius. He drove her to . . . Oh, hello, Cassandra." She broke off and took my bag, waving good-bye to the newspaper hacks. "And don't forget it's AddlePOOT—not PATE, author of numerous thrillers. . . . Come in, come in." She opened the low front door and stooped to show me in. "Oh, the media rats. We love to hate them."

I suspected that Andrea loved them more than she hated them. It was only since her career had slipped that she'd begun to speak of them in disparaging terms. During the years that the feminist thriller had been in fashion, Andrea's name had shone brighter than anyone's. "If Jane Austen were alive today and writing detective stories, she would be named Andrea Addlepoot," gushed one reviewer. All of her early books—*Murder at Greenham Common, Murder at the Small Feminist Press, Murder at the Anti-Apartheid Demonstration*—had topped the *City Limits* Alternative Best Seller lists, and she was regularly interviewed on television and in print about the exciting new phenomenon of the feminist detective.

Alas, any new phenomenon is likely to be an old phenomenon soon and thus no phenomenon at all. It never occurred to Andrea that the feminist detective was a bit of a fad and that, like all fads in a consumer culture, its shelf life was limited. Oh, Andrea and her detective, London PI Philippa Fanthorpe, had tried. They had taken on new social topics—the animal rights movement, the leaky nuclear plants on the Irish Sea—but the reviews were no longer so positive. Too "rhetorical," too "issue-oriented," too "strident," the critics wrote wearily, and Andrea Addlepoot's fortunes declined. In the bookstores feminist mysteries were replaced with the latest best-selling genre: women's erotica.

And Andrea, who had never written a sex scene in her life, retired for good to Dorset.

"Cassandra, it's shocking how this is being reported," she announced as we sat down in the tiny parlor. She took off her safari hat and her gray curls bristled. "Peter Putter is here giving interviews to the BBC news every few hours. And now the Americans have gotten in on it. Cable News Network is here and I've heard Diane Sawyer is arriving tomorrow."

"Well, Francine Crofts was born in America," I said. "And that's where a lot of her papers are, aren't they?"

"Yes, everything that Putter couldn't get his hands on is there."

"I read somewhere that he destroyed her last journal and the manuscript of a novel she was working on."

"Oh, yes, it's true. He couldn't stand the idea of anything bad about himself coming to the public's attention."

"Any chance he could have removed the bones himself?" I asked.

Andrea nodded. "Oh, I would say there's a very good chance indeed. All this rowing over her headstone has not been good publicity for our Peter Putter. It puts him in a bad light, it keeps bringing back the old allegations that he was responsible in great measure for Francine's death. It's quite possible, I think, that he began to read about the appearance of all these new blue plaques and thought to himself, 'Right. I'll get rid of the grave entirely, blame it on the radical feminists and there'll be an end to it.' I'm sure he's sorry he ever thought to bury the body here in the first place and to put 'Putter' at the end of her name. But he can't back down now, so the only solution was to arrange for the bones to disappear."

"I don't suppose we could go over to the graveyard and have a look?"

Andrea peered out her small-paned front window. "We'll go when it's quieter. Let's have our tea first."

We had our tea, lavish with Devonshire cream and fresh scones, and then Andrea went off for a brief lie-down, and I, left to my own resources in the parlor, went to the bookcase and found the volume of Crofts's most celebrated poems.

They struck me with the same power now as they had when I read them twenty years ago, especially the poems written at the very end, when, translucent from rage and hunger, Francine had struck out repeatedly at the ties that bound her to this earth and that man. Even as she was starving herself to death in the most barbaric and self-punishing way, she still could write like an avenging angel.

Around five, when the autumn mists had drifted down over the small village in the valley, Andrea roused herself and we walked across the road to the tiny churchyard of St. Stephen's. The small church was from the thirteenth century and no longer in use; its front door was chained and padlocked. The churchyard was desolate as well, under the purple twilight sky, and covered with leaves that were damp with rain. It was enclosed on all sides by a low stone wall and shielded by enormous oaks. We went in through the creaking gate. The ground was trampled with footprints, and many of the graves were untended.

I could barely see my feet in front of me through the cold, wet mist, but Andrea led the way unerringly to a roped-off hole. There had been no effort to cover the grave back over, and the dirt was heaped hastily by the side.

It had the effect of eerie loneliness and ruthless desecration, and even Andrea, creator of the cold-blooded Philippa Fanthorpe, seemed disturbed.

"You can see they didn't have much time," she murmured.

Suddenly we heard a noise. It was the gate creaking. Without a word Andrea pulled me away from the grave and around the side of the church. Someone was approaching the site of the theft, a woman with a scarf, heavy coat, and Wellington boots. She stood silently by the open grave a moment. And then we heard her begin to cry.

Ten minutes later we were warming ourselves in the local pub, The King's Head. A few journos were there, soaking up the local color, the color in this case being the golden yellow of lager. Andrea bought me a half of bitter and a pint of Old Peculiar for herself, and we seated ourselves in a corner by the fireplace. The woman in the churchyard had left as quickly as she had come. We were debating who she could be when the door to the pub opened and a paunchy man in his fifties came in, wearing a tweed jacket and carrying a walking stick.

"That's how he dresses in the country," Andrea muttered. "Sodding old fart."

It was Putter, I assumed, and I had to admit that there was a certain cragginess to his face that must have once been appealing. If I had been a young American working at a publishing house as a secretary in the early sixties, perhaps I, too, would have been flattered if Chatup and Windows's rising male author had shown an interest in *me* and asked *me* if I'd like to do a spot of typing for him. Putter's first novel, *The Man in the Looking Glass*, had been published to enormous acclaim, and he was working on his second. An authentic working-class writer (his father was actually a bank clerk, but he kept that quiet)—who would have guessed that this voice of the masses would eventually degenerate into a very minor novelist known mostly for his acerbic reviews of other people's work in the *Sunday Telegraph*? Poor Francine. When she was deserted by her young husband, with just one book of poetry published to very little acclaim at all, she had no idea that within two years their roles would have completely reversed. Peter Putter would in the years to come be most famous for having been Francine Crofts's husband.

"I wish it were possible to have a certain sympathy for him," Andrea said gruffly, downing the last of her Old Peculiar. "After all, we both know what it is to experience the fickleness of public attention."

I went up to the bar to order us another round and heard Putter explaining loudly to the journos, "It's an outrage. Her married name was Francine Putter and that's how I planned to have the stone engraved in the first place. I only added Crofts because I knew what she had brought off in that name, and I wished in some small way to honor it. But the radical feminists aren't satisfied. Oh, no. It didn't satisfy them to vandalize the headstone over and over; they had to actually violate a sanctified grave and steal Francine's remains. No regard for me or her family, no regard for the church, no regard for her memory. God only knows what they plan to use her bones for. One shudders to think. Goddess rituals or some sort of black magic."

"You're suggesting a Satanic cult got hold of Francine?" a journo asked, and I could see the story in the *Daily Mail* already.

"Wouldn't surprise me in the least," Putter said, and he bought a round for all the newspapermen.

I returned to Andrea. "If you were a radical feminist and/or Satanic cultist, how would you have stolen the bones?"

She glowered at Putter. "It was probably dead easy. Drive over from London in a minivan, or even a car with a large boot. Maybe two of you. In the hours before dawn. One keeps watch and the other digs. The wooden casket has disintegrated in twenty years. You carefully lay the bones in a sheet—so they don't rattle around too much—wrap the whole thing up in a plastic bag, and Bob's your uncle!"

I shuddered. Blue plaques were one thing, but grave robbery and bone-snatching, even in the cause of justified historical revisionism, were quite another.

"Why not just another gravestone, this time with the words Francine Crofts?"

"Do you really think Putter"—Andrea shot him a vicious look—"would allow such a stone to stand? No, I'm sure whoever did it plans to rebury her."

"What makes you think that?" I asked. "Maybe they'll just chip off pieces of bone and sell them at American women's studies conferences."

"Don't be medieval," Andrea said absently. "No, I think it's likely they might choose a site on the farm not far from here where Francine and Peter lived during the early days of their marriage. The poems from that period are the lyrical ones, the happy ones. A simple monument on the top of a hill: Francine Crofts, Poet." Andrea looked up from her Old Peculiar and turned to me in excitement. "That's it. We'll stake the farm out, we'll be the first to discover the monument. Maybe we'll catch them in the act of putting it up."

"What good would that do?"

"Don't be daft," she admonished me. "It's publicity, isn't it?"

* * *

Andrea wanted to rush right over to the farm, but when we came outside the pub the fog was so thick and close that we decided to settle in for the night instead. I went up to the guest room under the eaves with a hot-water bottle and Crofts's *Collected Poems*. I'd forgotten she had been happy until Andrea reminded me. Her memory was so profoundly imbued with her manner of dying and with her violent despair that it was hard to think of her as celebrating life and love. But here were poems about marriage, about the farm, about animals and flowers. It made one pause: if she had married a faithful and loving man, perhaps her poetry would have stayed cheerful and light. Perhaps Putter did make her what she was, a poet of genius; perhaps it was right that he still claimed her by name. But no—here were the last poems in that first collection, the ones that had been called prefeminist, protofeminist and even Ur-feminist. Some critics now argued that if only Francine had lived to see the women's movement, her anger would have had a context; she wouldn't have turned her fury at being abandoned against herself and seen herself a failure. But other critics argued that it was clear from certain poems, even early ones, that Francine understood her predicament quite well and was constantly searching for ways out. And they quoted the poem about Mary Anning, the early nineteenth-century fossil collector who was the first to discover the remains of an ichthyosaurus in Lyme Regis, not far from here, in 1811. It was called "Freeing the Bones."

The next morning Andrea and I drove over to the farm and skirted the hedges around it looking for a spot that the unknown gravediggers might decide was suitable for a memorial of some sort.

"This is such a long shot," I said. "I think it's quite possible that some Americans were involved, and that they've taken the remains back to America. Wasn't she from Iowa? They'll bury them in Cedar Rapids."

"Francine would hate that if she knew," said Andrea. "She was such an anglophile she couldn't wait to get out of Cedar Rapids. It was the pinnacle of happiness for her to study at Oxford and then to get a job afterward. No one, not even her family, tried to make a case for sending her bones back to Iowa."

The farm was owned by an absentee landlord; it was solitary and lovely on this mid-autumn day. We broke through a weak hedge and tramped the land, settling on one or two likely little rises where the monument might go. Francine's spirit seemed all about us that afternoon, or perhaps it was just because I'd been reading her poetry. It would be nice if she were reburied out here in the open, rather than in that dank little closed-in churchyard. I imagined picnics and poetry readings under the oak trees. With bowls of food left on the grave to feed her starved soul.

* * *

Late in the afternoon we returned to the village and decided to have tea in Francine's sister-in-law's tea shop. It had occurred to me that perhaps it had been Jane Fitzwater crying at Francine's grave last night.

The Cozy Cup Tea Shop was packed with journalists, however, and one look at Jane was enough to convince me that it had not been she in the dowdy coat and Wellingtons. Jane, a bit younger than her brother, was less craggy but still imposing, with bleached blond hair and a strong jaw that gave her the look of a female impersonator. Her dress was royal blue and so was her eye shadow, coordinated, no doubt, for the cameras.

She barely gave Andrea and me a second glance when we entered, but consigned us to an out-of-the-way table and a waitress who looked to be only about twelve and who brought us very weak tea, stale scones, and whipped cream instead of clotted cream.

"*Whipped* cream?" said Andrea severely to the little waitress, who hunched her shoulders and scurried away.

Jane Fitzwater had seated herself at a table of journalists and was holding forth in quite loud tones on the absolutely undeserved amount of publicity that Francine had gotten through her death. "I say, if you're unhappy, take a course in weaving or a holiday abroad. Don't stew in your own self-pity. And I tried to tell Francine that. All marriages go through difficult times, but Peter would have come back to her eventually. Men will be men. Instead she had to hide away in that little flat of hers and stop eating. Oh, I tried to talk to her, I even brought her a casserole one day—I could see she'd gotten thinner—but it never occurred to me, I'm sure it never occurred to Peter, that she was deliberately trying to starve herself to death. And then he gets all the blame. It's made a broken man of him, you know. Never recovered from the shock of it, he hasn't. Ruined his career, his life. She should have thought of that when she did it, but no, always thinking of herself, that's how she was right from the beginning, my mum and dad noticed it right off. 'Seems a little full of herself,' my dad said the first time Peter brought her to Dorset. 'Talks too much.' My mum felt sorry for her, of course. Francine didn't have a clue about life, really, her head was in the clouds. 'It will end in tears,' my mum said. And she was right."

"I've got to get out of here," Andrea muttered to me. "Or it will end in something redder than tears."

We left the tea shop and strolled through the village, which was scattered with posh cars and vans emblazoned with the logos of television stations, native and foreign. Peter Putter was over in the churchyard giving an interview to what appeared to be a German film crew.

"It's enough to make one lose one's appetite entirely," Andrea said and slammed the door to her little cottage.

* * *

That night I was awakened from a deep sleep by the sound of a car driving down the road to the village. Normally it would not have been anything to wake up to, but I had a sudden odd feeling that it was my car. I staggered over to the little garret window, but saw nothing. I crept down the steep stairs and peeked into Andrea's room.

She was not there.

I went out the back door and saw that my little Ford was gone.

Since Andrea didn't have a car, I supposed she'd taken mine. Perhaps she'd decided to visit the farm by herself to stake out the gravediggers; perhaps she'd heard someone else's car driving down the road and decided to follow it. Whatever my suppositions, my actions were limited. The farm was a good four miles away, it was raining, and—I finally looked at the clock— four in the morning. I got dressed just to keep warm and paced around a bit, then remembered that Andrea had a bicycle out in the shed behind the cottage. With the feeling that there was nothing else to do, I steeled myself for cold and rain and set off into the dark night.

With water streaming down my face, I pedaled furiously, wondering why roads that always seemed to be perfectly flat when you drove over them by car suddenly developed hills and valleys when you were traveling by bicycle. Still the cold rain gave me an incentive for speed, and I arrived at the farm in record time. There were no cars at the side road leading to the farmhouse, so I got off the bike and began to reconnoiter on foot around the hedges. There must be another road leading to the farm, but I would waste more time looking for it than going on foot.

By this time my clothes were soaked and my boots caked with mud. I tried to retrace the steps Andrea and I had taken the day before, but in the darkness it was hard to see the difference between land and sky, much less between a rise and a fall in the earth. Then, through the hedges, I saw a small light. I broke through and started staggering over the land toward it. It was joined by another small light.

The lights seemed to be dancing together, or were they struggling? One of the lights vanished. I began to hear voices. Had Andrea discovered the perpetrators; was she fighting with them?

But then I heard a voice I thought I recognized. "Put those bones down! I'll have you in court for this. Grave robbing is a criminal offense as well as a sin!"

"What you did to Francine is a sin and a crime," another even more familiar voice shot back. "Give me back my shovel. She deserves to have a better resting place than the one you gave her."

"I was her husband, I have a right to decide where she's buried."

"You gave up your rights long ago."

Then there was only the sound of grunts as they grappled again.

"Peter," I said. "Andrea. Stop this. Stop this right now."

I picked up one of the flashlights and shone it at each of their faces in turn. "What's going on here?"

"I suspected her from the beginning," said Peter, looking like a large wet muskrat in his brown oilskin jacket. "I've been keeping an eye on her. Lives right across from the churchyard; easy enough to break into the grave. Tonight I heard the car starting up and decided to follow her. Called the journalists first, they'll be here in a minute. You'll go to jail for this, Addlepoot!"

"Oh, Cassandra," groaned Andrea. "I'm sorry. I had it planned so differently."

But she didn't have time to exonerate herself. The journalists were suddenly on us like a pack of hounds; there were bright lights everywhere, illuminating a stone marker that said, FRANCINE CROFTS, POET, and a muddy sheet piled, haphazardly, with thin white bones.

Some weeks after this, when I was back in London, Andrea came up to see me. If it hadn't been for the surprising intercession of Mrs. Putter, Peter's mother (for she had been the woman we'd seen crying at the grave), Andrea would have been on trial now. As it was, Francine's bones were back in the churchyard of St. Stephen's and Andrea had closed up her cottage and was thinking of moving back to London.

"I didn't have completely ignoble motives," she said. "I always did believe that Francine deserved better than a Putterized headstone or no headstone in a grim little grave under the eye of people who had hated her. But I have to admit that I saw an opportunity. When the blue plaques started to appear I thought, why not? Someone's bound to do it, why not me? I wouldn't say I was the one who'd done it, of course. I'd steal the bones, rebury them, erect a marker and then—with you as a witness—I'd discover the new site, and let the media know. It would have been the best kind of publicity, for me *and* for Francine. I would have solved a mystery, my name would have been back in the news, my publisher might have decided to reissue my books . . . but instead . . ."

"Instead the newspapers called you a grave robber and filled the pages of the tabloids with photos that made you look like a refugee from *Nightmare on Elm Street.* And they spelled your name wrong."

Andrea shuddered. "I'm going to have to put all this behind me. Start over. Science fiction, perhaps. Or why not feminist horror? Skeletons that walk in the night, the ghosts of Mary Wollstonecraft and Emily Brontë that haunt us still today . . ."

"I did read in the newspaper today," I interrupted, "that the owner of the farm has decided to put up a marker to Francine himself, and to open the farm up to readings and poetry workshops. Apparently he's something of an artist himself, in addition to being a stockbroker. He said he never knew that Francine had lived there. So something good came of it."

Andrea cheered up. "And Putter didn't look so terribly fabulous in those photographs either."

We started to laugh, embarrassed at first, and then with gasping and teary amusement, recalling our wet night in the mud.

And then we went out for a walk to look at some of the blue plaques that had gone up recently. For, you see, the remembering and honoring hadn't stopped. There were now more blue plaques to women than ever.

One of the fastest rising stars of mystery fiction, **SUSAN DUNLAP** has created three memorable detectives—Berkeley-based Jill Smith, in novels like *Diamond in the Buff;* PI Kiernan O'Shaughnessy, who works out of San Diego in books like *Rogue Wave;* and the only meter reader sleuth in history, Vejay Haskell, in the wonderfully named (and wonderful) *The Last Annual Slugfest.* Ms. Dunlap makes her home in Albany, California.

DEATH AND DIAMONDS

Susan Dunlap

 "The thing I like most about being a private investigator is the thrill of the game. I trained in gymnastics as a kid. I love cases with lots of action. But, alas, you can't always have what you love." Kiernan O'Shaughnessy glanced down at her thickly bandaged foot and the crutches propped beside it.

"Kicked a little too much ass, huh?" The man in the seat beside her at the Southwest Airlines gate grinned. There was an impish quality to him. Average height, sleekly muscled, with the too-dark tan of one who doesn't worry about the future. He was over forty but the lines around his bright green eyes and mouth suggested quick scowls, sudden bursts of laughter, rather than the folds of age setting in. Amid the San Diegans in shorts and T-shirts proclaiming the Zoo, Tijuana, and the Chargers, he seemed almost formal in his chinos and sports jacket and the forest green polo shirt. He crossed, then recrossed his long legs and glanced impatiently at the purser standing guard at the end of the ramp.

The gate 10 waiting area was jammed with tanned families ready to fly from sunny San Diego to sunnier Phoenix. The rumble of conversations was broken by children's shrill whines and exasperated parents barking their names in warning.

"We are now boarding all passengers for Southwest Airlines flight twelve forty-four to Oakland, through gate nine."

A mob of the Oakland-bound crowded closer to their gate, clutching their blue plastic boarding passes.

Beside Kiernan the man sighed. But there was a twinkle in his eyes. "Lucky them. I hate waiting around like this. It's not something I'm good at. One of the reasons I like flying Southwest is their open seating. If you move fast you can get whatever seat you want."

"Which seat is your favorite?"

"One-B or one-C. So I can get off fast. *If* they ever let us *on.*"

The Phoenix-bound flight was half an hour late. With each announcement of a Southwest departure to some other destination, the level of grumbling in the Phoenix-bound area had grown till the air seemed thick with frustration, and at the same time old and overused, as if it had held just enough oxygen for the scheduled waiting period, and now, half an hour later, served only to dry out noses and to make throats raspy and tempers short.

The loudspeaker announced the Albuquerque flight was ready for boarding. A woman in a rhinestone-encrusted denim jacket raced past them toward the Albuquerque gate. Rhinestones. Hardly diamonds, but close enough to bring the picture of Melissa Jessup to Kiernan's mind. When she'd last seen her, Melissa Jessup had been dead six months, beaten and stabbed, her corpse left outside to decompose. Gone were her mother's diamonds, the diamonds her mother had left her as security. Melissa hadn't been able to bring herself to sell them, even to finance her escape from a life turned fearful and the man who preferred them to her. It all proved, as Kiernan reminded herself each time the memory of Melissa invaded her thoughts, that diamonds are *not* a girl's best friend, that Mother (or at least a mother who says "don't sell them") does *not* know best, and that a woman should never get involved with a man she works with. Melissa Jessup had done all those things. Her lover had followed her, killed her, taken her mother's diamonds, and left not one piece of evidence. Melissa's brother had hired Kiernan, hoping that with her background in forensic pathology she would find some clue in the autopsy report, or that once she could view Melissa's body she would spot something the local medical examiner had missed. She hadn't. The key that would nail Melissa's killer was not in her corpse, but with the diamonds. Finding those diamonds and the killer with them had turned into the most frustrating case of Kiernan's career.

She pushed the picture of Melissa Jessup out of her mind. This was no time for anger or any of the emotions that the thought of Melissa's death brought up. The issue now was getting this suitcase into the right hands in

Phoenix. Turning back to the man beside her, she said "The job I'm on right now is baby-sitting this suitcase from San Diego to Phoenix. This trip is not going to be 'a kick.' "

"Couldn't you have waited till you were off the crutches?" he said, looking down at her bandaged right foot.

"Crime doesn't wait." She smiled, focusing her full attention on the conversation now. "Besides, courier work is perfect for a hobbled lady, don't you think, Mr.—uh?"

He glanced down at the plain black suitcase, then back at her. "Detecting all the time, huh?" There was a definite twinkle in his eyes as he laughed. "Well, this one's easy. Getting my name is not going to prove whether you're any good as a detective. I'm Jeff Siebert. And you are?"

"Kiernan O'Shaughnessy. But I can't let that challenge pass. Anyone can get a name. A professional investigator can do better than that. For a start, I surmise you're single."

He laughed, the delighted laugh of the little boy who's just beaten his parent in rummy. "No wedding ring, no white line on my finger to show I've taken the ring off. Right?"

"Admittedly, that was one factor. But you're wearing a red belt. Since it's nowhere near Christmas, I assume the combination of red belt and green turtleneck is not intentional. You're color-blind."

"Well, yeah," he said buttoning his jacket over the offending belt. "But they don't ask you to tell red from green before they'll give you a marriage license. So?"

"If you were married, your wife might not check you over before you left each morning, but chances are she would organize your accessories so you could get dressed by yourself, and not have strange women like me commenting on your belt."

"This is the final call for boarding Southwest Airlines flight twelve forty-four to Oakland at gate nine."

Kiernan glanced enviously at the last three Oakland-bound passengers as they passed through gate 9. If the Phoenix flight were not so late, she would be in the air now and that much closer to getting the suitcase in the right hands. Turning back to Siebert, she said, "By the same token, I'd guess you have been married or involved with a woman about my size. A blonde."

He sat back down in his seat, and for the first time was still.

"Got your attention, huh?" Kiernan laughed. "I really shouldn't show off like that. It unnerves some people. Others, like you, it just quiets down. Actually, this was pretty easy. You've got a tiny spot of lavender eyeshadow on the edge of your lapel. I had a boyfriend your height and he ended up sending a number of jackets to the cleaners. But no one but me would think to look at the edge of your lapel, and you could have that jacket for years and not notice that."

"But why did you say a blonde?"

"Blondes tend to wear violet eyeshadow."

He smiled, clearly relieved.

"Flight seventeen sixty-seven departing gate ten with service to Phoenix will begin boarding in just a few minutes. We thank you for your patience."

He groaned. "We'll see how few those minutes are." Across from them a woman with an elephantine carry-on bag pulled it closer to her. Siebert turned to Kiernan, and giving her that intimate grin she was beginning to think of as *his look,* Siebert said, "You seem to be having a good time being a detective."

The picture of Melissa Jessup popped up in her mind. Melissa Jessup had let herself be attracted to a thief. She'd ignored her suspicions about him until it was too late to sell her mother's jewels and she could only grab what was at hand and run.

Pulling her suitcase closer, Kiernan said, "Investigating can be a lot of fun if you like strange hours and the thrill of having everything hang on one maneuver. I'll tell you the truth—it appeals to the adolescent in me, particularly if I can pretend to be something or someone else. It's fun to see if I can pull that off."

"How do I know you're not someone else?"

"I could show you ID, but, of course, that wouldn't prove anything." She laughed. "You'll just have to trust me, as I am you. After all, *you* did choose to sit down next to me."

"Well, that's because you were the best-looking woman here sitting by herself."

"Or at least the one nearest the hallway where you came in. And this is the only spot around where you have room to pace. You look to be a serious pacer." She laughed again. "But I like your explanation better."

Shrieking, a small girl in yellow raced in front of the seats. Whooping gleefully, a slightly larger male version sprinted by. He lunged for his sister, caught his foot on Kiernan's crutch and sent it toppling back as he lurched forward, and crashed into a man at the end of the check-in line. His sister skidded to a stop. "Serves you right, Jason. Mom, look what Jason did!"

Siebert bent over and righted Kiernan's crutch. "Travel can be dangerous, huh?"

"Damn crutches! It's like they've got urges all their own," she said. "Like one of them sees an attractive crutch across the room and all of a sudden it's gone. They virtually seduce underage boys."

He laughed, his green eyes twinkling impishly. "They'll come home to you. There's not a crutch in the room that holds a *crutch* to you."

She hesitated a moment before saying, "My crutches and I thank you." This was, she thought, the kind of chatter that had been wonderfully seductive when she was nineteen. And Jeff Siebert was the restless, impulsive type of man who had personified freedom then. But nearly twenty years of mistakes—her own and more deadly ones like Melissa Jessup's—had shown her the inevitable end of such flirtations.

Siebert stood up and rested a foot against the edge of the table. "So what else is fun about investigating?"

She shifted the suitcase between her feet. "Well, trying to figure out people, like I was doing with you. A lot is common sense, like assuming that you are probably not a patient driver. Perhaps you've passed in a no-passing zone, or even have gotten a speeding ticket."

He nodded, abruptly.

"On the other hand," she went on, "sometimes I know facts beforehand, and then I can fake a Sherlock Holmes and produce anything-but-elementary deductions. The danger with that is getting cocky and blurting out conclusions before you've been given evidence for them."

"Has that happened to you?"

She laughed and looked meaningfully down at her foot. "But I wouldn't want my client to come to that conclusion. We had a long discussion about whether a woman on crutches could handle his delivery."

"Client?" he said, shouting over the announcement of the Yuma flight at the next gate. In a normal voice, he added, "In your courier work, you mean? What's in that bag of your client's that so very valuable?"

She moved her feet till they were touching the sides of the suitcase. He leaned in closer. He was definitely the type of man destined to be trouble, she thought, but that little-boy grin, that conspiratorial tone, were seductive, particularly in a place like this where any diversion was a boon. She wasn't surprised he had been attracted to her; clearly, he was a man who liked small women. She glanced around, pleased that no one else had been drawn to this spot. The nearest travelers were a young couple seated six feet away and too involved in each other to waste time listening to strangers' conversation. "I didn't pack the bag. I'm just delivering it."

He bent down with his ear near the side of the suitcase. "Well, at least it's not ticking." Sitting up, he said, "But seriously, isn't that a little dangerous? Women carrying bags for strangers, that's how terrorists have gotten bombs on planes."

"No!" she snapped. "I'm not carrying it for a lover with an M-1. I'm a bonded courier."

The casual observer might not have noticed Siebert's shoulders tensing, slightly, briefly, in anger at her rebuff. Silently, he looked down at her suitcase. "How much does courier work pay?"

"Not a whole lot, particularly compared to the value of what I have to carry. But then there's not much work involved. The chances of theft are minuscule. And I do get to travel. Last fall I drove a package up north. That was a good deal since I had to go up there anyway to check motel registrations in a case I'm working on. It took me a week to do the motels, and then I came up empty." An entire week to discover that Melissa's killer had not stopped at a motel or hotel between San Diego and Eureka. "The whole thing would have been a bust if it hadn't been for the courier work."

He glanced down at the suitcase. She suspected he would have been appalled to know how visible was his covetous look. Finally he said, "What was in that package, the one you delivered?"

She glanced over at the young couple. No danger from them. Still Kiernan lowered her voice. "Diamonds. Untraceable. That's really the only reason to go to the expense of hiring a courier."

"Untraceable, huh?" he said, grinning. "Didn't you even consider taking off over the border with them?"

"Maybe," she said slowly, "if I had known they were worth enough to set me up for the rest of my actuarial allotment, I might have."

"We will begin preboarding Southwest Airlines flight seventeen sixty-seven with service to Phoenix momentarily. Please keep your seats until preboarding has been completed."

She pushed herself up and positioned the crutches under her arms. It was a moment before he jerked his gaze away from the suitcase and stood, his foot tapping impatiently on the carpet. All around them families were hoisting luggage and positioning toddlers for the charge to the gate. He sighed loudly. "I hope you're good with your elbows."

She laughed and settled back on the arm of the seat.

His gaze went back to the suitcase. He said, "I thought couriers were handcuffed to their packages."

"You've been watching too much TV." She lowered her voice. "Handcuffs play havoc with the metal detector. The last thing you want in this business is buzzers going off and guards racing in from all directions. I go for the low-key approach. Always keep the suitcase in sight. Always be within lunging range."

He took a playful swipe at it. "What would happen if, say, that bag were to get stolen?"

"Stolen!" She pulled the suitcase closer to her. "Well, for starters, I wouldn't get a repeat job. If the goods were insured, that might be the end of it. But if it were something untraceable"—she glanced at the suitcase—"it could be a lot worse." With a grin that matched his own, she said, "You're not a thief, are you?"

He shrugged. "Do I look like a thief?"

"You look like the most attractive man here." She paused long enough to catch his eye. "Of course, looks can be deceiving." She didn't say it, but she could picture him pocketing a necklace carelessly left in a jewelry box during a big party, or a Seiko watch from under a poolside towel. She didn't imagine him planning a heist, but just taking what came his way.

Returning her smile, he said, "When you transport something that can't be traced, don't they even provide you a backup?"

"No! I'm a professional. I don't need backup."

"But with your foot like that?"

"I'm good with the crutches. And besides, the crutches provide camouflage. Who'd think a woman on crutches carrying a battered suitcase had anything worth half a mi—Watch out! The little girl and her brother are loose again." She pulled her crutches closer as the duo raced through the aisle in front of them.

"We are ready to begin boarding Southwest Airlines flight number seventeen sixty-seven to Phoenix. Any passengers traveling with small children or those needing a little extra time may begin boarding now."

The passengers applauded. It was amazing, she thought, how much sarcasm could be carried by a nonverbal sound.

She leaned down for the suitcase. "Preboarding. That's me."

"Are you going to be able to handle the crutches and the suitcase?" he asked.

"You're really fascinated with this bag, aren't you?"

"Guilty." He grinned. "Should I dare to offer to carry it? I'd stay within lunging range."

She hesitated.

In the aisle a woman in cerise shorts, carrying twin bags, herded twin toddlers toward the gate. Ahead of her an elderly man leaned precariously on a cane. The family with the boy and girl were still assembling luggage.

He said, "You'd be doing me a big favor letting me preboard with you. I like to cadge a seat in the first row on the aisle."

"The seat for the guy who can't wait?"

"Right. But I got here so late that I'm in the last boarding group. I'm never going to snag one-B or one-C. So help me out. I promise," he said, grinning, "I won't steal."

"Well . . . I wouldn't want my employer to see this. I assured him I wouldn't need any help. But . . ." She shrugged.

"No time to waver now. There's already a mob of preboarders ahead of us." He picked up the bag. "Some heavy diamonds."

"Good camouflage, don't you think? Of course, not everything's diamonds."

"Just something untraceable?"

She gave him a half wink. "It may not be untraceable. It may not even be valuable."

"And you may be just a regular mail carrier," he said, starting toward the gate.

She swung after him. The crutches were no problem, and the thickly taped right ankle looked worse than it was. Still, it made things much smoother to have Siebert carrying the suitcase. If the opportunity arose, he might be tempted to steal it, but not in a crowded gate at the airport with guards and airline personnel around. He moved slowly, staying right in front of her, running interference. As they neared the gate, a blond man carrying a jumpy toddler hurried in front of them. The gate phone buzzed. The airline rep picked it up and nodded at it. To the blond man and the elderly couple who had settled in behind him, Kiernan, and Siebert, he said, "Sorry, folks. The cleaning crew's a little slow. It'll just be a minute."

Siebert's face scrunched in anger. "What's 'cleaning crew' a euphemism for? A tire fell off and they're looking for it? They've spotted a crack in the engine block and they're trying to figure out if they can avoid telling us?"

Kiernan laughed. "I'll bet people don't travel with you twice."

He laughed. "I just hate being at someone else's mercy. But since we're going to be standing here awhile, why don't you do what you love more than diamonds, Investigator: tell me what you've deduced about me."

"Like reading your palm?" The crutches poked into her armpits; she shifted them back, putting more weight on her bandaged foot. Slowly she surveyed his lanky body, his thin agile hands, con man's hands, hands that were never quite still, always past *ready*, coming out of *set*. "Okay. You're traveling from San Diego to Phoenix on the Friday evening flight, so chances are you were here on business. But you don't have on cowboy boots, or a Stetson. You're tan, but it's not that dry tan you get in the desert. In fact, you could pass for a San Diegan. I would have guessed that you travel for a living, but you're too impatient for that, and if you'd taken this flight once or twice before you wouldn't be surprised that it's late. You'd have a report to read, or a newspaper. No, you do something where you don't take orders, and you don't put up with much." She grinned. "How's that?"

"That's pretty elementary, Sherlock," he said with only a slight edge to his voice. He tapped his fingers against his leg. But all in all he looked only a little warier than any other person in the waiting area would as his secrets were unveiled.

"*Southwest Airlines flight number seventeen sixty-seven with service to Phoenix is now ready for preboarding.*"

"Okay, folks," the gate attendant called. "Sorry for the delay."

The man with the jittery toddler thrust his boarding pass at the gate attendant and strode down the ramp. The child screamed. The elderly couple moved haltingly, hoisting and readjusting their open sacks with each step. A family squeezed in in front of them, causing the old man to stop dead and move his bag to the other shoulder. Siebert shifted from foot to foot.

Stretching up to whisper in his ear, Kiernan said, "It would look bad if you shoved the old people out of your way."

"How bad?" he muttered, grinning, then handed his boarding pass to the attendant.

As she surrendered hers, she said to Siebert, "Go ahead, hurry. I'll meet you in one-C and D."

"Thanks." He patted her shoulder.

She watched him stride down the empty ramp. His tan jacket had caught on one hip as he balanced her suitcase and his own. But he neither slowed his pace nor made an attempt to free the jacket; clutching tight to her suitcase, he hurried around the elderly couple, moving with the strong stride of a hiker. By the time she got down the ramp the elderly couple and a family with two toddlers and an infant that sucked loudly on a pacifier crowded behind Siebert.

Kiernan watched irritably as the stewardess eyed first Siebert, then her big suitcase. The head stewardess has the final word on carry-on luggage, she knew. With all the hassle that was involved with this business anyway, she didn't want to add a confrontation with the stewardess. She dropped the crutches and banged backward into the wall, flailing for purchase as she slipped down to the floor. The stewardess caught her before she hit bottom. "Are you okay?"

"Embarrassed," Kiernan said, truthfully. She hated to look clumsy, even if it was an act, even if it allowed Siebert and her suitcase to get on the plane unquestioned. "I'm having an awful time getting used to these things."

"You sure you're okay? Let me help you up." The stewardess said. "I'll have to keep your crutches in the hanging luggage compartment up front while we're in flight. But you go ahead now; I'll come and get them from you."

"That's okay. I'll leave them there and just sit in one of the front seats," she said, taking the crutches and swinging herself on board the plane. From the luggage compartment it took only one long step on her left foot to get to row 1. She swung around Siebert, who was hoisting his own suitcase into the overhead bin beside hers, and dropped into seat 1-D, by the window. The elderly couple was settling into seats 1-A and 1-B. In another minute Southwest would call the first thirty passengers, and the herd would stampede down the ramp, stuffing approved carry-ons in overhead compartments and grabbing the thirty most prized seats.

"That was a smooth move with the stewardess," Siebert said, as he settled into his coveted aisle seat.

"That suitcase is just about the limit of what they'll let you carry on. I've had a few hassles. I could see this one coming. And I suspected that you"— she patted his arm—"were not the patient person to deal with that type of problem. You moved around her pretty smartly yourself. I'd say that merits a drink from my client."

He smiled and rested a hand on hers. "Maybe," he said, leaning closer, "we could have it in Phoenix."

For the first time she had a viscerally queasy feeling about him. Freeing her hand from his, she gave a mock salute. "Maybe so." She looked past him at the elderly couple.

Siebert's gaze followed hers. He grinned as he said, "Do you think they're thieves? After your loot? Little old sprinters?"

"Probably not. But it pays to be alert." She forced a laugh. "I'm afraid constant suspicion is a side effect of my job."

The first wave of passengers hurried past. Already the air in the plane had the sere feel and slightly rancid smell of having been dragged through the filters too many times. By tacit consent they watched the passengers hurry on board, pause, survey their options, and rush on. Kiernan thought fondly of that drink in Phoenix. She would be sitting at a small table, looking out a tinted window; the trip would be over, the case delivered into the proper hands; and she would feel the tension that knotted her back releasing with each swallow of scotch. Or so she hoped. The whole frustrating case depended on this delivery. There was no fallback position. If she screwed up, Melissa Jessup's murderer disappeared.

That tension was what normally made the game fun. But this case was no longer a game. This time she had allowed herself to go beyond her regular rules, to call her former colleagues from the days when she had been a forensic pathologist, looking for some new test that would prove culpability. She had hoped the lab in San Diego could find something. They hadn't. The fact was that the diamonds were the only "something" that would trap the killer, Melissa's lover, who valued them much more than her, a man who might not have bothered going after her had it not been for them. Affairs might be brief, but diamonds, after all, are forever. They would lead her to the murderer's safe house, and the evidence that would tie him to Melissa. *If* she was careful.

She shoved the tongue of the seat belt into the latch and braced her feet as the plane taxied toward the runway. Siebert was tapping his finger on the armrest. The engines whirred, the plane shifted forward momentarily, then flung them back against their seats as it raced down the short runway.

The FASTEN SEAT BELT sign went off. The old man across the aisle pushed himself up and edged toward the front bathroom. Siebert's belt was already unbuckled. Muttering, "Be right back," he jumped up and stood hunched under the overhead bin while the old man cleared the aisle. Then Siebert headed full-out toward the back of the plane. Kiernan slid over and watched him as he strode down the aisle, steps firmer, steadier than she'd have expected of a man racing to the bathroom in a swaying airplane. She could easily imagine him hiking in the redwood forest with someone like her, a small, slight woman. The blond woman with the violet eyeshadow. She in jeans and one of those soft Patagonia jackets Kiernan had spotted in the L.L. Bean catalog, violet with blue trim. He in jeans, turtleneck, a forest green down jacket on his rangy body. Forest green would pick up the color of his eyes and accent his dark, curly hair. In her picture, his hair was tinted with the first flecks of autumn snow and the ground still soft like the spongy airplane carpeting beneath his feet.

When he got back he made no mention of his hurried trip. He'd barely settled down when the stewardess leaned over him and said, "Would you care for something to drink?"

Kiernan put a hand on his arm. "This one's on my client."

"For that client who insisted you carry his package while you're still on crutches? I'm sorry it can't be Lafite-Rothschild. Gin and tonic will have to do." He grinned at the stewardess. Kiernan could picture him in a bar, flashing that grin at a tall redhead, or maybe another small blonde. She could imagine him with the sweat of a San Diego summer still on his brow, his skin brown from too many days at an ocean beach that is too great a temptation for those who grab their pleasures.

"Scotch and water," Kiernan ordered. To him, she said, "I notice that while I'm the investigator, it's you who are asking all the questions. So what about you, what do you do for a living?"

"I quit my job in San Diego and I'm moving back to Phoenix. So I'm not taking the first Friday night flight to get back home, I'm taking it to get to my new home. I had good times in San Diego: the beach, the sailing, Balboa Park. When I came there a couple years ago I thought I'd stay forever. But the draw of the desert is too great. I miss the red rock of Sedona, the pines of the Mogollon Rim, and the high desert outside Tucson." He laughed. "Too much soft California life."

It was easy to picture him outside of Show Low on the Mogollon Rim with the pine trees all around him, some chopped for firewood, the ax lying on a stump, a shovel in his hand. Or in a cabin near Sedona lifting a hatch in the floorboards.

The stewardess brought the drinks and the little bags of peanuts, giving Jeff Siebert the kind of smile Kiernan knew would have driven her crazy had she been Siebert's girlfriend. How often had that type of thing happened? Had his charm brought that reaction so automatically that for him it had seemed merely the way women behave? Had complaints from a girlfriend seemed at first unreasonable, then melodramatic, then infuriating? He was an impatient man, quick to anger. Had liquor made it quicker, as the rhyme said? And the prospect of unsplit profit salved his conscience?

He poured the little bottle of gin over the ice and added tonic. "Cheers."

She touched glasses, then drank. "Are you going to be in Phoenix long?"

"Probably not. I've come into a little money and I figure I'll just travel around, sort of like you do. Find someplace I like."

"So we'll just have time for our drink in town then?"

He rested his hand back on hers. "Well, now I may have reason to come back in a while. Or to San Diego. I just need to cut loose for a while."

She forced herself to remain still, not to cringe at his touch. *Cut loose*— what an apt term for him to use. She pictured his sun-browned hand wrapped around the hilt of a chef's knife, working it up and down, up and down, cutting across pink flesh till it no longer looked like flesh, till the flesh mixed with the blood and the organ tissue, till the knife cut down to the bone and the metal point stuck in the breastbone. She pictured Melissa Jessup's blond hair pink from the blood.

She didn't have to picture her body lying out in the woods outside Eureka in northern California. She had seen photos of it. She didn't have to imagine what the cracked ribs and broken clavicle and the sternum marked from the knife point looked like now. Jeff Siebert had seen that too, and had denied what Melissa's brother and the Eureka sheriff all knew—knew in their hearts but could not prove—that Melissa had not gone to Eureka camping by herself as he'd insisted, but had only stopped overnight at the campground she and Jeff had been to the previous summer because she had no money and hadn't been able to bring herself to sell the diamonds her mother had left her. Instead of a rest on the way to freedom, she'd found Siebert there.

Now Siebert was flying to Phoenix to vanish. He'd pick up Melissa's diamonds wherever he'd stashed them, and he'd be gone.

"What about your client?" he asked. "Will he be meeting you at the airport?"

"No. No one will meet me. I'll just deliver my goods to the van, collect my money, and be free. What about you?"

"No. No one's waiting for me either. At least I'll be able to give you a hand with that bag. There's no ramp to the terminal in Phoenix. You have to climb down to the tarmac there. Getting down those metal steps with a suitcase and two crutches would be a real balancing act."

All she had to do was get it into the right hands. She shook her head. "Thanks. But I'll have to lug it through the airport just in case. My client didn't handcuff the suitcase to me, but he does expect I'll keep hold of it."

He grinned. "Like you said, you'll be in lunging range all the time."

"No," she said firmly. "I appreciate your offer, Jeff; the bag weighs a ton. But I'm afraid it's got to be in my hand."

Those green eyes of his that had twinkled with laughter narrowed, and his lips pressed together. "Okay," he said slowly. Then his face relaxed almost back to that seductively impish smile that once might have charmed her, as it had Melissa Jessup. "I want you to know that I'll still find you attractive even if the bag yanks your shoulder out of its socket." He gave her hand a pat, then shifted in his seat so his upper arm rested next to hers.

The stewardess collected the glasses. The plane jolted and began its descent. Kiernan braced her feet. Through his jacket, she felt the heat of his arm, the arm that had dug that chef's knife into Melissa Jessup's body. She breathed slowly and did not move.

To Kiernan he said, "There's a great bar right here in Sky Harbor Airport, the Sky Lounge. Shall we have our drink there?"

She nodded, her mouth suddenly too dry for speech.

The plane bumped down, and in a moment the aisles were jammed with passengers ignoring the stewardess's entreaty to stay in their seats. Siebert stood up and pulled his bag out of the overhead compartment and then lifted hers onto his empty seat. "I'll get your crutches," he said, as the elderly man across the aisle pushed his way out in front of him. Siebert shook his head. Picking up both suitcases, he maneuvered around the man and around the corner to the luggage compartment.

Siebert had taken her suitcase. *You don't need to take both suitcases to pick up the crutches.* Kiernan stared after him, her shoulders tensing, her hands clutching the armrests. Her throat was so constricted she could barely breathe. For an instant she shared the terror that must have paralyzed Melissa Jessup just before he stabbed her.

"Jeff!" she called after him, a trace of panic evident in her voice. He didn't answer her. Instead, she heard a great thump, then him muttering and the stewardess's voice placating.

The airplane door opened. The elderly man moved out into the aisle in front of Kiernan, motioning his wife to go ahead of him, then they moved slowly toward the door.

Kiernan yanked the bandage off her foot, stepped into the aisle. "Excuse me," she said to the couple. Pushing by them as Siebert had so wanted to do, she rounded the corner to the exit.

The stewardess was lifting up a garment bag. Four more bags lay on the floor. So that was the thump she'd heard. A crutch was beside them.

She half heard the stewardess's entreaties to wait, her mutterings about the clumsy man. She looked out the door down onto the tarmac.

Jeffrey Siebert and the suitcase were gone. In those few seconds he had raced down the metal steps and was disappearing into the terminal. By the time she could make it to the Sky Lounge he would be halfway to Show Low, or Sedona.

Now she felt a different type of panic. *This* wasn't in the plan. She couldn't lose Siebert. She jumped over the bags, grabbed one crutch, hurried outside to the top of the stairs, and thrust the crutch across the hand rails behind her to make a seat. As the crutch slid down the railings, she kept her knees bent high into her chest to keep from landing and bucking forward onto her head. Instead the momentum propelled her on her feet, as it had in gymnastics. In those routines, she'd had to fight the momentum; now she went with it and ran, full-out.

She ran through the corridor toward the main building, pushing past businessmen, between parents carrying children. Siebert would be running ahead. But no one would stop him, not in an airport. People run through airports all the time. Beside the metal detectors she saw a man in a tan jacket. Not him. By the luggage pickup another look-alike. She didn't spot him till he was racing out the door to the parking lot.

Siebert ran across the roadway. A van screeched to a halt. Before Kiernan could cross through the traffic, a hotel bus eased in front of her. She skirted behind it. She could sense a man following her now. But there was no time to deal with that. Siebert was halfway down the lane of cars. Bent low, she ran down the next lane, the hot dusty desert air drying her throat.

By the time she came abreast of Siebert, he was in a light blue Chevy pickup backing out of the parking slot. He hit the gas, and, wheels squealing, drove off.

She reached toward the truck with both arms. Siebert didn't stop. She stood watching as Jeffrey Siebert drove off into the sunset.

There was no one behind her as she sauntered into the terminal to the Sky Lounge. She ordered the two drinks Siebert had suggested, and when they came, she tapped "her" glass on "his" and took a drink for Melissa Jessup. Then she swallowed the rest of the drink in two gulps.

By this time Jeff Siebert would be on the freeway. He'd be fighting to stay close to the speed limit, balancing his thief's wariness of the highway patrol against his gnawing urge to force the lock on the suitcase. Jeffrey Siebert was an impatient man, a man who had nevertheless made himself wait nearly a year before leaving California. His stash of self-control would be virtually empty. But he would wait awhile before daring to stop. Then he'd jam a knife between the top and bottom of the suitcase, pry and twist it till the case fell open. He would find diamonds. More diamonds. Diamonds to take along while he picked up Melissa Jessup's from the spot where he'd hidden them.

She wished Melissa Jessup could see him when he compared the two collections and realized the new ones he'd stolen were fakes. She wished she herself could see his face when he realized that a woman on crutches had made it out of the plane in time to follow him to point out the blue pickup truck.

Kiernan picked up "Jeff's" glass and drank more slowly. How sweet it would be if Melissa could see that grin of his fade as the surveillance team surrounded him, drawn by the beepers concealed in those fake diamonds. He'd be clutching the evidence that would send him to jail. Just for life, not forever. As Melissa could have told him, only death and diamonds are forever.

KILL THE MAN FOR ME

Mary Wings

"It was okay," you said after the first time we'd made love. You said it very neutrally as if you'd been talking about the weather. Or snowflakes. Or cornflakes. "It was okay."

"Nobody's ever told me that before," I joked.

You were lying next to me saying, "It's no big deal. No big deal to say, 'It's okay.' "

You leaned up on your elbow. I traced your collarbone with my eyes. You tried tracing my eyes with your eyes.

"It's our first time," you said. "We need to learn some more things about each other." Your voice was warm, instructive. Of course, you'd been in practice a long time. Or so *they* had said.

"Sure!" I crowed. "Learn some more things. Discourse about intercourse! Sex as perception," I burbled at you. "Sure!" But I also knew that you were telling me that we had a future. I laughed in the darkness. I would get what I wanted. And I would get you.

Later I would tell you that when I made love with you, the memories of former lovers abandoned all claim upon my body. I told you I was free.

We curled up together and fell asleep. The next day we would be stuck in gridlock traffic for three hours. On the way home.

I joined in the sighs of relief when you spoke at public gatherings. You'd summarize, make the contradictions manageable. We'd been anxious. You'd satisfy us. One of *them* came to a lecture once. But it wasn't a problem. You were attentive to me at these gatherings. You'd ruffle my hair. I was a portrait by your side. You'd let me know with the slightest of gestures at the end of a publicly spoken phrase that you were, in fact, only speaking to me. Of course, all you told anyone was what they wanted to hear. Pure pap.

Except this morning when you said, after we'd come out of the shower, "Don't you ever comb your hair?"

And then I remembered, that's what you used to tell *them*.

You were laughing, "What did your parents ever do to you?" You were hardly exasperated at all. And I'd spilled the garbage bag on the floor for the third time that week. I was on the floor too.

I was watching Jackson the terrier make pesto sauce paw prints the color of avocado. She was making them on the rug of desert tan. I was crying. And I was tan. We were all tan. We lived in Los Angeles.

"What did your parents ever do to you?" you repeated. But you knew better than I did what my parents had done to me. You'd been my shrink. You'd been *theirs* too.

You'd never thought about advertising. Not that I'd ever suggest it. But I'd asked Mr. Geramus, the neighbor to the north of us, for tennis doubles. Then he asked you to join the agency. I knew he would.

It was autumn and you said your soul had been searched. You said yes. But later you didn't seem too happy to me.

And the first time you did it you felt really bad. It was the loss of control. You were so devastated it was easy to want to comfort you. And eventually you let me.

Later you didn't even comment when I spent extra time at the mirror powdering my bruise.

They had bought me oil-based foundation. It's better because it doesn't run with the sweat, they told me. And always follow up with matte powder.

Then it was Christmastime and the agency had fired you right before having to give you your Christmas bonus. Your old shrink circle had laughed when you said you were going into advertising. Marketing, you'd called it. They'd envied your salary, and now they were triumphing over your unemployment.

Yes, your old shrink circle had shrunk, but we were going to one of those parties anyway.

Mrs. Watkin, the neighbor to the south of us, peered out her window as we walked down the driveway in our festive holiday attire. You always opened the door for me, and this time you had to. And we always wore our safety belts.

We floated in with a liquor delivery. If I was very quiet it was because my arm hurt. But it was one more bond between us. It was our private story about how you'd lost control and I'd given it back to you by forgiving you.

As the people floated by, faces talked about auto insurance, termites, weekend resort prices. Those subjects would latch on to other topics and become health care, roach motels, and freeway ramps. But you knew and I knew that you'd come damned close to breaking my arm last night. The throbbing and swelling of that arm filled up the whole room for me; the pain devoured hours of small talk generated by holiday anxieties and large quantities of hard liquor.

And I knew that next time I'd make enough noise, near a south window, that the neighbor would call the cops.

Patrol Officer Laura Deleuse:

The call was a 418-DV on Del Mar Drive. Domestic violence. In a neighborhood that is usually just domestic.

All assaults used to be lumped together as 418s, now we sort out the DVs. Makes it easier for the people at the university to study the statistics. These calls are never my favorites. The worst are the "hold me back" couples. When you arrive on the scene, they really go out of control. Because they know that now that *you're* there, nothing really bad is going to happen.

But, of course, this wasn't the story with these folks. We pulled up to Malibu lighting, alarm systems, and bleached oak designer fencing. Of course, the husband with the big excuse opened the door. The sobbing wife would be in the background somewhere. This would take application of social skills. I thought I'd done all that on my dinner date last night.

I explained that a neighbor phoned, complaining about noise. I asked him the usual questions: "What's happened here?" "Has there been an accident?" "Is someone hurt?" *(That* scared him.)

He mumbled some polite denials.

"Who else is at home? Where's your wife? May I see her, please?"

He invited us in, opening the door too quickly, too widely, as if to say, "What do you think this is, a torture chamber?"

What it was was a sea of chintz upholstery and a woman with a cut above her eye sinking into it. She had long hair and short legs. Her hair was pulled up in a complicated chignon (not a hair-pulling fight, apparently) and her feet were curled up underneath her. A fresh fire crackled on the grate of a marble fireplace.

I squinted my eyes, looking at that cut, but when her husband glanced at her she turned her face away. *The skin is so delicate there,* I thought, *if you get hit, your cheekbone can actually cause a tear in the skin.* I looked over at my partner Kevin. His eyes were roaming the room; there were no weapons or anything that could be construed as a weapon lying around. But these days a fist is enough to cause corporal injury and can be regarded as a weapon in court.

"What can I do for you?" she asked, and as I approached she uncurled her legs and bent over to poke at the fire, which was beginning to smolder. She fumbled with the iron, the only sign of nervousness.

She was wearing stockings without a snag or run. She kept her face averted from me, although she had given me a good enough look when I'd first come in. But other than that she didn't act like your usual humiliated upper-middle-class victim.

What a difference from the scene I'd visited last week. Basically a couple trying to tear each other to shreds. The technique of separating them and defusing the fight wouldn't be necessary here. When that couple made eye contact, it set them to spitting—spitting!—at each other.

This woman, in her stocking feet, poking at the fire, with the husband nervously shifting his weight from side to side, was a different setup altogether. But the reason I was there was that phone call, and the cut above her eye. As in all these cases, I had to get her alone.

"I'd like to ask you a few questions; could we speak privately?"

She nodded and slipped on her black pumps, which were neatly paired by the skirt of the sofa. She led me down a hallway into a phony English library setup, with leather books and leather furniture. We settled into wing chairs, but I didn't want to be too comfortable. I didn't want *her* to be too comfortable either.

"I assume there's some sort of injury here." I pointed with my pencil to the cut beneath her eye.

"You assume correctly. I fell down the stairs." Her tone was too measured, I thought; this woman was too smart not to know that that is *the* cliché. She was almost throwing it in my face.

"I've never seen an eye cut like that from a fall down stairs, ma'am. A blow to the face is usually what causes this sort of thing." I could hear irritation in my voice. "Are you sure?"

"I'm sure."

I sighed. What a waste of my time and the taxpayers' money. And the laws have changed in California too. Used to be they'd have to press charges. Hire a lawyer. Still hubby would get out the same night. Now all we have to do is get her to admit that he hit her and we can cool his heels in jail, at least overnight, until he can get before a judge. But this woman wasn't going to help herself out.

"You sure about that? If you can just confirm that he hit you—that's all you have to do—"

"He didn't."

"And the bruise on your arm?"

She looked down and moved the skin on her upper arm around to see a purple spot. She looked surprised. She hadn't noticed it. So maybe she just wasn't even feeling pain.

"Must have happened on the stairs."

"Looks a few days old."

She shrugged.

I shrugged. "That's all, I guess."

Later I thought, maybe if my social skills had been better I could have charmed the words out of her. But now I was getting hungry. Kevin and I were helping each other out with our diets. I wondered who would try and talk whom out of the late-night salad bar this time.

We stood up and walked back into the living room. She had her head tilted up high, but not with the pride of the humiliated or the pain of a broken jaw. I liked the tilt of her head and something else, some strength I couldn't place. Or maybe she was just crazy.

I watched her eyes settle upon her husband as we walked into the room, and saw how much space she chose to put between them. *She's not afraid of him,* I thought. *Maybe she did fall down the stairs.* It didn't matter anymore.

Kevin had a crush on the hamburger joint waitress with great repartee and I was dating a paramedic with awesome social skills. That's the way it was with night work. Your society becomes waitresses at all-night restaurants, nurses, lap dancers, paramedics, and criminals. Couples with Malibu lighting were the exception.

Kevin and I made our polite good-byes and went back to the car to call in and write up a report.

"My feeling is, we won't have to go back there again tonight."

"I've never seen a DV so calm after the storm."

"If everybody's so copacetic, what can you do? I'll bet that guy doesn't ever have to be up before the judge."

But what I was thinking was, I hope he doesn't cut her up into little tiny pieces either.

We settled on hamburgers and drove to a neon-lighted, late-night part of town.

They were right. Things got much easier after that. It became so simple to fuck up. I not only burned your shirts when I ironed them, I developed a cowering posture, lowering my eyes that darted only over to your shoe soles. And I knew that as things became worse for you, as the pressure started to mount, you'd beat me.

But you were dependent upon me. I was the only thing you could control in your life. Or so you thought. You had no idea how out of control you really were!

I went to several doctors, under assumed names, but I never wore sunglasses. I looked them straight in the face. And I introduced memorable topics with the receptionist at every appointment.

Of course, I had to show some kind of escalation. But I wasn't about to rent slasher films for your at-home video entertainment (besides, I was afraid the video places would have receipts). But I didn't know how to time it. It was like taking a wishbone and pulling on it, hoping that it would break in the right place. The place that would be in my favor. And that's what I wanted to do. I didn't want to get broken anymore.

But I didn't know then how easy it would be, once I'd remembered what *they'd* told me.

When I showed them the photos (probably not admissible in court, but nevertheless interesting), it was emotionally upsetting for them. To see the photos. The pictures traced bruises with bilious yellow centers that blossomed into purple and black. Or red welts, like bars across my back. It brought back memories that were not pleasant for them. And they expressed sympathy for me. They encouraged me to finish the work soon.

I knew I would get all the elements right. It was Christmas again (I'd disconnected the heater in your car) and you were worried about losing the rather menial lectureship that you had finally landed. After you arrived, with nearly frostbitten fingers (I'd hidden your gloves), I arranged for my cousin to stop by, blow marijuana smoke in your face, shout loudly at you some story about a sports victory, and slap you on the back.

We were having a dinner party (read potential job prospect) and I lied to you about the arrival time of our guests. So you were caught off guard when they came half an hour early. I managed to burn the roast anyway.

Later I made insipid comments and quite frequently had no opinion at all (although four times I managed to contradict you over matters at hand: the brand of the oven, the age of Alexander Dubček, and the cost of pouring a cement patio last summer). You bickered with me publicly until you remembered where you were and with whom. You were hating me really good by the time your no-longer-potential employer left.

Patrol Officer Laura Deleuse:

It's easier to take on a violation of a restraining order. These women don't want to be hassled and have made their demand public record. They don't cover up for someone that's causing them corporal injury.

I put personal interest in carrying out violation of restraining orders. One particular weasel was calling a woman twenty times a day at her work. Her boss had sympathy for her, but after a few months it was getting seriously in the way of business. What could he do? She was going to lose her job.

I got to know her, going over there and taking reports quite often. She had a daughter and two kittens. Two kittens! She was just trying to raise her kid, a working mom, and here was some jerk ruining her life. Hanging on her doorbell. Standing outside her window at night. And the stupid bastard had his timing down right. She'd call the station, but he never lingered more than three or four minutes after she'd noticed him. We can't make it in less than five minutes and he knew it. He was always gone before we made the scene.

So who hasn't known somebody pretty unstable, even gotten involved with them? You only really find out when you try and pull away. There's not too much you can do. Get a restraining order.

But if somebody wants to harass you, make your life miserable, if that somebody is making that his career, even with bodyguards there's not much to be done. But a restraining order is the only way to start.

That's why I really wanted to get this particular weasel. She called and said he was calling her from a pay phone. He said that he was watching her, that he could see her from where he was. In between calls she reached the dispatch unit, and I just drove up to that lighted booth, recognized him from a mug shot, threw him on the hood, cuffed him up, and case closed.

This particular woman had great documentation; that's what I tell them all. Write it down: where it happened, when, what was said, how many times he rang the doorbell, whatever. Few think to do that. First of all you don't want to believe that this person in your life has turned out to be crazy. Then you just want them to go away. It doesn't inspire you to play secretary.

So when the 418-DV at Del Mar Drive came up again, I wasn't happy. I was going to get the cold shoulder and the short stockinged legs all over again. But I didn't have any choice after the anonymous tip from the neighbor had been received.

After the first visit, such types would usually learn to keep their voices to a provocative growl. But this growl had had quite different consequences.

We walked up the Malibu-lighted path. I rang the bell. This time it wasn't the husband with the big excuse. It was the wife with a little gun.

It hung off her hand like ripe fruit. The elegant chignon had come apart, and hair was falling off her shoulders, pointing in all directions; a ratty knot was caught behind her left ear. Her stocking had been ripped; on one leg it hung nearly down to her ankle, beige cobwebs covering her foot.

She didn't turn her head to avoid my glance this time. Her face told of a pummeling that was physically painful to see. And the front of her blouse. I took the gun from her; it was easy—it just fell into my hand.

An acrid whiff of gunpowder was in the air, and we ran into the house. We ran past the chintz L-shaped sofa, past the library (a wing chair was overturned), and into the kitchen. We looked down the stairs. He was lying at the bottom.

I ran down to check his pulse, stepping around a pool of sticky blood surrounding his big back. A knife lay close by his side, a large German meat knife.

Even without a pulse (excluding gray matter, or maggot face as even the coroner calls it, and oh, yes, decapitation) we can't make a death call. Even paramedics can't pronounce a 187, death on the scene, without pretty obvious physical decomposition. This guy was going to get an ambulance like every other dead citizen.

I wondered which paramedic would be on duty tonight. Dinner dates had stopped because my social skills apparently weren't up to snuff (meaning her friends didn't like me). I didn't like to think her elitism was so compelling. The payoff was still some great compliments I'd garnered.

I went back upstairs and started cuffing our suspect. She was compliant, but I was still glad when it was over and I didn't have to sort of hold hands with her. She was talking the whole time too. "He pushed me down the stairs," she was saying. "He threatened me. I had the gun. He laughed. He said I didn't have the nerve. And he came closer and closer."

Kevin wasn't asking her any questions, and spontaneous statements are admissible in court. Didn't sound like she was incriminating herself in any event. I sat her down and recited Miranda to her anyway. Self-defense would be the case made for her, no doubt. I wondered when the court date would come up and how sleepy I'd be, having to get up in the middle of the day. I remembered the details of my first visit to Del Mar Drive. I remembered how my social skills were never up to snuff. I didn't feel good about seeing her months earlier, immune to pain, denying that anything had happened to her. So maybe this was the natural consequence, but why did I have to see it, on my beat, tonight? I could just guess which paramedic would be showing up too.

I called the supervisor on the radio; the sergeant would make notifications. The on-call homicide inspector and the on-call photographer would come, and I'd go to the hospital with her, for a quick checkup before she got booked on the sixth floor of the Hall of Justice.

After I'd shot you (it was so easy—you came after me like Attila the Hun, rattling your saber, roaring epithets), I felt so relieved. It was simple to pull that trigger. I aimed for your heart, but I think I ended up shooting you in the head. Your body actually fell on me (I'd run to the bottom of the stairs, "away from you" as I'd explain later). So there you were, staining my silk blouse with your blood and gray matter, pinning me to the floor.

I pushed you off me, keeping hold of the gun. I waited a few minutes, standing over you, looking at your back, not believing that I wouldn't have to follow your orders anymore, not believing you were actually dead, and knowing that this sort of shock response would be the most believable to the police. Later they'd take me to the hospital (I think I had a broken rib) and then to the sixth floor of the Hall of Justice (I'd done my homework; I knew just what would happen to me).

I would explain to them how the fight started in your study. I would say that I grabbed the gun there, but actually I had already gotten it that afternoon. I wasn't going to take any chances when I finally had you ready with rage.

But the story began almost a year ago, my dear. When you, the doctor, at my most vulnerable and trusting moment (I had thought I was losing my mind), had sat next to me on the couch and caressed me, talking to me about trust and transference!

Since you were my only reality check at the time, I was pretty disconcerted. I ran out of your office. After a few days I decided that my reality check deserved to be researched.

It was only later that I decided on revenge.

Public records revealed that you had been arrested once on charges of assaulting a woman you were living with; but she dropped charges. I remembered the name of the building receptionist who had left shortly after I started treatment. She was somewhat bitter over sexual misconduct on your part and mentioned that you had gone out with one of your former patients. I got her name and called her.

And then there was your first wife, a woman perhaps even angrier than I was. You'd never abused your doctor-client privilege with her, but I found out after interviewing her personally that she had suffered mental and physical torment before getting out of the marriage with no alimony and the minimum of child support. You were late with the checks too. She didn't know about the distraught ex-client who had you arrested but later dropped charges. But she did know about the whole life insurance policy you'd taken out at thirty, when your practice was booming, when you were making five, even pushing six digits a year. And I knew that an insurance policy more than two years old was incontestable to the beneficiaries, which at the moment included your son. And could include a new wife.

As we talked it over, your former wife and I, we decided to call your other former patient. The one who had suffered the broken jaw and the cracked ribs when she suggested she'd turn you in to the Board of Medical Quality Assurance. And that's when we all agreed. We weren't going to turn you in. We were going to turn you over.

Patrol Officer Laura Deleuse:

I hate going to court. I hate standing up in front of people. And I hated remembering that night.

I had to sit through a bunch of testimony for the defense before my turn came up. Seems the guy had beaten up a woman who was an ex-client, and there was an ex-wife who had some gruesome stories. Locked her in a closet while he beat the kid. Public humiliation, rape, we got to hear it all. And a chorus line of doctors attesting to the multifarious wounds of the defendant. It didn't make me want to get up and go to work the next day either.

So it was open and shut. With him coming down the stairs at her like that, imminence wasn't even a remote improbability. But that's not why I didn't want to remember that night. It was the paramedic who strolled up the driveway, hung out waiting for the photographer, and pretty much ignored me, walking right past me like I was a tree. I got her out of earshot, when she was busy inspecting her manicure, and said, "Hi, remember me? The one you had an affair with last week."

"Yeah." She looked up, and some kind of recognition played across her face. "Oh yeah," she said. "I was there."

Sometimes her social skills weren't too good either.

Do I have any regrets? No. Well, maybe only one. I was a bit hasty in organizing our victory lunch. Lee, your ex-wife, was there, and Rachel, the girl friend (she's not only going to get her jaw fixed, she's going for a facelift, and a Ph.D. in media studies). Lee and I always wanted to learn Italian, so we'll buy a villa on Capri (we chose one already, through an estate agent). You see, what we didn't count on was that "accidental death" clause that includes self-defense and awards a double policy. We've well endowed every charity that remotely tugged on our heartstrings.

I was a bit worried about being hasty with the luncheon. After all, we were supposed to have set eyes on each other only in court. And there we were, chatting away like old friends (after all, they'd seen me through bruises, and beatings, fixed me up—and sent me back). We were drinking champagne, high on the knowledge of total financial security for life, jubilant that we'd done it ourselves (we'd never had a conflict about the split either) when I saw her. That police officer. She was behind a pillar, lunching, in fact, with the sour-faced paramedic that had scooped up the gray matter around your head. I did something I'd never done before. I looked her straight in the eye and raised my champagne glass to her. She spotted me and her eyes swept with mounting recognition across the faces of my luncheon companions. I saw her process the whole thing; she seemed to freeze. But then slowly she turned her back (the whole time I was thinking about my research, double indemnity, double jeopardy, and insurance companies that are not mandated to recollect), and as she turned around I saw what was in her hand. A champagne glass, and she raised it toward me.

The cases of police detectives Carlos Cruz and Jay Goldstein have entertained readers for several years, and such excellent novels as *A Single Stone, A Case of Loyalties,* and *Primary Target* are among the best books of their type. The last-named combines an excellent puzzle with strong political commentary. In addition, **MARILYN WALLACE** is the editor of the very successful *Sisters in Crime* series of anthologies. Ms. Wallace resides in San Anselmo, California.

THE CUTTING EDGE

Marilyn Wallace

 If I weren't Rico's mother and if I didn't live 3,000 miles away, I probably would have reacted differently to Catherine's two-sentence note, and to the invitation.

Someone slipped this under the gallery door. What do you make of it? her curlicued scrawl asked.

The note was paper-clipped to an invitation to the opening of Porterfield's, her new art gallery on West 51st Street. Thursday, December 4. Seven to nine P.M. Meet the artists, etc. I was familiar with the text not only because Rico was one of the artists but because my New York office, Happenings East, was coordinating the event.

It wasn't until I turned the invitation over to look at the image on the other side, a montage portrait of the three artists each standing in front of one of their paintings, that I noticed a gash running from the right edge in toward the center of the card. It cut right across the picture of Rico. The edge of the cut appeared to be smeared with dried blood.

Dried blood? Surely I was imagining that.

Like my attempts to persuade him to finish his undergraduate studies, any implied threat would only make Rico—full of promise, so damned stubborn

—more determined to pursue painting. My shudder of fear was his frisson of excitement. So what else was new?

I showed the card to David. After twenty-five years of marriage, we still count on each other to put a new spin on things. He held it close to the light, touched his finger to the cut.

"Why don't you call Rico and see what he thinks? I'd guess it's probably just a tear, a coffee stain, nothing to get worked up about." He kissed my cheek; he seemed more concerned about my worrying than he was about Catherine's note.

I granted the possibility that someone had slipped the note under the gallery door, that it had caught on a splinter, that perhaps coffee or something—wine, paint—had been spilled on it. But my anxiety level continued to rise as I dialed Rico's number and listened to the phone ring and ring, unanswered.

I've never been very good at waiting and that seemed to be all I could do: wait for Rico to answer the phone, wait for Thursday when David and I were scheduled to fly to New York for the opening. David was just starting a four-night piano gig at Yoshi's and couldn't get away earlier.

By nine o'clock, despite David's calm assurances, I had convinced myself that my New York staff needed my help. After all, the final mailing had to be done, the wine and hors d'oeuvres ordered, the work hung. I turned over the details of the California events to my Happenings West staff and bought a night-flight ticket from SFO to JFK.

I sat by the window, watching for those staccato glitters of light that are the small towns of nocturnal America. I tried to occupy my mind with one of Monk's atonal melody lines that resolves itself three bars later than I always expect it to, and with keeping the plane in the air by the strength of my will.

After a while, convinced that the plane would be fine on its own, my mind was free to tend to other things. I thought about my friend Catherine. After struggling for twenty years to gain critical or commercial recognition for her own paintings, she had given up. A mother for the first time at forty-two, she spent a year at home with Michael before she decided that if she couldn't paint, at least she would make a place for herself in the art world and open a gallery.

Images of Rico kept intruding. I remembered the moment I first held him and looked at his red, wrinkled face and knew that my most difficult task as the mother of this miracle would be to learn how to let him go. I pictured his delight when he uncurled his fingers from mine and took three steps on his own. I recalled the pained confusion when he found out that two of his seventh-grade friends forgot to ask him to go to the movies with them.

Somewhere over Nebraska, I demoted the torn invitation to a prank perpetrated by some bored art-scene crisis junkie. No one would want to hurt Rico

—why should they? I put on the earphones and let the jazz channel distract me the rest of the way across the continent.

The gray mist that hung over the city welcomed me home, the light so familiar that I wanted to embrace it. I headed for the first cab in the long yellow line and got in. Murray Feldman, number 3905467, nodded when I gave him Catherine's Brooklyn address. I needed to hear what she thought before I laid my mother-worries on Rico. The cab careened into the Kennedy exit maze.

"Take the Van Wyck to Atlantic Avenue," I said.

Murray grumbled and pulled into the proper lane and I closed my eyes, happy to be on the ground.

Sooner than I expected, the cab turned left onto Tenth Street and pulled to the curb in a squeal of brakes. I squinted to see the meter through the dingy plastic shield.

"That's twenty-four and sixty-eight," the cabbie said. "If you'da took the subway, you coulda bought a new pair of glasses."

I love New York.

I peeled a ten and a twenty from the roll in my wallet and waved away Murray's change. He flashed me his best you-ain't-a-bad-tipper-for-a-broad smile.

"Hey, you have a nice day, lady," he said with enthusiasm.

I groaned. The city was deteriorating, losing its old abrasive edge. At least Park Slope, a neighborhood of brownstones and gaslights and brave little window boxes, hadn't changed much. Even though David and I moved to California two years earlier, I had insisted on keeping the Happenings East office open. Brooklyn still felt like home.

Brooklyn is a state of mind. Ask Walt Whitman or Marianne Moore. A genuine Brooklyn soul doesn't last too long without forsythia in March, egg creams in July, and the minimum daily requirement of unidentified particulate matter blowing into your eyes in October.

Catherine, more a creature of the ether than of Brooklyn, met me at the door. Without makeup, her dark eyes and her springy brown curls made her look particularly vulnerable. We exchanged hugs and niceties in the entry foyer, its oatmeal-colored walls lined with Japanese artifacts. I purposely kept my back to her husband's collection of Samurai swords. I would wait until we were comfortable—in the kitchen, where we told all our secrets—to ask about the slashed invitation.

Michael led the way down the hall. He had a sixteen-month-old's round-faced, squat-legged chubbiness and looked somehow already bigger than Catherine, who was still exotically small. No one has ever accused me of being willowy, but I can still shop the outlets for size-ten samples. Still,

Catherine is the one friend who makes me feel like a Valkyrie in full armor. That hadn't changed in twelve years, nor had her questions.

"Do you ever sabotage yourself, Gina?" She spoke in a whisper, as though saying it aloud would make some negative reality more tangible.

Catherine always had questions. I used to think of it as a sign of some mild mental disorder, a *dementia inquisitas* manifesting itself in an inability to follow the rules of normal conversation. Then I discovered that I enjoyed looking for answers to give her. I even, quite consciously at some point, started to ask Catherine-questions myself.

"You didn't tamper with that invitation just to get some free publicity for the gallery, did you?" I hadn't slept much; that thought must have crept up when my mental censors were off duty. Maybe this was how Catherine lived all the time.

She made a face. "Your office can manage better publicity than that. Did you come out early because of that invitation? I mean, I'm glad you're here and happy you're working on the event, but I think you're overreacting, Gina. I guess I *was* a little worried at first but now it seems, I don't know, silly." She held out a half sandwich, tiny moon shapes scalloping the crust edge, about at Michael's mouth level, and he pulled her hand down to take a bite.

When he was a toddler, Rico had settled for nothing less than holding the sandwich in his own dimpled hands.

"Rico's age is enough to get some good press. Featured in a major gallery at twenty-two. Patrick says they'll call him a wunderkind." She laughed, a small sound, and licked grape jelly from her fingers. "I asked him if he slipped that invitation under the gallery door, and he looked at me like I had finally lost my mind. I believe him. About not doing it, I mean."

Did she mean Rico or Patrick? Before I could ask, she wrinkled her nose and said, "I don't have enemies and I doubt that Rico does. It's probably not a threat at all."

"Maybe you're right. But why was the invitation stained only along that slash?"

With a shrug and a noisy sigh, Catherine sat in the rocking chair and folded her hands in her lap, Madonna becalmed.

I drank my coffee and remembered that April day, seven months earlier, when Catherine and I sat on the steps in front of her brownstone, hands wrapped around mugs of hot coffee. We had pretended that the sun was warm, but it was our friendship that felt so good.

"Did you ever wish Rico would disappear," Catherine had said, "just be unborn? I mean not ever have been born."

A real Catherine-question.

"Not once. Not ever," I said, unable to entertain the notion of no Rico. The stone steps felt cold, hard.

"I stopped painting when I got pregnant." Her dark eyes had looked into my very heart as though she were asking me to change something. "Rico will never have to face that."

Now, as I sat in her kitchen, I wondered whether she would blame Michael, later, secretly, for this transformation from painter to purveyor of paintings.

Michael plopped himself at her feet and she reached down and stroked his cheek. "The gallery has to work. The rest isn't enough for me," she said. The silver gleam of the sky framed by the window behind her hurt my eyes.

"Not enough how . . . intellectually? . . . emotionally?" I asked.

She was quiet; Catherine's pauses took some getting used to. It was her timing, I had learned. Not my fault, just her way.

"I want to soar. I don't soar at home."

Catherine wanted a poet to play his words in accompaniment to her rapture, to join her in freedom from the law of gravity.

"Aren't things good with you and Patrick?" I had meant to ask her if she soared in her marriage. It hadn't come out that way.

"Staying home, I don't get much, you know, stimulation during the day. At first, when I told him my idea—about the gallery—Patrick said he wanted me to stay home with Michael for a few more years." Her face was lost behind those wild curls. "But then he changed his mind. Just like that. He's even financing the first twelve months."

"That sounds good." Almost too good, I thought. Patrick indulged this whim too readily and helped Catherine give up on herself as a painter. "So when the gallery opens, you'll be happy."

Catherine stood, stretched on her toes, and reached both arms up, her fingers pointing. I expected her to lift off the ground and float to the ceiling, to beat her wings against the window until someone opened it and let her out to catch the smoky November wind moving among the city's spires.

"Mostly," she said. "I guess, mostly."

I left Catherine's and wheeled my suitcase down the street. *Just a tear . . . nothing to get worked up over,* David had said. *I think you're overreacting,* Catherine had told me. Probably they were right and I had fixed on this for some mother-reason born of my struggle to let my son live his own life. Surely Rico would consider my worries proof of a relapse into the role of overprotective mother with an overactive imagination.

He was, after all, a grown-up, a man whose dark hair, long-lashed brown eyes, broad shoulders, and narrow hips are attractive to women. His natural reserve gives way easily to his genuine interest in people. He keeps himself in cadmium yellow by working at a record store called Riffs, shelters neighbor-hood strays, likes old movies, and returns library books on time.

He's good but not perfect.

What he hasn't yet acquired, even after two years in New York, is an everyday instinct for self-preservation. He lives mainly on salami and Mal-lomars and would never buy a new toothbrush unless his old one fell into the toilet. He rides the subway at all hours, falls in and out of love with The Most Terrific Woman several times a year, and is determined to be a painter and not acquire any credentialed, marketable skills.

We all have our blind spots, and I had to allow Rico *his* and keep mine from getting in his way. I resolved not to mention the slashed, stained pic-ture.

I set my bag in front of the grillwork gate, pressed the buzzer, looked through the just-below-street-level window. Inside, a Tiffany table lamp glowed in the midday pallor. Ribbons of light fell to the floor through a jungle of foliage. In lieu of paying rent to David and me, Rico has been restoring the three-level brownstone to its original Victorian glory. He calls the jungle room "the conservatory." Shades of Colonel Mustard. The room was empty.

The tips of my fingers curled toward my palms in an attempt to get warm. The cold bit at my toes through the thin leather of my pumps, which had been fine for the 71 degrees I'd left in California.

Then Rico's face appeared in the window, his expression leaping from wariness to surprise and finally settling into a broad smile. I hoped he would still be smiling in fifteen minutes.

I hugged him; his face felt good against my chilled cheek. He smelled good. When he pulled back, I noticed a scrap of toilet paper stanching a shaving cut on his jaw.

I suppressed a shudder and began. "I tried to call last night but you weren't home and Riffs was closed. I didn't decide I was coming until late. About nine. California time." So much for urbane patter.

He set my suitcase beside the hall table, a spindly-legged affair sporting a drop cloth covered with plaster dust. "You could have had Dad call me or something. I know this is your house, but you said you'd give me some notice. I didn't expect you until Thursday."

It *was* a lame excuse. Clearly, I had lost some ground in the struggle to let go. "I'm sorry for the lack of warning."

On cue, a rumpled little redhead wrapped in a wrinkled terry-cloth robe appeared at the top of the stairs.

"Mom, this is Laura. She plays keyboards for the Rompettes. Laura, this is my mom, Gina Capobella."

Laura smiled and said hello and disappeared. Another of his women—we'd discussed safe sex since he was fifteen but maybe we needed a little brushup talk about safe relationships.

He hung my coat on a brass hook in the hall and we went into the kitchen. His mouth was tight, his shoulders up around his ears. He lit a burner on the stove and set a teakettle over the flame. In the tense silence, I heard my own breathing and the pounding water filling the upstairs bathtub.

"I hope Laura's not in any *hot water*," I said, emphasizing the key phrase as I pointed at the ceiling, in the general direction of the bathroom.

Rico's face was blank, his silence stony. He was turning down the invitation to our old game.

"I hope she's not *in too deep*," I said, giving it one last try.

The corners of his mouth edged into a smile. "She's prepared to *sink or swim* on her own," he said. "She'll talk about it when she's ready to *come clean*."

We both grinned, but I knew that punning our way to familiar ground was only a start. Rico had lived in this house on his own since his twentieth birthday, two years ago. It *was* peremptory to claim territorial prerogatives on such short notice; I really should have tried harder to call. "Maybe you could think of my being here as a double-reverse empty-nest syndrome," I offered.

"You've been reading *Good Housekeeping* again. That's dangerous." He lifted a serrated knife out of its slot and cut a French bread in half.

"Very funny. Listen, I'm quiet in the mornings and I might even be persuaded to make you some bracciola." I smiled sweetly.

"Home cooking and word games can't make everything all right, Mom."

It's good when your kid keeps you honest. Reminds you that you've done a decent job of it. Knife in hand, he hugged me and then set to piling turkey, cheese, lettuce, mustard, and mayo on the bread. He sawed through the huge tower with a knife, then scooped the sandwiches onto plates and carried them to the table. "Does this visit have anything to do with Catherine? She's seemed a little weird or something the past couple of days."

"She desperately wants the gallery to be a success. I thought it would put her at ease if I was here." Every word true, but sins of omission would surely be my undoing. They felt too much like getting away with something.

"She's more anxious about the gallery than I thought." Concern for my friend—his friend, too—creased his brow.

What a face. Not only a mother could love it.

"It's been so hard on her, trying to make it as a painter. She's giving up her dreams. Don't you think"—*What? That he should give up before he's given it a try? What are you trying to tell your child?*—"that she's entitled to be a little weird?"

Rico didn't answer.

"Enough water for me to have some tea?" Rico's friend, her face scrubbed

and sparkling but her hair still a wiry auburn tangle, stood in the doorway.
The terry-cloth robe had been traded for jeans, a citrus-green turtleneck, and
a tattered purple sweater that looked big enough for her to hold a party in.

Rico wiggled his eyebrows like Groucho Marx, then disappeared into the
pantry and emerged with a teabag dangling between two fingers. "Almond
Sunset for you, my lovely."

"You two look just like each other." The girl made a circle of her thumb
and forefinger and held it up to her right eye, closing her left eye as though
she were looking through a lens. "I'd recognize you anywhere. Not just from
the pictures but because your mouth is so much like Rico's and your eyes. It's
neat." She put one hand in her lap, propped her head on the other fist, and
watched Rico prepare the tea.

"What kind of music do the Rompers play?" I envisioned a band for the
Sesame Street set. Somehow this pretty, sleepy woman didn't seem the type,
but maybe the small ruby stud in her left nostril gave the wrong impression.

"Romp*ettes*. Ska." Laura smiled benignly at my blank look. "You know,
kind of like world beat or reggae. We're not very good, but my boyfriend is
making a documentary about us. He's studying filmmaking. NYU, graduate
level."

Rico's back was to me; this was a little confusing. Her boyfriend?

"Interesting," I said. Rico looked over his shoulder and smiled. *Interesting*
was a long-shared code for *judgment temporarily deferred*.

"He got very intense a couple of weeks ago. Watching me like he was
framing every action for a scene—it made me nuts. So I came here and got
my mother to promise not to tell him where I was. With the unlisted phone
here, I don't even have to talk to him unless *I* want to. The quiet feels . . .
healing, I guess you'd say in California. Rico was terrific to offer me a place."
She got up and stood behind Rico, massaging his shoulders.

So she was another of his strays, not a romantic relationship at all.

"I never met her boyfriend," Rico said as he set the teapot on the table,
"but she swears he's handsomer than me."

"Well, he is. Anyway, you can't compare dark and dashing with blond and
brooding." Laura stared at her crimson-tipped nails and then arranged her
face in a smile. "Are you staying long?" she asked me.

I told her I would be in Brooklyn until the day after the gallery opening.
The three of us sipped our tea and talked about friends and school, the art
scene, and old neighbors. Rico showed me the five paintings he'd be exhibit-
ing at Porterfield's. They were abstract, with the suggestion of a face serving
as the focal point for each. "This one's a self-portrait," he said pointing to
the largest canvas.

I balanced my swelling pride with the desire to shield him from the frustra-
tions of being a painter. Catherine and Patrick were doing things right with

the gallery, Rico said, except that Patrick got stuck in traditional thinking sometimes—but what else could you expect from someone whose family had lived in the Hudson Valley since Rip Van Winkle went to sleep? She needed someone like that, I said, to gaze at her fondly while she explored her place in the arts.

By Thursday morning I had sublimated any leftover worries about Rico with vast and unnecessary expenditures of energy. Despite the presence of my willing and competent staff, I took care of everything personally: I hired the harpist, selected the champagne, calculated the number of hors d'oeuvres, tested the lighting, and called my media contacts. Only a few times during those hectic days did I catch myself staring at Rico, memorizing the details of his face, the angle of his cheekbones, the ridge of his jaw, the clear, taut skin.

Only one last detail to settle—what to wear.

"Do you like this one better?" I swirled into the kitchen with what I hoped was the grace of a runway model. In the bulky gray suit with the leather trim, I felt more like a 747.

"No contest. The white jumpsuit. My boyfriend says white is the ultimate sophistication. He wants me to wear white all the time. He says it enhances inner purity." Laura wrinkled her nose, tugged at the collar of her houndstooth jacket, pulled down the sleeve of her cinnamon-and-nutmeg striped jersey. "Maybe wear the green silk. I like what it does for your eyes."

That sounded nice. "What about you, Rico? You're the star. What are you wearing?" I asked.

Rico, who had become involved with a cleaver, garlic, celery, and bok choy, said through his gritted teeth, "I've done okay dressing myself for the past two years, Mom. I'll figure out something."

That told me.

"Mothers are supposed to care about these things, Rico." Laura gave Rico's cheek a pinch before she turned to me. "If you wear the silk, you need some outrageous earrings. I'm going to see my boyfriend before I go to the opening, so remind me before I leave and I'll lend you mine."

Did she mean the safety pins or the Christmas ornaments? I was saved from a reply by the insistent shrill of the doorbell.

I unlocked the inner door. A blast of arctic air swept into the vestibule as I opened the grillwork gate. Shivering, I moved aside to let a grape-colored woolen bundle step in.

Catherine's face was barely visible between the wool beret and the scarf pulled up around her nose. Her eyes warned that this was not a simple social call.

"Come into the kitchen and stand by the stove," I said.

She didn't budge. With her gloved hand she reached into her coat pocket and handed me an envelope. "Someone slipped this under the gallery door early this morning. I just found it."

I opened the envelope and pulled out a folded page from the New York *Post* entertainment section. Great—they were doing a piece on the gallery. Not the *Times*, to be sure, but maybe after the opening . . . I unfolded the page. Rico's face, centered in front of one of his paintings, stared up at me. A slash outlined in reddish brown sliced through the page. Dried blood or cranberry juice, it hardly mattered; the intent was clear enough.

"This doesn't feel like a prank, Catherine. Someone is sending a message that they intend to hurt Rico."

"Or me. Or the gallery." Her eyes downcast, she jammed her hands into her pockets. "Rico's not the only possible target. And no, I don't know anyone who thinks Rico cheated them out of a place in the show. Patrick already asked me that."

Exasperated with her self-indulgence and fearful for Rico, I sent her home and called Frankie Fretelli, an old friend with an NYPD desk job. If I brought along some Johnnie Walker Black instead of art gallery white wine, Frankie said, he'd come to the opening and keep an eye on things. David would be there too, if the weather didn't delay his flight. We'd all keep our eyes open.

Now, despite my neat avoidance of the subject, Rico would have to be told. I could no longer convince myself that it was just a prank. Perhaps professional jealousy was the poison here. How many times had Catherine pointed out how *young* Rico was? Other artists, embittered after years of struggle, might also resent Rico's success.

The delicious smell of vegetables sizzling in sesame oil filled the kitchen. Rico stirred them, then grated fresh ginger into the wok.

"Was that Catherine? I thought I heard her voice but it sounded kind of funny."

Time to plunge in. *Lettuce begin,* I thought. "She's worried. She, uh . . ." *Orange you going to tell him?* I demanded of myself. "She found a newspaper article. Slipped under the gallery door. A picture of you and one of your paintings. It was cut and the edge was stained with something that looked like dried blood."

Rico dribbled tamari over the vegetables and I went on. "That's the second time. The first was eight days ago. It looks like someone is threatening you, Rico."

He set the wooden stirrer on the stove. "Me? Who would threaten *me?*"

His bewilderment was genuine. I hated asking him to think the way I'd been thinking, off and on, for the past week, but I had to. "Another artist, maybe? Someone whose girl you stole? Someone you had an argument with at the record store?"

With each suggestion he shook his head. "None of the above. Listen, I get to have my first gallery opening once in my life. And nobody—no nameless enemy, no one playing jokes—nobody is going to keep me from enjoying it."

He smiled at me and stopped just short of admonishing me to do the same.

It was ten after five when the taxi deposited me at the curb in front of the gallery. Fat snowflakes drifted lazily to the ground, dusting everything with a sugary whiteness. No wind, temperature hovering near thirty. If I could let go of the nagging anxiety that had kept me company all afternoon, the weather might even feel festive.

I pushed open the door and surveyed the gallery.

The minifloods cast an even, untinted light on the paintings. White movable walls, arranged with enough angles to keep the space from feeling predictable, carried attention to the paintings rather than to the room itself. False modesty aside, Catherine and I had done a superb job of hanging this show and of placating artists' egos, sensitive to such questions as which was the better wall and what critics would see first when they entered the gallery.

Rico's large canvases, those faces emerging from abstract swirls of strong, clear colors, hung at the far end of the room. To the left of the door, a profusion of tiny paintings—florals à la O'Keeffe but signed Siandra—dotted the wall. On the right, Ken Arcie's monochromatic, detailed landscapes of New England scenes served as somber balance. The total effect was stunning.

"Hello. Anybody here?" I called.

"I'll be out in a moment."

The voice was exactly as I remembered, a rich baritone, a little haughty but approachable, redolent of old money and Harvard.

I brushed the snow from my hair and peeled off my gloves, took off my coat, and shook it.

"Very fetching. You look like a Mary Cassatt, high-necked demure dress, dark eyes." Patrick was tall, golden-haired, and polished; if he had been bald, he would have resembled an Oscar statuette wearing a gray wool suit.

"Thanks. I think. How do you like it?" I said, sweeping my arm to take in the whole room.

A flicker of something I didn't understand shone in his eyes. "You've both done a fine job of it," he said. "Fine."

I gathered my coat and walked toward the small rear office, thinking about faint praise and damning myself for not pursuing my uneasiness over his feelings about the gallery. "Catherine's a little nervous about tonight," I said as I deposited the Johnnie Walker in a desk drawer. "She's done a wonderful job. She has some terrific artists."

"Even if you do say so yourself." His voice was flat.

When I walked back into the gallery, he was standing in front of one of Rico's paintings, arms crossed against his chest, the habitual skeptic's pose. His head was tilted; considering that he was a corporate attorney, his hair curled toward his collar in an almost decadent way.

The man had taste. This was the painting on the invitation, the one in the newspaper. Catherine and Rico had chosen carefully; it was the best work Rico had ever done. The painting surged with compressed power that swept the eye to the upper left quadrant where a web of magenta lines delineated eyes, nose, mouth, and a spidery jumble of hair amid the gradations of blue and gray. If I squinted, it really did resemble Rico. Particular about titles, he had called it *Feature This*.

"I'm terribly old-fashioned," Patrick said, stepping back from the canvas. "I believe that paintings should be of recognizable things, that music should have a melody one can hum, and that books should tell a story."

And that women belong in the kitchen and the bedroom? I wondered. "Well, then it's a good thing Catherine has such an eclectic trio of artists. Something for everyone, you might say."

"Old-fashioned doesn't mean ineducable. Maybe someday I'll get the point of these paintings." Patrick's smile made him look less like the portrait of a disapproving Mather paterfamilias—Cotton, not Jerry—and more like someone my friend Catherine might fall in love with. "Anything I can do to help?" he asked.

"Thanks, but it's all under control. Bound to be surprises—there always are—but as far as I can tell, there's nothing to do now."

Patrick's gaze swept the room. "How about if I slice up this meat?" he said as he held up a crusty, wrinkled Italian salami.

"The caterer would kill me if I let anyone else touch her food." The knife lay on the table, gleaming fiercely in the light. I wanted to hide it, throw it away.

The door swung open and the harpist and her unwieldy burden stumbled in. I pointed her to a corner to practice and busied myself with checking artists' statements, price lists, champagne glasses, half listening as she brought David's composition to life. The music was solid, lithe, fanciful, substantial; the notes flew around the room or marched, as the theme changed.

I couldn't wait to see David. I shifted some of my anxiety to concern about his plane landing in the snow, pushed away the imagined sight of Rico's face with a raw scar running down his cheek, left my worries in one corner of my mind while I attended to the problem of the three cases of Chablis that had arrived instead of the champagne I'd ordered.

By six forty-five, the caterer's assistant had replaced the wine, everything else was in order, and I was holding David's hand. His tumbled hair glistened with snow and his smile as the music spilled from the harp thrilled me nearly as much as his whispered description of how he intended to make up for lost time.

I had just finished telling him about this morning's slashed newspaper when the door flew open and Catherine hurried in, stomping her feet and rubbing her hands.

"This is terrible. No one's going to come out in this weather. The press will be covering the first snow of the season and the opening will be a flop. The whole thing is a terrible idea, and the critics are going to crucify me." She shrugged out of her coat, mumbling all the way to the back room.

In fact, it had crossed my mind that the weather might keep some people away. I wondered if our correspondent would show up. Unless he (she?) was already here.

"Nonsense. The same reporters don't cover snow and gallery openings, you know that. The guest list is loaded with people with a personal interest in you, the artists, or being seen at the new and happening place. And tonight, my dear, this is it."

Catherine tried not to smile. "You really think so?"

"I'm sure of it." Patrick took her in his arms. "You look wonderful. Your artists are marvelous and Porterfield's is going to be a success."

So supportive for someone who just a while ago told me how much he favored traditional values, at least in art and music.

Just then the door tinkled and a round woman swathed in a rainbow of gauzy stuff, a gold turban wound around her head, undulated toward the coat rack. "Cath-er-ine," she purred. "The ten of pentacles in the future spot! I did a reading on the gallery and that's what it said. Pentacles! Money, money, money. The tarot never lies." She blew on her fingers and frowned. "Isn't it cold in here?"

The thermostat was set for seventy but the red temperature indicator pointed to sixty. This was one of those things that ages an event coordinator beyond the mere passage of time. Like the broken water pipe outside the Central Park tent where four elephants were waiting for their cue in the benefit performance of *Aïda*, this was something I had to fix.

I soon discovered that the only piece of electrical equipment not on a circuit breaker was the furnace. By the time I found a fuse, installed it, and then made the necessary repairs to my dress and makeup, the party was well under way.

I scanned the bright, noisy crowd for Rico. A man in a dark suit and white shirt nodded to me: one of Frankie's NYPD buddies, no doubt. Any others would be easy to spot, too. The invited guests dressed along a fashion continuum from Hell's Angels chic to Kamali slouch, with hardly any room for Brooks Brothers, *faux* or *vrai.*

I finally spotted Rico on the other side of the room. I would *not* transmit my worries to him. I would *not,* tonight of all nights, be the hovering, overprotective mother. I would not ruin this celebration.

The lighting and the harp music and the tinkle of glasses and conversation *were* festive; I couldn't help smiling as Rico, elegant in a camel-colored sweater and dark slacks, walked through the crowd toward me.

"You want a name tag? How about 'Capobella's Mother'?" Rico, his arm around David, grinned down at me. Frankie Fretelli stood nearby, clutching his glass half filled with amber liquid.

"A chiaroscuro mom in a rocking chair? No, thanks." I hugged Rico, a little longer than he would have liked but a little shorter than would have pleased me. He was beautiful, radiating pleasure from his smile, from his perfect, unmarred skin. "The paintings look wonderful," I whispered as I kissed his cheek and squeezed his arm.

"Thanks. So do you." He kissed me back; then a leather-skirted lady appeared, slipped her arm through his, and led him into a thicket of wellwishers in the middle of the floor. Frankie stuck close behind him.

"You're Rico's friend?" A blue-eyed, platinum-haired, classically handsome young man stood beside me. A smile crinkled his face. In his right hand he held a champagne flute. The cast on his left arm was cradled in a sling, as fresh and white as his shirt and the scarf around his neck.

"How did you know?"

"I saw the two of you talking." He shifted his arm.

I nodded; I would make pleasant talk with this fellow and not pursue Rico, with my eyes, all over the room. "I hope you're not left-handed and not a painter."

"I'm not a painter. I'm an aficionado. A particular fan of Rico's." He sipped from the champagne glass. "Can I get you some?"

"Thanks, no." I craned my neck to look for David's tousled head, which should have been towering above the crowd. I caught Catherine's eye; she beamed back a message of gratitude.

"So Rico's living with his girlfriend now, right? They must be really serious about each other. I mean, to be living together." The young man's gaze flitted around the room, resting for microseconds here and there. Then he turned to look at me; his eyes were blue, intense, and direct.

The conversation had taken a decidedly personal turn. "What did you say your name was?"

"Peter. Peter Webster."

Harp music wafted through the din; the angel with blond hair and a cast on his arm grinned at me, but before I could say anything, Rico materialized at my right side. His worried eyes scanned the crowd. "You see Laura yet? I thought she'd be here by now."

"She'll be here soon," I assured him. Now I could worry about *her,* too. I expected that Laura, who had seemed almost as excited about the opening as Rico, would have been here an hour ago. His leather-clad lady called his name and he winked at me and walked away.

He hadn't said a word to this supposed friend standing beside me. Not even hello.

"You've known Rico a long time?" I smiled because it seemed the thing to do.

"We've got a mutual friend," he said, his pale face expressionless. "You're his mother aren't you?"

My smile this time was genuine. "It shows, doesn't it?"

"Since Rico came into my life, I can't work, can't concentrate."

Before I could ask why, he turned and was gone, maneuvering through the crowd to the large silver coffee urn.

He'd said he was a fan. But he never really said a fan of the paintings. It was Rico himself. He had a crush on Rico, and Rico, trying to discourage Peter, was ignoring him.

I stepped back to let someone pass and almost bumped into Catherine. "The *Times* critic told someone that Rico is a—quote—bright new talent—unquote," she said. "I really *am* soaring." And she drifted away, not quite on the ground.

The crowd should have been thinning but, apparently reluctant to go out into the snow, they continued to pick over the last crumbs of pâté and drain the last sips of wine. Rico was at my side again, beaming as the front door flew open. "There's Laura. I wonder how things worked out with her boy-friend. She was going to tell him that she's ready to start seeing him again."

Snow swirling around her head, Laura waved and stepped inside. Rico went to greet her.

I let out my breath and relaxed. The evening was almost over. David was here, Laura was here, and no one had tried to cut Rico's face. Rico and Laura swept toward the champagne table. As I followed their progress, I noticed the young man, Peter what's-his-name, standing with his back to Rico's largest canvas.

Sling knotted at his neck, Peter held his good arm up. His thumb and forefinger closed into a circle and he held the circle up to his eye. As though he were looking through a lens.

As Laura had, that first morning I met her.

Her filmmaker boyfriend.

He was neither admirer nor art aficionado. His questions now made sense, not like Catherine-questions at all, but attempts to trick me into offering him information to confirm his suspicions.

I was half a room away. Peter backed up, two large steps, his fingers still held to his eye like a make-believe camera.

The air, vibrating with chatter and laughter and harp music, parted as I pushed my way toward Peter.

A glint of light caught an object in his right hand. A silver pen, perhaps, or a cigarette lighter. Or a knife.

He took a step toward one of Rico's paintings, arm raised.

"Stop!" I screamed as I pushed past three people who stood frozen between me and Peter.

I was two steps away when Peter's arm came down, dragging the knife across a corner of the canvas. I could almost hear the image-face scream, could almost feel the ooze of warm blood and fluid leak through the rent cloth. Peter pulled the knife out and raised his arm again.

I grabbed his elbow and slid my hand down to his forearm. I dug my thumb into the soft inner flesh of his wrist. The knife clattered to the floor and I snatched it up.

"What are you doing?" I snapped.

Someone took the knife from me. Frankie clamped his beefy hand on Peter's good arm.

"I was evening the score," Peter said, his body slack as Frankie led him toward the door. "A little suffering. A little pain. For both of them. For the hurt I feel every time I think of them together." His misplaced jealousy and those sad, beautiful eyes filled his twisted angel-face.

Shocked and pale, Rico put his arm around me. "My painting . . . I'm glad you . . ." He shook his head and drew me closer; we watched Laura run to Peter.

Tears spilled over onto her cheeks when Peter shrugged away from her touch. Poor girl, all she had wanted was some quiet.

I turned away from her pain and found myself staring at the square white card beside the painting. In neat letters, dark and clear, it announced the title of the painting: *Feature This*.

The self-portrait.

Rico's face *had* been slashed.

"Mom, it's a pretty small rip," Rico said, examining the canvas. "Don't get all *torn up* about it. You stopped him just in the *nick* of time."

I didn't feel at all casual but I joined the old game anyway. "Maybe someday what happened tonight will seem like just another *slice of life*."

Rico hugged me a good, long time and then smiled sadly. "I wonder if it's always like this out here on the *cutting edge*."

Born in South Africa, **GILLIAN SLOVO** has lived in England since she was twelve. A journalist and television producer, she has written several excellent mystery novels featuring London-based Kate Baeier, including *Morbid Symptoms* and *Death by Analysis*.

LOOKING FOR THELMA

Gillian Slovo

 I was in the middle of doing my accounts when the doorbell rang. Or, to be more accurate, my accounts were in the middle of doing me. The center column was being cooperative: it was the ones either side of it that were making trouble.

The bell sounded again. I ignored it: I didn't feel like visitors, and besides, I'd just made a momentous decision. I'd decided to compromise—a few pence to the left subtracted from the right would achieve the proper balance. It wasn't entirely on the level, but if the customs and excise noticed, all they would learn was what they must already know—namely, that I couldn't add to save my life.

"The door was open," a timid voice said.

Frowning at the distraction, I looked toward the door. My eyes came to rest not on a face but on a wide patent-leather belt. I shifted my gaze upward.

The man in front of me was huge—nearer to seven than to six feet—with a body to match. He was made to be noticed, and he flaunted the fact. He had shaved his head clean, and his bald pate shone a deep black against the rest of his clothes. It was quite an outfit—his three-piece suit was tailored to fit his broad frame and sewed from all colors of the rainbow, a broad silver tie nestled under the garish waistcoat, and a pair of shining black shoes that seemed to go on forever had silver buckles the size of my hands. I gulped.

"The door was open," he said again.

The voice was not only small but melodic with it. On the principle that there was no point in antagonizing giants, even ones with ingratiating voices, I threw a smile his way. My neck hurt with the effort of twisting so I stood in an attempt to equalize the distance. He strode toward me.

The man was big, real big, and close up he towered above me. There was no point in competing. I sat.

"Can I help you?" I asked. *Good,* I thought, *my voice sounds normal.*

He smiled, and the long gray-brown scar that ran the full length of his left cheek smiled with him. He lowered himself onto the chair in front of me and planted two huge fists on my desk. I backed away and hit the wall with my head. I rubbed it surreptitiously.

"I hope you can help," he said.

I turned the rub into an encouraging nod and waited. I was ready for anything.

"I want you to find somebody for me," he said. "Name of Thelma."

Something clicked in my head, so tangibly that I bet I lost a hundred thousand brain cells making the connection. *Got it in one,* I thought. Smiling cynically, I leaned my chair against the wall and stretched my legs out so that my feet landed on the desk, right in the middle of my accounts book. My only regret was that I didn't have a cigarette to hang out of the side of my mouth and complete the impression.

"And what's your name?" I asked. "Moose, by any chance?"

He looked puzzled. "Moose?" he thought about it a bit. "No, Martin. Martin Malloy."

I smiled again, and this time the cynicism was not an act. "That figures," I said.

He leaned across and shifted my feet to the right, uncovering the columns of numbers. His thick index finger pointed at the center row.

"But this doesn't," he said. "You've inverted one of those numbers, there in the middle. Easily done."

I returned my legs to the ground and pulled the book nearer to me, meaning to close it. But I couldn't help looking at where his finger had once been, and I couldn't help seeing that he was right. I frowned.

He grinned almost by way of apology. "I'm good at figures," he explained. "Always have been. And I learned to read upside down when I was inside."

"You've been in prison, then," I stated.

He nodded.

"And this Thelma put you there."

His brow creased, and I remembered his size and the scar that creased in its redness on his cheek. He was no longer doing an impression of the genial giant: I had angered him. I pulled at the telephone wire, edging the instrument closer to me.

"Thelma didn't put me there," he said. "In fact, if anybody got me out, it was Thelma." He glared at me. "I don't like people who say bad things about Thelma," he concluded.

With a supreme effort of will I fixed his eyes with mine. I kept looking at him while I nudged the receiver off the phone and let it drop on my lap. I rested my hand on the headless phone, thanking the heavens that I now had digital dialing. His frown deepened.

"Tell me more," I said in a voice that was more fear than fake. I hit the first nine on the phone while I tried to work out whether I could manage to make a successful break for the door.

In one effortless motion he reached across the desk and pulled the receiver from my lap. He put it down on the desk. He stretched across again.

He put a finger on one of the buttons and pressed it down.

"That makes two nines," he said. "You've only got to dial one more and you're connected. Go ahead, I won't stop you."

The brain cells were going fast by now. It was a dare, I thought; he'd get me before my first cry for help. He was toying with me, and probably enjoying it. And yet what option did I have? I was isolated and alone, up in my grimy office in the center of London. A cry for help wafting to the street would be cause for a quickening of pace rather than investigation. I had no choice: without the phone, I had no line to the world.

I lifted my hand slowly as the seconds expanded. I could try it, I thought, and maybe I'd succeed. My hand began to shake.

"I'm really a gentle guy," he said slowly, watching that hand. "My size militates against me, but I wouldn't harm a fly. Certainly not a woman, that's for sure."

"And what's that?" I asked, using the poised finger to point at his scar. "Shaving accident?"

He shrugged, and I saw how the rocks in his shoulders bulged. "Prison's a rough place," he said. "It makes you or it breaks you."

"And it made you?"

"Thelma made me," he said. "That's why I want to find her."

We were both back in fiction land. I replaced the receiver on the phone and breathed out. I no longer felt scared, only foolish—a foolishness tinged with anger. He was a pro, I thought, a real good actor, and I might as well face the fact that he had me. He and whoever had sent him—and I had a good idea as to who that was. Well, all I had to do was get rid of him, finish my accounts, close the office for perhaps the last time, and then be free to wreak my own kind of revenge.

But I'd do it subtly, I thought. I reached into the top drawer of my desk and pulled out a pad. As a heading I chose the name M. MALLOY. I underlined it: it looked better that way. On the next line I inscribed the name THELMA in block capitals.

"Parsons," he said. "Thelma Parsons."

"A dancer?" I asked without looking up.

"A social worker," he said. He blinked. "But she did like to dance. She showed me pictures of herself when she was a kid. All dressed up in a white tutu, she was."

Social worker, I wrote, *failed ballet dancer.*

"Thelma never failed at anything," he said loudly. It was the first time he had raised his voice.

I smiled placatingly. It took two to tango, I thought, and I was finally in step. I wasn't going to break my rhythm for any fake display of righteous anger by a giant gullible enough to involve himself in one of Sam's pranks.

"Why don't you tell me the whole story?" I suggested.

He leaned back in the chair. It creaked. He frowned and began to toy with the gold watch fob that was attached to his waistcoat. "Thelma liked to visit me in prison," he began. "She turned me on to books."

I glanced up and my eyes strayed to my accounts.

He laughed, or at least I think that was what described the creaking that issued from his big mouth. "Not those kind," he said, "I always had a knack with them. That's what got me into trouble in the first place. No, Thelma revealed the world of literature to me."

Social worker reforms con by opening his eyes to the joys of the nineteenth century, I wrote.

"Modern literature," he said loudly.

I gulped. I kept forgetting that he could read upside down.

"It changed my whole world view," he continued. "Opened new horizons. I want to be able to thank her, not in the claustrophobia of prison, but in the real world. In the free world."

Free world, I thought, *more like anticommunist modern literature, then.*

"So go round to her office and thank her," I said.

He shook his head unhappily. "She's left her job," he said. "She was never happy with it, it cramped her style, she said, and now she's had the courage to leave. They won't tell me where she went—they don't do that on principle in case some ex-con has a grudge against them."

"And you want me to find her?" I stated.

"That's it," he said, delighted that the slow pupil had finally caught on. "And then you will thank her."

He nodded. He reached a fist into a pocket of his garish plaid suit. *Here comes the punch line*, I thought.

He placed a piece of paper in front of me, right side up. On it was written the name Thelma Parsons along with an address in Islington.

"That's where Thelma used to work?" I asked.

For reply he reached once more into his pocket. *Ahaa*, I thought, *here it comes.*

I was wrong again. In front of me, dead in front, he placed a wad of new bank notes. I stared at him, and he smiled. I picked up the notes and felt their crispness.

"Two hundred and fifty pounds," he said. "Retainer."

"Is that what they said it would cost?" I asked.

"They?" He frowned. I resolved in future not to aggravate the scar. "It's a guess," he continued. "Your retainer plus something toward expenses. Give me a record when you finish, and I'll settle up with you. I'm good at figures, you know."

I didn't say anything, and he had finished as well. I watched as he stood up and began to stride to the door.

"I suppose that you'll be in touch with me rather than leaving me your address," I said.

He turned. "That's right," he said. "Circumstances have conspired to make me a bit of an itinerant at the moment." He waved a hand in my direction before turning away again. "I'll be in touch," he said.

"One more thing," I called just as he had bent his head down far enough to fit. "Ever read any Chandler?"

"No, I haven't," he replied without bothering to look back. "And my reading days are over. I only want to thank Thelma and then I can get on with my life."

They were conveniently seated around the kitchen table when I arrived, all three of them, the ones I had decided were guilty. Sam was doing what he liked best—explaining in layperson's terms a particularly neat solution to the latest space-time continuum problem—while Anna and Daniel were doing what they did best—pretending to understand.

Into this cozy scene I strolled. I took a swig from the half bottle of Bells I'd picked up on the way.

"Bad day?" Sam asked.

I shoved the bottle into my jacket pocket. It bulged in the linen, but you can't have everything. At least I was suitably crumpled, I thought. I shook my head.

"Great day," I said. "I was having problems balancing the books, but Moose solved that for me."

They looked at one another, and the first hint of a doubt insinuated itself into my mind. They were giving a good impression of confusion, I thought, but then I discarded the thought. Anna and Daniel must surely have picked up some tips from the actors they directed, and as for Sam, well, he'd learned impassivity from years of teaching aspirant Nobel winners.

I changed tack. I reached into my bag, pulled out the wad of money, and threw it at them. It landed just where I had wanted it to, plum in Sam's lap. Both Anna and Daniel stretched across the table to get a better look.

"Nice crisp notes," Daniel commented. "Did this Moose rob a bank?"

"Maybe Sam did," I said. "Let's ask him."

Sam looked at the notes in that abstracted way he had. "Moose," he said speculatively. *"The Big Sleep?"*

"Farewell, My Lovely," Daniel said impatiently. "I thought mathematicians were literate these days."

Sam opened his mouth to defend himself. I decided that it was time to stop playing.

"I know you think I should give up the business," I said. "As a matter of fact, I was coming to the same conclusion myself. But sending a nine-foot Moose to my office is not what I call a subtle hint. Nor is it funny."

This time there was no mistaking the confusion in their eyes. I knew them well, these three, and they knew me. They wouldn't, I thought, continue the game this far. Would they?

"Except he said his name was Martin," I told them in a voice that was no longer so certain. "Martin Malloy. Looking for Thelma."

They glanced briefly at one another, but they didn't speak. I saw Anna's eyes come to rest on my jacket pocket. The concern in her eyes spoke of her innocence, spoke of all their innocence. I gulped, took the whiskey out, walked to them, and deposited it on the table. I pulled myself a chair and sat heavily on it.

"I better start again," I said.

I told them all about it, each piece of stinted dialogue, and by the time I had finished I was sure they weren't involved. Which left me with a problem. A big one.

"So who sent him?" I asked.

They had no answer to that, and neither did I. Like most individuals I knew people who didn't like me, and I knew people I didn't like, but they could hardly be called enemies. Not the kind who would go to such elaborate lengths to hoax me—never mind produce 250 crisp new ones to aid them.

"Any dissatisfied clients?" Daniel asked.

No disatisfied clients—no clients at all, come to think of it.

"So what are you going to do?" Anna's voice broke into my reverie.

I drew myself up straight as if I had already made the decision that was only then forming in my brain.

"Investigate," I answered. "Find Thelma. What else can I do?"

"What if the money's stolen?"

I shrugged. "I guess I'll cross that bridge when I come to it," I said. I picked up the bottle of Bells and dropped it lightly into the dustbin. "Let's celebrate with a real whiskey," I said, "now that I'm no longer filing for a divorce from the lot of you."

I was nicely oiled by the time I arrived at Tony's Golders Green office.

Street Times was peopled by hacks like Tony who'd wakened up one day to the realization that their ulcers were never going to get any smaller. A few of them got together and decided that if they were going to start developing bosses' diseases, they might as well be their own bosses. They'd started a London-based magazine that—now in its middle age—no longer tried to compete for the youth market. In a way, I suppose, they were one of the few remaining relics of the sixties although they had long since grown away from nostalgia or angst and had settled, instead, for what they could do in a world grown increasingly hostile.

Their new offices were, however, not exactly friendly. Workaday would be a better description, sited between a Dorothy Perkins and a grimy solicitor, with a smell courtesy of Grodzinski, the baker, giving the only hint of atmosphere. I made a mental note to pick up a sliced rye and some cheese Danish as I located Tony in his glass cubicle. His shirt sleeves, I observed, were held up by rubber bands.

"Still preserving the image," I commented.

Tony glanced up from his computer and shot what, for him, approximated a smile.

"Bloody kid bit the buttons off," he said.

"And how is she?"

This time the smile was definite. "Great," he gushed. Catching himself, he ran a hand through his mousey brown hair. "For a monster. Want a coffee?"

"If it comes with a Danish," I said.

Tony frowned. "They make them by machine now," he said, "in some warehouse out in Bromley. The smell's bottled to give us the impression that the good old days are still with us."

"I'll pass then," I said. I perched myself on the edge of his desk and peered around in an attempt to read his screen. "Impressive symbols," I said. "*Street Times* going postmodernist?"

Tony moved the screen away. "Accounts," he said curtly. He didn't need to say more; I knew all about accounts. Which brought me to my business.

"Name of Martin Malloy mean anything to you?" I asked.

Tony yawned. "I'm losing my knack," he said. "You're no longer even bothering with the foreplay." He yawned again. "You used to at least pretend to be giving me something in exchange for my gems of information," he explained, "but since we've been exiled to the Green, I suppose you think I come cheap."

I shrugged. "Nothing much to offer," I said. "Business is slow."

"Slow to get off the ground, or slow to die?"

"The latter."

"Well, in that case," Tony said. He hit a cue on his keyboard and the machine began to whir. "Bloody noisy, this new technology," he said. "Now let's see if the data base moved with us." He typed fast with two fingers. "Malloy," he said out loud. "Martin, Mr."

I waited while he squinted his eyes at the screen, and then, a few seconds later, he hit a key and the bytes of information stopped rolling. "Thought I remembered him," Tony said. "An interesting case, Martin Malloy."

So he actually existed, I thought—interesting indeed.

"Martin, aka 'Mouse,' Malloy," Tony offered.

"Mouse?"

"A reference to his size. Never met him, but apparently he's on the big side."

"You could say that."

"And Mouse as well on account of the fact that he never talked to the cops." Tony's eyes scanned rapidly down the screen. "Malloy's a genius with numbers," he said. "When his face first hit the front pages, the gutter press got excited and tried to pin an idiot-savant label on him. He wouldn't play ball, so they dumped him."

"What was their interest in the first place?" I asked.

"Malloy was associated with some East End hoods," Tony answered, "part of a crack gang—you know the scene—New York comes to London. The word was that the police picked the Mouse up in an attempt to get him to finger the big men. He didn't, and someone started to kick up a stink about habeas corpus. The cops eventually got themselves out of trouble by persuading the inland revenue to charge him with tax evasion."

"Tax evasion?"

Tony grinned. "Modern, innit? The case against him was weak, but all the jury saw was a giant, and a black giant to boot, who refused to talk. They threw the book at him. Sad, really, although by the sounds of his physique, he'd have no trouble in jail."

I thought about the scar and wondered. "Any woman involved?" I asked.

Tony hit another key. "Not that I can see." He rolled the screen on again and then, finding nothing, wiped it clear. "Want me to check this out further?"

"If you have the time."

Tony yawned again. "Sure," he said. "I'll be in touch if . . ." He didn't finish the sentence: he started up on his computer again. That was it, no good-bye, he had done with me. It wasn't personal—Tony never was one for social niceties, and I knew he'd contact me if he found anything of interest. And besides, who was I to stand between a man and his collective's accounts? I left him to them.

Or tried to. I'd forgotten how much Tony liked to hold his conversations in transit. "Kate," he called when I was almost at the door.

I turned.

"Maybe you should let the business die," he said.

I shrugged and left.

I spent the evening on my own—alone, that is, so long as you don't count my alto. I counted it, I'd just had the whole thing resprung, and I spent a few hours rediscovering both its range and my limitations.

I usually played to get away from work, but this time I failed. An image of a man they called the Mouse kept weaving its way through the blues I played. I saw him as he stood there in my office, his bright clothes, contrasting with those sad eyes, a man with no home trapped for tax evasion. I was beginning to feel sorry for him—sorry that I had treated his visit as a hoax, sorry that I hadn't asked him more. That, I thought, was why I liked the job—and why I would miss it so much when I was forced to close. It wasn't often that you get the opportunity to meet giants who want to thank their social worker for introducing them to literature. Thelma must be quite a woman, I thought—certainly more trusting than I. I should have been more friendly; I should have tried harder.

I shook my head, moved the beat up tempo to fit with my version of South African township jazz, and put a brake on my regrets. Thelma, if she existed, was the social worker, not me. I would try and find her, that's all I could do. I had enough troubles of my own, I had the business to worry about.

Without noticing I slipped back into the blues.

It was hot when I got up, the kind of heat that visits London once every thirteen years. I opened the wardrobe in the hall, the one where I stored the clothes I never got a chance to wear, and stared at the uninspiring choices. In the end I decided to go for broke, fitted myself out in a tight black cotton skirt and flimsy pink T-shirt, threw a pair of thonged sandals on my feet, and took a jacket for protection from the vagaries of the English climate.

The flimsy pink number was already showing signs of wilting when I arrived at the address Martin Malloy had given me. What's more, it clashed with my destination.

The building was plum in the middle of the Arsenal, a cheerful item if ever I saw one. It was round and squat, and red and yellow—a low thing in the middle of a long row of detached gray brick. A kind of eighties version of a sixties domed tent, it was part of the council's attempt to decentralize its services in order to benefit the community.

The community, consisting mainly of women and children, who were crowded into a big room with narrow slanted windows, did not look impressed. I can't say I blamed them: the place was hot and, although cheerful, downright uncomfortable. When I asked for the duty social worker, I was told to take a seat. I gingerly lowered myself into a red plastic item that, bolted to the floor, resembled a bucket with large holes.

"Gets to your bum after an hour or two," said the woman to my left.

"Our Johnny got stuck in one once," said the woman to my right. "Had to get the fire brigade to cut him out. They blamed me, of course." She reached over and slapped her Johnny, who seemed to be making a second bid for fire brigade fame.

"Miss Baeier," a voice called.

I was shown into a small cubicle of a room, airless and lit by fluorescent, in which stood two chairs, a table, and a woman in her early thirties. She smiled at me from her seat and gestured to the second one. When I sat, I could hardly see her for the mound of papers piled in front of her.

She shifted to the right, pulled a manila file from the pile, and opened it. It was, I saw, lined with blank paper. She frowned, turned to her side, dug into a bag that could have doubled as a haversack and that hung on the back of her chair, and pulled out a biro. I saw that it was doing extra work as an advert for sausages. She used the pen to transfer my name from the slip I had filled in onto the first sheet of paper.

"What can I do for you?" she asked.

"I'm trying to find someone," I said.

The woman glanced up sharply, saw that I wasn't joking, and shut the file with a bang. "Ms. Baeier," she said clearly, "we are not all-powerful. We have strict guidelines to which we always adhere. I can tell you, without needing to check, that we draw the line at tracing missing persons. You might care to try the police—we never have much luck with them, but don't let that stop you." The lines in her face belied the aggression in her voice: she looked too tired to have only just started work.

I smiled at her. "Bad morning?"

She half returned my smile. "The worst," she said. "Except for yesterday and tomorrow."

"I won't waste your time then," I said. "I'm looking for a Thelma Parsons."

A look of alarm crossed the woman's face, a flash of response quickly concealed as she ducked behind the pile of papers. When she reemerged, she had gone bland again: I wondered whether I'd been imagining the sheer panic that had cut through her fatigue. She raised an eyebrow.

"Thelma was a social worker," I continued, "based here once. Hated the job as much as you all do and managed to escape. She's an old friend of mine. I was hoping you could help me find her."

It was weak and I knew it. Marlowe would have done better. But then I wasn't Marlowe, was I? I was just a private detective in a land that didn't like detectives, and a woman, not a man.

But then, I thought brightly, as her face seemed to soften at the mention of my friendship with Thelma, neither was this woman a reluctant witness with something to hide—just an overworked social worker fighting the disillusionment that seemed to come with the job these days. Maybe it would work.

It didn't. "We never release addresses of former employees," she said. "Nor, for that matter, of current employees." She was good at her job, but not good enough. Her eyes were narrowed, beaming hostility, contradicting her seeming unconcern.

I opened my mouth to try again, but she shook her head in the general direction of the door, dismissing me with a determined finality. She discarded the manila file and began her way through the one underneath. I got the message: I left.

My way out was blocked by a woman who thrust a small child toward me.

"Here, do me a favor and watch him for a second," she said. "Got to change the baby, and those chairs are useless." She was a pro: she sped down the corridor with yelling infant in arms. I looked down at the abandoned child.

He was a cute enough item if you managed to ignore the effluent issuing from his nose. I couldn't ignore it, so I took a tissue from my bag and moved it downward. He was out of range before the tissue had even a chance of reaching his face.

I recognized him. "Johnny?" I asked.

He wiped his nose with the back of his hand and nodded sullenly. I smiled. A gift from heaven, I thought, snot and all.

"How'd you like to earn fifty pence?" I asked.

Visibly he sized me up. "A pound," he said.

"Seventy pence?"

"A quid or nuffing," he said firmly. He folded his small arms together and stood there, facing me, his feet planted stubbornly on the ground.

I knew when I was beaten. I knelt down beside him and explained what I wanted. He nodded. When I had finished, he held out his hand, palm up. Into it I placed a pound coin that rapidly disappeared into his pocket. Then he nodded again.

As agreed, I walked away from him until I had rounded the corner. Then I waited.

Nothing happened. I waited some more—still nothing. *I've been had,* I thought. *Maybe Tony's right, I'm no detective.* Then suddenly, from around the corner, issued a scream, a bloodcurdling scream, the likes of which I had never before had the privilege of hearing. Once it came, paused, and then once again.

It worked like a dream. I heard a door open and a woman, my woman, call out, "What the hell's going on?"

She got another scream for a reply and some words this time. "My brovver," Johnny screamed. "My brovver, he's stuck."

"Oh save me," the woman muttered.

Johnny screamed again.

"All right, all right," she said. "I'll get him out. Just do me a favor and stop screaming, will you?"

They rounded the corner at a brisk pace, Johnny leading, the woman following. As they passed me, Johnny let out another yell and the woman quickened her pace, giving him a push as she did so.

I walked fast in the opposite direction, running when I had rounded the corner. I opened the door of her office and stumbled over to her chair. I grabbed her bag and began to rifle through it, one ear on the commotion outside.

It was a bottomless chasm I faced and a messy one at that. I pulled things out at random. The screaming had stopped and I heard the sound of a slap. I had little time left.

The bag was incredible. I dug deep, throwing out old Kleenex, keys, a plethora of credit cards (*social workers must be better paid these days,* I thought), and the occasional half-eaten nut. None of the contents fitted my preconception of what should be there. I dug again.

I was on the verge of giving up when I found what I'd been looking for— an address book, small and black. Except I was probably too late. I heard footsteps outside.

I opened the book to the *P* section. No Parsons there. The footsteps were coming closer.

I turned to the *T* section. And there it was, the name Thelma, no surname, just Thelma. Except it did me no good because underneath the name was a blank piece of paper, stuck on, tight. I know it was tight because I tried to get it off. No luck: I heard a rustling outside the door. So I did what I had to. I pulled the page out, shoved the book along with the rest of the garbage back into the bag, threw the bag over the chair, and ran for the door.

I collided with her there.

"Forgot my pen," I said. "One day I'll forget my head."

The anger in her face faded. "Tell me about it," she muttered before closing the door on me.

In a workers' café across the road I sat over a cup of milky hot water masquerading as tea and stared at the stolen page. There was no way I could remove the covering blankness. I'd tried again and all I'd managed to do was to tear a corner off it.

I turned the paper over. I could see the writing there, faint and inviting, but still indecipherable. I held the page up to the light and it became clearer but still incomprehensible. *Well, it would be,* I thought. *It's backward.*

I left my tea to its own devices and went to the toilet. I held the back of the page up to the scratched mirror above the basin—again the writing appeared, but still illegibly. I got a pen out of my bag and, holding the paper up to the exposed bulb, I slowly started to trace the lines that I could see.

It took a long time, but I managed it in the end. And when I'd finished, I could see, in writing that was not mine, an address, clearly written.

My tea was still waiting for me. I put some coins beside it and left them all to their own devices.

Thelma lived in a small terraced house almost opposite the football ground. Hers was in the middle of a row of look-alikes, all built from dingy gray brick, with lace curtains covering small square windows, low front gardens whose walls could never hold back the tide of litter from the fans, and dark-red-stained front steps that would once, in another age, have been daily scrubbed.

I stood on the steps and rang her bell. I got no response, no sound at all. I rang again but again without luck. I turned to go and it was then that, out of the corner my eye, I saw a portion of the dingy lace twitch. I waited but still nothing happened. I got the message. I turned away and walked back to my car, climbed in, revved it ostentatiously, and drove off. I drove around the block and then returned to her street, parking a few doors down, away from the lace curtain. I switched off the engine and waited.

It was two hours before anything happened. I concentrated mostly on my business or lack of it. I sat and I boiled and I wondered what I was doing, trapped in my own car on a sunny day, watching the minutes tick by and the money diminish, waiting for a fictional Thelma to make a move so I could report back to the fantastic Mouse. Tony was right, I thought, and Sam as well—it was time to move on, time to reenter the real world.

My hand was on my car keys, ready to switch on and leave, when I heard the footsteps. I ducked down, landing heavily on the floor. I strained my neck as I peered through the side mirror. It was her, all right, the woman from Thelma's old office, walking briskly down the pavement. She crossed in front of my car, so close that I could almost smell the anxiety emanating from her, and walked purposively up to Thelma's door.

It was opened almost immediately and kept open. I saw a hint of blue, but otherwise my social worker concealed her protagonist from me. For protagonists they obviously were: I didn't need to hear their conversation to guess that it was ugly—I could see it in the gestures of the social worker, in the hard set of her back, in the way she reached into her bag and flung something toward the door, in the way she walked away, and in the bang that sounded as the door closed.

I crouched down as she passed by me, but I needn't have bothered. She walked fast and angrily, lost in a world of her own making, muttering to herself. At one point she stopped and hit herself—quite literally hit herself on the head with the flat of her hand. I heard the sound of the blow from twenty yards away.

She started up again, and only when she had turned the corner did I get out of my car. I ignored the front of the house and instead walked round the block, counting houses until I reached Thelma's back gate. I pressed against it and it yielded slightly. One long push was enough to break the lock.

I made my way down the narrow path, past the overflowing dustbin and the small outhouse that must once have been the house's only toilet until I reached the kitchen door. I put my hand on the doorknob, and it opened as if it had been waiting for me. I stepped in.

I found myself in a ꞏitchen that stank of neglect. Dishes were piled on both sides of the sink, unwashed and uncleared. On the floor stood two saucers, one with the dregs of old milk, the other piled high with cat food. Plants wilted on the windowsill, geraniums that instead of enjoying the sun were being finished off by it.

And yet it was not a kitchen that I would ever have described as poor. It was packed with consumer durables, with microwaves, coffee percolators, automatic juicers, stainless steel knives, still wrapped and shining, and a variety of food processors of the latest design. An ideal home gone mad, I thought, as I walked through the room and into the hall.

I was faced with the choice of two doors that opened onto the narrow corridor, and I chose the one at the front, the one from which the lace curtain movement had originated. I found myself in a small room, dirty but tastefully furnished. There was one person in it, a woman in her middle thirties, clad in jeans and a low-slung silk blouse, her thin blond hair hanging weakly down the sides of her long face. She was standing by a small antique maple desk, staring at something on it.

She turned and saw me as soon as I entered, but otherwise she didn't move. Her face did, but not her body. On that pale face, a gamut of emotions crossed—displays of shock, of fear, and finally of a kind of resignation.

"What are you doing here?" she asked dully.

"The door was open," I said. "The back door."

"Have you got a warrant?" she asked.

I shook my head. "I'm not the police," I said. I watched as the resignation turned to slow anger.

"Well, in that case," she said, "I'll call them." She reached across the desk for the phone and picked up the receiver. But the movement seemed to have exhausted her. She stood still, holding it and staring at me. "What do you want?" she asked. The anger was replaced with despair.

I walked over and looked behind her. On the desk, I saw, were pieces of paper, scrawled with writing. There was some tracing paper there too, askew on one piece of the writing, but when she saw my eyes light on it she brushed against it, catapulting it to the floor. She stared at me defiantly.

"My name's Kate Baeier," I said. "I'm a private detective. A man called Martin Malloy hired me to find you."

"Martin?" Her voice rose and she repeated it. "Martin?"

"You used to visit him in prison," I said.

Her face cleared as she remembered and then it disintegrated again, not in fear, this time, but rather in hilarity. The laughter came slowly at first, from deep inside her, surfacing as a giggle but soon transformed into near hysteria. I stood and waited as she laughed in my face, laughed and laughed until the tears streamed down her cheeks.

Gradually the laugh subsided. She sniffed and wiped her eyes with the back of one hand. She looked at me and giggled again, controlling herself only by looking away.

"A private detective," she muttered. "You're not for real."

I shrugged. "Martin wants to see you," I said.

"Well, he can't." Her words had a final ring to them.

"He just wants to thank you," I explained.

The look she threw me was one of pure contempt, not for me, I thought, but for Martin.

"Gimme a break," she said.

"To thank you for opening up the world of fiction to him."

She looked as if she was going to laugh again, and I didn't really blame her. Put like that, it sounded ridiculous. If I hadn't met Martin Malloy, I too would have laughed.

And Thelma had met Martin. She didn't laugh. She smiled but not in mirth.

"He taught me something too," she said in a voice that was pure malice. "The dumb bastard."

I didn't know until then how much I had cared, how much I wanted to deliver to Martin Malloy what he had requested. I acted without thinking. First, I saw the tracing paper on the floor with new eyes, with eyes that were looking at a mirror, then I took in the writing on the desk, and then I acted. I quickly moved behind her and wrenched open a drawer. She was too surprised to prevent me, and we both watched as it tumbled to the floor, spilling its contents. She flung herself on them, but too late to stop me from confirming what I had already guessed.

"Fraud," I said. "That's what it is."

From the floor she looked up at me, surrounded by small pieces of plastic, her eyes flashing anger. I remembered the social worker's bag, and the visit that she had just paid, and I remembered the goods in the kitchen. It made sense.

"Credit card fraud," I said, thinking out loud. "The tracing paper is how you copy the signatures."

She was down but not out, no longer vulnerable, in a way. She glared up at me. "So what are you going to do about it?" she shot.

I didn't answer and she didn't need me to.

"Nothing," she said. "You're the do-gooder type, aren't you? I should know, I've tried that game. It gets you nowhere."

"Except the occasional thanks," I commented.

"Don't give me that," she said. "Thanks never buttered any bread. I've met enough Martin Malloys in my time, I don't need to meet any more. A casualty of the system, that's all he is, a well-meaning idiot without a chance. He even gave me tips on how to forge signatures, until he realized that my interest was more than academic. Then he had the cheek to lecture me, as if I was the one who had been jailed. Well, I've served my own kind of time, I'm free now. I don't owe anybody anything; I don't owe Martin Malloy the time of day. I can tell you . . ."

I knew she was right; she could have told me. She looked set to go on for a good few hours. I didn't need to listen. I walked out of the room, through the hall, opened the front door, and stepped into the bright sunshine. I left the door open, hoping that some of the air would flow in. I wasn't optimistic.

Martin Malloy turned up two days later. I was in my office waiting for him. I had nothing else to do but wait, and I couldn't shake off the feeling of uselessness that had settled on me ever since I'd met Thelma.

I'd left the door open and he didn't bother to ring the bell this time. He just arrived in my office, a huge man with a surprisingly light tread.

"Did you find her?" he asked.

I nodded.

When he smiled, his face opened up like an exotic flower that the scar did nothing to spoil. "When can we meet?" he asked.

I stood up. "She doesn't want to see you," I said.

I don't know what I expected—fury, sorrow, violence even, but all I got was a vague look of disappointment. He nodded and made as if he were about to go. But then he changed his mind.

"Is Thelma all right?" he asked.

Wrong-footed, I didn't know how to answer. I looked into those warm brown eyes and I shivered. I remembered the sight of that smile, and I knew that I didn't want to disappoint it.

"She's fine," I lied. "Just busy."

I should have known better: Malloy was no fool.

"Don't try and kid me," he said, and his voice was as hard as his body. "Don't treat me like a child."

I sat down. "I'm sorry," I said. "I shouldn't have pretended. Thelma is far from fine. She's involved in some kind of credit card fiddle." I paused. "And I'm not sure she's doing too well." I finished quickly, feeling somehow that I had betrayed someone. I looked away, out the window and at the faultless blue sky.

"Anything I could do to help?" he asked. "She helped me, you know." His voice was sad.

I shook my head and looked at him again. "I'm not sure—" I started.

But he was lost in his own thoughts, and he spoke them out loud. "I knew it was something stupid," he said. "I tried to tell her that people like us just don't win. I thought if I was no longer behind bars, she would listen to me."

I remembered what Thelma had said about him, and I couldn't help myself. "She's a bitch," I snapped. "Beyond saving."

"Don't say that," he said. "She's just confused. Nobody's beyond saving."

I nodded in recognition of sentiment rather than in agreement with the meaning. I reached into my desk and pulled out his money, the money that I had not yet touched.

"It didn't take me long," I said. "You're due some back."

He looked at me and smiled, but his smile was no longer open. "Keep it," he said airily. "There's plenty more where that came from. Payment for keeping my trap shut. Guilt money for doing hard time." His face softened. "I knew Thelma was desperate," he said. "That's why I wanted to thank her. I thought if somebody, anybody, told her how much she'd done for them, it might give her hope. I guess I was too late."

I didn't say anything. What was there to say?

He hadn't finished.

"Did you get somebody to look for me?" he asked.

I nodded.

"My landlord chucked me out," he said. "You should have known nobody wants to house a convict. Especially one who looks like me. Why did you do it?"

I felt I owed him the truth and so I gave it to him. "Because I wasn't sure you really existed," I said.

He nodded, to himself rather than me. "I feel sorry for your type, you know," he said, again almost as if to himself. "I came to literature late, but there's one thing I can do that you can't. I can distinguish between fact and fiction."

I shrugged and I looked at him, at this huge man, dressed this time in gold threads that shimmered when he moved. I smiled. "It's not always easy," I said.

He saw my look and he returned my smile. He strode over to me, enfolded one of my hands in his big paws, and clasped it. "Nice to have met you, Kate Baeier," he said. He let go of my hand. "Can I give you one last piece of advice?"

"How can I refuse?"

"Open the windows," he said. "Let the sun shine in. Breathe the air."

"Thanks," I said.

He shrugged and looked at me. "A balance sheet isn't everything," he said. "I should know, I'm good at numbers. Business will pick up. You're good at your job—you found Thelma, didn't you?"

He left the room as quietly as he had arrived. I climbed on my chair so I could watch him in the street, but somehow I missed his exit.

I was in the right position, so I took his advice.

I opened the windows.

It was difficult, but I managed.

MARGARET MARON's books featuring the New York Police Department's Sigrid Harald are both complex mysteries and intense character studies. Harald appears in over half a dozen books to date, including such notable works as *Corpus Christmas* and *One Coffee With.* Ms. Maron lives in Raleigh, North Carolina.

DEBORAH'S JUDGMENT

Margaret Maron

"And Deborah judged Israel at that time."

An inaudible ripple of cognizance swept through the congregation as the pastor of Bethel Baptist Church paused in his reading of the text and beamed down at us.

I was seated on the aisle near the front of the church, and when Barry Blackman's eyes met mine, I put a modest smile on my face, then tilted my head in ladylike acknowledgment of the pretty compliment he was paying me by his choice of subject for this morning's sermon. A nice man but hardly Christianity's most original preacher. I'd announced my candidacy back in December, so this wasn't the first time I'd heard that particular text, and my response had become almost automatic.

He lowered his eyes to the huge Bible and continued to read aloud, *"And she dwelt under the palm tree of Deborah, between Ramah and Bethel in Mount Ephraim; and the children of Israel came up to her for judgment."*

From your mouth to God's ear, Barry, I thought.

Eight years of courtroom experience let me listen to the sermon with an outward show of close attention while inwardly my mind jumped on and off a dozen trains of thought. I wondered, without really caring, if Barry was still the terrific kisser he'd been the summer after ninth grade when we both drove tractors for my oldest brother during tobacco-barning season.

There was an S curve between the barns and the back fields where the lane dipped past a stream and cut through a stand of tulip poplars and sweetgum trees. Our timing wasn't good enough to hit every trip, but at least two or three times a day it'd work out that we passed each other there in the shady coolness, one on the way out to the field with empty drags, the other headed back to the barn with drags full of heavy green tobacco leaves.

Nobody seemed to notice that I occasionally returned to the barn more flushed beneath the bill of my baseball cap than even the August sun would merit, although I did have to endure some teasing one day when a smear of tobacco tar appeared on my pink T-shirt right over my left breast. "Looks like somebody tried to grab a handful," my sister-in-law grinned.

I muttered something about the tractor's tar-gummy steering wheel, but I changed shirts at lunchtime and for the rest of the summer I wore the darkest T-shirts in my dresser drawer.

Now Barry Blackman was a preacher man running to fat, the father of two little boys and a new baby girl, while Deborah Knott was a still-single attorney running for a seat on the court bench, a seat being vacated against his will by old Harrison Hobart, who occasionally fell asleep these days while charging his own juries.

As Barry drew parallels between Old Testament Israel and modern Colleton County, I plotted election strategy. After the service, I'd do a little schmoozing among the congregation—

Strike "schmoozing," my subconscious stipulated sternly, and I was stricken myself to realize that Lev Schuster's Yiddish phrases continued to infect my vocabulary. Here in rural North Carolina schmoozing's still called socializing, and I'd better not forget it before the primary. I pushed away errant thoughts of Lev and concentrated on lunch at Beulah's. For that matter, where *was* Beulah and why weren't she and J.C. seated there beside me?

Beulah had been my mother's dearest friend, and her daughter-in-law, Helen, is president of the local chapter of Mothers Against Drunk Driving. They were sponsoring a meet-the-candidates reception at four o'clock in the fellowship hall of a nearby Presbyterian church, and three of the four men running for Hobart's seat would be there too. (The fourth was finishing up the community service old Hobart had imposed in lieu of a fine for driving while impaired, but he really didn't expect to win many MADD votes anyhow.)

Barry's sermon drew to an end just a hair short of equating a vote for Deborah Knott as a vote for Jesus Christ. The piano swung into the opening chords of "Just as I Am," and the congregation stood to sing all five verses.

Happily, no one accepted the hymn's invitation to be saved that morning, and after a short closing prayer we were dismissed.

I'm not a member at Bethel, but I'd been a frequent visitor from the month I was born; so I got lots of hugs and howdies and promises of loyal support when the primary rolled around. I hugged and howdied right back and thanked them kindly, all the time edging toward my car.

It was starting to bother me that neither Beulah nor J.C. had come to church. Then Miss Callie Ogburn hailed me from the side door, talking sixty to the yard as she bustled across the grass.

"Beulah called me up first thing this morning and said tell you about J.C. and for you to come on anyhow. She phoned all over creation last night trying to let you know she's still expecting you to come for dinner."

That explained all those abortive clicks on my answering machine. Beulah was another of my parents' generation who wouldn't talk to a tape. I waited till Miss Callie ran out of breath, then asked her what it was Beulah wanted to tell me about J.C.

"He fell off the tractor and broke his leg yesterday, and he's not used to the crutches yet, so Beulah didn't feel like she ought to leave him this morning. You know how she spoils him."

I did. J.C. was Beulah's older brother, and he'd lived with her and her husband Sam almost from the day they were married more than forty years ago. J.C. was a born bachelor, and except for the war years when he worked as a carpenter's helper at an air base over in Goldsboro, he'd never had much ambition beyond helping Sam farm. Sam always said J.C. wasn't much of a leader but he was a damn good follower and earned every penny of his share of the crop profits.

Although I'd called them Cousin Beulah and Cousin Sam till I was old enough to drop the courtesy title, strictly speaking, only Sam Johnson was blood kin. But Beulah and my mother had been close friends since childhood, and Beulah's two children fit into the age spaces around my older brothers, which was why we'd spent so many Sundays at Bethel Baptist.

When Sam died seven or eight years ago, Sammy Junior took over, and J.C. still helped out even though he'd slowed down right much. At least, J.C. called it right much. I could only hope I'd feel like working half days on a tractor when I reached seventy-two.

Five minutes after saying good-bye to Miss Callie, I was turning off the paved road into the sandy lane that ran past the Johnson home place. The doors there were closed and none of their three cars were in the yard, but Helen's Methodist and I'd heard Beulah mention the long-winded new preacher at her daughter-in-law's church.

Helen and Sammy Junior had remodeled and painted the shabby old two-story wooden farmhouse after old Mrs. Johnson died, and it was a handsome place these days: gleaming white aluminum siding and dark blue shutters, sitting in a shady grove of hundred-year-old white oaks.

Beulah's brick house—even after forty years, everyone in the family still calls it the "new house"—was farther down the lane and couldn't be seen from the road or the home place.

My car topped the low ridge that gave both generations their privacy, then swooped down toward a sluggish creek that had been dredged out into a nice-size irrigation pond beyond the house. As newlyweds, Sam and Beulah had planted pecans on each side of the lane, and mature nut trees now met in a tall arch.

The house itself was rooted in its own grove of pecans and oaks, with underplantings of dogwoods, crepe myrtles, redbuds, and flowering pears. Pink and white azaleas lined the foundation all around. On this warm day in late April, the place was a color illustration out of *Southern Living*. I pulled up under a chinaball tree by the back porch and tapped my horn, expecting to see Beulah appear at the screen door with her hands full of biscuit dough and an ample print apron protecting her Sunday dress against flour smudges.

A smell of burning paper registered oddly as I stepped from the car. It wasn't cool enough for a fire, and no one on this farm would break the fourth commandment by burning trash on the Sabbath.

There was no sign of Beulah when I crossed the wide planks of the wooden porch and called through the screen, but the kitchen was redolent of baking ham. J.C.'s old hound dog crawled out from under the back steps and wagged his tail at me hopefully. The screen door was unhooked, and the inner door stood wide.

"Beulah?" I called again. "J.C.?"

No answer. Yet her Buick and J.C.'s Ford pickup were both parked under the barn shelter at the rear of the yard.

The kitchen, dining room, and den ran together in one large L-shaped space, and when a quick glance into the formal, seldom-used living room revealed no one there either, I crossed to the stairs in the center hall. Through an open door at the far end of the hall, I could see into Donna Sue's old bedroom, now the guest room.

The covers on the guest bed had been straightened, but the spread was folded down neatly and pillows were piled on top of the rumpled quilt as if J.C. had rested there after Beulah made the bed. He wouldn't be able to use the stairs until his leg mended, so he'd probably moved in here for the duration. A stack of *Field and Stream* magazines and an open pack of his menthol cigarettes on the nightstand supported my hypothesis.

The house remained silent as I mounted the stairs.

"Anybody home?"

Beulah's bedroom was deserted and as immaculate as downstairs except for the desk. She and Sam had devoted a corner of their bedroom to the paper work connected with the farm. Although Sammy Junior did most of the farm records now on a computer over at his house, Beulah had kept the oak desk. One of my own document binders lay on its otherwise bare top. I'd drawn up her new will less than a month ago and had brought it out to her myself in this very same binder. I lifted the cover. The holographic distribution of small personal keepsakes she had insisted on was still there, but the will itself was missing.

For the first time since I'd entered this quiet house, I felt a small chill of foreboding.

Sammy Junior's old bedroom had been turned into a sewing room, and it was as empty as the bathroom. Ditto J.C.'s. As a child I'd had the run of every room in the house except this one, so I'd never entered it alone.

From the doorway, it looked like a rerun of the others: everything vacuumed and polished and tidy; but when I stepped inside, I saw the bottom drawer of the wide mahogany dresser open. Inside were various folders secured by brown cords, bundles of tax returns, account ledgers, bank statements, and two large flat candy boxes, which I knew held old family snapshots. More papers and folders were loosely stacked on the floor beside a low footstool, as if someone had sat there to sort through the drawer and had then been interrupted before the task was finished. Beulah would never leave a clutter like that.

Thoroughly puzzled, I went back down to the kitchen. The ham had been in the oven at least a half hour too long, so I turned it off and left the door cracked. The top burners were off, but each held a pot of cooked vegetables, still quite hot. Wherever Beulah was, she hadn't been gone very long.

Year round, she and J.C. and Sam, too, when he was alive, loved to walk the land, and if they weren't expecting company, it wasn't unusual to find them out at the pond or down in the woods. But with me invited for Sunday dinner along with Sammy Junior and Helen and their three teenagers? And with J.C.'s broken leg?

Not hardly likely, as my daddy would say.

Nevertheless, I went out to my car and blew the horn long and loud.

Buster, the old hound, nuzzled my hand as I stood beside the car indecisively. And that was another thing. If J.C. were out stumping across the farm on crutches, Buster wouldn't be hanging around the back door. He'd be right out there with J.C.

It didn't make sense, yet if there's one thing the law has taught me, it's that it doesn't pay to formulate a theory without all the facts. I headed back inside to phone and see if Helen and Sammy Junior were home yet, and as I lifted the receiver from the kitchen wall, I saw something I'd missed before.

At the far end of the den, beyond the high-backed couch, the fireplace screen had been moved to one side of the hearth, and there were scraps of charred paper in the grate.

I remembered the smell of burning paper that had hung in the air when I first arrived. I started toward the fireplace, and now I could see the coffee table strewn with the Sunday edition of the Raleigh *News and Observer.*

As I rounded the high couch, I nearly tripped on a pair of crutches, but they barely registered, so startled was I by seeing J.C. lying there motionless, his eyes closed.

"Glory, J.C.!" I exclaimed. "You asleep? That must be some painkiller the doctor—"

I suddenly realized that the brightly colored sheet of Sunday comics over his chest was drenched in his own bright blood.

I knelt beside the old man and clutched his callused, work-worn hand. It was still warm. His faded blue eyes opened, rolled back in his head, then focused on me.

"Deb'rah?" His voice was faint and came from far, far away. "I swear I plumb forgot . . ."

He gave a long sigh and his eyes closed again.

Dwight Bryant is detective chief of the Colleton County Sheriff's Department. After calling the nearest rescue squad, I'd dialed his mother's phone number on the off chance that he'd be there in the neighborhood and not twenty-two miles away at Dobbs, the county seat.

Four minutes flat after I hung up the phone, I saw his Chevy pickup zoom over the crest of the lane and tear through the arch of pecan trees. He was followed by a bright purple TR, and even in this ghastly situation, I had to smile at his exasperation as Miss Emily Bryant bounded from the car and hurried up the steps ahead of him.

"Damn it all, Mother, if you set the first foot inside that house, I'm gonna arrest you, and I mean it!"

She turned on him, a feisty little carrottop Chihuahua facing down a sandy-brown Saint Bernard. "If you think I'm going to stay out here when one of my oldest and dearest friends may be lying in there—"

"She's not, Miss Emily," I said tremulously. J.C.'s blood was under my fingernails from where I'd stanched his chest wound. "I promise you. I looked in every room."

"And under all the beds and in every closet?" She stamped her small foot imperiously on the porch floor. "I won't touch a thing, Dwight, but I've got to look."

"No." That was the law talking, not her son; and she huffed but quit arguing.

"Okay, Deborah," said Dwight, holding the screen door open for me. "Show me."

Forty-five minutes later we knew no more than before. The rescue squad had arrived and departed again with J.C., who was still unconscious and barely clinging to life.

Sammy Junior and Helen were nearly frantic over Beulah's disappearance and were torn between following the ambulance and staying put till there was word of her. Eventually they thought to call Donna Sue, who said she'd meet the ambulance at the hospital and stay with J.C. till they heard more.

A general APB had been issued for Beulah, but since nobody knew how she left, there wasn't much besides her physical appearance to put on the wire.

Dwight's deputies processed the den and J.C.'s room like a crime scene. After they finished, Dwight and I walked through the house with Sammy Junior and Helen; but they, too, saw nothing out of the ordinary except for the papers strewn in front of J.C.'s bedroom dresser.

Sammy Junior's impression was the same as mine. "It's like Mama was interrupted."

"Doing what?" asked Dwight.

"Probably getting Uncle J.C.'s insurance papers together for him. I said I'd take 'em over to the hospital tomorrow. In all the excitement yesterday when he broke his leg, we didn't think about 'em."

He started to leave the room, then hesitated. "Y'all find his gun?"

"Gun?" said Dwight.

Sammy Junior pointed to a pair of empty rifle brackets over the bedroom door. "That's where he keeps his .22."

Much as we'd all like to believe this is still God's country, everything peaceful and nice, most people now latch their doors at night, and they do keep loaded guns around for more than rats and snakes and wild dogs.

Helen shivered and instinctively moved closer to Sammy Junior. "The back door's always open, Dwight. I'll bet you anything some burglar or rapist caught her by surprise and forced her to go with him. And then J.C. probably rared up on the couch and they shot him like you'd swat a fly."

I turned away from the pain on Sammy Junior's face and stared through the bedroom window as Dwight said, "Been too many cars down the lane and through the yard for us to find any tread marks."

Any lawyer knows how easily the lives of good decent people can be shattered, but I'll never get used to the abruptness of it. Trouble seldom comes creeping up gently, giving a person time to prepare or get out of the way. It's always the freakish bolt of lightning out of a clear blue sky, the jerk of a steering wheel, the collapse of something rock solid only a second ago.

From the window I saw puffy white clouds floating serenely over the farm. The sun shone as brightly as ever on flowering trees and new-planted corn, warming the earth for another round of seedtime and harvest. A soft wind smoothed the field where J.C. had been disking before his accident yesterday, and in the distance the pond gleamed silver-green before a stand of willows.

My eye was snagged by what looked like a red-and-white cloth several yards into the newly disked field. Probably something Buster had pulled off the clothesline, I thought, and was suddenly aware that the others were waiting for my answer to a question I'd barely heard.

"No," I replied. "I'd have noticed another car or truck coming out of the lane. Couldn't have missed them by much, though, because the vegetables on the stove were still hot. Beulah must have turned them off just before going upstairs."

"It's a habit with her," Sammy Junior said. He had his arm around Helen and was kneading her shoulder convulsively. It would probably be bruised tomorrow, but Helen didn't seem to notice.

"Mama burned so many pots when we were kids that she got to where she wouldn't leave the kitchen without turning off the vegetables. She'd mean to come right back, but then there was always something that needed doing, and you know how Mama is."

We did. We surely did. "Whatsoever thy hand findeth to do" must have been written with Beulah in mind. She always reacted impulsively and couldn't pass a dusty surface or a dirty windowpane or anything out of place without cleaning it or taking it back to its rightful spot in the house.

Maybe that's why that scrap of red-and-white cloth out in the field bothered me. If I could see it, so would Beulah. She wouldn't let it lie out there ten minutes if she could help it, and it was with a need to restore some of her order that I slipped away from the others.

Downstairs, the crime scene crew had finished with the kitchen; and for lack of anything more useful to do, Miss Emily had decided that everybody'd fare better on a full stomach. She'd put bowls of vegetables on the counter, sliced the ham, and set out glasses and a jug of sweet iced tea. At this returning semblance of the ordinary, Helen and Sammy Junior's three anxious teenagers obediently filled their plates and went outside under the trees to eat. Their parents and Dwight weren't enthusiastic about food at the moment, but Miss Emily bullied them into going through the motions. Even Dwight's men had to stop and fix a plate.

No one noticed as I passed through the kitchen and down the back steps, past the Johnson grandchildren, who were feeding ham scraps to Buster and talking in low worried tones.

The lane cut through the yard, skirted the end of the field, then wound circuitously around the edge of the woods and on down to the pond; but the red-and-white rag lay on a beeline from the back door to the pond and I hesitated about stepping off the grass. My shoes were two-inch sling-back pumps, and they'd be wrecked if I walked out into the soft dirt of the newly disked field.

As I dithered, I saw that someone else had recently crossed the field on foot.

A single set of tracks.

With growing horror I remembered the red-and-white hostess aprons my aunt Zell had sewed for all her friends last Christmas.

I ran back to my car, grabbed the sneakers I keep in the trunk, and then rushed to call Dwight.

It was done strictly by the book.

Dwight's crime scene crew would later methodically photograph and measure and take pains not to disturb a single clod till every mark Beulah had left on the soft dirt was thoroughly documented; but the rest of us hurried through the turned field, paralleling the footprints from a ten-foot distance and filled with foreboding by the steady, unwavering direction those footsteps had taken.

Beulah's apron lay about two hundred feet from the edge of the yard. She must have untied the strings and just let it fall as she walked away from it.

The rifle, though, had been deliberately pitched. We could see where she stopped, the depth of her footprints where she heaved it away from her as if it were something suddenly and terribly abhorrent.

After that, there was nothing to show that she'd hesitated a single second. Her footprints went like bullets, straight down to the pond and into the silent, silver-green water.

As with most farm ponds dredged for irrigation, the bottom dropped off steeply from the edge to discourage mosquito larvae.

"How deep is it there?" Dwight asked when we arrived breathless and panting.

"Twelve feet," said Sammy Junior. "And she never learned how to swim."

His voice didn't break, but his chest was heaving, his face got red, and tears streamed from his eyes. "Why? In God's name, *why*, Dwight? Helen? Deb'rah? You all *know* Uncle J.C. near 'bout worships Mama. And we've always teased her that J.C. stood for Jesus Christ the way she's catered to him."

It was almost dark before they found Beulah's body.

No one tolled the heavy iron bell at the home place. The old way of alerting the neighborhood to fire or death has long since been replaced by the telephone, but the reaction hasn't changed much in two hundred years.

By the time that second ambulance passed down the lane, this one on its way to the state's medical examiner in Chapel Hill, cars filled the yard and lined the ditch banks on either side of the road. And there was no place in Helen's kitchen or dining room to set another plate of food. It would have taken a full roll of tinfoil to cover all the casseroles, biscuits, pies, deviled eggs, and platters of fried chicken, sliced turkey, and roast pork that had been brought in by shocked friends and relatives.

My aunt Zell arrived, white-faced and grieving, the last of three adventuresome country girls who'd gone off to Goldsboro during World War II to work at the air base. I grew up on stories of those war years: how J.C. had been sent over by his and Beulah's parents to keep an eye on my mother, Beulah, and Aunt Zell and protect them from the dangers of a military town, how they'd tried to fix him up with a WAC from New Jersey, the Saturday night dances, the innocent flirtations with that steady stream of young airmen who passed through the Army Air Forces Technical Training School at Seymour Johnson Field on their way to the airfields of Europe.

It wasn't till I was eighteen, the summer between high school and college, the summer Mother was dying, that I learned it hadn't all been lighthearted laughter.

We'd been sorting through a box of old black-and-white snapshots that Mother was determined to date and label before she died. Among the pictures of her or Aunt Zell or Beulah perched on the wing of a bomber or jitterbugging with anonymous, interchangeable airmen, there was one of Beulah and a young man. They had their arms around each other, and there was a sweet solemnity in their faces that separated this picture from the other clowning ones.

"Who's that?" I asked, and Mother sat staring into the picture for so long that I had to ask again.

"His name was Donald," she finally replied. Then her face took on an earnest look I'd come to know that summer, the look that meant I was to be entrusted with another secret, another scrap of her personal history that she couldn't bear to take to her grave untold even though each tale began, "Now you mustn't ever repeat this, but—"

"Donald Farraday came from Norwood, Nebraska," she said. "Exactly halfway between Omaha and Lincoln on the Platte River. That's what he always said. After he shipped out, Beulah used to look at the map and lay her finger halfway between Omaha and Lincoln and make Zell and me promise that we'd come visit her."

"I thought Sam was the only one she ever dated seriously," I protested.

"Beulah was the only one *Sam* ever dated seriously," Mother said crisply. "He had his eye on her from the time she was in grade school and he and J.C. used to go hunting together. She wrote to him while he was fighting the

Japs, but they weren't going steady or anything. And she'd have never married Sam if Donald hadn't died."

"Oh," I said, suddenly understanding the sad look that sometimes shadowed Beulah's eyes when only minutes before she and Mother and Aunt Zell might have been giggling over some Goldsboro memory.

Donald Farraday was from a Nebraska wheat farm, Mother told me, on his way to fight in Europe. Beulah met him at a jitterbug contest put on by the canteen, and it'd been love at first sight. Deep and true and all-consuming. They had only sixteen days and fifteen nights together, but that was enough to know this wasn't a passing wartime romance. Their values, their dreams, everything meshed.

"And they had so much fun together. You've never seen two people laugh so much over nothing. She didn't even cry when he shipped out because she was so happy thinking about what marriage to him was going to be like after the war was over."

"How did he die?"

"We never really heard," said Mother. "She had two of the sweetest, most beautiful letters you could ever hope to read, and then nothing. That was near the end when fighting was so heavy in Italy—we knew he was in Italy though it was supposed to be secret. They weren't married so his parents would've gotten the telegram, and of course, not knowing anything about Beulah, they couldn't write her."

"So what happened?"

"The war ended. We all came home, I married your daddy, Zell married James. Sam came back from the South Pacific and with Donald dead, Beulah didn't care who she married."

"Donna Sue!" I said suddenly.

"Yes," Mother agreed. "Sue for me, Donna in memory of Donald. She doesn't know about him, though, and don't you ever tell her." Her face was sad as she looked at the photograph in her hand of the boy and girl who'd be forever young, forever in love. "Beulah won't let us mention his name, but I know she still grieves for what might have been."

After Mother was gone, I never spoke to Beulah about what I knew. The closest I ever came was my junior year at Carolina when Jeff Creech dumped me for a psych major and I moped into the kitchen where Beulah and Aunt Zell were drinking coffee. I moaned about how my heart was broken and I couldn't go on and Beulah had smiled at me, "You'll go on, sugar. A woman's body doesn't quit just because her heart breaks."

Sudden tears had misted Aunt Zell's eyes—we Stephensons can cry over telephone commercials—and Beulah abruptly left.

"She was remembering Donald Farraday, wasn't she?" I asked.

"Sue told you about him?"

"Yes."

Aunt Zell had sighed then. "I don't believe a day goes by that she doesn't remember him."

The endurance of Beulah's grief had suddenly put Jeff Creech into perspective, and I realized with a small pang that losing him probably wasn't going to blight the rest of my life.

As I put my arms around Aunt Zell, I thought of her loss: Mother gone, now Beulah. Only J.C. left to remember those giddy girlhood years. At least the doctors were cautiously optimistic that he'd recover from the shooting.

"Why did she do it?" I asked.

But Aunt Zell was as perplexed as the rest of us. The house was crowded with people who'd known and loved Beulah and J.C. all their lives, and few could recall a true cross word between older brother and younger sister.

"Oh, Mama'd get fussed once in a while when he'd try to keep her from doing something new," said Donna Sue.

Every wake I've ever attended, the survivors always alternate between sudden paroxysms of tears and a need to remember and retell. For all the pained bewilderment and unanswered questions that night, Beulah's wake was no different.

"Remember, Sammy, how Uncle J.C. didn't want her to buy that place at the beach?"

"He never liked change," her brother agreed. "He talked about jellyfish and sharks—"

"—and sun poisoning," Helen said with a sad smile as she refilled his glass of iced tea. "Don't forget the sun poisoning."

"Changed his tune soon enough once he got down there and the fish started biting," said a cousin as he bit into a sausage biscuit.

One of Dwight's deputies signaled me from the hallway, and I left them talking about how J.C.'d tried to stop Beulah from touring England with one of her alumnae groups last year, and how he'd fretted the whole time she was gone, afraid her plane would crash into the Atlantic or be hijacked by terrorists.

"Dwight wants you back over there," said the deputy and drove me through the gathering dark, down the lane to where Beulah's house blazed with lights.

Dwight was waiting for me in the den. They'd salvaged a few scraps from the fireplace, but the ashes had been stirred with a poker and there wasn't much left to tell what had been destroyed. Maybe a handful of papers, Dwight thought. "And this. It fell behind the grate before it fully burned."

The sheet was crumpled and charred, but enough remained to see the words *Last Will and Testament of Beulah Ogburn Johnson* and the opening paragraph about revoking all earlier wills.

"You were her lawyer," said Dwight. "Why'd she burn her will?"

"I don't know," I answered, honestly puzzled. "Unless—"

"Unless what?"

"I'll have to read my copy tomorrow, but there's really not going to be much difference between what happens if she died intestate and—" I interrupted myself, remembering. "In fact, if J.C. dies, it'll be exactly the same, Dwight. Sammy Junior and Donna Sue still split everything."

"And if he lives?"

"If this were still a valid instrument," I said, choosing my words carefully, "J.C. would have a lifetime right to this house and Beulah's share of the farm income, with everything divided equally between her two children when he died; without the will, he's not legally entitled to stay the night."

"They'd never turn him out."

I didn't respond and Dwight looked at me thoughtfully.

"But without the will, they could if they wanted to," he said slowly.

Dwight Bryant's six or eight years older than I, and he's known me all my life, yet I don't think he'd ever looked at me as carefully as he did that night in Beulah's den, in front of that couch soaked in her brother's blood. "And if he'd done something bad enough to make their mother shoot him and then go drown herself . . ."

"They could turn him out and not a single voice in the whole community would speak against it," I finished for him.

Was that what Beulah wanted? Dead or alive, she was still my client. But I wondered: when she shot J.C. and burned her will, had she been of sound mind?

By next morning, people were beginning to say no. There was no sane reason for Beulah's act, they said, so it must have been a sudden burst of insanity, and wasn't there a great-aunt on her daddy's side that'd been a little bit queer near the end?

J.C. regained consciousness, but he was no help.

"I was resting on the couch," he said, "and I never heard a thing till I woke up hurting and you were there, Deb'rah."

He was still weak, but fierce denial burned in his eyes when they told him that Beulah had shot him. "She never!"

"Her fingerprints are on your rifle," said Dwight.

"She never!" He gazed belligerently from Donna Sue to Sammy Junior. "She never. Not her own brother. Where is she? You better not've jailed her, Dwight!"

He went into shock when they told him Beulah was dead. Great sobbing cries of protest racked his torn and broken body. It was pitiful to watch. Donna Sue petted and hugged him, but the nurse had to inject a sedative to calm him, and she asked us to leave.

I was due in court anyhow, and afterwards there was a luncheon speech at the Jaycees and a pig-picking that evening to raise funds for the children's hospital. I fell into bed exhausted, but instead of sleeping, my mind began to replay everything that had happened Sunday, scene by scene. Suddenly there was a freeze-frame on the moment I discovered J.C.

Next morning I was standing beside his hospital bed before anyone else got there.

"What was it you forgot?" I asked him.

The old man stared at me blankly. "Huh?"

"When I found you, you said, 'Deborah, I swear I plumb forgot.' Forgot what, J.C.?"

His faded blue eyes shifted to the shiny get-well balloons tethered to the foot of his bed by colorful streamers.

"I don't remember saying that," he lied.

From the hospital, I drove down to the town commons and walked along the banks of our muddy river. It was another beautiful spring day, but I was harking back to Sunday morning, trying to think myself into Beulah's mind.

You're a sixty-six-year-old widow, I thought. You're cooking Sunday dinner for your children and for the daughter of your dead friend. *(She's running for judge, Sue. Did you ever imagine it?)* And there's J.C. calling from the den about his insurance papers. So you turn off the vegetables and go upstairs and look in his drawer for the policies and you find—

What do you find that sends you back downstairs with a rifle in your hands and papers to burn? Why bother to burn anything after you've shot the person who loves you best in all the world?

And why destroy a will that would have provided that person with a dignified and independent old age? Was it because the bequest had been designated "To my beloved only brother who has always looked after me," and on this beautiful Sunday morning J.C. has suddenly stopped being beloved and has instead become someone to hurt? Maybe even to kill?

Why, *why*, WHY?

I shook my head impatiently. What in God's creation could J.C. have kept in that drawer that would send Beulah over the edge?

Totally baffled, I deliberately emptied my mind and sat down on one of the stone benches and looked up into a dogwood tree in full bloom. With the sun above them, the white blossoms glowed with a paschal translucence. Mother had always loved dogwoods.

Mother. Aunt Zell. Beulah.

A spring blossoming more than forty-five years ago.

I thought of dogwoods and spring love, and into my emptied mind floated a single *what if—?*

I didn't force it. I just sat and watched while it grew from possibility to certainty, a certainty reinforced as I recalled something Mother had mentioned about shift work at the airfield.

It was such a monstrous certainty that I wanted to be dissuaded, so I went to my office and called Aunt Zell and asked her to think back to the war years.

"When you all were in Goldsboro," I said, "did you work days or nights?"

"Days, of course," she answered promptly.

The weight started to roll off my chest.

"Leastways, we three girls did," she added. "J.C. worked nights. Why?"

For a moment I thought the heaviness would smother me before I could stammer out a reason and hang up.

Sherry, my secretary, came in with some papers to sign, but I waved her away. "Bring me the phone book," I told her, "and then leave me alone unless I buzz you."

Astonishingly, it took only one call to Information to get the number I needed. He answered on the second ring and we talked for almost an hour. I told him I was a writer doing research on the old Army Air Forces technical schools.

He didn't seem to think it odd when my questions got personal.

He sounded nice.

He sounded lonely.

"You look like hell," Sherry observed when I passed through the office. "You been crying?"

"Anybody wants me, I'll be at the hospital," I said without breaking stride.

Donna Sue and Helen were sitting beside J.C.'s bed when I got there, and it took every ounce of courtroom training for me not to burst out with it. Instead I made sympathetic conversation like a perfect Southern lady, and when they broke down again about Beulah, I said, "You all need to get out in the spring sunshine for a few minutes. Go get something with ice in it and walk around the parking lot twice. I'll keep J.C. company till you get back."

J.C. closed his eyes as they left, but I let him have it with both barrels.

"You bastard!" I snarled. "You filthy bastard! I just got off the phone to Donald Farraday. He still lives in Norwood, Nebraska, J.C. Halfway between Omaha and Lincoln."

The old man groaned and clenched his eyes tighter.

"He didn't die. He wasn't even wounded. Except in the heart. By you." So much anger roiled up inside me, I was almost spitting my words at him.

"He wrote her every chance he got till it finally sank in she was never going to answer. He thought she'd changed her mind, realized that she didn't really love him. And every day Beulah must have been coming home, asking if she'd gotten any mail, and you only gave her Sam's letters, you rotten, no-good—"

"Sam was homefolks," J.C. burst out. "That other one, he'd have taken her way the hell away to Nebraska. She didn't have any business in Nebraska! Sam loved her."

"She didn't love *him*," I snapped.

"Sure, she did. Oh, it took her a bit to get over the other one, but she settled."

"Only because she thought Farraday was dead! You had no right, you sneaking, sanctimonious Pharisee! You wrecked her whole life!"

"Her life wasn't wrecked," he argued. "She had Donna Sue and Sammy Junior and the farm and—"

"If it was such a star-spangled life," I interrupted hotly, "why'd she take a gun to you the minute she knew what you'd done to her?"

The fight went out of him and he sank back into the pillow, sobbing now and holding himself where the bullet had passed through his right lung.

"Why in God's name did you keep the letters? That's what she found, wasn't it?"

Still sobbing, J.C. nodded.

"I forgot they were still there. I never opened them, and she didn't either. She said she couldn't bear to. She just put them in the grate and put a match to them and she was crying. I tried to explain about how I'd done what was best for her, and all at once she had the rifle in her hands and she said she'd never forgive me, and then I reckon she shot me."

He reached out a bony hand and grasped mine. "You won't tell anyone, will you?"

I jerked my hand away as if it'd suddenly touched filth.

"Please, Deb'rah?"

"Donald Farraday has a daughter almost the same age as Donna Sue," I said. "Know what he named her, J.C.? He named her Beulah."

Dwight Bryant was waiting when I got back from court that afternoon and he followed me into my office.

"I hear you visited J.C. twice today."

"So?" I slid off my high heels. They were wickedly expensive and matched the power red of my linen suit. I waggled my stockinged toes at him, but he didn't smile.

"Judge not," he said sternly.

"Is that with an *N* or a *K*?" I parried.

"Sherry tells me you never give clients the original of their will."

"Never's a long time, and Sherry may not know as much about my business as she thinks she does."

"But it *was* a copy that Beulah burned, wasn't it?"

"I'm prepared to go to court and swear it was the original if I have to. It won't be necessary though. J.C. won't contest it."

Dwight stared at me a long level moment. "Why're you doing this to him?"

I matched his stare with one about twenty degrees colder. "Not me, Dwight. Beulah."

"He swears he doesn't know why she shot him, but you know, don't you?" I shrugged.

He hauled himself to his feet, angry and frustrated. "If you do this, Deborah, J.C.'ll have to spend the rest of his life depending on Donna Sue and Sammy Junior's good will. You don't have the right. Nobody elected you judge yet."

"Yes, they did," I said, thinking of the summer I was eighteen and how Mother had told me all her secrets so that if I ever needed her eyewitness testimony I'd have it.

And Deborah was a judge in the land.

Damn straight.

A former journalist, **SHELLEY SINGER** is the author of the popular Jake Samson/ Rosie Vicente mysteries. The latter sleuth is almost certainly the only carpenter detective in the history of the genre. They have starred in such excellent novels as *Free Draw, Full House, Spit in the Ocean, Samson's Deal,* and *Suicide King.* Ms. Singer lives in the San Francisco Bay Area.

A MAN'S HOME

Shelley Singer

 The woman spoke slowly in a deep voice edged with tears; the message she left on the office answering machine was concise. She needed help. Her husband had been murdered. Would I please call her?

The name, Wittles, sounded familiar. I glanced through that morning's *San Francisco Chronicle* and Oakland *Tribune* and found brief follow-up stories in both. Of course. Alan Wittles. The Berkeley attorney who'd been shot to death in his living room a couple of nights before. Signs of a break-in, the papers said. I had to wonder—didn't the dead man's wife have anything better to do with her money than pay a private investigator for a job the police were already doing?

Still, I dialed the number she'd left on the tape. While the phone rang, I thumbed quickly through the phone book to verify that the number actually belonged to her and not to some stray lunatic who'd seen her name in the paper. The call was legitimate; I found Alan and Julia Wittles in the book, at the right number and at a very right address.

She answered with her name, as though she were an upscale clothing store.

"This is Barrett Lake," I told her. "I'm returning your call to Broz Investigations. How can we help you?"

"Oh, yes. Thank you for calling back quickly. But I'd rather talk to Mr. Broz himself."

"I'm sorry, Mr. Broz isn't available. He's left me in charge." Very impressive. I didn't tell her I was an apprentice, working out my term under Tito's license. She hesitated for a good ten seconds.

"You're a woman."

"Yes. I am." I was a little surprised that a proper Berkeley matron would be caught dead expressing what sounded like unfeminist thoughts, but she redeemed herself.

"All right. Good. That might be even better. I'd like you to come over right away so we can talk. So you can get started and clear this all up."

Not so fast, I told myself. "Perhaps first you could tell me a bit more about what you want me to do for you."

She sighed and spoke in her slow, soft way. "My husband was shot to death here. At home. Three nights ago."

"Yes. I know. I'm sorry. But aren't the police working on the case?"

"They are." *Did I have a point,* her tone of voice was asking.

"Well, we don't like to compete with the Berkeley police. They have resources—"

"Oh, they never catch anyone. They're busy. They have too much to do. Please, just come over here and talk to me about it. I know you can help me."

Ridiculous, I thought. If anyone could find a homicidal burglar, it would be the police. But she sounded so desperate, and so unhappy.

I glanced at the work sheet on Tito's desk. According to him, I didn't have anything to do that day—nothing, really, to be in charge of—except stick around in case something showed up.

And here was a poor, sad woman in obvious distress, certainly needing someone's help. Wasn't that the whole point? Besides making a living? Even Tito the semipractical admitted he had thought I was a natural for the investigating business the first time he came to my apartment and saw the suit of armor in the entry.

He enjoys my romantic delusions, and I enjoy the ones he says he doesn't have.

I told Julia Wittles I was on my way.

The house was about $750,000 worth of stucco and Spanish tile in the upper Elmwood section, one of Berkeley's best. I noticed a man sitting in a car parked across the street, an ordinary-looking car with a long radio aerial. Were the police with her now? I headed for the door, up a terra-cotta walk flanked by two large palm trees. When I pressed the bell button, I heard a chord sound somewhere deep inside; the door opened almost immediately.

The woman and I appraised each other. We were about the same height, five seven or so, the same age—early forties—and the same build, a bit on the thin side. But her coloring was much lighter. My French and Chippewa ancestors are more dominant genetically than the Minnesota Swedes, but all her material came from northern Europe. She had pale blond hair, long and fine, pale blue eyes, and pale skin. She also had a limp handshake, but I thought that had more to do with environment than heredity.

The day was hot; the house was cool. The entry hall, two stories high with a sweep of staircase leading to a gallery, was bright and airy, but in the living room the windows were heavily curtained. The only light came from the far end of the room, a good thirty feet away, where a young man dressed in T-shirt and jeans, standing in the bright sun of the patio, was working on the open French doors. From inside the dark room I watched him turn away and walk a couple of paces through the sunlight to a toolbox lying on the patio stones.

"This is the room where it happened," she said. "Make yourself comfortable. I'll get us some iced tea." She disappeared through a swinging door. I glanced around in the dimness—nice fireplace, hardwood floor. As for the furnishings, though, my mother would have said they were "different." A tactful condemnation. Except for a couple of overstuffed couches that looked like relatives of the Pillsbury Doughboy, the furniture was flimsy-looking and looked as though it had been painted gaudily by children.

My possible client returned with two glasses and two coasters on a tray and placed the tray on the red-white-and-green coffee table between the couches.

"This is a very lovely house, architecturally," I said.

She smiled, a radiant smile of white teeth against pale lips. An ivory woman.

"Thank you. Would you like to see more of it?" She was eager, happy. To refuse would have been almost cruel. Clearly she wanted to postpone talking about what had happened to her husband.

She led me first to the dining room, a large, light expanse furnished with a gigantic table, eight chairs, a sideboard, and two smaller cupboards. The table was a simple rectangle, soft edged, carved from hard, reddish wood. The chairs were more free form, with blob-shaped solid wood backs. The sideboard matched the table. I had seen furniture like this once before, at a gallery show of handmade pieces. Each of the chairs, I knew, cost several hundred dollars. The prices of the table and sideboard I did not even want to think about. The two smaller cupboards looked like some of the pieces I had seen in the living room. Here, in the bright uncurtained dining room, I recognized the style. There are a couple of shops in the Bay Area that specialize in amazingly expensive Southwest-style handmade furniture. Some of it is charming, bright, and whimsical, even if it doesn't seem to stand quite right on its legs. But some of it goes beyond artistic whimsy to artist's joke, and the two small cupboards in Julia Wittles's dining room fit into that last category. They were particularly rickety versions of that genre, or school, or whatever they were calling it. Both were covered with crude shapes painted in bitingly sharp primary colors. One of them had little tin cutouts of coyotes, or maybe wolves, tacked to the wood above the open shelves.

"Those cupboards were made by Ian Feather," she said, "a very famous artist who lives in Taos." I nodded and smiled. "It took months to get them, months."

After demonstrating that the cupboard doors actually opened, she led me upstairs to a master bedroom and bath, both of which had a bit too much brass for my taste. The quilt on the bed, though, was a beautiful geometric creation in blues and greens.

"The quilt was made in 1905 by a woman in Nebraska, a farmer's wife," she said. "It was in that quilt show at the art museum in San Francisco? About five years ago?"

"Interesting," I said politely. My compassion was slipping away. I was beginning to feel restless. I have always disliked guided museum tours.

As she led me through the rest of the upstairs, lovingly pointing out skylights, alcoves, and window seats, and telling me where and how she had acquired each piece of furniture, I thought about how much it had all cost. This woman had spent more on furniture than I'd earned in half my twenty-year teaching career.

"I do love this house so much," she said, as we trailed down the stairs again. "I've dedicated my life, these past eight years, to decorating it, to setting off its beauty properly."

"Certainly," I said, as we walked into the kitchen, "everything you have is unique."

"Exactly. That was the effect I wanted. Everything is perfect. Just the way I wanted it." The kitchen was basic California modern, with a greenhouse window and a center island stove top, a big fireplace, and lots of redwood and copper—all the things you see in the magazines dentists buy for their waiting rooms.

"You mentioned eight years," I said. "Is that how long you've lived here?"

We were back in the living room at last. I took a long swallow of my reclaimed iced tea and sat on one of the soft couches.

"Yes. That was when I married Alan and moved in. His first wife had done the house in Victorian. It didn't work at all."

"Was he divorced?"

"No, she died. Years before I met him. They bought the house together. It was theirs. And then it was his. And then it was ours. And now"—she sighed —"it's mine."

I didn't like sitting on the couch, after all. I felt as though it might begin to digest me. I moved to an unpadded wooden chair and placed my coaster, and then my tea, on the foot-square, red-and-white-paint-spattered table beside me. I was relieved when the table didn't collapse.

"Now," I said, "we need to talk about your husband's death. Although I know how difficult that must be for you."

She dropped her head, drawing her hand across her forehead.

"It is."

"You say it happened in this room. I take it the intruder broke in through those doors?"

I nodded toward the French doors. The young blond man was reaching up toward the top of the doorframe with a screwdriver. As he stretched, his T-shirt rode up to expose a hairless expanse of muscular stomach.

"Yes. You find him and I'll identify him, and we can get this whole thing over with once and for all. I saw him. I saw him running away. But the police haven't asked me to a single lineup yet." She made it sound like they'd neglected to invite her to tea.

"Let's back up just a little bit, Ms. Wittles. You were here when it happened?"

"I was upstairs. I heard Alan shout, and then I heard all these terrible noises—furniture crashing, yelling—and then a gunshot. I ran downstairs, and there was this man, standing over Alan with a gun, the patio doors open, furniture everywhere, and Alan lying on the floor. The man looked at me, dropped the gun, and ran back out the door."

A power tool whined. I followed her gaze as she looked anxiously toward the light. The carpenter was running a belt sander up the side of the door.

"Oh, no!" she shouted, waving at him, catching his eye. He turned off the sander and looked at her quizzically. "The dust is coming into the house." He nodded thoughtfully and began to take the door off its hinges.

I turned back to Julia Wittles. "He dropped the gun? He didn't shoot at you?"

"No. He dropped it. It was Alan's gun. And the killer was wearing gloves. Did I say that?"

"No. And you saw him clearly enough to identify him." She nodded. I glanced back toward the doorway. The carpenter had removed the door and was carrying it across the patio in the sunshine. Everything out there, the stones, the shrubs, the man himself, looked warm and bright. I turned back to Julia Wittles, the sad-faced woman sitting across from me in the cool dimness.

I concentrated on that face.

"Where was your husband when you found him?"

"On the rug in front of the fireplace."

There was no rug in front of the fireplace. She anticipated my next question.

"It's at the cleaners."

"So what must have happened, then, is that your husband caught this man breaking in, and went to get his gun. Where did he keep it, usually?"

She pointed to a small blue desk near the patio doors. "In there, always."

"Okay. So he grabbed his gun, but there was a struggle . . . ?"

"Yes, that's what I think. There was a struggle, the burglar got the gun, and shot him."

"The room must have been a mess," I said. It was a stupid thing to say, but everything looked so perfectly tidy now, every piece just so, every rug straight and lint free, the hardwood floor mirrorlike where there was light to reflect. I couldn't quite imagine this room tossed around.

She frowned at me, studied my face for a moment. "It was. And poor Alan, lying there." She dropped her head into her hands for a moment, sat up straight again, and took a deep breath.

"And you gave the police a description of the man. Did they do one of those drawings from your description?"

"We tried to do that, but I wasn't very good at it. But I'd know him if I saw him. And I'm sure you could find him down in West Berkeley, where all the bums are, down on San Pablo or Sacramento."

"You say you think the police aren't working on the case."

"Oh, they're working on it, I suppose. But they certainly haven't asked me to identify anyone."

"I think they're working on it. I think there's a plainclothesman parked across the street right now. Have they been watching the house?"

Her small mouth dropped open, her eyes widened. She stared at me. We were both silent for a moment. Out on the patio the power sander whined.

"They're going to try to blame me," she said, shaking her head. "Isn't that what they always do? Blame the spouse? You have to help me. We can go down to San Pablo together. I'll point him out to you." She was gripping the mushy arm of her couch, her voice rising.

I was getting a pain in my right temple. I rubbed it. "Why do you think the police are after you?"

"People know we've been having problems."

"What kinds of problems were you having?"

"He wanted a divorce. Did I show you the conservatory? I had it added to the house last year. Would you like to see it?"

Her eyes were pleading. She was like a lost kitten, sitting demurely, prettily, tail wrapped around her paws, hoping to please.

No, I thought. *No more museum tours, no more digressions.* We needed to stick to the subject, which was getting more complicated.

"Possibly later. He wanted to divorce you?"

"Yes. And make me leave the house."

"Wasn't it legally half yours, community property?" Had she signed some sort of prenuptial agreement?

"Yes, I suppose so, but he wouldn't have let me have it. He would have sold it. He said it was his home, his and Marsha's. His first wife."

"But you'd get half the money."

"That's not enough. I wouldn't get this house. I wouldn't get enough to buy one like it."

"Did you talk to a lawyer about all this?"

"No. No, Alan *was* a lawyer. All the lawyers I knew were his friends. I couldn't fight him legally. I wouldn't have known how." Her voice had risen in pitch again, high and breathless and soft. She sounded startlingly like Marilyn Monroe. Like an echo out of the past, bouncing around the room. I wanted to scream at her: Where had she been for the past three decades?

She was watching me warily. "We need another glass of tea," she said, and fled to the kitchen with our glasses.

I got up and walked to the square of sunlight, crossed the flagstones to where the young man stood, screwdriver in one hand, a new lock in the other. The French door he'd removed rested across a pair of sawhorses.

I couldn't even bring myself to flirt with him.

"Was there a lot of damage to the doors?" I asked.

He smiled at me. "No. Hardly any. The wood was barely marked. The burglar pried real gently until the lock gave way. Must have taken a long time. And the bolts top and bottom"—he pointed at the top of the door with his screwdriver—"they weren't shot, so there wasn't anything broken there. Not bad at all."

"Thank you."

He looked at me oddly. *Yes,* I thought, *you're very pretty and very charming and you have a sweet smile, and you're not used to women staring at you dully and walking away. Sorry.*

Julia Wittles was standing at the coffee table, waiting for me. The tea glasses were full again.

"Well, what are you going to do?" she demanded.

I went to the big front windows and pulled open the drapes. Then I turned on a few lamps.

"Tell me how the furniture was that night, when you came into the room."

She pointed out various pieces and described their positions, although she said she couldn't remember exactly in all cases. A couch was overturned. One chair was on its back near the entry door. "And some of the tables were thrown around the room, and that rug and that one were out of place."

"And that's how it was when the police came?" She nodded. I examined the chair that had been displaced, turning it over, looking at it carefully. I looked at the coffee table, the end tables.

"Where was this?" I asked, touching the small red-and-white-spattered table.

"Over there." She pointed to a spot near the kitchen door, some fifteen feet away. I crossed the room and studied the floor. Then I went back to the table, took a deep, compassion-expelling breath, and gave it a good kick. Julia Wittles yelled. The table shot up, hit the floor, and skidded a few feet, coming to rest about where she had pointed. I walked over to it, gingerly, because I'd hurt one of my toes.

The floor had a new, shallow, six-inch scratch with a flake of blue paint in it. The previously pristine table now had one loose leg and one chipped corner.

She came to stand beside me. I didn't look at her.

"I hope that wasn't one of your favorite pieces," I said. She didn't answer. "None of this furniture has a scratch on it. The only scratch on the floor is the one I just made. Did you think the police were complete idiots?"

"You're smarter than they are."

"Even if they had called you in for a lineup, you know, you might have picked someone they knew couldn't be guilty. Sometimes they put cops in them."

She moved across the room, standing just two feet from me. Her eyes were red, and the fine wrinkles around them deepened as she stared into mine, trying, I suppose, to read my mind. "You're not going to help me."

"You need a lawyer." And a doctor or two.

The carpenter was back at the doorframe again, reinstalling the door. She turned to watch him.

"I don't want to do that," she said. "I don't like lawyers."

Millions of mystery readers love mystery bookstores, and **CAROLYN G. HART** has given them and the bookstore owners someone to cheer for—Annie Laurance, whose own store is the base for exciting and intellectually stimulating cases in such books as *A Little Class on Murder, Something Wicked,* and *Death on Demand.* Ms. Hart lives in Oklahoma City.

HER GOOD NAME

Carolyn G. Hart

 Annie Laurance Darling willed the telephone to ring.

But the undistinguished garden-variety black desk telephone remained mute.

Dammit, Max could at least call!

The more she thought about it, the more she wished that she had gone. Of course, it was undeniably true that Ingrid wasn't available to mind the bookstore, but it wouldn't have been a disaster to close for a few days in November. She didn't let herself dwell on the fact that Saturday had been her best fall day ever. She'd sold cartons of the latest by Lia Matera, Nancy Pickard, and Sara Paretsky.

But there was Max, off to Patagonia and adventure. And here *she* was, stuck in her closed bookstore on a rainy Sunday afternoon with nothing to do but unpack books and wonder if Max had managed to spring Laurel. Even Laurel should have known better than to take up a collection for Amnesty International in the main hall of the justice ministry in Buenos Aires! A tiny worm of worry wriggled in Annie's mind. She knew, of course, that her husband was absolutely capable, totally in command, unflappable, imperturbable. Annie snapped the book shut and bounced to her feet. But oh, sweet Jesus, who knew what kind of mess Laurel had—

The phone rang.

Annie leaped across the coffee area and grabbed up the extension behind the coffee bar. She didn't bother saying "Death on Demand." The finest mystery bookstore on the loveliest resort island off the coast of South Carolina wasn't open.

"Hello." She tried not to sound concerned. But maybe if she caught a jet tonight—

"Maxwell Darling." The tone was peremptory, cut-through-to-the-bone direct.

Annie's shoulders tensed. She immediately recognized the dry, crackly voice that rustled like old paper. What did Chastain, South Carolina's most aristocratic, imperious, absolutely impossible old hag, want with Annie's husband?

"Miss Dora, how are you?" Annie could remember her manners even if some others could not. Annie could imagine the flicker of irritation in Miss Dora's reptilian black eyes.

"No time to waste. Get him to the phone."

"I wish I could," Annie snapped.

"Where *is* he?"

"Patagonia."

A thoughtful pause on the other end, then a sniff. "Laurel, no doubt." The old lady's voice rasped like a rattlesnake slithering across sand as she disgustedly pronounced the name of Max's mother.

"Of course," Annie groused. "And I darn well should have gone. He might need me. You know how dangerous it is in Argentina!"

A lengthening pause, freighted with emanations of chagrin, malevolence, and rapid thought.

"Well, I've no choice. You'll have to do. Meet me at one-oh-three Bay Street at four o'clock."

Annie's eyes narrowed with fury. Miss Dora was obviously the same old hag she'd always been. And just who the hell did she think she was, ordering Annie to—

"A matter of honor." The phone banged into the receiver.

Annie stalked down the storm-dark street, the November rain spattering against her yellow slicker. Clumps of sodden leaves squished underfoot. The semitropical Carolina Low Country was not completely immune to winter, and days such as this presaged January and February. Annie felt another quiver of outrage. Why had she succumbed to the old bat? Why was she even now pushing open the gate and starting down the oystershell path to 103 Bay Street?

The aged, sandpapery voice sounded again in her mind: *A matter of honor.*

The sign to the right of the front door hung unevenly, one screw yielding to time and weather. An amateur had painted the outstretched, cupped hands, the thumbs overlarge, the palms lumpy. The legend was faded but decipherable: HELPING HANDS.

Annie was almost to the steps of the white frame cottage when she saw Miss Dora standing regally beneath the low spreading limbs of an ancient live oak. Annie was accustomed to the gnomelike old lady's eccentric dress—last-century bombazine dresses and hats Scarlett would have adored—but even Annie was impressed by the full gray cloak, the wide-brimmed crimson hat protecting shaggy silver hair, and the ivory walking stick planted firmly in front of high-topped, black leather shoes.

A welcoming smile tugged at Annie's lips, then slid to oblivion as Miss Dora scowled and thumped the stick. "You're late. The carillons play at four o'clock."

"Carillons?"

A vexed hiss. "Come, come. We'll go inside. Wanted you to hear the carillons. It's too neat, you know. The shot at precisely four o'clock. Know it must have been then. Otherwise somebody would have heard." Thumping stiffly to the door, Miss Dora scrabbled in her oversize crocheted receptacle. "No one's taking Constance's character into account. Not even her own brother! Blackening her name. A damnable lie." She jammed a black iron key into the lock.

As the door swung in, Miss Dora led the way, a tiny, limping figure. She clicked on the hall light, then regarded Annie with an obvious lack of enthusiasm. "Would do it myself," she muttered obscurely. "But sciatica. With the rain in November."

The parchment face, wrinkled with age, also held lines of pain. Annie almost felt sorry for her. Almost.

The stick swished through the air. "A dependency, of course. Small. Cramped. Cold floors in the winter. Constance had no use for her own creature comforts. Never gave them a thought. Sixty years she took care of the poor and the helpless here in Chastain. Everybody welcome here." The rasp muted to a whisper. "And may her murderer burn in hell."

The hair prickled on the back of Annie's neck. She looked around the dimly lit, linoleum-floored hallway. Worn straight chairs lined both sides of the hall. Near the door, turned sideways to allow passageway, sat a yellow pine desk.

The stick pointed at the desk. "Manned by volunteers, ten A.M. to four

P.M., every day but Sunday. Emma Louise Rammert yesterday. You'll talk to her."

The calm assumption irritated Annie. "Look, Miss Dora, you're taking a lot for granted. I only came over here because you hung up before I could say no. Now, I've got things on my mind—"

"Murder?"

Annie fervently hoped not. Surely Max and Laurel were safe! Max had promised to be careful. He was going to hire a mercenary, fly in to the secret airstrip, hijack Laurel from her captors (a potful of money always worked wonders, whatever the political persuasion), and fly right back out. Oh, hell, she should have gone! What if he needed her?

"Oh, who knows?" Annie moaned.

"Don't be a weak sister," the old lady scolded. "Asinine to fret. He'll cope, despite his upbringing." A thoughtful pause. "Perhaps because of it. Any event, you've work to do here." The cane pointed at a closed door. "There's where it happened." The rasp was back, implacable, ice hard, vindictive.

The old lady, moving painfully, stumped to the door, threw it open, turned on the light.

"Her blood's still there. I'm on the board. Gave instructions nothing to be disturbed."

Annie edged reluctantly into the room. She couldn't avoid seeing the desktop and the darkish-brown splotches on the scattered sheets of paper. The low-beamed ceiling and rough-hewn unpainted board walls indicated an old, lean-to room. No rugs graced the warped floorboards. An unadorned wooden chair sat behind the scarred and nicked desk. In one corner, a small metal typewriter table held a Remington—circa 1930.

Gloved fingers gripped Annie's elbow like talons. The walking stick pointed across the room.

"Her chair. That's the way the police found it."

Propelled by the viselike grip, Annie crossed the few feet to the desk and stared at the chair. The very unremarkable oak chair. Old, yes. But so was everything in the room. Old, with a slat missing.

The ivory stick clicked against the chair seat. "No pillow. Constance always sat on a pillow. Bad hip. Never complained, of course. Now, you tell me, young miss, where's that pillow? Right at four o'clock and no pillow!"

Annie was so busy wondering if Miss Dora had finally gone around the bend—which would be no surprise to her, that was for sure—that it took her a moment to realize she was "young miss."

Annie slanted a sideways glance.

Miss Dora hunched over her stick now, her gloved hands tight on the knob. She stared at the empty chair, her lined face sorrowful. "Sixty years I knew Constance. Always doing good works. Didn't simper around with a pious whine or a holier-than-thou manner. Came here every day, and every day the poor in Chastain came to her for help. No electricity. They came here. Husband beat you, son stole your money, they came here. A sick child and no food. They came here."

A tear edged down the ancient sallow cheek. "I used to tell her, 'Constance, the world's full of sorrow. Always has been. Always will be. You're like the little Dutch boy at the dike.'"

The old lady reached out a gloved hand and gently touched the straight chair. Then the reptilian eyes glittered at Annie. "Know what Constance said?"

"No." The dark little room and the blood-spattered desk held no echo of its former tenant. This was just a cold and dreary place, touched by violence.

"Constance said, 'Why, Dora, love, it's so simple. "I was hungry and you gave me meat, I was thirsty and you gave me drink, I was a stranger and you took me in. Naked, and you clothed me; I was sick, and you visited me; I was in prison and you came unto me."' "

Beyond the dry whisper was an echo of a light and musical voice.

Miss Dora's stick cracked sharply against the wooden floor. She stared at Annie with dark and burning eyes. "A woman," she rasped, hard as stone against stone, "who saw her duty and did it. A woman who would never"— the cane struck—"never"—the cane struck—"never"—the cane struck— "quit the course."

Annie reached for the telephone, then yanked her hand back. Dammit, she dreaded making this call. Miss Dora had almost persuaded her yesterday afternoon. Indeed, Constance Bolton's life did argue against her death. Annie studied the picture Miss Dora had provided of a slender, white-haired woman in a navy silk dress. Constance Bolton looked serious, capable, and resourceful, a woman accustomed to facing problems and solving them. Her wide-set brown eyes were knowledgeable but not cynical; her mouth was firm but not unpleasant. Stalwart, steady, thoughtful—yes, she had obviously been all of these and more. Yet—Annie glanced down at the poorly reproduced copy of the autopsy report on Constance Maude Bolton, white, female, age seventy-two—the answer seemed inescapable, however unpalatable to Constance Bolton's friends. Annie hated to destroy Miss Dora's faith. But facts were facts.

She dialed in a rush.

"Here."

"Miss Dora, this is Annie. I'm at the store. Listen, I got a copy of the autopsy report on Miss Bolton." Annie took a deep breath. "She was sick, Miss Dora. Dying. Bone cancer. She hadn't told many people, but she knew. Her doctor said so. And there were powder burns on her hand."

Gusts of polar wind could not have been colder than Miss Dora's initial silence. Then she growled, "Doesn't matter, young miss. Get to work. Think." The receiver thudded with the same force as the cane had struck the floor in that dingy office. *"Never—never—never quit the course."*

Annie slammed down her own receiver and glared at the phone, then jumped as it rang again.

"Death on Demand."

"The pillow," Miss Dora intoned. "The pillow, young miss. The pillow!" And the receiver banged again.

Annie jumped to her feet and paced across the coffee area. Agatha, the bookstore's elegant and imperious black cat, watched with sleepy amber eyes.

"Dammit, Agatha, the old bat's going to drive me crazy!"

Agatha yawned.

"Unreasonable, ill-tempered, stubborn"—Annie stopped at the coffee bar and reached for her mug—"but not stupid, Agatha."

As she drank the delicious French roast brew, Annie stroked Agatha's silky fur and thought about Miss Dora. Irascible, yes. Imperious, yes. Stupid, no. "And about as sentimental as an alligator. So if she knows in the depth of her creaky bones that Constance Bolton wasn't a quitter, where does that leave us?"

If it wasn't suicide, it had to be murder.

How could it be?

Powder burns on her right hand. Constance Bolton was right-handed. A contact wound—star-shaped—to the right temple. Bone cancer. And the gun —Annie returned to her table and riffled through the police report—the gun had been identified by Miss Bolton's housekeeper, Sammie Calhoun. A .32 caliber revolver, it had belonged to Constance Bolton's late brother, Everett. It had, as long as Sammie worked there, lain in the bottom drawer of the walnut secretary in the library. She had seen the gun as recently as late last week.

The fact that this gun had been brought from Miss Constance's home was another pointer to suicide.

But—*if* she had been murdered—the use of that gun sharply circumscribed the list of possible killers.

It had to be someone with access to the bottom drawer of that walnut secretary.

Suicide? Or murder?

On the one hand, terminal illness, powder marks, a contact wound, a gun brought from home.

On the other hand, Miss Dora's unyielding faith in her friend's character and a missing pillow.

Annie sipped at her coffee. A pillow. There didn't seem to be any reason—

She thumped the mug on the counter and clapped her hands. *Of course, of course. It could only have been done with a pillow. And that explains why the murder had to occur at four o'clock when the carillons sounded. It wouldn't have been necessary to mask a single shot. But it was essential to mask two shots. Oh, my God, the old devil was smart as hell!*

Annie pictured the dingy room and Constance sitting behind the desk. A visitor—someone Constance knew well, surely—standing beside the desk. The movement would have been snake-quick, a hand yanking the pistol from a pocket, pressing it against her temple and firing. That would have been the moment demanding swiftness, agility. Then it would have been a simple matter, edging the pillow from beneath her, pressing her hand against the gun and firing into the pillow. That would assure the requisite powder residue on her hand. The stage then was set for suicide, and it remained only to slip away, taking the pillow, and, once home, to wash with soap and water to remove the powder marks upon the killer's hand.

Oh, yes, Annie could see it all, even hear the tiny click as the door closed, leaving death behind.

But was there anything to this picture? Was this interpretation an illusion born of Miss Dora's grief or the work of a clever killer?

Annie could hear the crackly voice and behind it the musical tones of a good woman.

"I was hungry . . ."

By God, nobody was going to get away with the murder of Constance Bolton! Not if Annie could help it!

Annie focused on Miss Constance's last few days. If it was murder, why now? Why on Saturday, November 18?

The housekeeper agreed that Miss Constance was sick. "But she paid it no nevermind. Miss Constance, she always kept on keepin' on. Even after Mr. Peter was killed in that car wreck up north, that broke her heart, but she never gave in. Howsomever, she was dragged down last week. Thursday night, she hardly pecked at her supper."

Annie made a mental note about Thursday.

She compiled a list of Miss Constance's visitors at Helping Hands the past week.

The visitors were all—to the volunteers—familiar names, familiar troubles, familiar sorrows.

Except on Thursday.

Portia Finley said energetically, "We did have someone new late that afternoon. A young man. Very thin. He looked ill. A Yankee. Wouldn't tell me what his trouble was, said he had to talk to Miss Constance personally. He wrote out a note and asked me to take it in to her. She read it and said she'd see him immediately. They were still in her office talking when I went home."

It took all of Annie's tact, but she finally persuaded Portia Finley to admit she'd read that short note on lined notepad paper. "I wanted to be sure it wasn't a threatening note. Or obscene."

"Oh, by all means," Annie said encouragingly.

"It didn't amount to much. Just said he was a friend of Peter's and Peter had told him to come and see her."

Friday's volunteer, Cindy Axton, reluctantly had nothing out of the ordinary to report.

But Saturday's volunteer, Emma Louise Rammert, had a sharp nose, inquisitive steel-gray eyes, and a suspicious mind.

"Don't believe it was suicide. They could show me a video of it and I still wouldn't believe it. Oh, yes, I know she was sick. But she never spoke of it. Certainly *that* wouldn't be motive enough. Not for Constance. But something upset her that morning and *I* think it was the paper. The *Clarion.* She was fine when she came in. Oh, serious enough. Looked somber. But not nervy. She went into her office. I came in just a moment later with the mail and she was staring down at the front page of the *Clarion* like it had bitten her. Besides, it seems a mighty odd coincidence that on the afternoon she was to die, she'd send me off early on what turned out to be a wild goose chase. Supposed to be a woman with a sick child at the Happy Vale trailer court and there wasn't anybody of that name. So I think Constance sent me off so she could talk to somebody without me hearing. Otherwise, I'd of been there at four o'clock, just closing up."

Was the volunteer's absence engineered to make way for suicide—or for an appointment? Constance Bolton, had she planned to die, easily could have waited until the volunteer left for the day. But if she wanted to talk to someone without being overheard, what better place than her office at closing time?

Annie picked up a copy of the Saturday morning *Clarion* and took it to the Sip and Sup Coffee Shop on Main Street.

The lead story was about Arafat and another PLO peace offer. The Town Council had met to consider banning beer from the beach. Property owners attacked the newest beach nourishment tax proposals. Island merchants reported excellent holiday sales.

A story in the bottom right column was headed:

AUTOPSY REVEALS
CAR OCCUPANT
MURDER VICTIM

Beaufort County authorities announced today that a young man found in a burning car Thursday night, originally thought to have died in a one-car accident on a county road, was a victim of foul play.

Despite extensive burns, the autopsy revealed, the young man had died as a result of strangulation. The victim was approximately five feet seven inches tall, weighed 130 pounds, was Caucasian, and suffered from AIDS.

The car was found by a passing motorist late Thursday evening on Culowee Road two miles south of the intersection with Jasper Road.

The car was rented at the Savannah airport on Thursday by a Richard Davis of New York City.

Authorities are seeking information about Davis's activities in Chastain. Anyone with any information about him is urged to contact Sheriff Chadwick Porter.

Annie called Miss Dora. "Tell me about Peter."

"Constance's grandnephew. His father, Morgan, was the son of Everett, her older brother. Everett died about twenty years ago, not long after Morgan was killed in Vietnam. Peter inherited the plantations, but he never worked them. James did that. The other brother. But they went to Peter. The oldest son of the oldest son inherits in the Bolton family. Peter inherited from his mother, too. She was one of the Cinnamon Hill Morleys. Grieved herself into the grave when Morgan was killed in Vietnam. So Constance raised the boy and James ran the plantations. When he was grown, Peter went to New York. A photographer. Didn't come back much. Then he was killed last winter. A car wreck."

One car wreck had masked murder.

Had another?

Annie wished for Max as she made one phone call after another, but she knew how to do it. When it became clear that Peter Bolton didn't die in a car wreck—despite that information in his obituary, which had been supplied by his great-uncle James—she redoubled her efforts. She found Peter's address, his telephone number, and the small magazine where his last photograph had been published and talked to the managing editor.

But Peter wasn't murdered.

Peter died in a New York hospital of AIDS.

And Richard Davis had been dying of AIDS before he was strangled and left in a burning car in Beaufort County, South Carolina.

Richard's note to Constance Bolton claimed he was a friend of Peter's. More than a friend?

Maggie Sutton had the apartment above Richard's in an old Brooklyn brownstone.

Her voice on the telephone was clipped and unfriendly. "You want to know anything about Richard Davis, you ask—"

Before she could hang up, destroy Annie's link to Richard and through him to Peter, Annie interrupted quickly. "Richard's dead. Murdered. Please talk to me. I want to find his murderer."

It took a lot of explaining, then Maggie Sutton said simply, "My God. Poor Richie."

"Did you know Richard was coming to South Carolina?"

"Yes. He was sick—"

"I know."

"—and they fired him. They aren't supposed to, but they do it anyway. Before most people with AIDS can appeal, file a lawsuit, they're dead. Richie was almost out of money. His insurance was gone. They only want to insure healthy people, you know. Nobody with real health problems can get insurance. Richie and Peter lived downstairs from me. Nice guys." She paused, repeated forcefully. "*Nice* guys." A sigh. "God, it's all so grim. Richie took care of Peter. He died last winter. Last week, Richie told me he was going on a trip and he asked me to feed their cat, Big Boy, while he was gone. Richie said Peter had written a will before he died, leaving everything to Richie, but he didn't do anything about it then. I mean, he didn't want Peter's money. But now he was desperate. And he thought, maybe if he went down there, showed the will to the family . . ." Her voice trailed off.

The family.

The last surviving member of the family stood with his head bowed, his freshly shaved face impassive, his hands clasped loosely behind his back, as mourners dispersed at the conclusion of the graveside service on Tuesday afternoon. A dark-suited employee of the funeral home held a black umbrella to shield James Caldwell Bolton from the rain.

The day and James Bolton were a study in grays, the metallic gray of Constance Bolton's casket, resting over the dark pit of her grave, the steel gray of Bolton's pinstripe suit, the soft gray of weathered stones, the misty gray of the weeping sky, the silver gray of Miss Dora's rain cape, the flinty gray of the stubby palmettos' bark, the ash-gray of the rector's grizzled hair.

Annie huddled beneath the outspread limbs of a live oak, a thick wool scarf knotted at her throat, her raincoat collar upturned. Rain splashed softly against gravestones as mourners came forth to shake Bolton's hand and murmur condolences.

Annie stared at the man who had inherited the Bolton and Morley family plantations.

James Bolton didn't look like a murderer.

He looked—as indeed he was—like a substantial and respectable and wealthy member of the community. There was a resemblance to his dead sister, brown eyes, white hair, a firm chin. But where Constance's face was memorable for its calm pity and gentle concern, there was an intolerant and arrogant quality to his stolid burgher's face.

As the last of Miss Constance's friends trod away across the spongy ground of the graveyard, Annie left the oystershell path. Skirting behind a stand of pines, she moved into the oldest part of the cemetery, stopping in the shadow of a crumbling mausoleum some twenty-five yards distant from the new grave site.

Bolton waved away the undertaker with the umbrella.

Had any of the mourners looked back, they would have glimpsed his figure, head again bowed, lingering for a last moment with his sister.

But Annie could see his face. It was for a singular, heartstopping instant transformed. His lips curved up in satisfaction.

Annie knew, as clearly as if he'd shouted, that James Bolton was exulting. A murderer twice over, safe, secure, successful. A rich and powerful man.

"James."

His face re-formed into sad repose as he turned toward Miss Dora.

The old lady took her time, each step obviously a painful task.

Annie slipped free of her raincoat, unfurled a navy umbrella—Sammie Calhoun had quite willingly given her mistress's umbrella to Miss Dora—and undid the scarf covering the curly white wig.

Miss Dora, her wizened face contorted in a worried frown, peered up at James Bolton.

"James, I've had the oddest"—the raspy voice wavered—"communication. The ouija board. Last night. Never been a believer in that sort—"

"James . . ." Annie held a high, light, musical tone then let her voice waver and drop like the sigh of a winter wind. In her own ears, it didn't sound enough like the recorded interview the local radio station had found of Constance Bolton speaking out in a League of Women Voters forum on abortion. She tried again, a little louder. "James . . ."

It must have been better than she'd thought.

James Bolton's head whipped around, seeking out the sound. His face was suddenly gray, too, the color of old putty.

Annie glided from behind the cover of the mausoleum, one hand outstretched. "James . . ." Then she backed away, just as a dimly seen figure might drift forth, then disappear. Once out of Bolton's sight, she darted in a crouch from stone to stone until she gained the street. Quickly pulling on the scarf and raincoat, she hurried to Miss Dora's.

* * *

"Heh. Heh. Heh." Miss Dora's satisfied cackle would chill the devil. She poured a cup of steaming tea.

Annie sneezed. The heat against her fingers helped a little, but she didn't feel that her bones would ever warm from the graveyard cold.

Miss Dora glowered. "No time to flag. Young people today too puny."

"I'm fine," Annie retorted crisply and knew she was catching a cold. But she couldn't afford to sneeze tonight. She and Miss Dora weren't finished with James Bolton.

"Scared him to death," Miss Dora gloated. "He looked like bleached bones." Her raisin-dark eyes glittered. "Mouth open, whites of his eyes big as a platter. And when I pretended I hadn't seen or heard a thing, thought he was going to faint. That's when I told him about the ouija message: *Pillow. Find pillow.*" She cackled again.

Annie took a big gulp of tea and voiced her concern. "Miss Dora, how can we be sure he didn't destroy the pillow?"

Miss Dora's disdainful look infuriated Annie.

"Classical education taught people how to think!" the old lady muttered. "Crystal clear, young miss. He dared not leave it behind. He had to take it with him. Then what? He couldn't keep it in his house. Old Beulah Willen's his housekeeper. Not a single spot safe from *her* eyes. So, *not* hidden in his house. No incinerators permitted in the city. Besides it's too bulky to burn well. Joe Bill Tompkins drives James. So, *not* in his car. I talked here and there. He's not been out to any of the plantations since Constance died. So where is it? Somewhere not too far, young miss." Another malicious cackle. "James thinks he's so smart. We'll see, won't we?"

The rain had eased to a drizzle. Annie was warm enough. A black wool cap, thermal underwear, a rainproof jacket over a wool sweater, rainproof pants, sturdy black Reeboks. The nylon hose over her face made it hard to breathe, but it sure kept her toasty. From her vantage point she could see both the front and rear doors to James Bolton's house. She had taken up her station at nine thirty. Miss Dora was to make her phone call at nine thirty-five and play the recording Annie had made and remade until Annie's whispered, "James . . . I'm . . . coming . . . for . . . the . . . pillow," sounded sufficiently like Constance Bolton to satisfy Miss Dora.

The back door opened at nine forty. James Bolton, too, was dressed for night in dark clothing. He paused on the top step and looked fearfully around, then hurried to the garage.

Annie smiled grimly.

He reappeared in only a moment, carrying a spade.

Annie followed him across the Bolton property and through a dank and dripping wood. She stepped softly along the path, keeping his shaded flashlight in view, stopping when he stopped, moving when he moved.

Whoo-oo-ooo-ooo.

Annie's heart somersaulted and she gasped for breath.

Bolton cowered by a live oak.

Annie wasn't sure which one of them the owl had frightened the most.

Iron hinges squealed, and Bolton stepped through the opened gate to the old graveyard, leaving the gate ajar. He moved more cautiously now, and the beam from his flashlight poked jerkily into shadowy pockets.

Did he fear that his dead sister awaited him?

Annie tiptoed, scarcely daring to breathe. One hand slipped into her jacket pocket and closed around the sausage-thick canister of mace, a relic of the days when she lived in New York. The other hand touched the Leica that hung from a strap around her neck.

Bolton stopped twice to listen.

Annie crouched behind gravestones and waited.

When he reached the oldest section of the cemetery, he moved more boldly, confident now that he was unobserved. He walked directly to a winged angel atop a marble pedestal, stepped five paces to his right, and used the shovel to sweep away a mound of leaves.

Annie was willing to bet the earth beneath those leaves had been recently loosened.

He shoveled quickly, but placing the heaps of moist sandy dirt in a neat pile to one side.

Annie crept closer and closer, the Leica in hand.

She was not more than ten feet away and ready when he reached down and lifted up a soggy newspaper-wrapped oblong.

The flash illuminated the graveyard with its brief brilliant light, capturing forever and always the stricken face of James Bolton.

He made a noise deep in his throat. Wielding the shovel, he lunged blindly toward the source of light. Annie danced sideways to evade him. Now the canister of mace came out and as he flailed the shovel and it crashed against a gravestone, Annie pressed the trigger and mace spewed in a noisome mist.

Annie held her breath, darted close enough to grab up the sodden oblong where he had dropped it, paused just long enough—she couldn't resist it—to moan, "Jaaammees . . ." Then she ran faster than she'd ever managed in a 10 K, leaping graves like a fox over water hazards.

The headline in next morning's *Clarion* told it all:

JAMES BOLTON CHARGED
IN MURDER OF SISTER

Miss Dora rattled the newspaper with satisfaction, then poured Annie another cup of coffee. The old lady's raisin-dark eyes glittered. "We showed him, didn't we? Saved Constance's good name."

For once—and it was such an odd feeling—Annie felt total rapport with the ill-tempered, opinionated, impossible creature awaiting her answer.

Annie grinned. "Miss Dora, we sure as hell did!"

Annie bought her own copy of the newspaper before she took the ferry back to the island. She wanted to have it to show to Max. Especially since his telegram had arrived last night:

Retrieval accomplished. No fireworks. Boring, actually. Only action caused by fleas Laurel picked up in jail. Plus tourista tummy (me). Home soon. But not soon enough.

Love, Max.

A Brooklyn-based attorney, **CAROLYN WHEAT** naturally has a criminal lawyer, Cass Jameson, as her series detective. Cass has solved cases in at least two wonderful books, *Where Nobody Dies* and *Dead Man's Thoughts*. The latter novel was nominated for an Edgar Allan Poe Award.

GHOST STATION

Carolyn Wheat

 If there's one thing I can't stand, it's a woman drunk. The words burned my memory the way Irish whiskey used to burn my throat, only there was no pleasant haze of alcohol to follow. Just bitter heartburn pain.

It was my first night back on the job, back to being Sergeant Maureen Gallagher instead of "the patient." Wasn't it hard enough being a transit cop, hurtling beneath the streets of Manhattan on a subway train that should have been in the Transit Museum? Wasn't it enough that after four weeks of detox I felt empty instead of clean and sober? Did I *have* to have some rookie's casually cruel words ricocheting in my brain like a wild-card bullet?

Why couldn't I remember the good stuff? Why couldn't I think about O'Hara's beefy handshake, Greenspan's "Glad to see ya, Mo," Ianuzzo's smiling welcome? Why did I have to run the tape in my head of Manny Delgado asking Captain Lomax for a different partner?

"Hey, I got nothing against a lady sarge, Cap," he'd said. "Don't get me wrong. It's just that if there's one thing I can't stand . . ." Et cetera.

Lomax had done what any standup captain would—kicked Delgado's ass and told him the assignment stood. What he hadn't known was that I'd heard the words and couldn't erase them from my mind.

Even without Delgado, the night hadn't gotten off to a great start. Swinging in at midnight for a twelve-to-eight, I'd been greeted with the news that I was on Graffiti Patrol, the dirtiest, most mind-numbing assignment in the whole transit police duty roster. I was a sergeant, damn it, on my way to a gold shield, and I wasn't going to earn it dodging rats in tunnels or going after twelve-year-olds armed with spray paint.

Especially when the rest of the cop world, both under- and aboveground, was working overtime on the torch murders of homeless people. There'd been four human bonfires in the past six weeks, and the cops were determined there wouldn't be a fifth.

Was Lomax punishing me, or was this assignment his subtle way of easing my entry back into the world? Either way, I resented it. I wanted to be a real cop again, back with Sal Minucci, my old partner. He was assigned to the big one, in the thick of the action, where both of us belonged. I should have been with him. I was Anti-Crime, for God's sake. I should have been assigned—

Or should I? Did I really want to spend my work nights prowling New York's underground skid row, trying to get information from men and women too zonked out to take care of legs gone gangrenous, whose lives stretched from one bottle of Cool Breeze to another?

Hell, yes. If it would bring me one step closer to that gold shield, I'd interview all the devils in hell. On my day off.

If there's one thing I can't stand, it's a woman drunk.

What did Lomax think—that mingling with winos would topple me off the wagon? That I'd ask for a hit from some guy's short dog and pass out in the Bleecker Street station? Was that why he'd kept me off the big one and had me walking a rookie through routine Graffiti Patrol?

Was I getting paranoid, or was lack of alcohol rotting my brain?

Manny and I had gone to our respective locker rooms to suit up. Plain clothes—and I do mean plain. Long johns first; damp winter had a way of seeping down into the tunnels and into your very blood. Then a pair of denims the Goodwill would have turned down. Thick wool socks, fisherman's duck boots, a black turtleneck, and a photographer's vest with lots of pockets. A black knit hat pulled tight over my red hair.

Then the gear: flashlight, more important than a gun on this assignment, handcuffs, ticket book, radio, gun, knife. A slapper, an oversize blackjack, hidden in the rear pouch of the vest. They were against regulations; I'd get at least a command discipline if caught with it, but experience told me I'd rather have it than a gun going against a pack of kids.

I'd forgotten how heavy the stuff was; I felt like a telephone lineman.

I looked like a cat burglar.

Delgado and I met at the door. It was obvious he'd never done vandal duty
before. His tan chinos were immaculate, and his hiking boots didn't look
waterproof. His red plaid flannel shirt was neither warm enough nor the right
dark color. With his Latin good looks, he would have been stunning in an
L.L. Bean catalogue, but after ten minutes in a subway tunnel, he'd pass for a
chimney sweep.

"Where are we going?" he asked, his tone a shade short of sullen. And
there was no respectful "Sergeant" at the end of the question, either. This
boy needed a lesson in manners.

I took a malicious delight in describing our destination. "The Black Hole
of Calcutta," I replied cheerfully, explaining that I meant the unused lower
platform of the City Hall station downtown. The oldest, darkest, dankest
spot in all Manhattan. If there were any subway alligators, they definitely
lurked in the Black Hole.

The expression on Probationary Transit Police Officer Manuel Delgado's
face was all I could have hoped for. I almost—but not quite—took pity on
the kid when I added, "And after that, we'll try one or two of the ghost
stations."

"Ghost stations?" Now he looked really worried. "What are those?"

This kid wasn't just a rookie; he was a suburbanite. Every New Yorker
knew about ghost stations, abandoned platforms where trains no longer
stopped. They were still lit, though, and showed up in the windows of passing
trains like ghost towns on the prairie. They were ideal canvases for the aspir-
ing artists of the underground city.

I explained on the subway, heading downtown. The car, which rattled
under the city streets like a tin lizzie, was nearly riderless at 1:00 A.M. A
typical Monday late tour.

The passengers were one Orthodox Jewish man falling asleep over his
Hebrew Bible, two black women, both reading thick paperback romances,
the obligatory pair of teenagers making out in the last seat, and an old
Chinese woman.

I didn't want to look at Delgado. More than once I'd seen a fleeting smirk
on his face when I glanced his way. It wasn't enough for insubordination; the
best policy was to ignore it.

I let the rhythm of the subway car lull me into a litany of the AA slogans I
was trying to work into my life: EASY DOES IT. KEEP IT SIMPLE, SWEETHEART.
ONE DAY AT A TIME. I saw them in my mind the way they appeared on the
walls at meetings, illuminated, like old Celtic manuscripts.

This night I had to take one hour at a time. Maybe even one minute at a
time. My legs felt wobbly. I was a sailor too long from the sea. I'd lost my
subway legs. I felt white and thin, as though I'd had several major organs
removed.

Then the drunk got on. One of the black women got off, the other one looked up at the station sign and went back to her book, and the drunk got on.

If there's one thing I can't stand, it's a woman drunk.

ONE DAY AT A TIME. EASY DOES IT.

I stiffened. The last thing I wanted was to react in front of Delgado, but I couldn't help it. The sight of an obviously intoxicated man stumbling into our subway car brought the knowing smirk back to his face.

There was one at every AA meeting. No matter how nice the neighborhood, how well dressed most people attending the meeting were, there was always a drunk. A real drunk, still reeling, still reeking of cheap booze. My sponsor Margie said they were there for a reason, to let us middle-class, recovery-oriented types remember that "there but for the grace of God . . ."

I cringed whenever I saw them, especially if the object lesson for the day was a woman.

"Hey, kid," the drunk called out to Delgado, in a voice as inappropriately loud as a deaf man's, "how old are you?" The doors closed and the car lurched forward; the drunk all but fell into his seat.

"Old enough," Manny replied, flashing the polite smile a well-brought-up kid saves for his maiden aunt.

The undertone wasn't so pretty. Little sidelong glances at me that said, *See how nice I am to this old fart. See what a good boy I am.* I like drunks, *Sergeant Gallagher.*

To avoid my partner's sly face, I concentrated on the subway ads as though they contained all the wisdom of the Big Book. "Here's to birth defects," proclaimed a pregnant woman about to down a glass of beer. Two monks looked to heaven, thanking God in Spanish for the fine quality of their brandy.

Weren't there any signs on this damn train that didn't involve booze? Finally an ad I could smile at: the moon in black space; on it, someone had scrawled, "Alice Kramden was here, 1959."

My smile faded as I remembered Sal Minucci's raised fist, his Jackie Gleason growl. "One a these days, Gallagher, you're goin' to the moon. To the *moon!*"

It wasn't just the murder case I missed. It was Sal. The easy partnership of the man who'd put up with my hangovers, my depressions, my wild nights out with the boys.

"Y'know how old I am?" the drunk shouted, almost falling over in his seat. He righted himself. "Fifty-four in September," he announced, an expectant look on his face.

After a quick smirk in my direction, Manny gave the guy what he wanted.

"You don't look it," he said. No trace of irony appeared on his Spanish altar boy's face. It was as though he'd never said the words that were eating into me like battery-acid AA coffee.

The sudden jab of anger that stabbed through me took me by surprise, especially since it wasn't directed at Delgado. *No, you don't look it,* I thought. *You look more like seventy.* White wisps of hair over a bright pink scalp. The face more than pink; a slab of raw calves' liver. Road maps of broken blood vessels on his nose and cheeks. Thin white arms and matchstick legs under too-big trousers. When he lifted his hand, ropy with bulging blue veins, it fluttered like a pennant in the breeze.

Like Uncle Paul's hands.

I turned away sharply. I couldn't look at the old guy anymore. The constant visual digs Delgado kept throwing in my direction were nothing compared to the pain of looking at a man dying before my eyes. I didn't want to see blue eyes in that near-dead face. *As blue as the lakes of Killarney,* Uncle Paul used to say in his mock-Irish brogue.

I focused on the teenagers making out in the rear of the car. A couple of Spanish kids, wearing identical pink T-shirts and black leather jackets. If I stared at them long enough, would they stop groping and kissing, or would an audience spur their passion?

Uncle Paul. After Daddy left us, he was my special friend, and I was his best girl.

I squeezed my eyes shut, but the memories came anyway. The red bike Uncle Paul gave me for my tenth birthday. The first really big new thing, bought just for me, that I'd ever had. The best part was showing it off to cousin Tommy. For once I didn't need his hand-me-downs, or Aunt Bridget's clucking over me for being poor. *God bless the child who's got her own.*

I opened my eyes just as the Lex passed through the ghost station at Worth Street. Closed off to the public for maybe fifteen years, it seemed a mirage, dimly seen through the dirty windows of the subway car. Bright color on the white tile walls told me graffiti bombers had been there. A good place to check, but not until after City Hall. I owed Manny Delgado a trip to the Black Hole.

"Uh, Sergeant?"

I turned; a patronizing smile played on Delgado's lips. He'd apparently been trying to get my attention. "Sorry," I said, feigning a yawn. "Just a little tired."

Yeah, sure, his look remarked. "We're coming to Brooklyn Bridge. Shouldn't we get off the train?"

"Right." *Leave Uncle Paul where he belongs.*

At the Brooklyn Bridge stop, we climbed up the steps to the upper platform, showed our ID to the woman token clerk, and told her we were going into the tunnel toward City Hall. Then we went back downstairs, heading for the south end of the downtown platform.

As we were about to go past the gate marked NO UNAUTHORIZED PERSON-NEL BEYOND THIS POINT, I looked back at the lighted platform, which made a crescent-shaped curve behind us. Almost in a mirror image, the old drunk was about to pass the forbidden gate and descend into the tunnel heading uptown.

He stepped carefully, holding on to the white, bathroom-tile walls, edging himself around the waist-high gate. He lowered himself down the stone steps the exact replica of the ones Manny and I were about to descend, then disappeared into the blackness.

I couldn't let him go. There were too many dangers in the subway, dangers beyond the torch killer everyone was on the hunt for. How many frozen bodies had I stumbled over on the catwalks between tunnels? How many huddled victims had been hit by trains as they lay in sodden sleep? And yet, I had to be careful. My friend Kathy Denzer had gone after a bum sleeping on the catwalk, only to have the man stab her in the arm for trying to save his life.

I couldn't let him go. Turning to Delgado, I said, "Let's save City Hall for later. I saw some graffiti at Worth Street on the way here. Let's check that out first."

He shrugged. At least he was being spared the Black Hole, his expression said.

Entering the tunnel's blackness, leaving behind the brightly lit world of sleepy riders, a tiny rush of adrenaline, like MSG after a Chinese dinner, coursed through my bloodstream. Part of it was pure reversion to childhood's fears. Hansel and Gretel. Snow White. Lost in dark woods, with enemies all around. In this case, rats. Their scuffling sent shivers up my spine as we balanced our way along the catwalk above the tracks.

The other part was elation. This was my job. I was good at it. I could put aside my fears and step boldly down into murky depths where few New Yorkers ever went.

Our flashlights shone dim as fireflies. I surveyed the gloomy underground world I'd spent my professional life in.

My imagination often took over in the tunnels. They became caves of doom. Or an evil wood, out of *Lord of the Rings*. The square columns holding up the tunnel roof were leafless trees, the constant trickle of foul water between the tracks a poisonous stream from which no one drank and lived.

Jones Beach. Uncle Paul's huge hand cradling my foot, then lifting me high in the air and flinging me backward, laughing with delight, into the cool water. Droplets clinging to his red beard, and Uncle Paul shaking them off into the sunlight like a wet Irish setter.

Me and Mo, we're the only true Gallaghers. The only redheads. I got straight A's in English; nobody's grammar was safe from me—except Uncle Paul's.

I thought all men smelled like him: whiskey and tobacco.

As Manny and I plodded along the four-block tunnel between the live station and the dead one, we exchanged no words. The acrid stench of an old track fire filled my nostrils the way memories flooded my mind. Trying to push Uncle Paul away, I bent all my concentration on stepping carefully around the foul-smelling water, the burned debris I didn't want to identify.

I suspected Delgado's silence was due to fear; he wouldn't want a shaking voice to betray his tension. I knew how he felt. The first nighttime tunnel trek was a landmark in a young transit cop's life.

When the downtown express thundered past, we ducked into the coffin-sized alcoves set aside for transit workers. My heart pounded as the wind wake of the train pulled at my clothes; the fear of falling forward, landing under those relentless steel wheels, never left me, no matter how many times I stood in the well. I always thought of Anna Karenina; once in a while, in my drinking days, I'd wondered how it would feel to edge forward, to let the train's undertow pull me toward death.

I could never do it. I'd seen too much blood on the tracks.

Light at the end of the tunnel. The Worth Street station sent rays of hope into the spidery blackness. My step quickened; Delgado's pace matched mine. Soon we were almost running toward the light, like cavemen coming from the hunt to sit by the fire of safety.

We were almost at the edge of the platform when I motioned Delgado to stop. My hunger to bathe in the light was as great as his, but our post was in the shadows, watching.

A moment of panic. I'd lost the drunk. Had he fallen on the tracks, the electrified third rail roasting him like a pig at a barbecue? Not possible; we'd have heard, and smelled.

I had to admit, the graffiti painting wasn't a mindless scrawl. It was a picture, full of color and life. Humanlike figures in bright primary shades, grass-green, royal-blue, orange, sun-yellow, and carnation-pink—colors unknown in the black-and-gray tunnels—stood in a line, waiting to go through a subway turnstile. Sexless, they were cookie-cutter replicas of one another, the only difference among them the color inside the black edges.

A rhythmic clicking sound made Delgado jump. "What the hell—"

"Relax, Manny," I whispered. "It's the ball bearing in the spray-paint can. The vandals are here. As soon as the paint hits the tiles, we jump out and bust them."

Four rowdy teenagers, ranging in color from light brown to ebony, laughed raucously and punched one another with a theatrical style that said *We bad. We* real *bad.* They bounded up the steps from the other side of the platform and surveyed their artwork, playful as puppies, pointing out choice bits they had added to their mural.

It should have been simple. Two armed cops, with the advantage of surprise, against four kids armed with Day-Glo spray paint. Two things kept it from being simple: the drunk, wherever the hell he was, and the fact that one of the kids said, "Hey, bro, when Cool and Jo-Jo gettin' here?"

A very black kid with a nylon stocking on his head answered, "Jo-Jo be comin' with Pinto. Cool say he might be bringin' Slasher and T.P."

Great. Instead of two against four, it sounded like all the graffiti artists in New York City were planning a convention in the Worth Street ghost station.

"Sarge?" Delgado's voice was urgent. "We've gotta—"

"I know," I whispered back. "Get on the radio and call for backup."

Then I remembered. Worth Street was a dead spot. Lead in the ceiling above our heads turned our radios into worthless toys.

"Stop," I said wearily as Manny pulled the antenna up on his hand-held radio. "It won't work. You'll have to go back to Brooklyn Bridge. Alert Booth Robert two twenty-one. Have them call Operations. Just ask for backup, don't make it a ten-thirteen." A 10-13 meant "officer in trouble," and I didn't want to be the sergeant who cried wolf.

"Try the radio along the way," I went on. "You never know when it will come to life. I'm not sure where the lead ends."

Watching Delgado trudge back along the catwalk, I felt lonely, helpless, and stupid. No one knew we'd gone to Worth Street instead of the Black Hole, and that was my fault.

"Hey," one of the kids called, pointing to a pile of old clothes in the corner of the platform, "what this dude be doin' in our crib?"

Dude? What dude? Then the old clothes began to rise; it was the drunk from the train. He was huddled into a fetal ball, hoping not to be noticed by the graffiti gang.

Nylon Stocking boogied over to the old drunk, sticking a finger in his ribs. "What you be doin' here, ol' man? Huh? Answer me."

A fat kid with a flat top walked over, sat down next to the drunk, reached into the old man's jacket pocket, and pulled out a half-empty pint bottle.

A lighter-skinned, thinner boy slapped the drunk around, first lifting him by the scruff of the neck, then laughing as he flopped back to the floor. The old guy tried to rise, only to be kicked in the ribs by Nylon Stocking.

The old guy was bleeding at the mouth. Fat Boy held the pint of booze aloft, teasing the drunk the way you tease a dog with a bone. The worst part was that the drunk was reaching for it, hands flapping wildly, begging. He'd have barked if they'd asked him to.

I was shaking, my stomach starting to heave. God, where was Manny? Where was my backup? I had to stop the kids before their friends got there, but I felt too sick to move. *If there's one thing I can't stand, it's a woman drunk.* It was as though every taunt, every kick, was aimed at me, not just at the old man.

I reached into my belt for my gun, then opened my vest's back pouch and pulled out the slapper. Ready to charge, I stopped cold when Nylon Stocking said, "Yo, y'all want to do him like we done the others?"

Fat Boy's face lit up. "Yeah," he agreed. "Feel like a cold night. We needs a little fire."

"You right, bro," the light-skinned kid chimed in. "I got the kerosene. Done took it from my momma heater."

"What he deserve, man," the fourth member of the gang said, his voice a low growl. "Comin' into our crib, pissin' on the art, smellin' up the place. This here *our* turf, dig?" He prodded the old man in the chest.

"I—I didn't mean nothing," the old man whimpered. "I just wanted a place to sleep."

Uncle Paul, sleeping on our couch when he was too drunk for Aunt Rose to put up with him. He was never too drunk for Mom to take him in. Never too drunk to give me one of his sweet Irish smiles and call me his best girl.

The light-skinned kid opened the bottle—ironically, it looked as if it once contained whiskey—and sprinkled the old man the way my mother sprinkled clothes before ironing them. Nylon Stocking pulled out a book of matches.

By the time Delgado came back, with or without backup, there'd be one more bonfire if I didn't do something. Fast.

Surprise was my only hope. Four of them, young and strong. One of me, out of shape and shaky.

I shot out a light. I cracked the bulb on the first shot. Target shooting was my best asset as a cop, and I used it to give the kids the impression they were surrounded.

The kids jumped away from the drunk, moving in all directions. "Shit," one said, "who shootin'?"

I shot out the second and last bulb. In the dark, I had the advantage. They wouldn't know, at least at first, that only one cop was coming after them.

"Let's book," another cried. "Ain't worth stayin' here to get shot."

I ran up the steps, onto the platform lit only by the moonlike rays from the other side of the tracks. Yelling "Stop, police," I waded into the kids, swinging my illegal slapper.

Thump into the ribs of the kid holding the kerosene bottle. He dropped it, clutching his chest and howling. I felt the breath whoosh out of him, heard the snap of rib cracking. I wheeled and slapped Nylon Stocking across the knee, earning another satisfying howl.

My breath came in gasps, curses pouring out of me. Blood pounding in my temples, a thumping noise that sounded louder than the express train.

The advantage of surprise was over. The other two kids jumped me, one riding my back, the other going for my stomach with hard little fists. All I could see was a maddened teenage tornado circling me with blows. My arm felt light as I thrust my gun deep into the kid's stomach. He doubled, groaning.

It was like chugging beer at a cop racket. Every hit, every satisfying *whack* of blackjack against flesh made me hungry for the next. I whirled and socked. The kids kept coming, and I kept knocking them down like bowling pins.

The adrenaline rush was stupendous, filling me with elation. I was a real cop again. There was life after detox.

At last they stopped. Panting, I stood among the fallen, exhausted. My hair had escaped from my knit hat and hung in matted tangles over a face red-hot as a griddle.

I pulled out my cuffs and chained the kids together, wrist to wrist, wishing I had enough sets to do each individually. Together, even cuffed, they could overpower me. Especially since they were beginning to realize I was alone.

I felt weak, spent. As though I'd just made love.

I sat down on the platform, panting, my gun pointed at Nylon Stocking. "You have the right to remain silent," I began.

As I finished the last Miranda warning on the last kid, I heard the cavalry coming over the hill. Manny Delgado, with four reinforcements.

As the new officers took the collars, I motioned Manny aside, taking him to where the drunk lay sprawled in the corner, still shaking and whimpering.

"Do you smell anything?" I asked.

Manny wrinkled his nose. I looked down at the drunk.

A trickle of water seeped from underneath him; his crotch was soaked.

Uncle Paul, weaving his way home, singing off-key, stopping to take a piss under the lamppost. Nothing unusual in that, except that this time Julie Ann Mackinnon, my eighth-grade rival, watched from across the street. My cheeks burned as I recalled how she'd told the other kids what she'd seen, her hand cupped over her giggling mouth.

"Not that," I said, my tone sharp, my face reddening. "The kerosene. These kids are the torch killers. They were going to roast this guy. That's why I had to take them on alone."

Delgado's face registered the skepticism I'd seen lurking in his eyes all night. Could he trust me? He'd been suitably impressed at my chain gang of prisoners, but now I was talking about solving the crime that had every cop in the city on overtime.

"Look, just go back to Brooklyn Bridge and radio—" I was going to say Captain Lomax, when I thought better. "No, call Sal Minucci in Anti-Crime. He'll want to have the guy's coat analyzed. And make sure somebody takes good care of that bottle." I pointed to the now-empty whiskey bottle the light-skinned boy had poured kerosene from.

"Isn't that his?" Manny indicated the drunk.

"No, his is a short dog," I said, then turned away as I realized the term was not widely known in nondrunk circles.

Just go, kid, I prayed. *Get the hell out of here before—*

He turned, following the backup officers with their chain gang. "And send for Emergency Medical for this guy," I added. "I'll stay here till they come."

I looked down at the drunk. His eyes were blue, a watery, no-color blue with all the life washed out of them. Uncle Paul's eyes.

Uncle Paul, blurry-faced and maudlin, too blitzed to care that I'd come home from school with a medal for the best English composition. I'd put my masterpiece by his chair, so he could read it after dinner. He spilled whiskey on it; the blue-black ink ran like tears and blotted out my carefully chosen words.

Uncle Paul, old, sick, and dying, just like this one. Living by that time more on the street than at home, though there were people who would take him in. His eyes more red than blue, his big frame wasted. I felt a sob rising, like death squeezing my lungs. I heaved, grabbing for air. My face was wet with tears I didn't recall shedding.

I hate you, Uncle Paul. I'll never be like you. Never.

I walked over to the drunk, still sprawled on the platform. I was a sleep-walker; my arm lifted itself. I jabbed the butt of my gun into old, thin ribs, feeling it bump against bone. It would be a baseball-size bruise. First a raw red-purple, then blue-violet, finally a sickly yellow-gray.

I lifted my foot, just high enough to land with a thud near the kidneys. The old drunk grunted, his mouth falling open. A drizzle of saliva fell to the ground. He put shaking hands to his face and squeezed his eyes shut. I lifted my foot again. I wanted to kick and kick and kick.

Uncle Paul, a frozen lump of meat found by some transit cop on the aboveground platform at 161st Street. The Yankee Stadium stop, where he took me when the Yanks played home games. We'd eat at the Yankee Tavern, me wolfing down a corned beef on rye and a cream soda, Uncle Paul putting away draft beer after draft beer.

Before he died, Uncle Paul had taken all the coins out of his pocket, stacking them in neat little piles beside him. Quarters, dimes, nickels, pennies. An inventory of his worldly goods.

I took a deep, shuddering breath, looked down at the sad old man I'd brutalized. A hot rush of shame washed over me.

I knelt down, gently moving the frail, blue-white hands away from the near-transparent face. The fear I saw in the liquid blue eyes sent a piercing ray of self-hatred through me.

If there's anything I can't stand, it's a woman drunk. Me too, Manny, I can't stand women drunks either.

The old man's lips trembled; tears filled his eyes and rolled down his thin cheeks. He shook his head from side to side, as though trying to wake himself from a bad dream.

"Why?" he asked, his voice a raven's croak.

"Because I loved you so much." The words weren't in my head anymore, they were slipping out into the silent, empty world of the ghost station. As though Uncle Paul weren't buried in Calvary Cemetery, but could hear me with the ears of this old man who looked too damn much like him. "Because I wanted to be just like you. And I am." My voice broke. "I'm just like you, Uncle Paul. I'm a drunk." I put my head on my knee and sobbed like a child. All the shame of my drinking days welled up in my chest. The stupid things I'd said and done, the times I'd had to be taken home and put to bed, the times I'd thrown up in the street outside the bar. *If there's one thing I can't stand . . .*

"Oh, God, I wish I were dead."

The bony hand on mine felt like a talon. I started, then looked into the old man's watery eyes. I sat in the ghost station and saw in this stranger the ghost that had been my dying uncle.

"Why should you wish a thing like that?" the old man asked. His voice was clear, no booze-blurred slurring, no groping for words burned out of the brain by alcohol. "You're a young girl. You've got your whole life ahead a you."

My whole life. To be continued . . .

One day at a time. One night at a time.

When I got back to the District, changed out of my work clothes, showered, would there be a meeting waiting for me? Damn right; in the city that never sleeps, AA never sleeps either.

I reached over to the old man. My fingers brushed his silver stubble.

"I'm sorry, Uncle Paul," I said. "I'm sorry."

Born in Manacor, Majorca, Spain, **MARIA ANTONIA OLIVER** also maintains a home in Barcelona. A leading Catalan writer, she has written more than six novels and is also a noted translator of American and English classics into her native language. Her mystery novel *A Study in Lilac* was very well received in Europe and North America.

Her translator, Kathleen McNerney, is a professor of Spanish and Catalan at the University of West Virginia in Morgantown.

WHERE ARE YOU, MONICA?

Maria Antonia Oliver

I

 "Is Mr. Guiu here?" he asked.

"I'm Ms. Guiu," I said.

We looked each other over, eyebrows arched by surprise. He sure hadn't expected to find a female detective. For my part, I certainly never expected to find a man like him in my greasy office. What a man—tall, well dressed, well built, the kind that turns your head on the street, the kind you want a hug from when you have them nearby.

"May I help you?"

He took a chair from in front of Quim's desk and sat down in front of mine. His gestures were secure and indifferent, as if he hadn't done anything in his whole life except move chairs from one place to another in my office. He had gray eyes, and his fingernails were manicure-clean and polished.

"Look, I . . . it's kind of sensitive, you know? I mean . . ."

"Does it have to do with fucking around, by any chance?" I cut in quickly.

It was a system that on more than one occasion had spared me having to play the role of psychiatrist or confessor, and then lending a shoulder to cry on.

"What?"

"Your wife has a lover and you want us to catch them 'in flagrante,' right?"

"Good heavens, lady!"

"Then maybe your lover is messing around with someone else and . . ."

He smiled sadly. No, it wasn't that, either. He even seemed offended.

"Then . . ." I was about to let out another guess, but I withheld it. If I kept on chasing wild geese like that, I could lose my client, and Guiu Investigation Agency couldn't afford such a luxury.

"Look, it's that my wife disappeared three days ago."

So I wasn't so far off base after all, shit! He didn't need to put on such an act, for Christ's sake!

"Just like that?" I asked. "Has she called you, or did she leave a letter or anything?"

"No, nothing at all."

"Did you have a fight? I mean, do you have any idea why she might have wanted to disappear?"

"No, not at all."

"Are you very wealthy?"

"I'll pay whatever you charge."

"No, I didn't mean that. I wasn't worried about my fees. I was thinking of the possibility of a kidnapping."

He turned pale and looked scared. I thought he was going to fall off his chair.

"Why don't you tell me about it in more detail?" I said immediately.

"Okay, maybe, but . . ."

"But what?"

"Before giving you more details I want to know whether you're going to take on the job . . ."

"But our policy is not to accept any job until we know the details. . . . Have you called the police?"

"No, her family doesn't want that."

"Why not? What about what you want? Have they looked for her themselves?"

He gestured for me to stop. He was smiling, but barely.

"Look, her family, especially her father, doesn't want anyone to know about it, because they're high-class people, know what I mean? Me, I'd do anything to find her . . . just to know she's okay. You understand, right? If she doesn't want to come back, what can I do? We can't force people to do things they don't want to do, after all. . . ."

"So both you and her family believe that she ran away from home. . . ."

"No, no, we don't have any idea, not at all."

He didn't say anything for a while. I waited. I was prepared to be patient. After all, that morning's work was pretty mechanical, and for me it was a lot more fun to contemplate those eyes, that mouth half hidden by a moustache cultivated with a studied nonchalance. Much more fun than typing up reports on people who had purchased televisions or refrigerators and then tried to pay for them in installments.

"We started to call the hospitals," he finally said. "But then we figured there were professionals out there who could do it better, more discreetly, than we could—you know what I mean, don't you?"

"Yes, of course."

"So, will you take it on?"

"You said before that we wouldn't have to argue about money, or something like that, right?"

He smiled. It was sort of a suppressed smile, as if he didn't want to seem too satisfied. He brushed his hand across his forehead and installed himself more comfortably in the chair.

"You can send me the bill, Miss Guiu. To discuss money at the moment seems like an insult to my wife."

"But you might be able to find another agency that would do it cheaper."

"Perhaps, but I feel confident with you. I was surprised to find a woman doing this kind of work, but for the job I want you to do, I think it's better to have a woman than a man."

"Why?"

"Well, because it'll be easier for you to get inside the mentality of another woman, and that way you'll do better at tracking her down."

"Okay. Now let's start at the beginning," I said.

I reached for a notebook and turned on the tape recorder.

"Listen, Miss Guiu, why don't we go to a quieter place to discuss this?"

It seemed to me that it would be hard to find a quieter place. A more pleasant place, that would be easy.

II

When I got into the car, I was assaulted by an overly enthusiastic dog that jumped on me from the backseat and made itself comfortable on my lap.

"You're the first person she's paid any attention to since Monica's not around. She hasn't eaten a bite for two days, poor thing."

I was moved as I watched Victor and the dog leaving. When the two had left the bar, I began to go over the notes.

Monica Pradell, thirty-two years old, married for eight years to Victor Cabanes, only child of Mateu Pradell and Angela Comessa.

Mr. Pradell, head of a construction company. High social standing.

Mr. Cabanes, architect, partner of Mr. Pradell in several development projects. Architecture office together with A.M. and J.F.R.

Monica and Victor live in the pavilion located on Mr. and Mrs. Pradell's land. No kids. Ideal couple.

Both Monica and Ms. Comessa, housewives.

Monica fond of enamel work. Serene character, sure of herself, not a show-off, a real homebody, reserved, not many friends, a few girl friends from high school. Classical dressing style, with some extravagant details—scarves, jewelry, flowers. Very high heels, always. Very good-looking legs, almost sculptured. Loves the sea. Good health. Not a spendthrift, except for the beauty parlor. Lots of changes in hairstyle and color.

She didn't have any reason to run away: she was happy. She wasn't scatter-brained; reject the possibility of a prank of some kind. A lover or affair was out of the question. So was suicide. How about kidnapping, then? So far, no signs.

Afraid that something has happened to her, but she always carried a card in her purse; in case of accident notify . . .

Datebook on her desk, but no significant notations. Normal appointments at the beauty parlor and with some girl friends.

Not a member of any club or association.

Last time seen: Thursday, February 17. Beige suit with lilac silk blouse and a beige felt hat with a ribbon and fabric flowers. There don't seem to be any jewels missing, but they aren't exactly sure how many she had. No large withdrawal from her personal account. She usually carried a couple of hundred dollars with her, plus credit cards. She was supposed to go to the beauty parlor, but she didn't show up. Very curly hair, the color of mahogany.

The photograph Victor brought me didn't give any details away. It was of a group, a blurry snapshot, and that silhouette in a bathing suit surrounded by other silhouettes could have been me myself.

III

"Mr. Cabanes, please."

They put me through the sieve: the telephone operator, the head secretary, an overseer who insisted on knowing why and about what I wanted to talk to Victor. Finally the voice of his personal secretary said, as soon as I told her my name, that Mr. Cabanes was in a meeting but he had ordered that he should be notified right away if I called.

"Tell me, Miss Guiu . . . have you found something?"

"No, not yet. Listen, Mr. Cabanes, I'd like to talk to you, to find out more details."

"All right, right now, if you wish . . ."

"By the way, remember I need another photograph. I'd like to have another look at the datebook, too, and if possible, I'd like to see her clothes, her jewelry, the atmosphere, in a word. To get a better idea, you know?"

There was a pause. Finally:

"Very well, come over for dinner. To the pavilion, I mean, around nine, is that okay?"

"I warn you I'm a vegetarian . . ."

"Listen, Miss Guiu, it doesn't matter to me what you are or aren't. The only thing I'm interested in is the job I gave you to do. Nothing more."

Pedantic shit-head!

"All right then: your wife isn't in any clinic, hospital, or hotel in the city. Nor is she at the morgue. That's all I know at the moment. I'm not the Holy Ghost, you know."

"It's all right, don't get mad. Tonight, come in through the door on Modolell Street. That way you won't have to go through my in-laws' yard.

I was ringing the doorbell of the pavilion at nine on the dot. It was a cozy house, and very luxurious, of course. It was a rich people's nest, with all the comforts, both necessary and superfluous, and those are the most comfortable ones. Spacious. Pleasant. And Mr. Victor Cabanes—Jesus, I could have smothered him with kisses. But I kept my grip: a job was a job. Before dinner I scrutinized the belongings of the missing person. The quantity was indescribable: dresses, jackets, skirts, blouses, coats . . . lots of everything. Incredibly high heels, for sure.

"I couldn't tell you whether anything is missing or not," Victor told me. "But at least the suitcases are where they belong."

Then, the jewelry. Some real, some not. I mean costume jewelry. But good stuff, and lots of it.

"The only things missing are the enamel pendant and ring she made herself. She was very proud of them and never took them off."

We dined by candlelight and started on the photos.

"Monica doesn't like to have her picture taken. I couldn't find many at all . . . a few from my in-laws, some I had, and a couple from her desk."

The champagne was leaving the bottle little by little, and the warm atmosphere in the room almost made me forget why we were looking at the pictures. Let it be said in passing, they were all really bad. No works of art, that's for sure.

"Where was this taken?" I asked.

"The Aegean Sea. Didn't I tell you Monica was crazy about the sea? That must have been from our honeymoon."

"You're wearing the same sweater you're wearing now."

"Oh, yeah, it's true!"

He laughed. It was a romantic story: Monica had given him that sweater when they were on their honeymoon. And now, a few months ago, on their anniversary, she had given him another one just like it that she'd come across by chance in a shop. Victor's eyes watered a little as he told me the story, and I couldn't help feeling a touch of jealousy. It was hard to have to recognize, but that's what it was: jealousy.

"Is this the pendant you mentioned before?"

The photo we were looking at presented me with a woman with distinct features. She wasn't pretty, but she had character: eyes whose smallness was well disguised by skillful makeup, a nose difficult to hide, and a rather formless mouth. An enamel pendant with matching ring, long fingers with exaggerated nails. It was the only photo that was of any use to me at all.

"Did she always keep them so long?" I asked.

"What?"

"Her fingernails."

"Oh, yes, and picked up the habit of drumming her nails on the pendant, making a little noise like when you clink glasses together, and I'll tell you the truth, it made me nervous."

"Do you have the negative of this picture?"

"What do you want it for?"

"So I can make a copy for my partner . . . don't worry, man, he's going to help me find her."

"Surely you don't intend to go around showing pictures of my wife all over the place?"

"And I'm going to need the addresses of the people your wife sees the most."

"But are you planning to go see those people and ask them about Monica?"

He was really scared.

"Oh, yes, and the datebook. Perhaps you didn't find anything unusual, but I'm more experienced, and . . ." I said in a very professional tone of voice.

"I'm sure I told you, Miss Guiu, that we wanted the utmost discretion in this matter."

The man was capable of snapping up like an oyster. How exasperating! What did he expect me to do? How could I find a missing person who hadn't left a trace if not by trying to pick up a few traces?

I said all that in shouts. Offended. And the oyster opened up a little.

"Now how come you're sore, Miss Guiu?"

"I'm not sore. Well, could I see your wife's makeup? To judge by the picture, she must have been an expert at playing cutaneous dress-up."

"What do you mean?"

"Nothing, just she was real good at making herself up."

"Oh, well, yeah, of course."

He showed me to the bathroom.

But I had more lipstick myself than Monica had. Perhaps the only thing she took with her was her makeup. Among the few that were left, there was a gorgeous lipstick, of an incredible color, with a case that looked like gold. I fell in love with it.

"May I take this lipstick with me?" I asked.

"Sure . . . but what good can it do you?"

"A question of detail, Mr. Cabanes."

IV

"Yes, we're good friends, but I hadn't seen her for about a month. As far as I know, she was only seeing Patricia."

"Who's Patricia?"

"To be perfectly frank, miss, I think she's a little on the murky side."

"Where does she live?"

"Somewhere in the Eixample area, I think, but I'm not sure. But I think I do have her telephone number . . . that is, if she hasn't moved . . . you never know, with her type."

As I was leaving, Mrs. Culell held the door open and said, taking on a secretive tone:

"You may find out, miss, whether Monica and Victor are really the ideal couple they seem to be."

What a hypocrite! And here I thought that people with bucks weren't so gossipy, or at least that they had enough dignity to hide it.

I called from the first booth I could find. No answer.

I had another appointment that morning, with another of Monica's friends. It might be useful to compare the information the Culell woman had given me and figure out how much of it was bad blood; not that that would do me much good, but I was curious about it. However, the very thought of going through yet another session of good manners and hypocrisy had me in hysterics.

I pulled myself together and rang the doorbell. This lady had a maid.

"Victor must be beside himself," Mrs. Torres said with a glass of whiskey in her hand.

For me, the maid brought in some orange juice, the kind you make with real oranges.

"When was the last time you saw Mrs. Monica Pradell?"

"It must have been—wait a minute." She looked at her calendar. "Yes, two weeks ago. We ate together at the Pradells', in the big house."

"Do you know someone by the name of Patricia?"

She knew her, all right.

"I've never been able to understand it at all, such a close friendship. Wait, now that I think about it, I saw Monica with that girl, let's see, about a week ago, yeah, I saw them from a distance. I always tell Monica, 'I don't know how you can be such bosom buddies with that . . . blockhead.' "

"Do they get along? The couple, I mean."

"Victor and Monica? Oh, yeah, they make such a nice couple, both so good-looking. And so crazy about each other."

"What do you think could have happened to Mrs. Pradell? I mean, do you know or suspect whether she had some motive for disappearing just like that?"

"I've no idea. It's all so strange . . . poor Victor. I recall that they had an argument that night we had dinner, well, a friendly argument, anyway, nothing tragic, I don't want you to get the wrong idea, miss; I'm just telling you so you'll see how much they loved each other, well . . ."

"What was the argument about?"

That was the first I'd heard about the development. I pretended I wasn't too interested. I didn't want to jump the gun before I was pretty sure about it. When I left Mrs. Torres's place, I called Quim right away.

"I'm asking you as a professional favor, man."

"But I've never done anything like that, Lònia!" he whimpered.

"Tell them you're there on my behalf. They're not going to hassle you. And do it now, okay? I need to know by noon today."

"Why don't you go yourself, sweetie pie?"

"Because I have other things to do, sweetie pie yourself! Oh, come on, man. You owe me more than one favor, you know that." And I hung up.

I dialed again. Patricia still wasn't answering. I dialed again: my friend at the telephone company gave me the address.

When I got to the office I found a note from Quim on my desk: "Kid, I can see you really know how to get along with people. When I gave your name to those guys at the Property Registry, and at the College of Lawyers, too, they treated me like a king. How do you do it, honey? You'll have to clue me in. I include, under separate cover, the results of my research. I'm at your disposal for whatever might be necessary, Mrs. Paloni, you know that. I'm having dinner at that rabbit restaurant of yours and I'll have them put it on your bill. I deserve it, don't you think? Oh, yeah: your beloved client called—wants you to call."

Quim's research, as he called it, confirmed that Mr. Pradell was the owner of some land along the seashore. And that there was a project in the name of Victor Cabanes to develop it, already presented and approved, but held up "sine die." So far, okay.

Then to Patricia's place. But she'd already flown the coop. She'd left the apartment four days ago, without leaving a forwarding address.

"What if she gets mail?" I asked the doorlady.

"She said she was sure she wouldn't get any."

At the nearest telephone booth, Victor Cabanes's secretary asked me if it would be convenient to come by the office.

"Right away," I said.

Ten minutes after that "right away" they were showing me into Victor's office. He was waiting for me, looking as though he needed to ask me to do him a favor.

"What's up?" I asked.

"That's what I'd like to know," he answered with a sticky sweetness.

"Why did you want to see me, Mr. Cabanes?"

Naturally, he wanted to know how my investigations were going. What his wife's friends had told me. If studying Monica's datebook had turned anything up. Etc., etc.

"What do you know about Patricia?" I cut him off.

"Who's Patricia?"

"A very good friend of your wife."

"I remember she had a friend who was a little on the flaky side . . . but what does that have to do with Monica?"

"It turns out you're the only one who doesn't know anything about the friendship your wife had with this woman. It also turns out that she left her apartment exactly four days ago: the very day after Monica Pradell's disappearance. What do you think about that?"

He was taken aback. I took advantage:

"By the way, how's the development going?"

"Development? What development?"

"Blue Sea. It's a terrific project, Mr. Cabanes. Too bad it's being held up, isn't it? And I'm afraid that if your wife doesn't turn up, Mr. Pradell won't ever get around to closing the deal on it. . . ."

"I've no idea what you're getting at, Miss Guiu. . . ."

"Do you love Monica Pradell, Mr. Cabanes?"

"Listen, what did those reptiles tell you? What are you thinking, Miss Guiu? What do you suspect?"

It took God's help and then some to get him to confess. And once I had it,

I realized that the confession wasn't going to do me much good. No, he didn't love Monica anymore. He was looking for her because, in fact, her father wasn't about to let that land be developed if his heir didn't go along with it.

"And you don't know where she is, right?" I said with my very best sarcasm. "You don't suppose she could have run off precisely so she wouldn't be forced to say yes to something she didn't want, do you?"

I was beating him to death, and behaving like a spoiled kid, too. Victor was thrown completely out of gear.

"No, I don't think that," he said. "Nor do I know where she is, Miss Guiu. And I must say I don't care one bit for your attitude."

"Well, it's up to you. I'll drop the case."

"No, don't do that."

"Could this be revenge on your wife's part?"

"Revenge? For what?"

"You told me you didn't love her. . . ."

"Monica doesn't know that. Or if she knows, she doesn't care. She doesn't love me either."

"Why do you live together, then?"

But that was going beyond the limits of conjugal intimacy, propriety, appearances, and all that.

He invited me to dinner at his place again, this time not on working time, he said. What a pity to have met him under such circumstances.

The soiree was delightful, and I went home with Monica's dog. It seems the Pradells were heartbroken to see her so sad and thin, and Victor didn't want to take her to the kennels, but he couldn't take care of her, either. She paid so much attention to me, and maybe I'd like to keep her until Monica came back.

Sure, glad to.

When I left, he kissed me on the cheek.

"Tomorrow I'll start investigating Patricia," I told him. "I think we might just find something there."

"Fine. Give me a call."

V

"Hadn't she ever mentioned that she was thinking of moving out of the apartment?"

"She wasn't nice at all. If I didn't say hello to her, she never said a word to me. Why would she mention anything to me?"

"Did she live alone?"

"Yes, but she had a lot of company . . . especially men. Well, I don't want to bear false witness . . . sometimes women came over, too."

"What did she live on?"

"I don't know . . . I suppose the people who came to see her, don't you think?"

"She didn't have a job anywhere?"

"Not that I know. Listen, miss, has she done something?"

"Have you ever seen this woman?" I showed her Monica's picture.

She looked it over from every angle. Up close. Far away. She examined the details.

"This face looks familiar to me, it looks kind of familiar, all right."

"Could I have a look at the apartment?" I asked.

"I wouldn't be able to do that, miss. You'd have to go to the agency that rents it out. I . . ."

"You have the key, don't you?"

"Yes, but I can only show it to people with a card from the agency. Besides, there isn't anything of hers there anymore."

"How about if instead of a card from the agency, I give you one of mine?" I showed her a ten-dollar bill.

"Well, okay, just because I think you're okay. But don't go telling them at the agency that I let you in."

The elevator stank of trash, and it was slow.

"Did she live here for long?" I kept up the questioning.

"About two years, more or less."

"Did she get any mail?"

"A little, not much. Maybe one or two letters the whole time she lived here." She opened the apartment door. "Both from here, from banks . . . they weren't personal letters. The fact is that people don't get personal letters anymore, do they, miss? Just letters from the bank and junk mail."

The doorlady went on philosophizing and opening drawers. She took her job very seriously. Meantime, I was trying to get an idea of what Patricia's life must have been like in that apartment, so impersonal now.

There was a dresser scarf on the side table, with a rumple in it. A clump of starch maybe? No, it was a piece of paper.

"Could you open the blinds, please?" I said to the woman.

She obligingly hurried to do so. I stuck my hand under the cloth and stuffed the paper into my pocket.

Nothing else of significance in the apartment. Once I was on the street, I took a look at the paper. It was an empty envelope with the address written by hand. So Patricia had received a letter, but it didn't say from whom, or on what street.

I had to ask Quim for help again.

"Come on, with your detective ID card it'll be easy. You do these"—I gave him a list—"and I'll do the rest."

"Know what I think, sweetie? I think I like the easier cases better."

"Don't give me that stuff, Quim. Commercial reports are a piece of shit, and the skirt-chasing cases get boring. Have they brought in the copies of the photo?"

"Your problem is that that jerk has you wrapped around his little finger. He even stuck you with his dog. Yes, they brought the copies."

"The dog! Where's the dog?"

"I locked her up in the bathroom. I don't like having animals around in the office."

"I can't leave her home alone all day long, the poor thing is depressed . . . and you, you animal, you lock her up in the bathroom!"

"I wouldn't be surprised if you got into collecting dogs, crazy lady. Collecting lipsticks is more peaceful."

"Don't mess with me, Quim," I warned him severely. I went to let the dog out.

"It was doing weird things today, that animal," Quim was saying.

She'd taken a big leak in the bathroom. She came out with her tail between her legs. She took a leap when she recognized me, and when I picked her up, she licked my face.

"Okay, Quim, go ahead and start something. What weird things was she doing? The dog, I mean."

"She was sniffing my shoes and she started to howl and pull away from me. She's nuts."

"She's probably hungry, poor thing," I said. Then I went on: "Okay, that's it. I'll call you at Ton's bar at six o'clock to see if you've found anything. Go on, clear out, off with you. Hey, don't forget the picture!"

"I think I'm going to quit this job. I'm not the right type to take orders from a woman." He was still grumbling when he got in the elevator.

I fed the dog and then grabbed the other envelope of photos to take with me to visit my share of the travel agencies. Nothing, a total failure. Quim too. Not at six, not at eight.

"Maybe Patricia bought the ticket?" mused Quim.

"For sure. But I gave her name to the agencies, too, and nothing's turned up at all."

"You're so smart, Miss Paloni!" Quim said.

"A lot more than you. And don't call me Paloni!"

"Dirty rotten lie: I gave her name to the agencies too. But she must have bought the tickets under a false name."

VI

It felt as if I'd just gone to bed when the telephone rang.

"You're still in bed?" It was Quim's voice. "Isn't that nice! I play the early bird and you're still snoring!"

"What's up?"

"I have a lead. I'm at the Osborn Agency, on Muntaner Street, between . . ."

"I know where it is. I'm on my way."

I got dressed in a flash. The dog had destroyed the sole of one of my shoes. Luckily they were already worn out. The crepe soles stuck to the floor. All I had time to do was yell at her, and I left her curled up in a corner, trembling.

Quim was waiting for me at the door of the travel agency.

"They recognized Monica. Come in."

"How was she dressed, do you recall?" I asked the man on the other side of the counter.

"A tailored outfit, light color. Lilac blouse. Curly hair, sort of . . ." the man recited.

"Mahogany-colored?" I asked.

"Mahogany? Dark red, it was."

"That's right. You're very observant."

"No, not really. I noticed her because she was very . . . elegant . . . and especially because she made this constant noise."

I looked at him, surprised.

"Yes," Quim interrupted. "She was wearing that medal that's in the picture. And she kept tapping it with her fingernails."

"It sounded like glass," clarified the employee with satisfaction.

"She bought two tickets to Paris, the day after her disappearance. And she left a Paris address!"

"Well, make out a ticket for me. To Paris. For today, if possible," I said.

"Have you lost your senses altogether?" Quim yelled, appalled.

"Don't fail to feed the dog, you hear? We can't let her starve to death now that she's getting her appetite back."

"Okay, okay, go to Paris. And don't come back, dammit!"

VII

It was an apartment building. An old house that with some resources and a certain number of new doors had been transformed from a home for well-off bourgeois into a semiluxurious, semisnobbish Tower of Babel.

Patricia opened the door. She was an exuberant woman. She had on a rather transparent tunic and her hair was wound up in a towel. Her glasses were covered with rhinestones.

"Where's Monica?" I asked right away.

The smile froze on her face, and her extraordinarily fleshy lips, traced with a line darker than the color of her lipstick, filled up with little wrinkles. Her queenly pose tottered, and she didn't try to pretend.

"Who are you?" she asked.

She let me in, but she wouldn't tell me where Monica was. Nor what they were doing, the two of them. But I had that figured out, and the more Patricia did to hide it, the surer I was. Women's intuition, as they say, but also because of professional experience. The apartment was quite dark, but perhaps that would encourage secret-sharing.

"Do you realize I can turn you in for kidnapping, dear?"

"Why can't they just leave her alone, poor kid?" she said.

"Don't change the subject. Whether they leave her alone or not, that's up to her family. They're paying me to find her, and that's what I'm going to do, no matter what."

"So you'd ruin her life, now that she's starting to fix it up?"

"With you, right?"

She wouldn't go for it, though. She was just a childhood friend and she'd helped her escape, she said. Monica would have ended up in a nuthouse if it hadn't been for her. Victor hadn't told me that his wife was under the treatment of a psychiatrist, right? He hadn't told me because he didn't know.

So that was it! The three weekly *P*s in her datebook. At first I'd been convinced they meant the beauty parlor, and so had Victor. Then later I thought it stood for Patricia, and it turned out it meant psychiatrist. Now it was clear as a bell: all that was left was for Patricia to be willing to confess, and then Monica herself. Piece of cake. I was just sorry about how Victor was going to feel.

"Why was she under psychiatric care?" I asked.

"You didn't know about it, did you?"

"Of course I knew, naturally," I lied. "Victor knew too. And I know why, but I want you to tell me. So don't go making up any absurd stories."

"She was done in by her monotonous life. Depressed."

She didn't even buy that one herself, of course. She was good at keeping things under the rug, that poor excuse for a Sappho.

"And you, of course, decided to rescue her, out of generosity, right? What did you get out of this deal? What did you gain by deceiving the poor gal? She's got a pretty substantial bank account."

"I didn't do it for the money!"

Now we were getting somewhere. I spurred on:

"No? You did it out of the kindness of your heart, then? Come on, where's Monica? If I don't find her, it won't be just a kidnapping, it'll be murder."

It took pain and perspiration, threats, lies, promises. . . . She wouldn't budge, this gal, but I finally managed to get her between a rock and a hard place, and she began to fall apart altogether.

Her dark voice, with a foreign accent I wasn't able to identify, broke down. First she cried and cried, and then, sheltered by the darkness, she explained it all to me.

VIII

"Patricia made me swear I wouldn't make out my report until you're on your way to Australia," I said.

"Will you stick to that?" Monica asked.

"If you'll write a letter for me explaining the whole thing. It's a matter of professional pride."

We were in the bar of the Carse Hotel, near Westminster. Patricia had set up the appointment herself the previous day, but Monica still didn't quite trust me.

"Why did you come to London?" I asked, just to say something.

"To get ready to go to Australia. Patricia must have told you that, didn't she?"

"Just out of curiosity, personal not professional," I said. "Why didn't you take all the money out of your account? Because I assume your father will disinherit you."

"So I wouldn't leave any leads behind. But you can see that didn't do me any good. It didn't work, either, for us to stay apart until everything was ready. If my husband had hired a man instead of a woman, even if he'd found Patricia, she'd have gotten rid of him. But you put it all together, and now look."

I'd established some kind of complicity with Monica in spite of myself. I didn't like Patricia at all, but Monica was so pleasant, so peaceful, just the opposite of that gnawing tigress. But she did have, as Victor had told me, the habit of drumming her fingernails against that enamel pendant. It really was unnerving.

"Well, what's the deal then, about the letter?" she said.

"You can write it right now, if you like," I said.

"No, I want to really give it some thought. Tomorrow, same time, here, okay?"

"Absolutely."

She got up, stretching her arm out to caress me. I pulled back instinctively.

"You're still an uptight, repressed conservative, my friend," she said softly. I watched her leave, balancing on a set of spike heels that made me dizzy.

She must not have been too comfortable in them, because when she went to go up the two steps leading to the vestibule, she twisted an ankle and nearly ended up all over the floor. She turned around and smiled mischievously.

The next day, at the same time, Monica had had to go out, but she'd left the letter for me. Typewritten, shit! But I assumed that the signature would make it plenty valid.

That night I caught a plane for home. With the money I'd get for that job, I'd treat myself to a nice little week off.

IX

Victor was waiting for me at his pavilion. He was furious . . . he'd been calling me every day at the office, and Quim told him the truth at first, that is, that I was in Paris and then in London checking out some leads, and then lies, that is, that I was still in London. I'd given my word to the two women that I'd give them a little head start, ten days to be exact. Ten desperate days for Victor. I was sick to death of sticking around the house, and Quim was in a rage for having to deal with the details.

He ushered me in without saying a word, but he made up for that with the look on his face. His curiosity about what had happened overcame his anger at not being kept informed. After all, we had agreed to keep him abreast of all the details.

I gave him Monica's letter.

Dear Victor,
    By the time you read this letter, I won't be Monica anymore. Get used to the idea. Think of it as a death, because that's the truth. I haven't been your wife for a very long time, and I've had to make colossal efforts to keep you from noticing. It's not just a question of love worn out, it's a matter of total incompatibility, not just with you personally, but with you as a man, a male. I know it's going to hurt you, but I've been Pat's lover for a long time. My sexual relationship with you wasn't a disaster because I was frigid, but because I'm a lesbian. I hope you won't dismiss and scorn me—because I don't consider my condition shameful—but if you do, and if I disgust you, it's all the same to me, and I won't even be surprised, knowing you as I do. I hope you won't take all this as a big tragedy. Just try to understand, and try to make a new life, as I've done.
    Love, Monica
    P.S. Tell Daddy to let you go ahead with the development. My opposition was a silly childish stubbornness, totally illogical.

Victor looked at me, beside himself.

"Do you want to read my report?" I asked.

"What's the point?"

"Well, it would clear up a few details," I said, positive that what I was saying was absurd.

"It's all as clear as a bell," he mumbled.

A very long silence ensued. He stared at the letter, without seeing it. Finally, he exploded.

When the fireplace had consumed all the photographs, including the ones I'd made, he seemed to calm down a little.

"Listen, Lònia, I don't think I'm up to giving this letter to my in-laws. Would you mind? You could give them the report, too."

"Victor, read it yourself first, then decide whether you really want her parents to read it. There's some stuff . . ."

He wasn't listening to me. I left the report on the couch, went through the Pradells' yard with Monica's letter in my purse, and rang their doorbell.

X

"Hi, sweetie," Quim greeted me.

He was munching on a tired-looking old sandwich and reading the paper, as usual. Every day. I let the dog out and looked over the mail. All business letters, of course. Bank statements, junk mail.

"A crazed guy showed up," Quim said distractedly. "Seems his wife is fooling around. Shall I do it, or do you want to?"

I broke a toothpick and let him choose. Without even looking, he picked the shorter one.

"Guess I get to do it," I said.

"Let me finish reading the paper and I'll tell you all about it."

I finished looking over the mail. There was an impersonal note from Victor, accompanied by a check that knocked me over.

"Hey, Quim, you'll have to find the gal that's cheating on her old man after all. I just struck it rich!"

Quim dropped his sandwich when he saw the figure.

"We're partners, right, sweetie?" he said.

"Sure, but I'll just help myself to a few bucks first so I can get a permanent. This very day. I'm off to the bank, and then to the beauty parlor."

Quim's mouth fell open. He didn't know what to say. I don't know whether he grumbled or not, since I was already gone.

At the beauty parlor, with all kinds of critters running around in my head, I realized that Victor didn't want to have any more to do with me. My sorrow was somewhat assuaged by the roll of banknotes I had in my purse, though. A victim of the ups and downs, I leafed through one of those worn magazines, the kind that tell you all about how such and such a singer has the flu, or how Mr. Bullfighter gets terrible headaches.

Then I saw her: Mrs. Monica Pradell de Cabanes at a dinner in honor of who knows whom. And Victor two spaces away from her. Except that Monica wasn't Monica. While they were taking my curlers out, with the permanent half done, my little brain was in sixth gear. By the time I walked out the door, my strategy was set: it was the beginning of a crazy week.

Beauty parlor, Patricia, psychiatrist. The three *P*s. I called a dozen counselors before I found the one I was looking for. Naturally, they didn't want to tell me anything, not on the phone and not in person. Professional secrecy. Adela would help me out.

"I absolutely must have a look at Monica Pradell's file," I said to her. "Among colleagues, professional secrecy shouldn't be a barrier."

I told her about the case, with all the gory details. She called me that afternoon. Monica wasn't a lesbian or anything like it. And so on.

I took off for London. Just as I suspected, the Carse Hotel had no record of Monica Pradell's visit. Then I went to Paris. I surreptitiously entered Patricia's apartment and found more than I was counting on. They were so confident that they'd forgotten about me altogether and weren't even being careful.

Home again. Now it was absolutely necessary for me to get into the pavilion, and into the Pradells' main house, too, without the family realizing it. Or with some kind of believable excuse. The dog, of course.

I watched from the car, waiting until they would all be gone. The first day, Mrs. Pradell stayed home. The next day, she left an hour after her husband left, who had gone out an hour after their son-in-law.

"I've lost the dog, and I thought maybe she'd come back here," I said to the maid.

"I haven't seen her."

"Wouldn't you let me have a look around?" I begged. "Maybe she's hiding somewhere in the house. I'm so upset!"

We searched every corner of the house. No sign of the dog. But I did find out that the Pradells had put an oil painting of Monica up in their attic. The maid even let me see a photo album where there were pictures of Monica and Patricia hugging. Next to that scandalous photo there was one of Monica by herself, wearing flat shoes with crepe soles.

What a perfect setup they'd created, those two! Real pros, capable of deceiving a pro like myself. Or am I such a pro after all? Maybe I'm just picking daisies.

Then we went to the pavilion, me and the maid. The dog wasn't there either, of course, but it gave me a chance to lift a scarf without her noticing.

"Maybe she'll come home on her own," I said, all discouraged. "Listen, I'd rather they didn't know that I've lost the dog, you know what I mean?"

"Yes, of course," the maid said. "I won't say a word, and if she shows up, I'll let you know."

I started the car and two blocks away I let the dog out of the trunk, where she was having a nice nap.

I raced toward Blue Sea. They had already started the construction and it was a bees' nest of machines and people. Shit, I'd have to wait until Sunday. On Sunday it was deserted. Sleeping machines, but they'd already torn up the earth. Displaced cliffs, holes, piles, and puddles all over the place. It was a crime to see such a gorgeous landscape so mistreated. A real rape.

I put the scarf to the dog's nose. The animal barked, then she looked at me astonished, and it even seemed she remembered. She went crazy sniffing. She ran wild. I could hardly follow her. The coast went uphill, forming cliffs and little sandless beaches you could only get to by sea, at least for the moment. The dog was on top of a rock, quite a few feet below me: she was howling and trying to find a way to get down. I called her, but she didn't hear me. Or she heard but didn't pay any attention. In any case, she found a way to keep going down and I lost sight of her. I could still hear her whiny yelps.

I had to rescue her with a boat. She was soaked, exhausted, hoarse. We didn't find what the two of us were looking for. But at least she'd found a piece of crepe-heeled shoe.

It all meshed.

XI

I didn't ask for permission to go into Victor's office. I opened the door softly and said with my very best smile:

"Hi!"

I saw again the same surprised look I saw the first day he came to my office. Then, the same charming smile.

"I just came to tell you that Monica really was going to a psychiatrist. I thought you might be interested."

"I know that, it's in your report."

"I put it in my report because Patricia told me that. But it was a story you and she made up. A lie that turns out to be true, how about that! Only one thing is different: the motive. She didn't go to a psychiatrist because she was a lesbian, she went because you forced her to make love with you whether she wanted to or not. Naturally, she felt raped. So she didn't want you to develop the place she loved most. It's as if she wanted to save the land from being raped, since she wasn't able to save herself from it."

He was listening to me with a sarcastic smile, but I could see a spark of fear in his eyes.

"What's all this about? Where did you dream up a story like that? What are you getting at?"

He spoke with a harsh voice, the voice of a secure man. Too harsh and too secure to be real.

I put Monica's pendant on his desk.

"I saw Monica in London. She was wearing the pendant. But what do you know! I just happened to find it in Patricia's apartment in Paris. By the way, Monica doesn't look much like this picture, does she?"

He repressed himself perfectly when I showed him the magazine.

"Besides, you were in such a rush to burn those pictures you made me believe were of Monica, but in fact were of Patricia."

"Now you're really getting embroiled, honey. The profession's gone to your head!"

"Were you aware that Monica's dog whined and got scared whenever she came across crepe-soled shoes? My colleague's, for example. And she completely chewed up one of mine, a real old one. Then the poor old hound helped me find the crepe sole that drove her crazy in the first place."

I set the piece of shoe on his desk, Monica's, that is, the real Monica. Victor paled.

"They're the shoes Monica was wearing when this picture was taken, this picture I found in your in-laws' album. I found this one, too, Monica and Patricia together. Monica was prettier than Pat, but I have to admit that Pat carried off the part of Monica real well, and even better when she played herself in that dark Paris apartment. Oh, yeah, I found this in Paris, too!"

A very curly, mahogany-colored wig.

He sank into his chair with sagging shoulders. He looked so vulnerable I felt sorry for him. But I had to be strong now, I couldn't allow myself to be deceived again.

"It was an accident, Lònia . . . I was so enraged, and I—I loved her, I loved Monica, but sometimes she drove me wild. She was so harsh!"

"You're a disgusting liar. You loved Patricia. That's why Patricia agreed to pass for Monica. Or what?"

"That's where you're wrong." He was recovering little by little. "Patricia did it for the money. She was real palsy with Monica, but only because of what she could get out of it. No, they weren't lesbians, of course, but Monica did have a weird weakness for Pat, and after the accident, I schemed the whole thing and Pat agreed to take on the role. . . ."

"So in fact, what you wanted was a report from a pro and a letter from

Monica obtained by that pro so that Mr. Pradell would reject his daughter as a pervert, right? That way, you'd be the victim and get your in-laws' sympathy, plus the permit to begin the development."

"You've done a terrific job, Lònia. Seems like I should hire you full time, so you'll work just for me!"

The nerve! He took out his checkbook and raised his mocking eyes:

"What will your monthly salary be?" he smiled.

"I guess you'll have to ask Mr. Pradell that. He's just outside, waiting for me to open the door. I consider myself well paid with what I've learned. Now I know for sure that if I want to stay in this profession I'll have to get thicker skin. And that I can't trust male clients, no matter how good-looking and nice they are, when they tell me I'll do a better job because I'm a woman."

Mr. Pradell was waiting by the door, looking pretty grim.

I waited outdoors, with the dog in my arms. When Victor came out handcuffed, between two guys in raincoats, I still felt a touch of pity.

SETTLED SCORE

A V. I. WARSHAWSKI STORY

Sara Paretsky

For Bob Kirschner, who helped make it work

I

"It's such a difficult concept to deal with. I just don't like to use that word." Paul Servino turned to me, his mobile mouth pursed consideringly. "I put it to you, Victoria: you're a lawyer. Would you not agree?"

"I agree that the law defines responsibility differently than we do when we're talking about social or moral relations," I said carefully. "No state's attorney is going to try to get Mrs. Hampton arrested, but does that—"

"You see," Servino interrupted. "That's just my point."

"But it's not mine," Lotty said fiercely, her thick dark brows forming a forbidding line across her forehead. "And if you had seen Claudia with her guts torn out by lye, perhaps you would think a little differently."

The table was silenced for a moment: we were surprised by the violent edge to Lotty's anger. Penelope Herschel shook her head slightly at Servino.

He caught her eye and nodded. "Sorry, Lotty. I didn't mean to upset you so much."

Lotty forced herself to smile. "Paul, you think you develop a veneer after thirty years as a doctor. You think you see people in all their pain and that your professionalism protects you from too much feeling. But that girl was fifteen. She had her life in front of her. She didn't want to have a baby. And her mother wanted her to. Not for religious reasons, even—she's English with all their contempt for Catholicism. But because she hoped to continue to control her daughter's life. Claudia felt overwhelmed by her mother's pressure and swallowed a jar of oven cleaner. Now don't tell me the mother is not responsible. I do not give one damn if no court would try her: to me, she caused her daughter's death as surely as if she had poured the poison into her."

Servino ignored another slight headshake from Lotty's niece. "It is a tragedy. But a tragedy for the mother, too. You don't think she meant her daughter to kill herself, do you, Lotty?"

Lotty gave a tense smile. "What goes on in the unconscious is surely your department, Paul. But perhaps that was Mrs. Hampton's wish. Of course, if she didn't *intend* for Claudia to die, the courts would find her responsibility diminished. Am I not right, Vic?"

I moved uneasily in my chair. I didn't want to referee this argument: it had all the earmarks of the kind of domestic fight where both contestants attack the police. Besides, while the rest of the dinner party was interested in the case and sympathetic to Lotty's feelings, none of them cared about the question of legal versus moral responsibility.

The dinner was in honor of Lotty Herschel's niece Penelope, making one of her periodic scouting forays into Chicago's fashion scene. Her father—Lotty's only brother—owned a chain of high-priced women's dress shops in Montreal, Quebec, and Toronto. He was thinking of making Chicago his US beachhead, and Penelope was out looking at locations as well as previewing the Chicago designers' spring ideas.

Lotty usually gave a dinner for Penelope when she was in town. Servino was always invited. An analyst friend of Lotty's, he and Penelope had met on one of her first buying trips to Chicago. Since then, they'd seen as much of each other as two busy professionals half a continent apart could manage. Although their affair now had five years of history to it, Penelope continued to stay with Lotty when she was in town.

The rest of the small party included Max Loewenthal, the executive director of Beth Israel, where Lotty treated perinatal patients, and Chaim Lemke, a clarinetist with the Aeolus Woodwind Quintet. A slight, melancholy man, he had met Lotty and Max in London, where they'd all been refugees. Chaim's wife, Greta, who played harpsichord and piano for an early music group, didn't come along. Lotty said not to invite her because she was seeing Paul professionally, but anyway, since she was currently living with Aeolus oboist Rudolph Strayarn, she probably wouldn't have accepted.

We were eating at my apartment. Lotty had called earlier in the day, rattled by the young girl's death and needing help putting the evening together. She was so clearly beside herself that I'd felt compelled to offer my own place. With cheese and fruit after dinner Lotty had begun discussing the case with the whole group, chiefly expressing her outrage with a legal system that let Mrs. Hampton off without so much as a warning.

For some reason Servino continued to argue the point despite Penelope's warning frowns. Perhaps the fact that we were on our third bottle of Barolo explained the lapse from Paul's usual sensitive courtesy.

"Mrs. Hampton did not point a gun at the girl's head and force her to become pregnant," he said. "The daughter was responsible, too, if you want to use that word. And the boy—the father, whoever that was."

Lotty, normally abstemious, had drunk her share of the wine. Her black eyes glittered and her Viennese accent became pronounced.

"I know the argument, believe you me, Paul: it's the old 'who pulled the trigger?'—the person who fired the gun, the person who manufactured it, the person who created the situation, the parents who created the shooter. To me, that is Scholastic hairsplitting—you know, all that crap they used to teach us a thousand years ago in Europe. Who is the ultimate cause, the immediate cause, the sufficient cause and on and on.

"It's dry theory, not life. It takes people off the hook for their own actions. You can quote Heinz Kohut and the rest of the self-psychologists to me all night, but you will never convince me that people are unable to make conscious choices for their actions or that parents are not responsible for how they treat their children. It's the same thing as saying the Nazis were not responsible for how they treated Europe."

Penelope gave a strained smile. She loved both Lotty and Servino and didn't want either of them to make fools of themselves. Max, on the other hand, watched Lotty affectionately—he liked to see her passionate. Chaim was staring into space, his lips moving. I assumed he was reading a score in his head.

"I would say that," Servino snapped, his own Italian accent strong. "And don't look at me as though I were Joseph Goebbels. Chaim and I are ten years younger than you and Max, but we share your story in great extent. I do not condone or excuse the horrors our families suffered, or our own dispossession. But I can look at Himmler, or Mussolini, or even Hitler and say, they behaved in such and such a way because of weaknesses accentuated in them by history, by their parents, by their culture. You could as easily say the

French were responsible, the French because their need for—for—*rappresag-lia*—what am I trying to say, Victoria?"

"Reprisal," I supplied.

"Now you see, Lotty, now I, too, am angry: I forget my English. . . . But if they and the English had not stretched Germany with reparations, the situation might have been different. So how can you claim responsibility—for one person, or one nation? You just have to do the best you can with what is going on around you."

Lotty's face was set. "Yes, Paul. I know what you are saying. Yes, the French created a situation. And the English wished to accommodate Hitler. And the Americans would not take in the Jews. All these things are true. But the Germans chose, nonetheless. They could have acted differently. I will not take them off the hook just because other people should have acted differently."

I took her hand and squeezed it. "At the risk of being the Neville Chamberlain in the case, could I suggest some appeasement? Chaim brought his clarinet and Max his violin. Paul, if you'll play the piano, Penelope and I will sing."

Chaim smiled, relaxing the sadness in his thin face. He loved making music, whether with friends or professionals. "Gladly, Vic. But only a few songs. It's late and we go to California for a two-week tour tomorrow."

The atmosphere lightened. We went into the living room, where Chaim flipped through my music, pulling out Wolf's *Spanisches Liederbuch*. In the end, he and Max stayed with Lotty, playing and talking until three in the morning, long after Servino and Penelope's departure.

II

The detective business is not as much fun in January as at other times of the year. I spent the next two days forcing my little Chevy through unplowed side streets trying to find a missing witness who was the key to an eighteen-million-dollar fraud case. I finally succeeded Tuesday evening a little before five. By the time I'd convinced the terrified woman, who was hiding with a niece at Sixty-seventh and Honore, that no one would shoot her if she testified, gotten her to the state's attorney, and seen her safely home again, it was close to ten o'clock.

I fumbled with the outer locks on the apartment building with my mind fixed on a hot bath, lots of whiskey, and a toasted cheese sandwich. When the ground-floor door opened and Mr. Contreras popped out to meet me, I ground my teeth. He's a retired machinist with more energy than Navratilova. I didn't have the stamina to deal with him tonight.

I mumbled a greeting and headed for the stairs.

"There you are, doll." The relief in his voice was marked. I stopped wearily. Some crisis with the dog. Something involving lugging a sixty-pound retriever to the vet through snow-packed streets.

"I thought I ought to let her in, you know. I told her there was no saying when you'd be home, sometimes you're gone all night on a case"—a delicate reference to my love life—"but she was all set she had to wait and she'd'a been sitting on the stairs all this time. She won't say what the problem is, but you'd probably better talk to her. You wanna come in here or should I send her up in a few minutes?"

Not the dog, then. "Uh, who is it?"

"Aren't I trying to tell you? That beautiful girl. You know, the doc's niece."

"Penelope?" I echoed foolishly.

She came out into the hall just then, ducking under the old man's gesticulating arms. "Vic! Thank God you're back. I've got to talk to you. Before the police do anything stupid."

She was huddled in an ankle-length silver fur. Ordinarily elegant, with exquisite makeup and jewelry and the most modern of hairstyles, she didn't much resemble her aunt. But shock had stripped the sophistication from her, making her dark eyes the focus of her face; she looked so much like Lotty that I went to her instinctively.

"Come on up with me and tell me what's wrong." I put an arm around her.

Mr. Contreras closed his door in disappointment as we disappeared up the stairs. Penelope waited until we were inside my place before saying anything else. I slung my jacket and down vest on the hooks in the hallway and went into the living room to undo my heavy walking shoes.

Penelope kept her fur wrapped around her. Her high-heeled kid boots were not meant for streetwear: they were rimmed with salt stains. She shivered slightly despite the coat.

"Have—have you heard anything?"

I shook my head, rubbing my right foot, stiff from driving all day.

"It's Paul. He's dead."

"But—he's not that old. And I thought he was very healthy." Because of his sedentary job, Servino always ran the two miles from his Loop office to his apartment in the evening.

Penelope gave a little gulp of hysterical laughter. "Oh, he was very fit. But not healthy enough to overcome a blow to the head."

"Could you tell the story from the beginning instead of letting it out in little dramatic bursts?"

As I'd hoped, my rudeness got her angry enough to overcome her incipient hysteria. After flashing me a Lotty-like look of royal disdain, she told me what she knew.

Paul's office was in a building where a number of analysts had their practices. A sign posted on his door this morning baldly announced that he had canceled all his day's appointments because of a personal emergency. When a janitor went in at three to change a light bulb, he'd found the doctor dead on the floor of his consulting room.

Colleagues agreed they'd seen Servino arrive around a quarter of eight, as he usually did. They'd seen the notice and assumed he'd left when everyone else was tied up with appointments. No one thought any more about it.

Penelope had learned of her lover's death from the police, who picked her up as she was leaving a realtor's office where she'd been discussing shop leases. Two of the doctors with offices near Servino's had mentioned seeing a dark-haired woman in a long fur coat near his consulting room.

Penelope's dark eyes were drenched with tears. "It's not enough that Paul is dead, that I learn of it such an unspeakable way. They think I killed him—because I have dark hair and wear a fur coat. They don't know what killed him—some dreary blunt instrument—it sounds stupid and banal, like an old Agatha Christie. They've pawed through my luggage looking for it."

They'd questioned her for three hours while they searched and finally, reluctantly, let her go, with a warning not to leave Chicago. She'd called Lotty at the clinic and then come over to find me.

I went into the dining room for some whiskey. She shook her head at the bottle. I poured myself an extra slug to make up for missing my bath. "And?"

"And I want you to find who killed him. The police aren't looking very hard because they think it's me."

"Do they have a reason for this?"

She blushed unexpectedly. "They think he was refusing to marry me."

"Not much motive in these times, one would have thought. And you with a successful career to boot. Was he refusing?"

"No. It was the other way around, actually. I felt—felt unsettled about what I wanted to do—come to Chicago to stay, you know. I have—friends in Montreal, too, you know. And I've always thought marriage meant monogamy."

"I see." My focus on the affair between Penelope and Paul shifted slightly. "You didn't kill him, did you—perhaps for some other reason?"

She forced a smile. "Because he didn't agree with Lotty about responsibility? No. And for no other reason. Are you going to ask Lotty if she killed him?"

"Lotty would have mangled him Sunday night with whatever was lying on the dining room table—she wouldn't wait to sneak into his office with a club." I eyed her thoughtfully. "Just out of vulgar curiosity, what were you doing around eight this morning?"

Her black eyes scorched me. "I came to you because I thought you would be sympathetic. Not to get the same damned questions I had all afternoon from the police!"

"And what were you doing at eight this morning?"

She swept across the room to the door, then thought better of it and affected to study a Nell Blaine poster on the nearby wall. With her back to me she said curtly, "I was having a second cup of coffee. And no, there are no witnesses. As you know, by that time of day Lotty is long gone. Perhaps someone saw me leave the building at eight thirty—I asked the detectives to question the neighbors, but they didn't seem much interested in doing so."

"Don't sell them short. If you're not under arrest, they're still asking questions."

"But you could ask questions to clear me. They're just trying to implicate me."

I pinched the bridge of my nose, trying to ease the dull ache behind my eyes. "You do realize the likeliest person to have killed him is an angry patient, don't you? Despite your fears the police have probably been questioning them all day."

Nothing I said could convince her that she wasn't in imminent danger of a speedy trial before a kangaroo court, with execution probable by the next morning. She stayed until past midnight, alternating pleas to hide her with commands to join the police in hunting down Paul's killer. She wouldn't call Lotty to tell her she was with me because she was afraid Lotty's home phone had been tapped.

"Look, Penelope," I finally said, exasperated. "I can't hide you. If the police really suspect you, you were tailed here. Even if I could figure out a way to smuggle you out and conceal you someplace, I wouldn't do it—I'd lose my license on obstruction charges and I'd deserve to."

I tried explaining how hard it was to get a court order for a wiretap and finally gave up. I was about ready to start screaming with frustration when Lotty herself called, devastated by Servino's death and worried about Penelope. The police had been by with a search warrant and had taken away an array of household objects, including her umbrella. Such an intrusion would normally have made her spitting mad, but she was too upset to give it her full emotional attention. I turned the phone over to Penelope. Whatever Lotty said to her stained her cheeks red, but did make her agree to let me drive her home.

When I got back to my place, exhausted enough to sleep round the clock, I found John McGonnigal waiting for me in a blue-and-white outside my building. He came up the walk behind me and opened the door with a flourish.

I looked at him sourly. "Thanks, Sergeant. It's been a long day—I'm glad to have a doorman at the end of it."

"It's kind of cold down here for talking, Vic. How about inviting me up for coffee?"

"Because I want to go to bed. If you've got something you want to say, or even ask, spit it out down here."

I was just ventilating and I knew it—if a police sergeant wanted to talk to me at one in the morning, we'd talk. Mr. Contreras's coming out in a magenta bathrobe to see what the trouble was merely speeded my decision to cooperate.

While I assembled cheese sandwiches, McGonnigal asked me what I'd learned from Penelope.

"She didn't throw her arms around me and howl, 'Vic, I killed him, you've got to help me.'" I put the sandwiches in a skillet with a little olive oil. "What've you guys got on her?"

The receptionist and two of the other analysts who'd been in the hall had seen a small, dark-haired woman hovering in the alcove near Servino's office around twenty of eight. Neither of them had paid too much attention to her; when they saw Penelope they agreed it might have been she, but they couldn't be certain. If they'd made a positive ID, she'd already have been arrested, even though they couldn't find the weapon.

"They had a shouting match at the Filigree last night. The maître d' was quite upset. Servino was a regular and he didn't want to offend him, but a number of diners complained. The Herschel girl"—McGonnigal eyed me warily—"woman, I mean, stormed off on her own and spent the night with her aunt. One of the neighbors saw her leave around seven the next morning, not at eight thirty as she says."

I didn't like the sound of that. I asked him about the cause of death.

"Someone gave him a good crack across the side of the neck, close enough to the back to fracture a cervical vertebra and sever one of the main arteries. It would have killed him pretty fast. And as you know, Servino wasn't very tall—the Herschel woman could easily have done it."

"With what?" I demanded.

That was the stumbling block. It could have been anything from a baseball bat to a steel pipe. The forensic pathologist who'd looked at the body favored the latter, since the skin had been broken in places. They'd taken away anything in Lotty's apartment and Penelope's luggage that might have done the job and were having them examined for traces of blood and skin.

I snorted. "If you searched Lotty's place, you must have come away with quite an earful."

McGonnigal grimaced. "She spoke her mind, yes. . . . Any ideas? On what the weapon might have been?"

I shook my head, too nauseated by the thought of Paul's death to muster intellectual curiosity over the choice of weapon. When McGonnigal left around two thirty, I lay in bed staring at the dark, unable to sleep despite my fatigue. I didn't know Penelope all that well. Just because she was Lotty's niece didn't mean she was incapable of murder. To be honest, I hadn't been totally convinced by her histrionics tonight. Who but a lover could get close enough to you to snap your neck? I thrashed around for hours, finally dropping into an uneasy sleep around six.

Lotty woke me at eight to implore me to look for Servino's killer; the police had been back at seven thirty to ask Penelope why she'd forgotten to mention she'd been at Paul's apartment early yesterday morning.

"Why was she there?" I asked reasonably.

"She says she wanted to patch things up after their quarrel, but he'd already left for the office. When the police started questioning her, she was too frightened to tell the truth. Vic, I'm terrified they're going to arrest her."

I mumbled something. It looked to me like they had a pretty good case, but I valued my life too much to say that to Lotty. Even so the conversation deteriorated rapidly.

"I come out in any wind or weather to patch you up. With never a word of complaint." That wasn't exactly true, but I let it pass. "Now, when I beg you for help you turn a deaf ear to me. I shall remember this, Victoria."

Giant black spots formed and re-formed in front of my tired eyes. "Great, Lotty."

Her receiver banged in my ear.

III

I spent the day doggedly going about my own business, turning on WBBM whenever I was in the car to see if any news had come in about Penelope's arrest. Despite all the damaging eyewitness reports, the state's attorney apparently didn't want to move without a weapon.

I trudged up the stairs to my apartment a little after six, my mind fixed on a bath and a rare steak followed immediately by bed. When I got to the top landing, I ground my teeth in futile rage: a fur-coated woman was sitting in front of the door.

When she got to her feet I realized it wasn't Penelope but Greta Schipauer, Chaim Lemke's wife. The dark hallway had swallowed the gold of her hair.

"Vic! Thank God you've come back. I've been here since four and I have a concert in two hours."

I fumbled with the three stiff locks. "I have an office downtown just so that people won't have to sit on the floor outside my home," I said pointedly.

"You do? Oh—it never occurred to me you didn't just work out of your living room."

She followed me in and headed over to the piano, where she picked out a series of fifths. "You really should get this tuned, Vic."

"Is that why you've been here for two hours? To tell me to tune my piano?" I slung my coat onto a hook in the entryway and sat on the couch to pull off my boots.

"No, no." She sat down hastily. "It's because of Paul, of course. I spoke to Lotty today and she says you're refusing to stir yourself to look for his murderer. Why, Vic? We all need you very badly. You can't let us down now. The police were questioning me for two hours yesterday. It utterly destroyed my concentration. I couldn't practice at all; I know the recital tonight will be a disaster. Even Chaim has been affected, and he's out on the West Coast."

I was too tired to be tactful. "How do you know that? I thought you've been living with Rudolph Strayarn."

She looked surprised. "What does that have to do with anything? I'm still interested in Chaim's music. And it's been terrible. Rudolph called this morning to tell me and I bought an L.A. paper downtown."

She thrust a copy of the *L.A. Times* in front of me. It was folded back to the arts section where the headline read AEOLUS JUST BLOWING IN THE WIND. They'd used Chaim's publicity photo as an inset.

I scanned the story:

Chaim Lemke, one of the nation's most brilliant musicians, must have left his own clarinet at home because he played as though he'd never handled the instrument before. Aeolus manager Claudia Laurents says the group was shattered by the murder of a friend in Chicago; the rest of the quintet managed to pull a semblance of a concert together, but the performance by America's top woodwind group was definitely off-key.

I handed the paper back to Greta. "Chaim's reputation is too strong—an adverse review like this will be forgotten in two days. Don't worry about it— go to your concert and concentrate on your own music."

Her slightly protuberant blue eyes stared at me. "I didn't believe Lotty when she told me. I don't believe I'm hearing you now. Vic, we need you. If it's money, name your figure. But put aside this coldness and help us out."

"Greta, the only thing standing between the police and an arrest right now is the fact that they can't find the murder weapon. I'm not going to join them in hunting for it. The best we can hope for is that they never find it. After a while they'll let Penelope go back to Montreal and your lives will return to normal."

"No, no. You're thinking Penelope committed this crime. Never, Vic, never. I've known her since she was a small child—you know I grew up in Montreal—it's where I met Chaim. Believe me, I know her. She never committed this murder."

She was still arguing stubbornly when she looked at her watch, gave a gasp, and said she had to run or she'd never make the auditorium in time. When I'd locked the door thankfully behind her, I saw she'd dropped her paper. I looked at Chaim's delicate face again, sad as though he knew he would have to portray mourning in it when the picture was taken.

IV

When the police charged Penelope late on Thursday, I finally succumbed to the alternating pleas and commands of her friends to undertake an independent investigation. The police had never found a weapon, but the state's attorney was willing to believe it was in the Chicago River.

I got the names of the two analysts and the receptionist who'd seen Servino's presumed assailant outside his office on Tuesday. They were too used to seeing nervous people shrinking behind partitions to pay much attention to this woman; neither of them was prepared to make a positive ID in court. That would be a help to Freeman Carter, handling Penelope's defense, but it couldn't undo the damage caused by Penelope's original lies about her Tuesday morning activities.

She was free on $100,000 bond. Swinging between depression and a kind of manic rage, she didn't tell a very convincing story. Still, I was committed to proving her innocence; I did my best with her and trusted that Freeman was too savvy to let her take the witness stand herself.

I got a list of Paul's patients, both current and former, from a contact at the police. Lotty, Max, and Greta were bankrolling both Freeman and me to any amount we needed, so I hired the Streeter Brothers to check up on patient alibis.

I talked to all of them myself, trying to ferret out any sense of betrayal or rage urgent enough to drive one of them to murder. With a sense of shameful voyeurism, I even read Paul's notes. I was fascinated by his descriptions of Greta. Her total self-absorption had always rubbed me the wrong way. Paul, while much more empathic, seemed to be debating whether she would ever be willing to participate in her own analysis.

"How did Paul feel about your affair with Rudolph?" I asked Greta one afternoon when she had made one of her frequent stops for a progress report.

"Oh, you know Paul: he had a great respect for the artistic temperament and what someone like me needs to survive in my work. Besides, he convinced me that I didn't have to feel responsible—you know, that my own parents' cold narcissism makes me crave affection. And Rudolph is a much more relaxing lover than poor Chaim, with his endless parade of guilt and self-doubt."

I felt my skin crawl slightly. I didn't know any psychoanalytic theory, but I couldn't believe Paul meant his remarks on personal responsibility to be understood in quite this way.

Meanwhile, Chaim's performance had deteriorated so badly that he decided to cancel the rest of the West Coast tour. The Aeolus found a backup, the second clarinet in the Chicago Symphony, but their concert series got mediocre reviews in Seattle and played to half-full houses in Vancouver and Denver.

Greta rushed to the airport to meet Chaim on his return. I knew because she'd notified the local stations and I found her staring at me on the ten o'clock news, escorting Chaim from the baggage area with a maternal solicitude. She shed the cameras before decamping for Rudolph's—she called me from there at ten thirty to make sure I'd seen her wifely heroics.

I wasn't convinced by Greta's claims that Chaim would recover faster on his own than with someone to look after him. The next day I went to check on him for myself. Even though it was past noon, he was still in his dressing gown. I apologized for waking him, but he gave a sweet sad smile and assured me he'd been up for some time. When I followed him into the living room, a light, bright room facing Lake Michigan, I was shocked to see how ill he looked. His black eyes had become giant holes in his thin face; he apparently hadn't slept in some time.

"Chaim, have you seen a doctor?"

"No, no." He shook his head. "It's just that since Paul's death I can't make music. I try to play and I sound worse than I did at age five. I don't know which is harder—losing Paul or having them arrest Penelope. Such a sweet girl. I've known her since she was born. I'm sure she didn't kill him. Lotty says you're investigating?"

"Yeah, but not too successfully. The evidence against her is very sketchy—it's hard for me to believe they'll get a conviction. If the weapon turns up . . ." I let the sentence trail away. If the weapon turned up, it might provide the final caisson to shore up the state's platform. I was trying hard to work for Penelope, but I kept having disloyal thoughts.

"You yourself are hunting for the weapon? Do you know what it is?"

I shook my head. "The state's attorney gave me photos of the wound. I had enlargements made and I took them to a pathologist I know to see if he could come up with any ideas. Some kind of pipe or stick with spikes or something on it—like a caveman's club—I'm so out of ideas I even went to the Field Museum to see if they could suggest something, or were missing some old-fashioned lethal weapon."

Chaim had turned green. I felt contrite—he had such an active imagination I should have watched my tongue. Now he'd have nightmares for weeks and would wait even longer to get his music back. I changed the subject and persuaded him to let me cook some lunch from the meager supplies in the kitchen. He didn't eat much, but he was looking less feverish when I left.

V

Chaim's cleaning woman found him close to death the morning Penelope's trial started. Lotty, Max, and I had spent the day in court with Lotty's brother Hugo and his wife. We didn't get any of Greta's frantic messages until Lotty checked in at the clinic before dinner.

Chaim had gone to an Aeolus rehearsal the night before, his first appearance at the group in some weeks. He had bought a new clarinet, thinking perhaps the problem lay with the old one. Wind instruments aren't like violins—they deteriorate over time, and an active clarinetist has to buy a new one every ten years or so. Despite the new instrument, a Buffet he had flown to Toronto to buy, the rehearsal had gone badly.

He left early, going home to turn on the gas in the kitchen stove. He left a note which simply said: "I have destroyed my music." The cleaning woman knew enough about their life to call Greta at Rudolph's apartment. Since Greta had been at the rehearsal—waiting for the oboist—she knew how badly Chaim had played.

"I'm not surprised," she told Lotty over the phone. "His music was all he had after I left him. With both of us gone from his life he must have felt he had no reason to live. Thank God I learned so much from Paul about why we aren't responsible for our actions, or I would feel terribly guilty now."

Lotty called the attending physician at Mitchell Hospital and came away with the news that Chaim would live, but he'd ruined his lungs—he could hardly talk and would probably never be able to play again.

She reported her conversation with Greta with a blazing rage while we waited for dinner in her brother's suite at the Drake. "The wrong person's career is over," she said furiously. "It's the one thing I could never understand about Chaim—why he felt so much passion for that self-centered whore!"

Marcella Herschel gave a grimace of distaste—she didn't deal well with

Lotty at the best of times and could barely tolerate her when she was angry. Penelope, pale and drawn from the day's ordeal, summoned a smile and patted Lotty's shoulder soothingly while Max tried to persuade her to drink a little wine.

Freeman Carter stopped by after dinner to discuss strategy for the next day's session. The evening broke up soon after, all of us too tired and depressed to want even a pretense of conversation.

The trial lasted four days. Freeman did a brilliant job with the state's sketchy evidence; the jury was out for only two hours before returning a "not guilty" verdict. Penelope left for Montreal with Hugo and Marcella the next morning. Lotty, much shaken by the winter's events, found a locum for her clinic and took off with Max for two weeks in Portugal.

I went to Michigan for a long weekend with the dog, but didn't have time or money for more vacation than that. Monday night, when I got home, I found Hugo Wolf's *Spanisches Liederbuch* still open on the piano from January's dinner party with Chaim and Paul. Between Paul's murder and preparing for Penelope's trial I hadn't sung since then. I tried picking out *"In dem Schatten meiner Locken,"* but Greta was right: The piano needed tuning badly.

I called Mr. Fortieri the next morning to see if he could come by to look at it. He was an old man who repaired instruments for groups like the Aeolus Quintet and their ilk; he also tuned pianos for them. He only helped me because he'd known my mother and admired her singing.

He arranged to come the next afternoon. I was surprised—usually you had to wait four to six weeks for time on his schedule—but quickly reshuffled my own Tuesday appointments to accommodate him. When he arrived, I realized that he had come so soon because Chaim's suicide attempt had shaken him. I didn't have much stomach for rehashing it, but I could see the old man was troubled and needed someone to talk to.

"What bothers me, Victoria, is what I should do with his clarinet. I've been able to repair it, but they tell me he'll never play again—surely it would be too cruel to return it to him, even if I didn't submit a bill."

"His clarinet?" I asked blankly. "When did he give it to you?"

"After that disastrous West Coast tour. He said he had dropped it in some mud—I still don't understand how that happened, why he was carrying it outside without the case. But he said it was clogged with mud and he'd tried cleaning it, only he'd bent the keys and it didn't play properly. It was a wonderful instrument, only a few years old, and costing perhaps six thousand dollars, so I agreed to work on it. He'd had to use his old one in California and I always thought that was why the tour went so badly. That and Paul's death weighing on him, of course."

"So you repaired it and got it thoroughly clean," I said foolishly.

"Oh, yes. Of course, the sound will never be as good as it was originally, but it would still be a fine instrument for informal use. Only—I hate having to give him a clarinet he can no longer play."

"Leave it with me," I said gently. "I'll take care of it."

Mr. Fortieri seemed relieved to pass the responsibility on to me. He went to work on the piano and tuned it back to perfection without any of his usual criticisms on my failure to keep to my mother's high musical standard.

As soon as he'd gone, I drove down to the University of Chicago hospital. Chaim was being kept in the psychiatric wing for observation, but he was allowed visitors. I found him sitting in the lounge, staring into space while *People's Court* blared meaninglessly on the screen overhead.

He gave his sad sweet smile when he saw me and croaked out my name in the hoarse parody of a voice.

"Can we go to your room, Chaim? I want to talk to you privately."

He flicked a glance at the vacant faces around us but got up obediently and led me down the hall to a spartan room with bars on the window.

"Mr. Fortieri was by this afternoon to tune my piano. He told me about your clarinet."

Chaim said nothing, but he seemed to relax a little.

"How did you do it, Chaim? I mean, you left for California Monday morning. What did you do—come back on the red-eye?"

"Red-eye?" he croaked hoarsely.

Even in the small space I had to lean forward to hear him. "The night flight."

"Oh. The red-eye. Yes. Yes, I got to O'Hare at six, came to Paul's office on the El, and was back at the airport in time for the ten o'clock flight. No one even knew I'd left L.A.—we had a rehearsal at two and I was there easily."

His voice was so strained it made my throat ache to listen to him.

"I thought I hated Paul. You know, all those remarks of his about responsibility. I thought he'd encouraged Greta to leave me." He stopped to catch his breath. After a few gasping minutes he went on.

"I blamed him for her idea that she didn't have to feel any obligation to our marriage. Then, after I got back, I saw Lotty had been right. Greta was just totally involved in herself. She should have been named Narcissus. She used Paul's words without understanding them."

"But Penelope," I said. "Would you really have let Penelope go to jail for you?"

He gave a twisted smile. "I didn't mean them to arrest Penelope. I just thought—I've always had trouble with cold weather, with Chicago winters. I've worn a long fur for years. Because I'm so small people often think I'm a woman when I'm wrapped up in it. I just thought, if anyone saw me they would think it was a woman. I never meant them to arrest Penelope."

He sat panting for a few minutes. "What are you going to do now, Vic? Send for the police?"

I shook my head sadly. "You'll never play again—you'd have been happier doing life in Joliet than you will now that you can't play. I want you to write it all down, though, the name you used on your night flight and everything. I have the clarinet; even though Mr. Fortieri cleaned it, a good lab might still find blood traces. The clarinet and your statement will go to the papers after you die. Penelope deserves that much—to have the cloud of suspicion taken away from her. And I'll have to tell her and Lotty."

His eyes were shiny. "You don't know how awful it's been, Vic. I was so mad with rage that it was like nothing to break Paul's neck. But then, after that, I couldn't play anymore. So you are wrong: even if I had gone to Joliet I would still never have played."

I couldn't bear the naked anguish in his face. I left without saying anything, but it was weeks before I slept without seeing his black eyes weeping onto me.

A recipient of the Grand Master Award of the Mystery Writers of America, **DORO-THY B. HUGHES** is also the biographer of Erle Stanley Gardner. Although she wrote several novels featuring an Inspector Tobin, most of her work is in the suspense, rather than the mystery field. Three of her major works were successfully filmed—*The Fallen Sparrow, Ride the Pink Horse,* and the magnificent *In a Lonely Place.* Hughes lives in Ashland, Oregon.

THAT SUMMER AT QUICHIQUOIS

Dorothy B. Hughes

 Time and place do not matter. They are happenings. Simply happenings.

There are other happenings. Some you don't or won't remember. Some you will. Deliberately. It is not that you remember the important and don't remember the unimportant. Often it's the other way around. Like dancing with Voss.

Sometimes I think of Voss and I cry. Tears. Wet tears. I don't cry easily. I don't make myself cry. It's just a happening.

I didn't actually know him. He was just someone I danced with. When I was fourteen years old. By the accident of him being there and me being there when the music changed. Does anyone remember the "Paul Jones"? Sort of like a grand march only gentlemen going one way and ladies another. Touching hands but not clasping, touching in passing. Until the music changes. Without warning. Like in "Going to Jerusalem." Musical chairs.

And that happening was when the music changed. I was right beside Voss. So I danced with Voss. Close tight, chest to chest, feeling him surrounding me. Engulfing me. Almost as if I were an integral part of his body. For those few moments.

I was nothing to him. Not a happening to him. It was simply the way he danced. To him that was the happening. To dance. As if dancing were created by him, for him.

Except Elektra. When he danced with Elektra they were one person. Not two dancing. One. Transformed. Two become one. Tightly together. Never again one and one. Two melded. Like by flame. The flame of movement and music.

My cousin Katty was sixteen going on seventeen. She and her very best friends—four or five of them—would have none of Voss. He wasn't privileged. Their cant word of the summer. He worked in a *butcher shop!* Henschel's Butcher Shop. His uncle Gus. Underprivileged. As if Voss had blood spattered all over his clothes. Like Uncle Gus had on his white apron when he waited on my aunt Georgie. In those days in a small town, meat didn't come prepackaged and iced by Armour or Swift. It came from a nearby farm. The farmer butchered and brought the haunch to the butcher shop. It was hung in an icebox room out back. The butcher cut from the haunch what the customer wanted. Sometimes blood would spatter on his white apron.

Voss worked mostly at the front counter. By the cash register. By the big front window.

But the girls shrieked "underprivileged" when I asked about him. The girls accepted only the privileged. Like Katty's choice for the summer, Roddy Rockefeller. No, not the rich Rockefellers with the wizened old golfer who gave a dime-a-day tip to his caddy. Rockefeller is a common name in upstate New York.

"What's Claude?" I asked them. Deliberately to provoke them. Claude had to be privileged. He was a Clark. Founders of Clarksvale back in Revolutionary days. His father was owner and president of the bank. The one where Aunt Georgie used to work and now owned a big piece of.

Of course they shouted with laughter at my question. "Whey-face?" I did not ever understand "Whey-face." He had a round doughy face. Something about curds and whey.

They added their other names for him. "Toady." "Cipher." And one daring friend of Katty's who considered herself sophisticated, "Faggotty."

Voss let Claude hang around. That was about all. Voss was a loner. He didn't have friends. Didn't want them.

We went back to the village every other summer. We—my mother, the children—my eight-year-old brother and six-year-old sister, and me. My father wanted us to know his people. He didn't come with us. He had his business as excuse. He had had enough of villages before he walked away from them to make his mark in the city. And did, all the way to California.

Every other summer we took the train—there were trains in those days—from California to New York, upstate New York. Change at Chicago to the

N.Y. Central. Disembark at Albany. But not for the local train. Met there by Aunt Georgie and her chauffeur Fred. He was one of the garage men in a chauffeur cap. We stayed with Aunt Priscilla. George was the younger sister by two years. She was the businesswoman. She owned half the town by now. Aunt Priscilla was the stay-at-home who took care of her kinfolk's children.

Katherine—Katty—had always lived with Aunt Pris. Her mother died in childbirth and her father was in the air corps, a captain or something. He wasn't on land very often.

This summer Aunt Pris also had the Tompkin boys. Their father, a nephew, was an archaeology professor at one of the universities, and so was his wife. They were off to some big dig deep in South America. No place to take little boys. The boys were around my brother's age.

I shared Katty's room in summer and we didn't see much of the children. Not if we could help it.

The village itself was a happening. For a girl born and raised in a big city, it was like a storybook holiday. Walking around town. No traffic. No street-cars. No buses. A post office with its walls of neat little golden boxes. An ice-cream parlor with tables and chairs.

And every Saturday night there was dancing on the pavilion in the town park. Which was how a fourteen-year-old came to dance with an older young man. That summer at Quichiquois. That summer of Elektra.

An open pavilion up a flight of steps to raise it above the park benches and the paths below. The pavilion was also the bandstand. The band played there in summer every night. Except Saturday. On Saturday night there was an orchestra, a real orchestra. Live music, it is called today. Miss Estelle had for some twenty-five years taught classical piano to all the children of the village whose parents were music minded, but on Saturday night in summer she played mean jazz. Deacon Raven of some local church played violin for the service. For dancing at the pavilion, he played a jazz fiddle. The drummer was the owner of the local hay-and-feed store. He was in the National Guard band. On special occasions, the city fathers would enlist a clarinet player, a young farmer up the road a piece who played in his college band. Musicians who aren't professionals have a certain spirit. They play for the love of it, certainly not for the pittance they are paid.

Everyone danced. Little children capered with one another. Or now and again politely waltzed with their mums or dads. Even the grampaws and gramaws sashayed around the floor.

And I danced with Voss. A happening only that once. Although after that night the older girls taught me how to lag. Without appearing to lag. No one would know you were looking for one specific partner. When you saw him you would lag a step here or there until he was almost beside you. Katty and I would practice it at night in her bedroom. But I never had a chance to try it out for real.

Because Aunt George decided. She made all the decisions in the family. Aunt Priscilla acquiesced or did not. If she did not, it was the end of that happening. Aunt Pris was a woman of few words. Quietly spoken. Aunt Georgie was the talker. Emphatic. Accurate. Almost always. A business-woman, accustomed to dealing with men. With yea and nay. No palavering.

She decided that the children should have three weeks at Lake Quichi-quois. There are myriad small lakes all through the Berkshires. This was nearest to Clarksvale, about twenty miles. No resort. Just summer cottages. Friends of Aunt George offered theirs as they were going north to visit family for several weeks. The cottages were in the woods above the lake. Each was surrounded by woods, land was not costly, everyone had privacy. Just comfortably set far enough apart.

Aunt Priscilla acquiesced. My mother, being company, had no yea or nay. My mother preferred the busiest city street to the beauties of the woods. Not to the beauty but to the creatures that came with it, flies and spiders and bees and creepy crawlers. But my mother was company. Polite. Company was expected to acquiesce.

Of course, Aunt Georgie wasn't going. Shut up for three weeks surrounded by children? Like my father, she had business excuses.

After her decision, Aunt Georgie said, "I have a hired girl to go along. No sense of you and Elizabeth [my mother] turning your holiday into a wash and iron and cook for six children."

Aunt Priscilla was wary. "Who is the hired girl?"

"I hired Elektra." Aunt Georgie slid the name off her tongue as if she just recalled it.

A look. From one to another of the aunts. And returned the other to the one. Aunt Pris decided, half-reluctantly, "Well, she's as good as we could hope for this late in the summer."

Imperceptible. Aunt George had been apprehensive. Priscilla could have said no. She hadn't. Now Aunt Georgie could resume her position as head of the family. In name. She paid the bills.

"She's strong," Aunt George said. "Remember how she took up all your rugs last spring—beat them like a man would, the air was grimy."

"And laid them all again," Aunt Priscilla mentioned. "And she would carry the whole laundry in one load up the stairs."

There were twenty-three steps up from the living room to the second floor. I had counted them. I always count steps. Another eighteen up to the attic bedrooms where the boys slept, and live-in help when Aunt Priscilla tolerated it.

I don't know how many steps to the basement. I didn't go to the basement. The furnace was there and the storage. Years of the *Saturday Evening Post* and the *Geographic,* and old trunks filled with old clothes.

Elektra was strong. Elektra didn't natter. She was scrub clean. The aunts ticked off her good points. Nothing said of the bad. Of the cause for apprehension one to the other. Somehow I didn't want to ask Katty. Katty had a way of embroidering words to make a bland story an exciting one. If not exactly a true one.

I'd seen Elektra, of course. Someone must have said, "There's Elektra." Walking on Main Street. Or going into the post office. Or sitting at a soda table at the soda fountain. "There's Elektra." I could describe her as if I'd seen a snapshot of her. Tall. Man tall. Lean. Man lean. Straight black hair, held back by a barrette. Hanging to her waist. Not when she was working. Then piled in braids or in loops. High ruddy cheekbones. Straight nose. Like on an Iroquois.

I'd seen her. She delivered the ironing that Aunt Priscilla sent to Gammer Goodwife. Gammer lived in that big square yellow rooming house on the terrace you passed walking to town. The townsfolk called it the "Poor House." Elektra lived there too. She was kin to Gammer.

I'd seen Elektra. Dancing with Voss.

I couldn't but wonder if Katty had put the idea of Lake Quichiquois into Aunt Georgie's head. Linda, her best friend, was going up there for the rest of the summer. Her family owned a summer cottage there. There was a boys' camp across the lake. For little boys, but the counselors were privileged!

And so we went to Lake Quichiquois. Aunt George's chauffeur, Fred in the chauffeur's cap, drove us up there in the seven-seater. The ladies in the backseat. My younger sister squeezed in by my mother. Katty and I on the jump seats. The three little boys in front with Fred.

Elektra would be up the next day. Fred was borrowing a pickup truck from the garage to carry our trunks. The aunts always took trunks, even for a short stay. Elektra would ride with Fred in the cab of the pickup.

Time goes quickly by the water. Too quickly. We are water people. Quichiquois was a dream happening. Elektra would have the breakfast cooked and served before eight o'clock every morning. She'd red up the kitchen while we waited out the dictum: "Do not go in the water until one hour after eating." We wouldn't. But we would go down to our dock before the hour was up and the children would splash through the shore water. Elektra would get our rowboat turned over, ready to row out for anyone in trouble. Elektra was a strong swimmer. She cleaved the water as beautifully as a dolphin.

Dover Camp, a long established one, was just across the lake. The little boys and our boys could and did exchange taunts across the water.

And of the three counselors, two were already in college, lordly sophomores the coming year. The other was a senior in prep school. Katty and

Linda were in rhapsodies. New boys—or as they called them, men—and these girls were practiced at making boyfriends. The boys were at Brown, and the girls' college was just across the Massachusetts line. The talk became all about football games and weekend soirees. And house parties in the spring.

Across the lake was also Mr. Gruen's general store and soda fountain. The meeting place for all lakers. He had a year ago built on a room for the soda fountain. He had old-fashioned tables and chairs in there during the week, but they were moved out on Saturday and there was dancing to a juke box. No Paul Jones.

The Dover Camp boys only had to walk downhill a short way to the soda fountain. On our side it was a quarter-mile walk, after we reached the lane from the cottage, down to the bend that led to the store. It was much shorter to get into the rowboat and row right across to the store dock. If you knew how to row. We didn't. Elektra did. She tried to teach us. It isn't easy to learn to row. The boat goes around and around in circles. Unless you have a very strong arm. Muscles. Like Elektra. The children, Katty, and I were allowed to go with Elektra in the boat on Saturdays. My mother and Aunt Pris would walk over later to fetch the little children home early. Katty and I were allowed to stay until the eleven-fifteen closing. With Elektra.

Until our first Saturday evening, I had not known Voss was also working at the camp. Three afternoons a week. Instructing the young campers on the fine points of sailing.

And I couldn't help but wonder which one of them had decided to find a job up at the lake, when the other had been already hired.

The cottagers danced. Katty and Linda and the counselors danced. The little boys and girls tried to dance. Voss and Elektra danced together. I watched from the sidelines. So did Whey-face.

I never did find out why he was called Whey-face. The girls would simply explode into "curds and whey" when I asked. He was sort of doughlike, not fat but a bit puffy; he would always be a little off side. No matter how fine an education he would have. No matter that when he grew up he would take over the president's chair at the bank and his father would retire to chairman of the board.

Both Claude and I just sat on the bench in the corner and watched the dancers. Sometimes I'd get him up on his feet and would try to show him how to move to the music. But he never understood rhythm or timing or movement. Two left feet. He always came out to the lake on dance nights to drive Voss back to town. On weeknights Voss hopped a ride to Clarksvale with workers at the camp.

Once—just once at Quichiquois—I danced again with Voss. He walked over to where Claude and I were sitting to ask Claude something or other. I think he recognized how my feet were in rhythm even while sitting down there on the bench. He would understand because he was a dancer. Not a professional, but bred in the bone, roiling in the blood. Without warning, he took my hand and pulled me up from the bench, said, "Come on," and we danced out onto the floor. Entirely different from the Paul Jones. A jazz jazzy. Exhilarating.

When Elektra came back from powdering her nose or whatever, Voss sat me down. He winked at me as they went off. But ours had been the best jazzy of the evening. It even led to my having some dances with Katty's older boys. Yes, I too have dance in my blood and bones.

It was that same night that I asked Claude how Voss could know so much about sailing to be able to teach the boys. Claude looked at me aghast. How could I know Voss and not know that? I tried to explain that I didn't know Voss. It was our hired girl who knew Voss. I'd just happened to dance with him once in the Paul Jones at the pavilion.

So Claude told me, "He's going to join the coast guard. He's been studying all this year to pass their tests or whatever you have to do to get in. He used to sail when he was a boy and lived up the coast. His father was a sailor. On a cargo boat. His father sailed all the way to China." It could be so. Or a sailor's yarn to a small hero-worshiping boy. It didn't matter. Voss would be a sailor if that was what he wanted.

I remember so well everything about that last dance night. It was getting on to eleven thirty, and I didn't see Elektra anywhere. I excused myself to Claude and walked across to where Katty was whooping it up with her current favorite boyfriend. Katty didn't shoo me away. Maybe I looked that worried. "Where's Elektra?" I asked her.

She surveyed the dancers on the floor. "She's probably down at the boathouse," she said.

"What's she doing down there?" I asked. Innocence. Too young. For a beat Katty and her friends just looked at me. And Linda started laughing. Katty joined in. The boys were politely inexpressive. They were sophisticates.

After she'd stopped laughing, Linda said, as if everyone knew that, "It's where couples go."

Katty added, "When they want to be alone."

"Smooching," Linda said.

I caught on. I wasn't that innocent. Necking, they called it at my school.

"She'll be here after the music stops," Katty said. "She wouldn't dare not," she explained to her friends. "She knows Aunt Priscilla is waiting up."

Truly true. Aunt Priscilla wasn't as sharp-tongued as Aunt George. But you could bully Aunt George by a temper tantrum. Katty explained it to me early in the summer. Aunt Priscilla was immovable.

When Mr. Gruen dimmed the colored lights and set the juke box for the last dance, always "Three O'Clock in the Morning," I saw them. Elektra and

Voss. Dancing. Two become one. I watched through the whole record. Day-dreaming. Why call it "day" when it's at night? Someday I'd grow up and have a boyfriend who danced like Voss.

Voss and Claude said good night and walked off. Elektra rowed us home. Aunt Pris glanced at her watch. "It will be midnight before you get to sleep." This was a nudge to go to bed, not stay up talking. "And we have to start packing up tomorrow. Aunt George and Fred will be here Monday morning."

Katty and I didn't talk much. Too tired. Too much, each of us, to remember. From the beginning of summer through this our final night of the boys' farewell across the water. "Good Night, Ladies . . ."

We had to miss Sunday morning church when at the lake. The nearest was in Clarksvale, too far to walk. Aunt Priscilla read her Bible. The children were kept quiet, and Katty and I usually slept until noon. In the afternoon we were allowed to swim and splash by our dock.

This Sunday was different. I woke—it wasn't eight o'clock—to the children gabbling in loud voices. Loud voices. Like on a weekday. My mother and Aunt Pris were ahead of me to the kitchen. Mother with her hair still in kid curlers, Aunt Pris with her gray hair in a plait down her back. Both in their nightgowns and robes. Aunt Pris was asking, "Whatever is the matter?" and my mother saying to her two, "Quiet. Quiet now. What's wrong?"

The children all talked at once. Emerged, one question. "Where's Elektra?"

Aunt Pris was dubious. "She isn't here?"

"No. She isn't here," all talking again at once. Almost shouting. "She's not here. There's no breakfast."

"Perhaps she overslept," Aunt Pris said. She hesitated. Then made her way to the back of the house, past my room, sleepy-eyed Katty just emerging, saying, "What's wrong?"

On to Elektra's bedroom beyond. Aunt Priscilla proper. Knocking on the door. Calling gently, careful not to startle a sleeper. "Elektra . . . Elektra . . . it's Miss Priscilla."

No response. She tried it again, a bit louder. Again no response. Aunt Priscilla took hold of the doorknob. Reluctantly. It was against all the principles of good manners. To open another's bedroom door. Even a servant's. But with no sound within, she did open the door, one small slant. Enough to peep inside. Then wider. And she said, "She isn't here."

"She must be around someplace." Katty and I had followed into the room. Katty said, "She can't have left. She hasn't taken her things." The hairbrush was on the bureau. The box of powder and the puff also there. Her nightdress still folded neatly over the back of a chair. The bed already made up. Or was it used last night?

"She'll be back," Aunt Priscilla decided. "I'll dress and then I'll cook breakfast."

Mother said, "I'll give the children some cornflakes and milk to tide them over." She had already put the kettle on for Aunt Priscilla's morning tea.

Aunt George came up in the afternoon. She said the same as Aunt Priscilla. "She'll be back." Her reasoning was different. "I owe her five dollars. For last week. She won't leave without her pay."

But she didn't come back. Not that day.

Not the next day. My small suitcase was packed. All else was confusion. Katty trying to curl her hair before closing her suitcase. Aunt Priscilla had packed all of Elektra's belongings into her own trunk. There wasn't much. The skirt and shirt she wore to work in, the few cosmetics, even her toothbrush and toothpaste had been left behind, and her undergarments (one to wear, one to wash, one to dry), her bedroom slippers, and an old night-robe that Aunt Pris had given her. Of course she'd taken her purse with her; the one she carried last night wasn't in the room. There'd be a comb and lipstick and powder compact in it.

Aunt Priscilla was trying to get everything shipshape, as it had been when we arrived. Mother was trying to get her children ready to leave. Aunt George arrived and added to the confusion while insisting, "Of course Elektra's gone back to Clarksvale. For reasons of her own." She finally took the Tompkin boys out to Fred, let him keep them busy out by the truck.

I managed to slip out the side door at a propitious moment when all the others were in the house or in front by the cars. I skulked rapidly through the trees until I was on the path that led to High Peak. It wasn't a real path. Just bumpy earth, pebbles and rocks, bits of green that wasn't weeds or wild grass, just green stuff. I zigzagged up the path to the promontory at the top. High above the shore. Elektra's special place. One afternoon when Katty and Linda were being exceptionally boy-crazies, Elektra had let me go with her to the peak. This was her time off from children and chores—why would she take me with her? Maybe because Voss danced with me once in the Paul Jones.

She didn't talk about him. She didn't talk when we were there. She just stood on the promontory and looked at the sky or down at the water. Under the promontory but still high on the slope there was a shelf. Not far below the peak. No way to get to it except by zigzagging down the slope and stooping your way under the protruding upper slope. She didn't take me there. She didn't go there either. Just pointed it out to me as we leaned over the tip. Scary.

I didn't want to go there now. She wasn't there. But she had been here last night. With Voss? A farewell? In each other's arms. Two into one. "Stop dreaming," Katty would say. Or my mother. Or anyone if I spoke of it. But I knew. Before I saw the bead, the red glass bead on the green stuff scattered on the earth. She wore those beads to the dance last night. She always wore them with her summer dress, her white dress with the little roses sprinkled across the pattern. The beads almost looked like crystals. Not really. They were pretend, cut like crystals, but made of glass. They were a little handful of beauty to her. She must have searched for them when the strand was broken. Caught on a tree branch, or the button on a man's jacket. Too dark to find all of them. I looked. There was one out on the tip, but I didn't go there. I scruffed through the green and found another. And another, with leaf mold patterning it. No more. I hadn't time to search for more. I ran until the cottage was in sight. Then I just hurried, the beads tight in my left fist. Fred was loading the last of the suitcases.

My mother came to me with, "Emmy, where have you been?" and as she looked into my face, softly, "Saying good-bye?"

She understood the need to say good-bye. To the woods and the water. To some of summer memories. In some secret place you had marked as your own.

Another week and the end of August. Of summer. My mother and the children off for California and school days again. Long good-byes until Christmas. Behind the scenes it had been decided that I would enter Mount Academy this year, the school where the women of my father's family had all attended to be finished. Katty had graduated there this spring. My mother approved though as a Californian she had been finished there. I would stay on with Aunt Priscilla until school started. Aunt George had assured me that with a diploma from Mount Academy I could attend any college of my choice. Such was its academic standing. Even Cambridge? Yes, even Cambridge. I doubted. Cambridge wasn't exclusively female, and Aunt Georgie with all her modern ideas and bold businesss maneuvers did not hold with coeducation. It was all right for primary students. Although better for the girls to go to Miss Mastersons and the boys to Albany Cadet. No hanky-panky.

It was one of those last nights before Katty would depart for college. Aunt Pris, Katty, and I had had early supper and cleanup and were relaxing in the living room. Until Aunt Georgie came by. She was again all het up about Elektra. She'd been at some meeting and none of the women knew anything about the disappearance of Elektra. No one had seen her since she went to the lake with us. They seemed to think Aunt Priscilla and Aunt George were to blame.

Aunt Priscilla said, "Stop worrying your head about the five dollars. I was going to have to let her go anyway. She was beginning to show."

They exchanged a few of their wise looks and dropped the subject.

Later when Katty and I went up to our room, I asked her. "What did Aunt Pris mean? Beginning to show."

Katty just looked at me. Stared. Finally she said, "You know."

"I don't know. If I knew, why would I ask you? 'Beginning to show'? Do you know?"

"Of course I do. Everybody knows. That she's going to have a baby. That's what it means."

"She's married!" I could not believe it. But if she and Voss were married . . .

"No. She's not married," Katty stated.

But if she's not married, how can she—I didn't ask that question out loud. Some people did. We just didn't know people who did. I sighed to Katty. "How do you know all these things?"

"Emmy," she told me, "you find out a lot living with the aunts. You keep quiet and listen and they forget you're there. And you learn a lot."

I figured for myself. In a small town you learned things that city girls didn't know about. Small towns were evolved from farm country. Where life and death were the beginning and end, and in between were all manner of happenings.

Another week of flurry and then we drove with Katty to Albany to put her on the train for New York. Three of her friends were also going to the college on the Hudson. Linda, of course, and Willa and Maleen. The college proctors would meet the train with the school bus.

When we returned to the house late that afternoon, we collapsed into chairs, even Aunt Georgie. I would be the next to go. But only as far as Hudson, where I'd be met by the school bus.

I'd stopped listening to the aunts long before they were talked out. It became tiresome listening to all the memories of Aunt A and Uncle B and Cousins C, D, E, etc. When I didn't know any of them. They were reminiscing to each other, remembering their own college days.

Finally Aunt Georgie gathered her gloves and string bag and high-stepped to the front door. She'd sent Fred and the car home; she'd be walking. Of course she carried her umbrella as always, to ward off sun or rain.

She said to me, "You be ready in the morning, Emmy. I'll come by for you about ten o'clock."

Aunt Priscilla showed mild surprise. "You're taking Emmy along?"

"I certainly am." Evidently I'd missed something in their long conversation. "She's the last to see Elektra."

"I saw her," Aunt Pris corrected.

"You weren't with her all evening. Or in the boat."

I could have told them I knew no more than Aunt Pris. Elektra never talked. She spoke necessary words, but she never talked. Not even phrases like "Is my lipstick on straight?" "Does my petticoat show?" Things all females say to each other.

Instead I asked, "Where are we going?"

"We're going looking for Elektra. Find out where she is. Find out why she hasn't been around for her five dollars. You think of some questions yourself, Emmy. We'll both ask questions."

I reacted in my veins. In my bones. I was to be a Miss Paul Pry. I could ask a dozen questions. I could ask Voss: "Where did she spend the night? How did she get back to Clarksvale? How did she break her strand of red glass beads?" But I wouldn't. It was none of my business. Just the same, I carried the three red glass beads along in my party handkerchief deep in my little purse, where I had tucked them away while we were still at the cottage. While no one was looking at me. Before I got into the car and shared a jump seat with Katty.

I was ready for Aunt George when she arrived next morning. She had walked over. "No sense in taking the car. More trouble than it's worth." She was thinking out loud. "We have to prowl."

We prowled along Town Street, which carried you into Main Street. But we stopped before then. We stopped at the big yellow boarding house where Elektra had lived. A flight of wooden steps led up to the porch. Aunt George didn't ring or knock on the door, she opened it. She knew her way around here. I followed her. She walked past the staircase that mounted to a second floor, and strode down the uncarpeted corridor, all the way to a door near the back of the house. She knocked a ratatat on that door. And again, stronger. From within now came a voice shouting, "Who's that come knocking at my door?" Aunt George shouted back, "Just Aunt George, Gammer, that's who." Everyone in town called her Aunt George or Georgie.

Came another shout: "George Fanshawe?"

"What other George do you know, Gammer?"

Sometime along the years I'd heard, just like an aside from someone in the family, that Aunt George had been married once on a time. Not for long. That's why she wasn't a Davenport like Aunt Priscilla and my father and his family.

"Well, don't stand out there yammering, Georgie. Come on inside."

My aunt opened the unlocked door and went in, me following behind her.

"Gammer," she said, "this is my niece Emmy."

I managed to stammer a "How d'you do" to the diminutive old woman in the big rocker with varnish peeling from it. This was Gammer Goodwife, supposed to be kin of Elektra. Half-toothless, a browned corncob pipe clutched by the few remaining teeth. A squawky voice like something was caught in her throat. The ironing woman. Hard to believe that those rheumatic cramped fingers could iron ruffles until they rippled. Could iron linen napkins down to the very edge of the hand hem. Could iron lace as delicately as if she'd spun it. She took one look at me out of her spiteful black eyes and dismissed me as without interest.

She had three different ironing boards set up in her large untidy room. One, oversize, for sheets, tablecloths and such; a middle-size one for the usual clothes wash, and a baby one, a sleeve board it was called. Probably for the ruffles and laces. A screen closed off a corner of the room. Behind it, Aunt Georgie told me later, was the bed and washbasin. An old-fashioned rooming house with the bathroom down the hall.

"I don't have your laundry done," Gammer spat.

"I didn't come for my laundry," Aunt George informed her. "I didn't bring any this week."

"Then what you doing here?"

"I'm looking for Elektra."

"Well, you can see she an't here." Gammer set the rocker rocking hard again. "She's up at the lake with your sister."

"She isn't up at the lake. We've all left the lake."

"Did you bring her back here?"

"We couldn't," stated Aunt George. "She left before we packed out."

"Why did she leave?"

"That's what I want to know. I want to ask her."

"Well, she an't here."

"Where's her room?"

"She an't in her room."

"How do you know she isn't up in her room?"

Gammer cackled. A cackle laugh. I'd read of them. But I didn't know there was really such a sound.

She dug her fist into a voluminous pocket in her skirt. "Because I got her key." She unreeled a long chain attached inside the pocket. On the end of it was a large ring of keys. "She leaves it with me when she's out of town. So nobody gets into her things." She beetled suspiciously at Aunt George.

"You haven't seen her since she came back? You haven't had any message from her?"

Gammer kept humming "Nnnnoooo" and rocking harder. Like little boys do to make it go faster.

"Then where is she?" Aunt George said. Not exactly to Gammer. At her own frustration.

But Gammer responded. "She's a Canuck. I told you that before. A Canuck witch." She restarted the rocker. "She flew away—up high—way up high . . ."

"On your broomstick," Aunt George bristled. She'd had enough of Gammer's antics. She stood up and brushed the dust off her skirt, although the chair she'd sat on had been brushed by her handkerchief before she sat down on it. "If you do see her or hear from her," Aunt George instructed, "tell her I'm looking for her. To pay her the money I owe her."

The rocking stopped like that. "You can pay me. I'll give it to her."

"I'll pay her. No one else."

"You think I'd spend it on myself."

"I pay what I owe to the one I owe." With that she stalked out while Gammer was still embroidering her role as a caretaker of Electra's money as well as her room. I sidled out beside Aunt George. I didn't want to be left alone in that room with Gammer.

All the way to Main Street Aunt George kept talking to herself, not to me, about the perfidious Gammer and her grandniece. I managed to keep up with her fast walk by saving my breath. Only three blocks to Main Street.

Waiting to cross the street, I could ask, "Now where do we go?"

"We'll go to Gus Henschel's. I understand his nephew, Voss, and that girl were what we used to call an item."

"Did everybody know?" Somehow I'd thought it was a private affair, known only to Katty and her friends who saw them dancing together.

"It's the talk of this town the way she went after him." She was opening the door of the butcher shop before I could think of some excuse to keep from going in there. I didn't want Voss to see me and think I'd talked about him and Elektra.

Voss wasn't up front today. His uncle was. He was arranging steaks for his display case. "Morning, Miss Georgie," he said, but it was a glum morning from his expression. "What can I do for you today?"

"You can let me talk to that nephew of yours."

"Voss?"

"I understand that is the name."

He peered over the counter at me. I was too young to be a friend of Voss so he dismissed me from his answer. To Aunt George he growled, "I'd like to talk to him myself. That javel never come back from the lake. That camp has been calling and calling him. He hasn't been around there either."

Aunt George was only temporarily speechless. "You haven't seen Elektra?"

"That the pawky girl been hanging around him all summer?"

"She hasn't been around lately?"

"Not since she went up to the lake with your sister. Leastways that was what she told him."

Both of them gone. Together. But she wouldn't go without taking her belongings. Yes, she might. If he was in a hurry. He'd have some money with two jobs. He'd buy her a new hairbrush and nightgown.

"Good riddance to bad rubbish," Uncle Gus was saying. "But he'll be around once he runs out of money. I paid him before he went off to the lake that Saturday. He'll be back."

"I owe Elektra some money. I don't like to owe money. If either of them turns up, you let me know. Right off. Hear?"

"I ain't deaf, Aunt George. I hear."

And she stomped away, me trailing. Again talking to herself. "They'll turn up when they want money."

I could have told her they weren't coming back. They had each other. But she wouldn't have believed me.

II

Ten years ago. Eleven come summer. High school and college over and done. Two years assistant women's editor on a medium-small-town newspaper. You want to know what an assistant women's club editor covers? Women's club meetings. Women's club social teas. Women's club holiday occasions. Washington's birthday cardboard hatchets. Cotton Easter bunnies in straw bonnets. Fourth of July crepe paper firecrackers. September, miniature grandmothers' school slates. October, take your pick, witches, brooms, jack-o'-lanterns. November, yarn turkeys. No need to illustrate December and January. How often can you write that the decorations were so charming, unique, attractive, amusing—add your own adjectives.

I couldn't get out of the groove. The editor wanted me where I was. I could spell.

On a September morning, I read on the AP tape, DATELINE CLARKSVALE. HUMAN BONES FOUND AT LAKE QUICHIQUOIS.

I didn't have to read on. I knew exactly where, and, without knowing, I knew who. And a chance to break from my shackles. I knocked on Editor Briar's door. His office is a square of window glass, but we observed the courtesy of a knock. He was chewing his pencil. Obviously working on his weekend editorial. Yes, he uses a pencil. A yellow wooden pencil with very black lead.

"Mr. Briar," I said, "I'd like to leave now. My page has gone to press."

"Who's going to read proof?"

"You are," I told him. "Or one of those callow youths you call reporters." I'd known Mr. Briar a long time. Since I was subeditor on the college paper. I knew how to give him just enough information to whet his news appetite. "I have a story that takes investigative reporting, and I want to get at it ahead of the pack."

He stuttered and glowered and called anathema on my head. A hot story was for callow Quentin, the one he was training to be a star metropolitan reporter. Like he'd always wanted to be.

He was wasting my time. I interrupted him. "It just came over AP. Finding bones upstate. Human bones."

His pink face glistened. "I'll send Quent—"

"Indeed you won't," I countered. "I have the inside track. I was there." Stress on there. "When that girl disappeared. I can beat the city slickers. They'll be coming around. But I know these folks. See you Monday."

With which I was out the door, leaving him to his blood pressure.

I retrieved my car from our parking lot and took off for Clarksvale. Ninety miles upstate. I didn't stop to pack up anything. I could buy a toothbrush. Borrow everything else from Aunt Priscilla or Aunt George.

I stopped at Aunt Priscilla's house—it was on the way into town. After ejaculations of surprise, I told her, "I'm here to cover the big story. Finding human bones at Quichiquois."

"I'll call George. She'll want to hear about this."

Aunt George was over to Aunt Priscilla's in a trice. She must be well in her sixties now and just as spry and as domineering as ever. As that summer of Elektra.

"You think it's Elektra," she said after I'd given her a rundown on the news story.

I did think so. I'd always thought that she had never left the lake. But couldn't let myself say it back then. Didn't want it to be so.

"Aunt George, you come uptown with me," I invited. "You know all these local officials. In case they try to freeze me out. I want the story."

"You'll get it." She did not doubt. She was too accustomed to getting what she wanted from the town fathers.

As we came out on Aunt Priscilla's porch she asked, "Is that your car?" nodding to where it stood in the driveway.

"We'll walk," she told me, just as she always said ten, almost eleven, years ago. "Easier than trying to park. Talk to more people anyhow."

And there were plenty of people out on Main Street. Gossiping. Gawking. And there was Claude, near the bank, his father's bank. Also Aunt Georgie's.

He greeted us Claude-like. "Good morning, Aunt George. Hello, Emmy. You haven't been to Clarksvale for a long time." He was still a whey-face, but he had some assurance now. He had been appointed an attorney with the county. Aunt Priscilla had kept me informed of all Clarksvale news. She wrote me every week.

Claude and I shook hands. As visitors do.

Aunt Georgie said to us, "I'm going on down to the courthouse." Where she could gather information.

Claude said, "You're here about the bones."

I showed him my newspaper card. "It was on the AP wire this morning."

"We sent the bones to the lab in Albany. Two weeks ago. They're on the way back here now. With the report."

I was reluctant but I asked. "Do you know . . ."

"Yes." He said almost to himself, "The director informed me. I inquired . . ." It took a moment or so before he could continue. But he said it without inflection. "They are male bones. The bones of a young man probably in his twenties. The skull has been bashed."

I only half asked. "They were found under the promontory, the one called High Peak."

"There is a ledge, an open cave. The bones were there. Nothing left of clothing."

"No leather? A belt? A wallet?"

"Not after ten years. Pumas take refuge there if a winter storm interrupts their hunting. Sometimes there are bears."

I didn't want to say it but I had to. "She killed him."

"We don't know that."

"She loved him. He was going away. She couldn't let him go."

"If she did, we will never know," Claude said. "She cannot be brought back to trial. Not without evidence. Even if she is found."

"She was carrying his child. He was leaving her and their child."

Somewhere there is a little girl, near ten years old. Straight as a lance. Long dark hair hanging down her back. Or a sandy little boy. Agile. Scrawny but muscular. Strong.

"She loved him." I kept repeating it. Not for Claude. For myself.

Claude said, "I don't think she planned it. I don't think she intended it. I think it was by accident."

In a rage, she struck him. There were some sizable rocks on the promontory. There would be some in the cave. And kept striking him until he was gone. Before she knew what she was doing.

He broke the strand of beads trying to get away from her. She must have had a rock. He was stronger. If it had been possible to get away from her, he could have stopped her.

"I hope you won't mention her in your story. Why torment her further? She'll always live with this. An agony of loss."

He had loved Voss. The way he'd never love anyone else. Nothing homosexual about it. A teenage boy's hero-worship of his hero.

"I won't. There may be gossip but it will come to nothing. There aren't many who really knew her." And I hesitated. "Gammer . . ."

"Everyone knows Gammer makes up tall tales."

We were left with a pause of silence, each in his own thoughts. Then

Claude said, "Shall we go down to the courthouse? It's time for them to get here with the report. You can call your paper from my office."

Together we walked the half block. On the way he said, "I'm going to be married this spring. To Willa. Do you remember Willa?"

"She was one of Katty's very best friends."

"We'll have a church wedding. Bridesmaids, attendants. All the frills. Willa wants it. We'll send you an invitation. I hope you'll be able to come. Katty's coming from Maryland."

Katty's husband is in government.

It occurred to him. "You're not married?"

"Not yet. I'm a career woman. I'm younger than Katty and her friends."

"That's right," he recalled. "You were just a little girl. You sat on the bench with me and we watched Voss."

"That's right," I echoed. I closed my eyes and I could see him. "He was a wonderful dancer."

Maybe to keep from tears, he laughed. "You tried to teach me to dance."

I laughed for the same reason. "You had two left feet."

So we went into the courthouse to hear the full report on the bones. Just another happening.

But I did not tell Claude that I would give up the story. I wouldn't mention Elektra. Not unless someone else did. But I would try to find her. I'm an investigative reporter. I have to know the entire story.